THIS
IS
WHAT it
FEELS
LIKE

Also by Rebecca Barrow

You Don't Know Me but I Know You

THiS iS WHAT it FEELS LiKE

REBECCA BARROW

HARPER TEEN
An Imprint of HarperCollins Publishers

HarperTeen is an imprint of HarperCollins Publishers.

This Is What It Feels Like
Copyright © 2018 by Rebecca Barrow
All rights reserved. Printed in the United States of America.
No part of this book may be used or reproduced in any manner whatsoever
without written permission except in the case of brief quotations embodied in
critical articles and reviews. For information address HarperCollins Children's
Books, a division of HarperCollins Publishers, 195 Broadway, New York, NY
10007.
www.epicreads.com

ISBN 978-0-06-249423-8

Typography by Torborg Davern
18 19 20 21 22 CG/LSCH 10 9 8 7 6 5 4 3 2 1
❖
First Edition

To everyone sitting in their bedrooms in the 2am stillness,
listening to that song that makes your heart ache

prologue

It's hot the second the doors open. The kind of air that leaves you sticky straightaway, sweat trickling along your spine, and you almost can't wait for the sweet relief of the cold shower awaiting you at the end of the night.

The stage is empty; music thumps out of hidden speakers instead, electro Biggie and Blondie covers and sometimes Aaliyah, because of course Aaliyah.

A light-copper-skinned girl in hacked shorts and a Bikini Kill tee cuts through the crowd, holding tight to the wrist of another girl with hair bleached whiter than her pale skin. The first girl, natural curly hair blown out to wild proportions, hoists herself onto the stage. A third girl appears from the wings, the lights setting a sheen of purplish-pink on her deep-brown skin, and holds a hand out to the blonde.

All three duck back into the wings together, grabbing guitars, picks, drumsticks, courage. Then the music cuts, and the purple-green-red lights flash down, and a person with lime-green lipstick and a buzz cut squeezes past them. "Ready?" they say.

The blonde nods. "Always."

The buzz cut person walks out on the tiny stage, takes a position at the mic stand to cheers from the raucous crowd. "All right, everybody! Make some fucking noise for Fairground!"

The girl with the curls slouches up to the mic, a pick between her teeth. She tugs her shorts up on her hips and takes the pick from her mouth. She doesn't bother introducing herself or the others, but hits a jarring chord and runs into their first song at breakneck speed, the blonde banging hell out of her drums and the bassist kicking into frenetic rhythm, sweat slicking away from her basketball jersey.

They only have fifteen minutes, but it's fifteen minutes more than they used to have. They speed through their short set list, and the crowd cheers, raises their hands, and gives in to the weird mix of punk and grunge and R&B.

They sing themselves hoarse in that short time, and when it's over—too fast, too soon—they leave the stage, clutching their guitars and drumsticks like precious jewels. The next band will start soon, replace them in the crowd's memory, but it doesn't matter. They did what they came to do.

Sometimes they stay to listen to the other bands and dance themselves silly, but tonight they're forty minutes from home and they have a curfew. Out in the parking lot an older girl with lilies inked on her upper arm and locs to the middle of her back waits by a beat-up van.

"Good set," she says, and pulls out keys so they can load the drums into the back. "Dia, your turn to choose. McDonald's or Dairy Queen?"

"DQ," the curly-haired girl says. She craves a Blizzard.

The one in the jersey lifts it to wipe the sweat from her neck, sticky from in there. "They know us now, a little," she said. "Hanna, get up."

The blonde stands up from her crouch, unsteady. "You're not my mom, Jules," she says.

It's late and dark, and Dia opens her red-painted mouth wide and yells a note out into the California night, a release of residual energy.

Their tattooed chauffeur laughs at the echo. "Come on, we gotta go."

Jules rolls her eyes but doesn't mean it. "Yes, Ciara."

They pile into the front of the van, legs and arms and guitars. The blonde—Hanna—turns the radio to the nineties station and they wind the windows down and sing along to Mariah Carey as they peel off into the night.

Hanna

Hanna kicked her locker, the noise echoing down the empty hall. "Useless piece of shit," she said under her breath. *"Open."*

She gave it a final wrench and it opened, finally, the mess inside spilling out. Perfect.

She only needed her paper for last period, the last assignment she had to turn in before officially being done, *d-o-n-e*, with high school. Hanna found it, folded it in two, and put it in her backpack. Then she gathered everything else—old notebooks, candy bar wrappers, letters she'd never given to her parents—and carried it down the hall, where she dropped it all into a trash can. It made a satisfying thud as it landed, and Hanna smiled to herself.

Four hundred and seven.

She took her lunch outside, found an empty table, and ate her lukewarm slice of pizza while she watched her classmates whirl around without her. Everybody was so *excited*: all week long she'd kept seeing people hugging each other and bursting into fake noisy crying, everybody taking a thousand selfies everywhere she looked. Like now—Ali Siberski and Priscilla Nguyen posing by the vending machine, faces pressed together as they snapped away. Michael Brewer signing some skinny guy's yearbook. Gloria Vazquez sitting on the lap of some kid from the basketball team—Hanna couldn't remember his name. She couldn't remember a lot of people's names, actually, and yet still she felt a tug of sadness that this was the last time she'd see most of them.

She rested her chin in her hands and watched. They all probably knew her name, for the wrong reasons. But they wouldn't miss her after graduation. She wouldn't actually miss them, either.

Hanna tipped her face up to the sun. Five days till graduation. Four hundred and seven days since she'd given up drinking.

Given up drinking. That made it sound so much easier than it had been. It didn't take into account the blackouts and fallouts, the repeated attempts and failures to quit. The night her little sister had found Hanna in her bedroom in the middle of the night, not breathing, and called the ambulance all on her own. The night when Hanna had to be treated for alcohol poisoning for the *second* time, when she woke up from the blur of the past couple of years and finally realized that her only options were complete self-destruction or sobriety. The pleading from her parents, and the promising from herself, and the ending up in a rehab facility four hours away.

Four hundred and seven days. How long it had been since she'd realized that no one would be surprised if she drank herself to oblivion.

At least she had one thing to be proud of.

Hanna sat there until the bell rang, listening to her classmates' chatter, screams of laughter, plans for some "major prank" that Hanna was sure was most definitely *not* going to be good. When they all started to stream out, on their way to their last few classes, she joined them, let herself be carried back into the building and through the halls. And on the stairs up to her English class, she passed them.

Dia Valentine and Jules Everett. The two people who *really* weren't going to miss her after graduation.

Whatever, Hanna thought. *Who even cares anymore?*

They were gone in an instant, disappeared in a flash of long braids and ripped jeans, and Hanna kept on to class, shaking her head as she slipped into her seat and slammed her bag down.

"Good afternoon, Miss Adler." Mr. Matthews looked at her pointedly. "If you could try not to destroy my classroom before the end of the year, that would be great."

Hanna rolled her eyes as she sat down, looking up to see the teacher still watching her with this expression that was equal parts *Can you believe this girl is actually graduating?* and *How soon can I get her out of my class?* It was the same expression she'd seen on pretty much every teacher's face this week, with the exception of the few who'd actually helped her get back on track last year.

Well, sorry, she wanted to say to Mr. Matthews right now. *Sorry I'm not giving you one last thing to hold against me! And really, really sorry for not being the complete train wreck you expected me to be! You must be so sad to miss out on telling everyone how right you were.*

Hanna bit her tongue. That kind of stuff got filed away in the Don't Say This Out Loud folder in her head, the one where she put everything that would get her in more trouble than she needed.

"Sure," was what she said instead. "I'll try."

A few people snickered at that but Hanna ignored them, searching for a pen as Mr. Matthews walked up and down, handing out their final exam papers. "You have forty-five minutes," he said. "Once you're done, you can go, but make sure to hand your papers in on the way out. Okay?"

Hanna flipped to the first question: *Compare and contrast the presentation of loneliness in Shakespeare's* Hamlet *and* To Kill a Mockingbird.

Easy.

Dia

"Dia Gabrielle Valentine!"

Dia rubbed her red-painted lips together before fixing a smile on her face and marching across the stage to meet Principal Cho.

Finally, she thought. Four years of one-a.m. assignments and sleep-deprived morning classes, Jesse explaining math to her and panic-inducing finals, all over now.

All ceremony long the clapping had been constant, punctured by an occasional cheer or ear-splitting whistle. Now it warmed Dia and sent a zip of staticky excitement down her spine, because everybody out there was clapping for *her.* She'd done it. She'd actually graduated.

How's that for a Fuck You?

Dia shook Principal Cho's hand, the last time she'd ever be face-to-face with her, probably, and the principal gave her this wide smile.

"Congratulations, Dia," she said, and the unending applause

played a perfect backing track to her words. "You've earned it."

"Thank you," Dia said, and as she wrapped her fingers around the diploma she smiled hard enough to hurt.

She looked out into the rows and rows of families: Jules's parents and her brother, Danny, were right up front, and the sun hit right in her eyes as Dia searched farther back. She had to squint but there they were—her parents, cheering and standing up so Alexa could be hoisted high in the air.

She waved as she moved on, praying she didn't trip in her heels, and then she was down the steps and in line with the rest of her class. And then they were tossing caps in the air and everyone was yelling and Dia turned her face to the open blue sky and finally, finally, *finally.*

Once the ceremony was done, the formality fell away. Families and graduates mingled together, a singular mass on the field normally reserved for the girls' soccer team. Dia found Jules quickly, and they ducked out of the way of somebody's family photo session. "Can you believe it?" Dia laughed. "We're free! We're *actually* free."

"Oh, yeah," Jules said. "So free. Until we have to go to work tomorrow."

Dia waved her off. "Work, shmurk. At least work doesn't involve ten-page papers on Congress or constant fill-in-the-bubble tests."

"No," Jules said. "Just getting yelled at by people who think they're better than us and a hideous amount of polyester."

Dia almost tripped as her heels sank into the grass, a last-second grab for Jules's arm the only thing stopping her from face planting. "These shoes, I swear."

"This everything," Jules said, shaking her head so her box braids snaked over her shoulders. "I can't wait to get out of this gown."

"I can't wait to get out of this *dress*," Dia said, tugging at the stretchy green fabric that clung a little too much to her every in and out. "I feel like any second could be a nip slip."

"The Valentine tits," Jules said, cracking a smile and raising her voice. "They will not be denied!"

"Shut up!" Dia swatted at Jules, but she was laughing too much to get her aim right. She should have bought something new, but it seemed like a waste to spend money on a fancy dress she'd wear only once when there was so much else she needed.

"Okay, I have to go find my parents," Jules said, sounding less than enthused. "You should hear my dad today. 'It's your graduation! It's a big deal! You're going to college!' And I'm like, 'Dad, I'm going to community college. The college that *you* teach at. I'll still be tripping over your shoes every morning. Calm down.'"

"Don't get down on us," Dia said, narrowing her eyes at her friend. "This is a big deal. Hello, we are no longer high school students. We are *college* students. Sure, we're still going to live at home and we'll see your dad on campus, but we did it. We got ourselves here, so stop shitting on it."

Jules rolled her eyes. "Fine," she said. "It could be worse. But it could be better, too."

Dia gave her a warning look. "Don't," she said. "Didn't we agree not to play this game anymore?" The game where they fantasized about the life they could maybe have now, if things hadn't fallen apart so spectacularly. The life where they were leaving for LA tomorrow, instead of looking forward to a summer of working their minimum-wage jobs and warming milk at three a.m.

It used to be fun to imagine that life, but now it was depressing, and so Dia had said they couldn't do it anymore.

"Yeah, yeah," Jules said. "Am I not allowed to dream?"

"Only for today," Dia conceded. "And then we go back to reality."

"Fine," Jules said. "Are we still going to the party?"

Dia nodded. "Come over before so I can do your makeup."

"Yes, ma'am." Jules gave a mock salute. "Later."

Dia watched her walk away, and then she heard her name being called and turned to the sound. Her mom and dad, Nina and Max, waved, Alexa propped up on her mom's hip. "Over here!"

Dia steeled herself to cross the grass in her heels again, and began walking over. Alexa squirmed out of Nina's grip, straining toward Dia as she approached. Her mom lowered the toddler to the ground and Alexa took a second to find her balance before breaking into a run. "Mama!"

"Hi, baby." Dia crouched, holding her hands out toward her daughter. "C'mere!"

She ran into Dia's arms, and Dia swept her up before peppering her apple cheeks with kisses. "Did you see me, Lex?"

The little girl nodded. "And I saw Juju," she said before jamming her thumb into her mouth. Dia caught her smile before it really started—she knew that habit needed to be broken before it became a real problem, but god, if it didn't look cute. "No, no," she said gently, and eased Lex's hand from her face. "We don't do that."

"Oh, leave her be," her dad said. "It's not going to kill her."

"No," Dia said. "But it *is* going to mess with her teeth, and in ten years I'll be paying for braces."

"She's right, Max," her mom said, smoothing down her cropped, relaxed, jet-black hair.

"Point taken," he said with an easy smile. That was how it always went: her mom laid down the law and her dad gave in to whatever her mom said, too easy-going to ever want to cause an argument. Her mom the engineer, former military, sharp and strong, and her dad the musician, now EMT: an opposites-attract pair, always had been, always would be.

Her dad took out his phone. "Now, smile nice for me, both of you. Lala, say cheese."

"Cheese!" Lex yelled, and Dia laughed.

"Okay, okay," she said. Dia shifted the baby onto her hip and straightened the bow around her curls. She put on her brightest smile as her dad snapped picture after picture, hoping that her boobs weren't spilling out and that there wasn't lipstick on her teeth and that she didn't look too much like she was about to cry.

Because she really had done it. *Graduated!* Two years ago, no one had believed she could. Or, not no one: Jules had been behind her all the way, and her parents, and Jesse. Principal Cho, too, pulling strings and signing off on extra credits and making sure Dia got her chance. *Without them, I wouldn't be here,* she thought.

But everybody else? People she'd called her friends, teachers she'd liked, her mom's coworkers? They'd rolled their eyes when Dia had said she was still going to graduate and go to college. When she insisted that yeah, she had a baby, but that didn't mean those things were completely *impossible*.

You have no idea, people said. *Having a baby changes everything.* She imagined them thinking, *You're going to end up on welfare anyway, why put it off?* And *Stupid slut. Way to ruin your life.*

"Dia!" her mom called. "Look happy, huh? It's your big day!"

Alexa laid her head on Dia's chest, and Dia raised her chin, her skin almost vibrating with all the love she had for this little girl. Yeah, having Lex had made things more difficult, and yeah, she could have made a different choice, but in the haze of everything back then, this was what she'd decided on. And when she looked into her daughter's big, brown eyes, she knew that she wouldn't change the way things were. Not for anything.

Eventually Dia's cheeks began to ache from all the smiling, and Alexa began to fuss, her irritable *I'm hungry and I could use my words but I don't want to* whimper. "Are you done?" Dia said through her rictus smile. "Is ten thousand pictures enough, or do you need more?"

"Don't be smart," Max said, but he put his phone away and held up his hands. "I'm done, okay? Forgive me for wanting to preserve this momentous occasion."

Dia tipped her head back to feel the sun, warm on her face. The rubbing of her shoes, her too-tight dress; the slippery gown and crisp diploma; the scent of cut grass in the air—she didn't need a photograph to remember any of it.

jules

Jules rang the bell only as a formality, and then walked right in, announcing her presence as she opened the refrigerator. "I'm getting a soda," she called out.

"Jules!" Dia's dad came into the kitchen, a look of mild annoyance on his face. "You treat my house like a hotel."

Jules gave her best impression of an apologetic smile. "Only because you said I could."

"Hmm," Max said. "I might start regretting that." But then he laughed. "I didn't get to say congratulations earlier, to my second-favorite graduate."

"It's okay, Dia's not here," Jules said, pulling her mass of braids over her shoulder. "You can be honest."

Max narrowed his eyes. "I remember when you were a kid and actually showed me some respect," he said. "Where did it all go wrong?"

"Ask Dia."

He shook his head. "You hungry?"

"I'm good," Jules said. "We had a ton of food at the house. Thanks, though." Her mom had been cooking the whole day before: stewed chicken and rice and curry goat, mac pie and roast lamb, a true Barbados feast in California. They'd crowded around the kitchen table and Jules had eaten her body weight in all of it while her parents got all teary-eyed and started reminiscing about Jules's birth. That always led into the story of how they met, and then they'd started dancing around the kitchen, and Danny had rolled his eyes, but Jules loved to watch her parents' love.

Perfect celebration.

"All right," she said. "I guess I better go get ready for this party."

"At least act excited," Max said. "It's your graduation night. You only get one."

"It'll be the same as every other party we've ever been to," Jules said, shrugging.

"Go anyway," Max said, running a hand over his locs. "Take Dia and make her have fun, for once."

"Fine," Jules said, grabbing her soda and heading toward the stairs. "I'll try!"

Jules didn't knock before entering Dia's bedroom either, her friend at her computer, her honorary niece scribbling on the floor. Dia looked up at her, immediate annoyance on her face. "I have nothing to wear."

"Juju!" Alexa stretched her arms up toward Jules, hands grabbing at the air. "Up!"

Jules did as she was commanded, scooping Lex up from the floor and settling the baby's weight on her hip. "Hi, sweet one," she said, nuzzling her nose against Lex's cheek. Then she looked at Dia. "Don't even start with me."

Dia stood. "Have you seen that show with the two girls and they're dating, but one of them's a spy?"

Jules arched one eyebrow. "I'm an eighteen-year-old lesbian with internet access. I've seen everything that even *hints* at two girls being into each other. The GIFs are imprinted on my eyelids."

"Okay, well, in one episode the tall one has this amazing red jump-suit. *That's* what I want to wear."

"Let's start with something you actually own," Jules said.

Dia made a face. "I don't know if I even want to go to this thing anymore."

"Me neither," Jules said, sitting on the edge of Dia's bed. She let Alexa loose on the comforter and shrugged her backpack off. "But we promised."

"Who?"

"Each other." In the cafeteria, two weeks ago, looking at the text invite on Dia's phone. *When do we ever go anywhere?* Dia had said. *Me with Lex, you working all the time. This'll be our last high school party ever.*

I'm so sick of folding jeans, Jules said. *Bagging people's groceries. One day I'm going to do something different.*

Of course you are.

Okay, Jules said. *So let's go to this fucking party.*

Dia steepled her fingers underneath her chin, and then nodded. "Okay. We'll go. And if it sucks, we get to leave after an hour. Deal?"

"Deal."

"Right," Dia said. "Now let me work my magic."

They set up the way they always did—or always had, Jules amended, back when they used to party and go to shows and roll around the streets of their town without a care in the world. Electro remixes and old-school punk playing through the speakers, Dia's makeup spread across the bed, a bag of chips within easy reach. Dia eased Jules's braids—fresh for graduation, the ten hours and numb ass and hypnotic click-click-click of Stephy's acrylics whipping through her hair oh-so-worth it—into a high pony, then started on Jules's makeup. Moments like these were what made Jules glad that they were both staying home for college: being apart, being without her best friend, the girl she'd loved since preschool? It would have felt like losing a part of herself.

Jules examined her face in the mirror when Dia was done: a simple flick of black liner on each eye and her thick brows framing them, clear lip gloss, and something shiny gold on her deep-brown cheeks. She got dressed in black jeans from her mall job, hacked at with a razor to make them look like the expensive ones from the store three doors down, and a gray shirt with the sleeves cut off, dipping low enough beneath each armpit to flash her black bra.

She played with Alexa while Dia painted her own eyelids deep blue and her lips a bright, shiny red. "I heard High and Mighty Kallas are playing at Revelry tonight," Jules said, making a polka-dotted lion dance with a robot as Lex clapped her hands. "If we get out of this party early enough, we could catch them. I haven't been to a show in forever." She sighed with longing. Cheap beer and sweaty dancing and pounding, punky music? It was *so* good and she missed it *so* much. The music scene was real in Golden Grove; Jules and Dia had been going to backyard shows and all-ages clubs for years before they'd picked up their own instruments and become part of it.

(Jules made herself stop. That was before, and this was now. They had no band. They had no Hanna. It made Jules ache thinking about it all.)

"HMK are completely unoriginal and you know it," Dia said. "They're the worst Glory Alabama rip-off."

Jules snorted. Anyone could be, and often was, labeled a GA rip-off by them—when your town had an amazing band that actually broke out, headlined every big festival in the US and overseas, played with legends like Sleater-Kinney and Melissa Auf der Maur, featured on the cover of not only *Rolling Stone* but fucking *Vogue*, too, there was a certain loyalty. Jules smiled, ready to drop a bomb on Dia. "You know they're touring soon, right?"

"What? Glory Alabama?" Dia said, and her voice jumped an octave. "Shut up. *Why* is this the first I'm hearing of this?"

"First tour in five years," Jules said. "First time back here in almost *ten*."

Dia widened her eyes. "Oh my god, we're going," she said. "Oh my *god*, we're going to get to see them? I don't care how much tickets are, I will work a month straight of morning shifts, whatever. We need to be there."

"I thought you might like that," Jules said with a laugh, and Lex laughed with her. "We can be the creeper fans who wait outside their tour bus, if you want."

"That is my dream," Dia said. She got up and opened her closet, taking out a plain white shirt, which she looked at for a second before putting back. "Is a dress too much?" she asked. "I have no idea anymore. But I want to look hot. Not like a mom."

"You are a mom," Jules said, glancing over. "A hot mom."

"You know what I mean."

"Wear whatever you want," Jules said, and she sat up. "Y'know, it's really only going to be people from school at this party."

"Okay." Dia stepped out of her shorts and held a blue-and-white vintage-ish dress in front of herself. "What about this?"

"Yeah, great," Jules said impatiently. "I'm only saying, if you were maybe trying to look especially good for a certain specific somebody—"

Dia pulled the dress over her head, coming up laughing. "I'm not."

"And," Jules continued, "if that certain somebody happened to be one Jesse Mackenzie . . ."

"I already said I'm not." Dia smoothed her hands over the striped skirt of the dress. "Juliana, a person can want to put on nice makeup and dress up and look good for reasons other than wanting to impress somebody," Dia said. "A person can want to put on nice makeup and dress up and look good solely for themselves."

Jules held up her hands. "All right, I take it back."

"You should." Dia turned her attention to Alexa, her entire face suddenly beaming. "What do you say, Lex? Is Mommy good to go?"

Lex opened her mouth in a big yawn, a squeak her only response. "You and me both, kid," Dia said with a laugh, and Jules reached over to tickle the baby until she was giggling wildly, too, all three of them exited and happy.

"Let's get out of here," Jules said eventually, breathless. "One last time, right?"

The bus dropped them off on the edge of a wide cul-de-sac lined with tall trees, branches still in the warm night, and Jules stared up at them. This was the Nice Side of Town, the side of Golden Grove where the big houses had glittering blue pools and cutesy mailboxes. The cars on the drive were shiny, brilliant, brand new; the lawns were green and dotted with flowers.

It made Jules feel small sometimes, how awed she was by these things, but wouldn't it be nice? Wouldn't it be nice to sit in your pretty house, and look out at your beautiful yard, and feel proud?

That was what she really wanted. That was what she secretly feared she'd never have.

A pretty, happy, shiny life.

Dia was already walking down the street, and Jules took several long strides to catch up with her, bouncing in her fresh Nikes. "I changed my mind," she said. "Come on. Let's go to the show. It'll be so much better than this."

"We're already here!" Dia whirled around, the skirt of her dress spinning, and she looked like some fifties movie star. "We made a deal! It's going to be fine."

"It's going to be annoying." Jules slowed as they approached the house with the music pounding out from the open front door. "But whatever. You want your party, you get your party."

"Attagirl." Dia hooked her arm through Jules's. "Chin up, kid," she said, an impression of the old stars she looked like tonight. "Let's have fun."

Fun, Jules thought. *I can do that.*

Once they were inside it didn't take long for Jules to remember that yeah, parties were annoying—people spilled drinks on you and yelled way too loud in your ear—but they were also loose, wild, open. In the big living room two guys—one on drums, one behind a synth—made loud, bass-heavy music, impossible not to nod your head to.

Jules watched them play. She recognized them from around town, even disconnected as she was right now. They'd won the Sun City Originals contest last year, too, the contest that she and Dia and Hanna had always planned to enter, before everything. It was like a rite of passage around town and beyond to at least try to win. Not for the prize—five hundred dollars and your song on the station playlist was cool, but it was more about bragging rights. So that one day in the future, when you were selling out tours, you could say that was where you got your start and Look at Us Now.

"Jules." Dia was at her elbow. "I'm getting a drink. What do you want?"

Jules pulled her attention away from the music and raised her voice. "Whatever," she said. "And lots of it."

Because Dia was right: this was their last-ever high school party, the last time they'd see some of these people, and didn't they deserve to have a good time?

Yes, Jules decided, and so she let the girl she'd sat next to in freshman English spin her around the living room to that slick electronica. She took the shot offered by Oscar Rush and followed him out onto the deck. She watched Oscar and his buddies as they threw themselves fully clothed into the pool, and she stepped closer to the edge. She considered jumping herself, and thought about what it would be like to hit the cool water and disappear under the surface, how long she could swim around down there before her lungs began to ache.

Jules crouched down and dipped her hand into the blue. Oscar was dunking some kid under, water splashing everywhere, and Jules laughed. She looked up, searching for Dia. But the gaze she found was not Dia's.

It was Hanna Adler's.

They stared at each other.

Jules hadn't thought she would be here. Wasn't sure why she had thought that, because it used to be that Hanna was the life of any and every party. Why would that be different? Just because Jules wasn't at those parties anymore didn't mean that Hanna wasn't.

Jules stood and hitched up her jeans. Her skin was hot to the touch and her mouth had that sour-sweet nervous taste. *How do I look to her?* she thought. To Jules, Hanna looked . . . like Hanna. An inch of dark roots in her blond hair, dark circles beneath her eyes, the same way she looked every time Jules glimpsed her in the packed hallway at school. Well—that wouldn't happen anymore. Maybe this was it: maybe Hanna was one of those people Jules would never see again. That didn't stop the twitch in the back of her mind, the reminder that this girl used to be her friend.

But tonight wasn't meant for her to fixate on things from the past that she couldn't change. Or people, who wouldn't change.

A touch on her shoulder, and Jules turned away from Hanna's empty stare. "Hey." Dia handed her a cup filled to overflowing with a pinky-orange liquid. "What are you doing?"

"I—" Jules started to say *I saw Hanna, she's here,* but she stopped herself. What was the point? That was all so old now, the three of them. Forget it. "Nothing. Waiting."

Dia tipped her head to the side, her eyes so shiny and excited. "For what?"

Jules knocked her cup against Dia's and downed the contents—too warm, sticky, and syrupy but with enough sting to perk her up—before smiling at Dia. "Isn't that the question?"

Elliot

JULY

Elliot has no idea who this house belongs to.

He has no idea whose party this is.

But he knows he's having a good time.

"Nolan," he says—or yells, maybe—"what time is it?"

Nolan checks his phone. "Ten fifteen."

"Okay!" Elliot has to be home by eleven, according to his dad, and midnight, according to his mom. He'll roll in sometime between the two, probably, and if he's lucky he won't get grounded.

He wanders outside, sipping the punch that stings as it goes down. It's packed out here, all these people crowding a makeshift stage where a band plays. He might not know where he is but these parties are all the same: music outside, drinks in the kitchen, a circle of stoners in an off-limits bedroom.

A punch hits his arm and he swears. "Kwame, you asshole."

Kwame salutes. "I'm out, man. Early shift in the morning. You coming to Mike's tomorrow?"

"I'll be there."

He's left alone again, and pulls a hand through his curls as he gets closer to the band. It's these three girls going hell for leather up there, and the music's good, but what catches Elliot right away is the girl in the front, singing.

It's not just that she's hot—though she is. Short and curvy and in these skin-tight jeans that make Elliot think about pulling them off and—

He shifts. Calm down.

She's up there, playing her red guitar like she wants to hurt it, and singing in this raspy voice, and winding her body like no one's watching her. But Elliot is.

Then he looks around and realizes: so is everyone else.

Later.

Elliot's trying to ignore Nolan arguing with him over their last baseball game, the mistakes Elliot apparently made that cost them the win, his tendency to freeze. He's trying to ignore Nolan, because on the other side of the yard the girl from the band stands right in his eye line.

"Uh-huh," he says, nodding without looking at Nolan. "Whatever."

He can't hear the girl talking, but she's using her hands to tell a story, drawing swooping circles in the air, and the other band members are watching her intently. She looks like the kind of person you have to listen to, he thinks. If it was him standing in front of her, watching those dizzying hands, he'd be listening.

Go over, he thinks. *Say hello. Ask her name.*

Is that an asshole move? Butting in while she's busy talking? Or is it okay? He won't know her if he doesn't talk to her. But if he talks to her she might not want to know him.

Elliot cuts Nolan off. "I'm getting a drink," he says. "You want one?"

"I'm good."

In this stranger's kitchen he grabs a half-empty bottle of rum, then puts it back. The clock on the microwave says 11:20.

Hi, he practices in his head. *You were really good.*

I like your band.

I like your band? What is he, twelve?

Hi. Good set.

Better?

Hi. I'm Elliot.

A coppery-brown hand reaches for the stack of cups at the same time Elliot does and he looks up to see the band girl right there. "Sorry," she says with a shake of her head, and the tight spirals of her curls fan around her face. "You go."

"No," Elliot says, his mouth dry. "After you."

She smiles at him, creases appearing around her eyes. "Thanks."

Silence.

Well, not silence: the noise of other people coming for drinks, more music outside. But silence from Elliot, his closed mouth.

"You know you're on the wrong coast."

"What?"

The girl finishes filling her cup and then points at Elliot's chest. "Biggie," she says, and he looks down at his shirt, The Notorious B.I.G. in his chains and crown, and for a moment Elliot thinks she's being serious, her face is dead serious, but then she cracks. "It's a joke."

Elliot manages a laugh and pulls a hand through his hair, a nervous tic he can't stop doing tonight. "Right," he says. "It's my mom's fault. She's from New York."

"I guess you get a pass," the girl says, and then she sees something over his shoulder and her face clouds over. "God, that was fast."

Elliot turns right as a white girl in supershort shorts stumbles into the kitchen. "There you are!" the girl sings, swaying slightly. "I've been looking for you."

"Hanna, what are you doing?" The band girl has forgotten about Elliot entirely, he can tell, as she hurries to the girl he now recognizes as the drummer from earlier. "Whoa! Okay, it's time to call Ciara. You're going home."

They're gone in a second and Elliot's left kicking himself. He should've taken his chance.

This is exactly what Nolan means when he says Elliot freezes.

It's 12:17, according to Elliot's phone. He's definitely going to be grounded.

He waits outside for Nolan, still in the house flirting with this guy with two sharp bars through his eyebrow. It's a hot night, the kind where you wake up in a layer of your own stale sweat, and Elliot holds his hand out into the empty air.

"We need rain." The voice comes from somewhere to his left, and then the band girl steps into his sight. "California's thirsty."

"Right," Elliot says, and winces. Is he capable of saying anything multisyllabic to this girl? He clears his throats, shoves his hands in his pockets. "Is your friend okay?"

The girl makes a face that Elliot can only describe as Over It. "Yeah," she says. "Too much to drink. She does it all the time. It's fine." The way she says *It's fine* tells Elliot it's anything but.

"You played tonight, right?" he says next. "You were good."

She shoots him a look, like it's the most obvious thing in the world. "I know."

Confident. Elliot decides to match her. "I'm Elliot," he says. "What's your name?"

She looks him up and down like she's vetting him, deciding whether to trust him or not. Eventually she smiles and looks right at him, these deep, dark eyes, and Elliot feels like she's laid him open right there on the street. "Hi, Elliot," she says. "I'm Dia."

Hanna

Hanna matched her steps to the beat of the frenetic drums pounding in her headphones, stepping on every crack and flattened piece of gum. Bad luck couldn't hurt her any more than it already had.

Four hundred and twelve days, she thought. No; it was after midnight now. So four hundred and thirteen.

Hanna ducked into the alley, which was dark enough to make her clutch her keys between her fingers. It had been a complete waste of time, that party, and Hanna had known it even before she'd walked in to the sight of Oscar Rush dancing shirtless on his parents' dining table. She had only gone because everybody else was going, and did she really want to remember her graduation as another night she spent alone at home in her bedroom?

In hindsight: yes.

The moon was a skinny sliver above Hanna's head, whatever light it gave off masked by neon streetlights. She skipped through track after track as she walked, sometimes letting no more than three seconds elapse before moving on, searching for something to set her nerves alight. On Hayworth Boulevard she let Brody Dalle scream about underworlds and ghost towns, and the perpetual itch that crawled up and down her spine felt satisfied, for three short minutes. But then the song was over and the yearning flooded back and she stopped, to wonder, to stare up at that crescent moon.

If she'd known Jules and Dia were going to be there, she definitely wouldn't have gone. But from now on, she wouldn't have to see them, would she? At school it had been hard to avoid them, even though she tried; there were only so many places to go, and she couldn't miss them walking the halls together. And as much as she pretended it didn't, it hurt—hurt deep, far down, in the place she stored those shattered pieces of her heart, next to the guilt. Because it used to be the three of them, always. Sharing fries and going to watch the BMXers pulling tricks after school. Sleeping three to a bed and switching clothes and rolling into places like they were the most important people in the entire world. Singing themselves hoarse, throats raw, on makeshift stages in people's backyards. Those were *their* moments, Hanna and Dia and Jules, always.

Until they weren't.

For four hundred and thirteen days, she'd been sober. For all that time, plus eight months more, they had not been friends. Things had changed, fissures and cracks becoming an all-out chasm so quietly and slowly that Hanna almost missed it. And when she'd realized, it had been too late. Nothing she could fix.

And she was alone.

Hanna sped up as she started down the long hill that eventually turned into her street. That was then and this was now, and now she was free. She didn't have to see them anymore, as long as she avoided their parts of town. And in September she'd start working full time, doing admin at a medical company, and she'd save all the money she made, and in a few years she'd be able to leave. And leave so much behind—her ex-friends, her mom's constant criticism, this whole town.

The music in her ears sped up, some discofied girl band, and Hanna matched her pace to it. She was almost running when she passed the Dempseys' place with its front yard of wildflowers, the biggest burst of color on the block. Finally her key slipped soundlessly into the lock of her own house and Hanna stepped inside.

It was still and quiet, and Hanna exhaled into the comfort of it. "You are okay," she whispered out loud, fast breaths. "You are here. You are okay."

She waited until her heart had slowed to its normal rhythm before climbing the stairs. She bypassed her bedroom and eased open the door plastered in pretty flower cutouts.

Molly's eyes flickered open as Hanna entered, as she slipped off her shoes and stole under the covers into her little sister's bed. "Hey, birdy."

"Hey, birdbrain."

Hanna flicked Molly's arm. "Shut up."

Molly's laugh turned into a yawn, her tongue peeking out catlike. Molly hated all that, Hanna knew—the nicknames and being told how adorable she was—now that she was thirteen. But being annoying was Hanna's prerogative as big sister, right?

"Did you have a good time?" Molly whispered, her eyes shining bright in the dark. "Were there cute boys there? Or cute girls? Did anyone get in a fight?"

"Parties aren't like they show them on TV, Moll." Hanna tucked her hands under her armpits and screwed up her face. "Trust me, you'll understand once you get to high school. They're another ridiculous way for people to decide who's cool and who isn't, and to get drunk so they can do things they don't have the courage for otherwise."

Molly's eyes searched her face, cautious trust in that look. "You didn't, right?" she asked, and her voice held the fear that her face did not. "Get drunk?"

See, she might be thirteen, but sometimes she sounded thirty. "No," Hanna said, and god, the crushing wave of guilt that broke with Molly's words, it could have drowned her. She wasn't really asking, Hanna knew; Molly knew her drunk. She wouldn't have to ask. It was more like she was checking, making sure, that she could really believe the sister in front of her eyes. And Hanna knew that was nobody's fault but her own. That was what happened when you let your little sister find you unconscious among empty bottles. "No, I didn't. Don't worry."

"I wasn't worried," Molly said. "Just wondering." She rolled onto her back, blond hair mussed around her face, and did her trademark shoulder-shrug-eye-roll combo. "If you don't have anything good to tell me, then why did you wake me up?"

"It's my right as a big sister." Hanna smacked a kiss on Molly's cheek before slipping out of the twin bed. "It's late," she said. "Go to sleep, okay? I'll see you in the morning."

"Will you go with me to the bookstore tomorrow?" Molly widened her eyes. "Please?"

"After work, sure," Hanna said. "Whatever you want. Now go to sleep."

She left the room and pulled the door almost closed, and then she stood there watching through the gap as Molly fell asleep, a ball beneath the covers. Only when Hanna was satisfied that her sister was absolutely asleep did she go to her own room. She stripped to her underwear, put on an old shirt, and climbed into bed.

What she'd told Molly was true: parties weren't like they were on TV. Hanna used to love them—they'd been fun for her. Not so much for everyone around her, having to hold her hair back and pick her up off the floor and rescue her from her whirlwind of destruction. But being drunk made her feel invincible, gave her cover for so many things. She said whatever she wanted, she did anything and everything that she got the urge to, and when she fucked up (often, and in big ways), she'd brush it off: "I was drunk! It's no big deal."

Until it was a big deal, a rubber tube down her throat, no-oxygen-to-her-brain kind of big deal.

Hanna had thought that getting sober would make everything better. Turn her into this shiny, new Hanna. But she'd realized pretty quickly that the girl who said every little thing that came into her head, who did whatever she wanted without thinking, who was careless and said and did things that really hurt the people around her—that wasn't because of the drinking. It was her, the way she was wired.

She'd thought she'd be happy sober. But her problems didn't go away; they shifted. Now she was always working out how to keep herself in check, to not say those awful things, to not act out. How to rewire herself so her instinct was not complete and utter self-destruction. How to not let the guilt and resentment and anger sweep her up and carry her to the point of giving up, giving in, letting herself drink again because at least then she could forget about it all.

Hanna sighed into the dark. Every night now this happened to her—no sleep, thoughts racing. So she did what she usually did: got out of bed and crouched to yank open the bottom drawer of her nightstand. Inside, thin black notebooks stacked up, some battered and creased, some shiny-new.

Hanna pulled out one with the spine cracked but not yet falling apart, and a pen that always leaked black ink all over her fingers. This was the best way she had to combat the self-loathing—well, the best that wasn't relapsing. She sat with her back against her bed and flicked to a clean page, past all the words that sometimes felt like poetry, sometimes self-indulgent ramblings, but in the end, were always songs.

She and Dia and Jules weren't friends anymore, no. They didn't make music anymore, no. But they did not own her writing; the lyrics that came from her brain and heart and pit of her stomach were Hanna's and Hanna's alone.

Without thinking too much about it, she scratched out a first line.

She wears your face—I've seen her.

jules

They left the party when it got sloppy, spilled drinks on the living room rug and vomit in the kitchen sink. The last bus only took them as far as Dia's, and Jules walked the rest of the way home, exhausted when she finally got there. She crept in quietly, then stood over the kitchen sink to eat a bowl of cereal, the milk turning pink, and closed her eyes when she thought about having to go to work in five hours.

She rinsed her bowl out and tiptoed upstairs, past her parents' bedroom, past Danny's door. In her room she changed into a tank top and pajama shorts, and pushed her windows open as far as they would go. The still air inside her room had a suffocating thickness to it, and Jules could feel sweat already starting at the base of her spine. Tomorrow was the first day of . . . what? Summer? The rest of her life?

In the bathroom she wiped off the little makeup Dia had put on her and brushed her teeth, peed, piled her braids up, and secured them beneath a leopard-print satin scarf, and when she got back to her bedroom her phone was flashing.

Jules reached for the phone, expecting it to be Dia saying good night, and definitely not expecting the name that she actually saw.

Delaney Myers.

Jules sat on her bed, shuffled back until she was pressed into the corner, and crossed her legs. The slightest breeze blew through the open windows, a welcome coolness on Jules's clammy skin.

Ignore it, she thought. *I should ignore this. I'm going to ignore her.*

Jules had to tell herself that, had to remind herself of the decision she'd made six months ago, when she'd told Delaney that they'd be better apart, that she was done. She had to remind herself of *why* she'd broken up with Delaney: she and Jules were not good together. It was as simple as that.

Okay, so it was a *little* more complicated.

One: Delaney was not out, and Jules was. That was okay—Jules was not interested in pressuring Delaney into coming out or doing anything she wasn't comfortable with yet. But it did mean that they didn't go out much, and when they did go out, they didn't act like a couple.

Which didn't help problem two: Jules was a romantic, the worst kind, the kind who dreamed of kisses in the rain and bouquets of beautiful flowers bigger than her body and running hand-in-hand from the weight of the world. She wanted the kind of love her parents had, still giddy after so many years. And Delaney? That was not her at all. She tried sometimes, but it was always lacking—the wrong coffee from

Starbucks, wilting flowers from the gas station. She just didn't get it.

And really, that was problem number three: They had very little in common, besides finding each other attractive and that one murder mystery show they were both obsessed with. They couldn't agree on what movie to watch, what music to listen to, what food to order. And in a weird way, Jules kind of liked when they bickered about all that. It felt like Delaney cared, at least. So sometimes she'd pick a fight over nothing in particular, to piss Delaney off, and afterward she'd kiss Delaney extra sweet to make up for it, and she kidded herself that it was passion.

For almost six months, Jules had managed to keep the illusion going. But one day, on the bus, sitting on opposite sides of the aisle and arguing over fucking Twizzlers or Red Vines, she'd realized.

This was not good for either of them.

This was not what she wanted.

This was not what she deserved.

So she'd ended it not long after, and hadn't really spoken to Delaney since—sometimes a hi in the hall at school, but that was about it.

(Okay, and *one* slipup, after a late night at work. But everybody called their ex to come pick them up and then fooled around for forty-five minutes in the back parking lot at least once, right?)

Jules smiled despite herself, shaking her head as, against her better instincts, she opened the text.

Four small words:

You looked good tonight.

Jules grasped at the hem of her tank, feeling heat race through her.

Had Delaney been there, at the party? Jules hadn't seen her anywhere.

You looked good tonight.

That meant Delaney had been looking for her, though. Watching her. Deciding that she looked good. Deciding to tell her.

Why?

Jules slid down until she was lying on her side, one arm wrapped around her body. "She's drunk," she whispered to herself, to her empty bedroom. It was perfectly quiet, aside from the rushed in-and-out of her breathing, the air in her lungs crackling with confusion. "She's drunk and she thinks this is a good idea but it's not. It's a very bad idea. And she's drunk. That's all."

Saying it out loud made it easier to believe.

It didn't make it easier for her to stop remembering what it was like to kiss Delaney. She slipped her fingers beneath the neckline of her shirt, sighing as she pressed her hand to the space between her breasts, to feel her heart pounding there. Kissing Delaney was soft summer wind and a sugar rush of sweetness, the hot thrill of shoplifting and the want drumming-thrumming-humming in parts of her body that before then only Jules had reached. It was rushed and urgent and intoxicating.

Jules could get wild high from a minute of pure Delaney.

But that was all it was, really—physical, a brief relief from the way Jules felt almost all the time, ready to combust, this pent-up energy scalding inside her. (And she could give herself better relief; she was good at that.)

It was not, as her overindulgent brain and heart conspired to tell her, a sign of how much Delaney loved her. And this, tonight, this text? It was not some part of Delaney realizing that Jules was the only person for her, the start of some grand gesture for getting Jules back. For the entirety of their short relationship, Jules had gone along in the naive belief that this was only their beginning, the hard part that came before the movie climax, when Delaney would suddenly realize what a mistake she was making and chase Jules down, tell her she loved her, fight for her.

The sheets whispered as Jules rolled over and squeezed her legs together to ease the tension between them, rubbing her thumb across the words on the screen.

No more naivety. This was not a movie. And Jules deserved way more than alcohol-fueled texts in the middle of the night.

You looked good tonight.

She pressed Delete.

Dia

"Dia!" Her mom's voice came loud and insistent through the bedroom door. "Do you not hear your daughter crying? Come do something about it!"

Dia winced at the volume of her mom's voice mixed with Alexa's sharp wail. All Lex had been doing for the past three days was crying: when she had to eat, when she had to get dressed, when her pacifier fell on the floor, when Dia read her favorite stories. According to the books, this meant Lex was going through a "developmental leap," but now they were all starting to get frictiony and Dia was wondering when she might *leap* into *quiet*.

"Dia!"

"I'm coming!" Dia yelled, and then under her breath, "Jesus Christ."

She yanked a clean shirt on with her cutoffs and tossed her stained uniform in the hamper. All morning she'd been sweating in the kitchen of the bakery, pulling out sheet after sheet of sugar cookies and listening to her manager, Imelda, out front trilling, "Welcome to the Flour Shop!" She'd stolen a ten-minute break in the freezer, because another moment of Imelda's voice would have officially pushed her over the edge.

She pulled the elastic out of her hair and teased out her curls as she made her way to the living room. Her mom was pacing around the room, bouncing Lex almost aggressively, and when she saw Dia she let out this exasperated sigh. "Look, baby, it's your mama!"

Alexa kept on crying and Dia swooped in to take her before her mom lost it. "C'mere. What's wrong?"

Lex bumped her head into Dia's shoulder, weeping a wet patch on that fresh shirt. Dia looked over her head to her mom. "Do you think maybe she needs to see a doctor? She's been like this for days now."

Nina followed them into the kitchen. "No, it's just a phase."

"Great." Dia plunked the baby into her high chair and grabbed a handful of tissues to wipe the tears and snot from her face. "Has she eaten?"

"Uh-uh." Nina opened the refrigerator and took out a pitcher of iced tea. "She wouldn't let me near her with anything."

"Right." Dia crouched so she was eye level with her daughter. "Lex, I'm going to get you lunch. What do you want to eat? Use your words."

Alexa's howls quieted to whimpers, and between giant gulping breaths of air she said, "I . . . want . . . bannas."

"Bananas! We can do bananas, no problem." Dia watched Lex's

face light up. God, before Lex had come along she'd never imagined that she could be so infuriated yet so infatuated at the same damn time. If only the solution to everything was as simple as bananas. "And maybe after lunch we can go see the puppy, if Miss Candy's home."

"We see the puppy?" Lex asked, sniffling but beaming. "Waffles!"

"Yes, Waffles, that's right!" Nina said, all cheer, and then to Dia, sharper, "You'll spoil her, one day."

"I know." She added that to the running list she kept in her head, Rules for Being a Good Mother: *Be tough, don't stress, keep her calm, don't spoil her.* Simple.

"She makes it so easy, though." Nina grabbed Alexa's hand and kissed her chubby fingers. "I'm going to run to the store. You be good, okay?"

"Bye," Dia called as her mom left. When it was the two of them, Dia fixed her gaze on Lex, staring at each other with their serious eyes. "All right, Lex. What do you say we go on an adventure today?"

They took the bus to Golden Grove Gardens, Dia's absolute favorite place in town.

In the stillness of the park Lex didn't stop fussing, kicking her legs out of the stroller, and straining at the straps holding her in. She kept up the noise, too, and Dia ignored the pointed looks from the people they passed, focusing on calming herself with the beauty of the gardens. A year ago Dia would have been mortified by Alexa's tantrum. Now, though, she didn't really care. Let them stare all they wanted—what, like they'd never seen a kid losing it before? Besides, it didn't really matter whether Alexa was yelling or sleeping or being the most angelic, beaming baby in the world; Dia always got looks. To everybody in town she was one of two things. To the assholes, and people who didn't know, she was a walking, talking stereotype, another brown girl with a baby. (Like that was all she was—never mind that she was a musician, that she was a *person*.) And the people who did know . . .

Dia could always recognize those. They were the people who looked a little too long before smiling at her, or patted her on the hand when she served them at the Flour Shop. And sometimes she wanted to say to them, "He wasn't even officially my boyfriend, you don't have to feel so sorry for me." But she could never say that to anyone besides Jules, and the rest of the time she let them imagine whatever they wanted. Because she was still and always the girl who had the baby by the dead boy.

This was how the true story went: Dia met Elliot Mendes at a party, almost three years ago. He was cute, pretty eyes and a slow smile. They flirted for a couple weeks, made out at a few more parties. Then Elliot took her out to the drive-in movie theater, and when Dia teased him and said *This is a date, isn't it,* he said, *Don't make fun of me or I won't buy you any snacks* and kissed her so she'd stop laughing. And that was how it went for a few months, and Dia thought maybe he'd be it, her first love and all that.

They'd been at a party the last time she'd seen him. It had been a good night—they'd watched Ciara's band play; Hanna had been on her best behavior, Jules had been silly. They'd jumped on the trampoline in a stranger's yard. She still had the picture Elliot had taken.

He'd told her she was beautiful.

And sometime in the early hours of the morning, when Elliot was walking home, someone hit him with their car. Couldn't look up from their phone long enough to see the person in front of them and by the time he hit the ground, her dad had told her after, the only reassurance she could ask him for, he was already dead.

And that was that.

Except it wasn't, because then Dia took a positive pregnancy test and she decided, in a burst of selfish love and hurting broken-heartedness, to have the baby.

So now she was the Girl Who Had the Baby by the Dead Boy, she guessed.

The flowers were in full glorious bloom. They wandered the paths long enough that Lex finally ran out of steam and fell asleep with her thumb jammed in her mouth. Dia pushed the stroller in the direction of the rose gardens, and it was nice: the sun on her face, walking with no place to be, her baby content (for now), and all the beautiful scenery around them. See? Things could be good.

She was so far away that the *tick-tick-tick* of bicycle wheels only registered a second before her name was called out: "Dia!"

She whipped around, a finger to her lips as she faced the boy on the bike. Today his hands were bandaged, grimy white around his burnt-sienna skin. Always with the accidents.

To his credit, Jesse looked suitably chastised and hit the brakes, coasting toward her quietly now. "Hey," he said when he was close enough for normal volume, letting his feet drop to the ground. "Sorry."

"It's okay," Dia said, and she tipped her head in the direction of the stroller. "She's asleep, is all, and we're having kind of a rough day, so."

Jesse peered behind the hood of the stroller, pulled down so Lex didn't get too much sun, and then his face broke into that beautiful smile of his. "She looks like butter wouldn't melt."

"That's what she wants you to think," Dia said. "What are you doing here, anyway? You know you're breaking the rules." Dia pointed at a faraway sign that she knew had a big CYCLING PROHIBITED proclamation on it.

"That's not a real rule," he said. "And I came to see you. I went by your house but you weren't there, and then you weren't at the bakery, but you were here. So here I am."

I came to see you. See, it was pretty little words like that, always getting Dia in more trouble.

"You *love* him," Jules would always say to her when she felt like being annoying. "Everyone can see it." And Dia would say, "So? I don't have time for a boyfriend."

That was true—when they'd first met, Alexa had been tiny and Dia was busy with school and work and taking care of a baby, and so she'd told Jesse they could only be friends.

But the real reason she kept to herself. No one needed to know that her avoidance of Jesse had less to do with her busyness and more to do with how the last boy she might have loved was dead now. How afraid she was to lose another person, to feel that cold shock of loss steal the breath from her lungs.

So she pretended it was all Lex and graduating and getting

through, and Jesse got it, he understood, and Dia had put all thoughts of his almost-black eyes and full mouth, his rich brown skin and back muscles out of her brain. They were friends. It was fine.

Except for when he said things like *I came to see you*, or when she touched his hand a little too long, or when she caught him watching her like he thought no one could see him.

Now Dia found a bench and sat, keeping one foot on the front bar of the stroller so she could ease it back and forth, keep Lex sleeping. "Here you are," she said. "What are you doing tonight?"

"Working," Jesse said. He leaned on the handlebars of his black bike, dirt sprayed across the metal. "If you come by I'll hook you up."

Dia gave half a laugh. "Have you ever noticed that our entire friendship is based on free food?"

"But Giorgio's pizza *is* the best," Jesse said.

"No lie."

Jesse pushed back on his bike. "So you gonna come by?"

"Can't." She held up her hand to make the biggest air quotes. "We're having 'family dinner' tonight. My mom's cooking."

"Okay," Jesse said. "So I'll see you around eight, then?"

Dia reached out to smack him but he dodged her, too fast. "Shut up. It's not my mom's fault she's a terrible cook."

"I never said she was," Jesse said. "But, y'know, if you're still hungry after, we got you."

"Sure."

Jesse spun his handlebars. "Are you going to Revelry next week?"

"For what?"

"The Sun City contest. The launch night or whatever."

Dia lifted her head and eyed him. "A launch event? They never did that before. Who's playing?"

"Are you serious? You haven't heard?" Jesse shook his head as he swung his backpack around. "Sometimes I think you ignore this stuff on purpose. You know they're changing the contest, right? Everybody's losing their shit even more than usual."

He pulled a crumpled flyer out of his bag and handed it to her. "See?"

Dia snatched it and scanned the glossy words: *Sun City Radio presents . . . Originals contest . . . First Place prize $15,000 and the chance to open for Glory Alabama.*

Hold up.

Playing with Glory Alabama?

Fifteen.

Thousand.

Dollars?

"Holy shit," she said. "Holy *shit*. That's a lot of money." Not to mention the little thing of *playing with Glory Alabama*. She read it again and slapped her hand on the bench. "Wait, is this for real?"

"One hundred percent," Jesse said. "Like I said, everyone's losing it."

Understandably, Dia thought. She was on the verge of it, too, as she took in the words on the flyer.

This was way bigger than before.

This was *more*.

This maybe changed things.

"Oh my god," she said, looking up at Jesse. "Can I keep this?"

He shrugged. "Sure." And then his look turned suspicious. "Why?"

"Because," Dia said. "That's all."

"Because maybe you're thinking about doing it?"

Dia raised her eyebrows. "Me and what band? I don't know if you've noticed, but I don't play anymore."

"Okay," Jesse said, bouncing his front wheel on the sand-colored gravel. "No, you're not interested, not at all."

She got up and grabbed the stroller, accidentally turning it so sharply that Lex woke with a startled cry. "Don't be an ass."

"Me?" Jesse put on a hurt face, but his shit-eating grin couldn't be hidden. "Come on, Dee. I can see the wheels in your brain turning as you talk."

Dia folded the flyer in half, and then again, and slipped it into her back pocket. He never missed anything with her. Not that she was *really* thinking about entering, because it was true, she didn't play anymore. There hadn't been a band for years. They didn't speak to Hanna. Dia couldn't remember the last time she'd been to a show, let alone played one.

(That was a lie. Of course she remembered the last time they'd played: in Rexford, at the end of a skate competition. Under a wide-open sky, the sun glowing on them, Elliot buried a month. And all day long, trying in vain to keep Hanna sober so she could play. Sweet memories.)

And really, Dia thought, so what if she was intrigued? It was only fantasy, one she would cut off before it began to hurt too much. It wasn't like she was going to do it. How could she?

She turned the stroller and scuffed her toe in the gravel. "My wheels are turning, huh? You think you know me," she said to Jesse, her fingers plucking at the collar of his shirt. "But I have secrets like you can't even *imagine*."

Did that sound too flirty? It was so hard to toe the line she'd drawn and sometimes hated.

But Jesse held his hands up and gave that smile of his. "All right," he said. "Maybe I'm wrong."

Dia rolled her eyes again, over-exaggerated this time, because maybe he was right, too. "We'll see," she said.

Then they walked the rest of the park, through the rose garden and by the pond and back around, talking about anything but the contest, how bad Dia wanted to play again. It was easy enough; Dia didn't talk about it anymore. She had made Jules stop, too. They both knew how much they missed performing and recording and feeling the pulsating energy of an audience with its eyes on them. Talking about it when there was no hope of going back there was way too much of a downer.

And it was okay, Dia told herself now, leading Jesse through the flowers. She didn't *need* it. That was then, and this was now.

And right now, she definitely wasn't still thinking about the flyer in her back pocket, the contest.

Not at all.

Dia

Dia waited until Lex was asleep in her crib that night, uttering her soft toddler snores, and then plugged her headphones in to her laptop. She clicked through to find the folder buried deepest of all, labeled *EP*.

Five songs that they'd recorded in Hanna's garage, with the jankiest setup, but it had been all they'd known how to do, and it was exhilarating to be able to play their music back afterward.

She hovered the cursor over the Play button. This was silly, really. What did it matter if the prize money was big enough to mean something to her now? Or that one of her favorite bands was involved? Her life was still what it was. The contest didn't change that.

But. Still.

She clicked Play.

The first note hit and that was it: Dia was gone. No longer was she sitting cross-legged on her bed, the sun setting outside and her daughter lying near. She was fourteen again, precocious as hell and pleased by that.

It had started when Dia had dragged them to a party they weren't invited to, to watch this band she'd heard was cool: Graceland. And they didn't let her down—their sound was staticky, electric, and Dia had been fixated on the lead singer, a light-skinned girl with locs twisted into a crown and flowers tattooed on her arms. *I wanna do that,* she'd thought, carefully watching the girl's careless style on the makeshift stage.

She'd been all keyed up after and started saying, "We should make our own music. We could be as good as that. Better, even. That could be us."

Dia already played. Her dad had been teaching her since before she could talk. She practiced on his old acoustic, and a third-hand, cherry-red electric she'd saved enough birthday money for. When she begged, he got his old equipment out of storage for them—amps and mics and everything they needed. Hanna bought an almost-trashed drum kit from a kid at school and Jules blew her savings on a battered bass, and, like magic, they were a band.

They'd thrown themselves into writing, playing, listening over and over to five-second loops of Glory Alabama songs to figure out their intricacies. Spent lunch periods scribbling lyrics and chord changes in the back of their notebooks.

The first time they played through a ten-minute set of their own songs, Dia felt more than triumphant.

"Now what?" Hanna had asked.

"Now," Dia said. "We get a show."

They had already been going to the all-ages nights at Revelry for a year almost, and hanging out at backyard shows. There was this festival that happened every year, the biggest and best local bands coming together for free. And Dia decided that *that* was going to be their performance debut. All she had to do was convince the organizers to let them in.

Her first email had gotten her this response: "The lineup's full, sorry! Maybe next year."

But Dia was stubborn and emailed again, and again, every day with a new reason why Fairground—the name they'd chosen after a thousand hours—should be on that lineup. And when she got silence in return, she took herself down to Revelry and begged the manager for help. "Sorry, kid," the manager said. "No can do. Maybe—"

"Not next year," Dia said, already on her way out. "Now."

She'd stood out in the parking lot, wondering where to go next, and only noticed the girl coming toward her when she spoke. "You have the persistence down already," she'd called out to Dia. "And the attitude."

Dia had looked up and said the only thing she could think of. "You're Ciara Lennon." The Graceland singer.

"That's me," Ciara Lennon said. "I'm also the person you've been emailing every single day."

Dia's instinct was to apologize, but instead she straightened up and folded her arms. "Persistence," she said.

Ciara smiled. "The question is, are you actually any good?"

"Let us play the festival," Dia had said, "and you'll find out."

Then Ciara had laughed. "Fine," she'd said. "Only so you'll stop irritating me."

So they'd played ten lightning-fast minutes in the early afternoon to a scattered audience—but a girl came up to them after and said she really liked them and would they play at a party she was having?

They did that party, and then a whole bunch more, and practiced almost every day after school, and got good. Really good. They played a different backyard show at least once a month, and Ciara even got them a couple slots opening up for Graceland at clubs outside Golden Grove. They'd drive out and play, then watch from the wings and wait until Ciara was ready to take them home, eating French fries in the back of the van. And after one of those shows, a woman gave them her card, said she was A&R at an indie label and they should get in touch with her.

Dia had thought it then: *This is real.*

The third track played in Dia's ears, crackly and frenetic. Their music was all like that, two-minute snarls of anger and excitement. You could hear it: the impatience, the energy, everything waiting to break out and run wild. They were like lightning, burning bright and hot.

And in the end, just as brief.

Sophomore year started out good: they had more shows, that rep's card, and almost enough money for a slot at a recording studio in Longport. But then in November, Elliot died.

The day after Christmas, Dia took the first of many positive pregnancy tests.

On New Year's Eve they found Hanna passed out in the parking lot of Clark Bar, eyes rolled back, and had to take her to the hospital to get her stomach pumped.

(What's that saying about things in threes?)

Jules wanted to keep going, but Hanna was getting worse and Dia was tired, heartbroken, and half hated Hanna for not being good enough.

It was easy to avoid her once summer rolled around, once Lex made her screaming arrival. Easier than it should have been to tell Hanna that she couldn't be around the baby, that she was out of control.

And so by the time junior year came around, they were completely fractured.

Dia listened all the way through the five tracks of the EP, three originals and two covers (a punked-out version of "Crazy in Love" and a Placebo track). Then she skipped it back to track one and listened through. Back, and through. Back, and through. The sun disappeared and pink streaks raced across the sky, the curtains billowing in the breeze from her open windows, and she closed her eyes to the sound of the past.

After work the next day, Dia scooped Lex up off the floor, where she was sitting in her pajamas, bashing at her baby-tiny keyboard. She got into her bed, allowing herself fifteen minutes of luxurious snuggly Sunday-evening baby time. "Hi, baby," Dia said, rubbing the tip of her nose against her daughter's cheek. "Did you have fun with Grammy today?"

"I found bugs," Lex said, holding her hand out and wiggling her fingers like little creatures. "And I saw Waffles!"

"Wow," Dia said, making her eyes wide. "Did you say hi to Waffles? Did she lick your hand?" Dia pulled Lex's hand to her mouth and pretended to nibble on it. "Like this?"

Lex squealed, a wild giggle. "No, Mama!"

"Silly Mama," Dia said. "Hey, Lex. You're going to be two soon. Two! Can you believe it?"

"My birthday?"

"Yeah, your birthday. We're going to have balloons and cake and presents, all for you."

Lex yawned, her tiny teeth peeking out. "Presents," she said, sounding content. "Balloons."

"You're sleepy," Dia said. "You want a song?"

Her daughter nodded, thumb slipping into her mouth, and Dia gently took it out. "Okay." She flicked through her mental catalogue of lullabies and then, running her fingers through Lex's damp curls, she sang a rendition of something her dad used to sing to her. She couldn't remember all the words but she knew the melody, and it worked. Lex's eyelids fluttered shut and stayed that way.

Dia leaned down and placed the softest kiss on Lex's head. "I love you," she said. "Sweet dreams."

She slipped out of the bed—she'd move Lex to her crib in a little while, once she was fully out—and sat at her desk again, running her fingers over her laptop keyboard. She opened a new browser window, typed "sun city radio contest" in the search bar, and hit Enter, bouncing her feet off the floor.

It was almost too good to be true, right?

And Dia knew: when something seemed that way, it almost always was.

She clicked on the first search result and the radio site loaded, with a bright banner at the top of the page:

SUN CITY AND GLORY ALABAMA PRESENT
THE ORIGINALS CONTEST

She skimmed the intro and slowed down when she got to the main section, her lips moving as she read it.

> Round One: Submit an original track. The submission portal will close on 06/13. The entries will be judged by our expert panel of listeners, and those that meet our standards will go through to Round Two.
> Round Two: You'll perform for our judging panel, one-on-one. Three entrants will go through from this to the final round.
> Round Three: The winners will be announced at the Revelry Room on 07/27 and they'll receive $15,000 cash, the opportunity to open at one of Glory Alabama's Sunset Revue Tour dates, and more.
> Give us your music NOW.

June 13. That was a week and a half away.

She clicked through to an interview with Astrid Parker and Luisa Savante, the lead singer and drummer for GA. They wanted to give back, they said in it; they'd had the idea to come back home and partner up with Sun City to find new talent, give them the opportunity to kickstart their music career. Astrid said:

It's hard to even get on the bottom of the ladder if you can't afford new equipment or studio time or transportation to other places to play different venues. Golden Grove is where we started, and it's where we want to go back to so we can help people in the same position we were in thirteen years ago.

Dia read it through twice, and then went through the fine print again, to make sure she wasn't missing anything. But she wasn't. This wasn't a joke, someone's exaggerated rumor running wild. It was real.

All she had to do was enter one song and she could have the chance to win fifteen thousand dollars. Not only that, but an opening slot for Glory Alabama, too. No amount of money could buy you that.

She looked over her shoulder at Lex, fast asleep and snuffling-snoring now. Dia's hands were itchy and her stomach doing that adrenaline-fueled swirling. Yeah, she was going to take music classes at community college, but that was months away. This was different, what she *really* wanted to be doing. And it was only one song.

She could do this, and if she didn't win, everything would carry on the way it was. But if they liked her music, if she actually won?

One song. That was all it would take.

Her guitar was propped up in its usual corner. Dia got up and moved Lex from her bed into the crib, settling her carefully. She'd need a real bed of her own soon, especially now she was trying to escape more and more often. *The never-ending expenses of motherhood,* Dia thought. *Oh, did I say expenses? I meant wonders.*

With a last glance at Lex, Dia grabbed her guitar and left her bedroom. She passed by the living room and called in to her mom. "I'm getting some air," Dia said. "She's out like a light."

"Okay," Nina called back, the rustle of a magazine page turning. "Everything okay, baby?"

"Perfect," Dia said.

She slipped out the back door and closed it behind her, sitting down on the steps that led down to their tiny patch of lawn. One day Dia wanted to live in a house with a big yard, big enough for a swing set and a pool and a trampoline, and space for them to breathe. Alexa could run around and they could eat dinner outside under the setting sun, and it would be perfect. That was Dia's dream.

One of them.

She settled her guitar on her knee and dragged her thumb over the strings, listening intently for any discordance. A quick tighten until the flatness was pulled up, and she played an E minor chord: better. Dia shifted the capo down a fret and picked out a simple melody, something that'd been rattling around her head for a few months without her doing anything about it.

She wanted to enter this contest.

She was going to.

But she didn't want to do it alone. Jules could be convinced, she was pretty sure, but it might take some work. And Hanna—

Hanna wasn't part of them anymore.

We'll figure it out, Dia thought. *We'll find somebody new. This town is full of musicians. There are other drummers. Ones who won't let us down. And we'll enter and we'll win, and then . . . glory.*

Or maybe not.

But the possibility, the wonder of it, was enough. Dia wanted it, bad.

She took her phone out and typed out a text to Jules in a rush. *Come see me after your shift tomorrow. I need to tell you something.*

Then Dia tipped her head back and looked at the tiny sliver of moon high in the gray-blue sky. Good things were about to happen. She could feel it.

Hanna

"Molly, let's go!" Hanna wound her hair into a topknot as she waited for her sister to come downstairs. "You're going to be late on your first day!"

She pulled the car keys from her back pocket and weighed them in her hand, the weight of trust and responsibility. The night before, her parents had sat her down at the kitchen table and given her this set, staring her down as her mom outlined the rules: "You'll take me to work in the morning, and then you use to the car to drive Molly, and to go to work, and that's it. No road trips, no picking up your friends, nothing. And you drive it carefully—any scratches or bumps and you'll pay for them yourself. Understand?"

Road trips? Hanna had almost laughed. Who would she go with? The phantom friends her parents seemed to think she had?

But then Hanna had looked at her parents, really looked at them, with their foreheads creased and worry setting their mouths in hard lines, and felt the guilt swell. She only had these rules because she'd proven she needed them. They only looked so worn out because they had an alcoholic daughter to worry about. Rehab didn't come cheap; they were still paying off her two-week stay, four hundred and eighteen days later. *Plus* those two ER bills. And all that energy they'd spent, searching her room for bottles and making sure she hadn't lifted cash from their wallets. Yes: she'd brought this all on herself, hadn't she?

Then the guilt had given way, as it often did, to the burn of resentment. They were going to make her pay for it for the rest of her life, weren't they? Nothing she did would be good enough. Nothing she said would ever convince them.

But she'd nodded anyway, and promised to play by the rules. "I understand," she'd said. "Thank you."

"Molly!" Hanna stomped to the bottom of the stairs. "Come *on.*"

"I'm coming! God!" Molly appeared at the top of the stairs and flounced down, her mouth pouty and covered in shiny lip gloss. "Why are you yelling at me?"

"Because we're going to be late, and I'm going to get in trouble, and I'd really rather not," Hanna said.

"Well, I'd *really rather not* go to this boring thing at all," Molly snapped, and then her face lit up. "Oh! Let's go to the beach instead. Wouldn't that be fun?"

"No, it wouldn't." Hanna opened the front door and stepped out into the blazing heat of the day. Molly was right: it was a perfect day to head to the ocean, to cool off in the surf, eat boardwalk junk and inevitably spend the evening smearing aloe vera on their sunburns. She hadn't been to the beach in years, though, and she wasn't about to change that so Molly could get out of this. "Get in the car, Molls."

"It's not fair," Molly said. "I don't even like theater."

"Well, Dad says you can't stay at home by yourself all day *every* day, and it's cheap. And you'll have fun!" Hanna said, not even convincing herself. "If you really don't want to do the acting part . . . make costumes or something. Paint scenery. It'll be fine."

Molly turned to Hanna. "I'm thirteen! I don't need a babysitter," she said. "And besides, I wouldn't be alone at home. I'd be with you. Why can't I stay with you?"

"Because," Hanna said, and she faltered. Because maybe her parents trusted her to drive Molly around and hang out, but that was about it. If Hanna was left to watch over her for the whole summer—who knew what would happen? Molly might develop a taste for bleach-scented vodka, exactly like Hanna had.

"Because what?" Molly said.

Hanna looked at her sister's hopeful expression and shook her head. "Because Mom and Dad say you can't," she settled on. "That's it."

"Well, that's a stupid reason," Molly said, and Hanna wasn't sure she disagreed. But what else could she say? *Hey, Molls! Mom and Dad don't want me to fuck you up the way I fucked myself up, okay!*

It was funny, in a way. Her mom so badly wanted Molly to turn out different from Hanna, and she'd wanted so much from Hanna in the first place, and the pressure of it all—the constant arguments and her mom picking at her and stubborn silences at the dinner table—had been what pushed Hanna closer and closer to drinking. Her friends, her hair, her grades—everything was a way for Hanna to accidentally disappoint her mother. After a while, Hanna had gotten tired of trying to please her. And shortly after that, she'd found a way to forget it all for a few hours at a time.

Not that she blamed her mom, her problems were her own, but—she'd helped Hanna get there, for sure. And wouldn't it be hilariously tragic if her desperation to keep Molly pure had exactly the same effect as it had on Hanna?

Well, not hilarious. Just tragic. But maybe her mom would learn something, finally.

"Let's go."

Molly lingered in the doorway. "I don't want to."

Hanna took a second, pushing down the urge to snap at her sister. "Well, sometimes you have to do things you don't want to," she said. Like working two days a week at a secondhand furniture store, making just enough money for junk food and cheap clothes, because it was the only place that would hire her. Like talking to herself instead of other people, because other people didn't like to listen to her. "Like driving your little sister around when she's being a brat."

Molly glared. "I am not a brat."

"I didn't say you were," Hanna said. "I said you were *being* one. So let's go."

She held Molly's gaze until her sister gave in and dragged herself to the car. "Fine, whatever."

"That's more like it." Hanna slid behind the wheel and took a deep breath. A cigarette right now would cure her shakes. It wasn't healthy, she knew, but at least it was better than drinking. She'd only gotten her license three months ago, years behind everyone else. When she'd been drinking she'd been too out of it to ever care, and once she quit she'd been too focused on staying sober and finishing school. But now she'd passed all the tests and she had the keys and there was nothing stopping her.

She slid the keys into the ignition and turned, and the engine didn't so much roar to life as whimper, but that was all they needed, really.

Jules

Speed-scanning frozen vegetables and cereal was a skill Jules had come to perfect in her time working at Callahan's Grocery and Deli. It was a very necessary skill around Thanksgiving and Christmas and Fourth of July, when the whole town seemed to turn out to wrestle in the freezer aisle and yell at her when their out-of-date coupons wouldn't scan. And Jules actually liked those times—the more rush and crowds the better, because who had time to be bored when they were scanning, scanning, scanning?

In summer, though, on a weekday afternoon, it was a dead zone.

Jules shifted her weight and glanced at the door to the manager's office, closed tight. "Okay," she called. "Go!"

At the end of the cereal aisle, her coworkers Malai and Henry began stacking Pop-Tart boxes end on end, making precarious towers.

This was their daily ritual when their manager, Greg, wasn't around: Grocery Olympics. So far, Malai held the record in both Pop-Tart stacking and apple juggling. But Jules had a plan to beat her.

Henry dropped a box of chocolate frosted. "Penalty!" Malai yelled. "Minus five points."

"Aww, come on!" Henry said. "Ref?"

Jules held her hand up. "Call stands," she said. "Don't be whiny, Henry." She glanced at the office again, and this time the door was opening. "Shit. Clean it up!"

She busied herself straightening out the dividers, and when Greg came around the corner Malai and Henry were back where they were supposed to be, arranging paper towels. By the time he'd told them about the special delivery coming later and then left, Jules had customers. She scanned three carts of stuff and then she was five minutes past her break. "I'm out," she called, setting the LANE CLOSED sign on her register.

She made it through the almost-empty store, past the door marked Staff Only, and into the break room, which she'd expected to be empty. But a girl she'd never seen before was tying up her hair in front of the only window, and she looked at Jules and all of a sudden Jules felt the earth shift beneath her.

It was as fast as that.

One moment she was Jules in her world, and the next she was

Jules

on

another

planet.

A planet where a girl who could make Jules's heart stop

with

one

look

actually existed.

The girl did a double take, her eyes wide, and said, "Hi."

"Hi," Jules said, and did her voice sound breathless to this girl or was it in her head? "I didn't—" *Stop. Focus. On your words, not on her. Okay: try that again.* "Are you new?"

The girl finished putting up her hair—her hair in multiple shades of peachy pink and bright lilac and the blue of tropical waters—and nodded. "Autumn," she said. She looked at Jules and smiled slowly, shiny teeth sparkling. "Hi."

"Autumn," Jules repeated, and the fall name felt sunshine warm in her mouth. "I'm Jules."

Say your name again, she wanted to say. And *You are so beautiful.* And *Do you feel this, too?*

But to say any of those things aloud would have been ridiculous, right, and so Jules shook her head. *Come on. Get it together. This is clearly just a girl and you're losing it from lack of exposure to the outside world and also to girls as beautiful as this.* Girls with rainbow hair, wide hips and thick thighs, skin that looked pillow soft were not common occurrences in Jules's life. Because Jules did *not* live on a planet where girls who could make her heart stop with one look actually existed; don't be ridiculous.

(*Why is that ridiculous?* one part of her asked. *Stranger things have happened.*)

(*Not to you,* another part of her answered. *Life is not a romantic drama.*)

"Do I know you?" she asked, her words slow, quicksand for her tongue. "I feel like I should know you."

"I don't think you do," Autumn said, that smile still playing on her face.

"Oh," Jules said. They stared at each other, but it wasn't staring, it was more watching. Waiting.

For what?

Jules whirled into movement, digging a couple crumpled-up bills from her pocket. "Autumn," Jules said, trying to make her voice sound normal now and almost but not quite achieving it. "Do you like Skittles?"

Autumn tipped her head to the side, her mermaid ponytail swinging through the air, curiosity in her eyes. "Um . . . yeah?"

"Good." Jules went to the vending machine and fed two dollars into it, punched the right buttons, and watched her prizes fall. She bent to collect them, and then walked over to Autumn. In the tiny break room, it should have taken two seconds to cross the space, but it felt endless as Jules moved toward her, every step closer filling her with electricity. It was like wading into the cool water of a lake until you were too deep to stand and floated there, spinning, content. "A welcome gift," Jules said, with an uncontrollable smile, "from me to you."

She offered the candy, and the laugh Autumn let out was maybe the most delightful sound Jules had ever heard. "Thank you," she said sweetly.

Jules watched her reach out her hand and held her breath, waiting for the touch of this Autumn's fingers against her. When it came, fleeting and thrilling, Autumn's hand cool, Jules exhaled slowly.

What sacrifice could she make in order to get that moment back, to play it out over and over again? Whatever she had to offer, she'd do it.

"I have to get out there," Autumn said, but she didn't move to go. "I guess I'll see you in a sec. Right?"

"Right," Jules said.

"Okay," Autumn said, and now she did move, making her way to the door and half out of it before she said, "It was lovely to meet you, Jules."

She was gone before Jules could process that and it was good, because there was no way she could think of anything remotely adequate to say in response.

It was lovely to meet you.

Who said that? Moreover, who *meant* that?

Autumn did. Jules could tell.

She stood there, watching the space where this new girl had been, and her heart was racing so fast, and she wanted to laugh out loud. So she did, one breath of it before clapping a hand over her mouth, and she collapsed on the lumpy old couch to stare up at the ceiling.

Something very momentous just occurred in this room, she thought.
Let this moment be marked: the day that I,

Juliana Everett,

maybe lost my heart

to a near stranger.

Hanna

That afternoon Hanna was lying on her bed under her window, scratching her thoughts in a new notebook, when there was a knock on her open door. She tipped her head to the side and her face broke into a wide smile. "Ciara!"

"Your sister let me in," Ciara Lennon said, looking as out of place in Hanna's house as she always did.

So it wasn't one hundred percent true that all of Hanna's friends had given up on her; Ciara stuck around. At a distance, a text every once in a while that said, *Checking in from Vermont. The trees are beautiful. C* or *Greetings from Denver! Not everyone here is high. C* when she was on the road with her band, messages Hanna had read but never replied to.

But when the blurriness cleared, when she could see straight again,

Hanna had finally replied. *Greetings from Golden Grove,* she'd said. *The view is clear.*

So now Ciara dropped by sometimes, when she wasn't touring sticky, badly lit clubs or temping.

Hanna sat up and shoved a pile of dirty clothes off her bed so Ciara could sit. "Molly's mad at me," she said, shifting over. "I don't know why."

"She's a thirteen-year-old girl," Ciara said, stepping across more of Hanna's mess and sitting. "Does she need a reason?"

"Good point." Hanna pointed at the plastic wrapped around Ciara's right wrist. "New tattoo?"

Ciara nodded, the faded ends of her blue-dip-dyed locs falling loose. "Wanna see?"

She started to peel back the plastic and Hanna recoiled. "No! You know it grosses me out."

Ciara smiled wickedly, taking her hand back. "Yeah, I know." She swiped the notebook onto the floor. "So what's happening, graduate? Wait—you did, didn't you? Graduate?"

"Barely," Hanna said. "But at least it's over. And I, Hanna Christina Adler, am now the proud owner of a high school diploma. Aren't you impressed?"

Ciara dipped her head. "I know you're being sarcastic, but I am impressed. You could have given up. You turned yourself around, Hanna. You don't think that's impressive?"

Hanna looked around her room. The walls were still the pale pink they'd been since she was a baby, but covered in marks from old posters, pictures she'd stuck up, that one time she'd fallen and kicked a chunk of the baseboard out. An impressive home for an impressive girl. People liked to say saccharine-sweet things like that when you were sober, or defied whatever preconceived notions they had of you. Hanna hated it. "I guess," she said after a moment. "But whatever. I don't want to talk about me. What are you doing now? Are you going out of town again?"

Ciara leaned back and blew her cheeks out. "Nah. Pretty sure we're done."

"Done touring?"

"Done being a band," Ciara said. "Fletcher's getting married. Cole got accepted to med school. That leaves me and Penny, and I don't think either of us wants to stay together."

Hanna made a face. "Well, she did dump you."

"*Hanna.*" Ciara threw her hands up. "Really? God, twist the knife a little more, it feels real good."

"Sorry!" Hanna said. But it was true—Penny did dump her, for a chef guy somewhere in Indiana. And it wasn't like Ciara was going to want to live in a van with her ex for another three months, right?

Hanna pinched the skin between her left thumb and forefinger. *Just because it's true doesn't mean you have to say it,* she reminded herself sharply. *I am thinking before I speak, remember?* "What I meant was," she said, carefully this time, "you have been broken up for a while now, and I can see how that might not be fun anymore."

Ciara shook her head at Hanna, but a tired smile crept onto her face. "Yeah. I got my music out of it, but I'm done now."

"What about the Sun City contest?" Hanna asked. "You going to do it this year?"

Ciara laughed now. "I wish," she said. "Did you hear Glory Alabama's sponsoring it this year? The prize money's fifteen fucking thousand dollars. Do you know what I could do with that?"

"It's a lot of money," Hanna said. "Like, a *lot*. And you could totally win, and then you'd have all that money, and I'm sure you wouldn't mind tossing your best friend Hanna a couple grand, right?"

"Please," Ciara said. "If I had that money, I'd take it and run. Everybody round here's a leech. You give 'em enough and they'll bleed you dry. Nah, it's not my year. Maybe next time." Her eyes gleamed. "What about you?"

Hanna rolled up the bottoms of her jeans and wiggled her toes. "No," she said. Not that she hadn't thought about it, because it was a *lot* of money, and she'd always wanted to win Sun City, *and* opening a show for Glory Alabama was a literal daydream of hers. They'd planned to enter, her and Jules and Dia, but that was a long time ago now. Still, she'd thought about it. But she couldn't enter by herself, couldn't play the music on her own, and even though for a minute she'd entertained the idea of forming a new band, *her* band, she hadn't done anything more than think about it. It would mean finding people to play with, people who didn't know her as either the drunk drummer or *that girl who always sits by herself*, and where would she find them? And then she'd gotten exhausted at the thought of it and decided it wasn't worth it.

Fifteen thousand dollars, though.

A car of my own. Money to move out. Put it in savings for college, eventually?

Hanna shook herself. Why was she thinking about it when she wasn't going to get it? "Nah," she said finally. "Maybe next time."

Ciara nodded like they weren't both talking shit and like *next time* didn't really mean never. "What about the others? Do you think they'll do it?"

Hanna got up and went to the window, pushing it open another inch, like that might make an actual breeze appear. "I have no idea," Hanna said. "You know that."

"I don't know," Ciara said, her voice hitting Hanna's back. "I've been gone for three months. Maybe you spoke to them while I was gone, what do I know?"

"Right. Yeah, I should have told you, we all made up while you were away." Hanna turned, her delivery dry. "We're the absolute bestest besties in the world again. Yay!"

Ciara rolled her eyes and stretched out on Hanna's bed now. "God, I forget how moody you are," she said. "And I was only asking. Is it beyond the realm of belief that they might be entering?"

"I guess not." Hanna hadn't thought about that. That Dia and Jules might enter the contest together. Without her.

Obviously without me, she thought. *Maybe they'll find some other drummer.*

Replace me.

"Maybe they are," Hanna said, ignoring the spike of jealousy and hurt in the pit of her stomach. "I guess we'll have to wait and see."

Ciara bounced to her feet. "Okay, that's enough. You're pissy, I'm starving. Let's go get something to eat." She grabbed Hanna's hand and wove their fingers together. "I miss you being a pain in my ass when I'm gone."

"You're so sweet," Hanna said, but she smiled and meant it. "If we get food, Molly has to come too."

"That's cool," Ciara said. "Me and the Adler sisters, causing trouble."

"No trouble," Hanna said, taking her hand from Ciara's to lift her hair from the back of her sticky neck. "Or my mom will kill us all."

Ciara grinned. "Okay."

Hanna warmed to Ciara's smile. She went away, but she always came back. That was more than Hanna could say about any of the other people she'd called her friends in the past.

jules

Jules's other job was at the mall, folding jeans and mass-manufactured tees with ridiculous slogans on them, ringing up people who were always in a rush and asking them, *Would you like to get our store card? It's a great deal!*

Usually she was good at it, efficient and forcing a necessary smile. Today she smiled without meaning to, and accidentally rang up some woman's items at three times the price. Eventually she got switched to dressing-room duty, where her mess-ups would be harmless. But that was okay, because she got to stand there thinking about Autumn.

Autumn standing at the register opposite Jules's, laughing sweetly at her old lady customers. The tie of her uniform apron looped in a bouncy bow right above her ass. The swing of her blue-pink-purple hair. To stand there for hours with this distance between them, and customers insisting on interrupting their conversations, was torture.

Not that their conversations were anything wild—not to anyone listening. Only words floated across the space between their registers: "How long have you worked here?"

"Two years."

"Do you like it?"

"Some days more than others."

"I like it so far."

"I like it today most of all."

And a smile from Autumn, like a bolt to Jules's heart.

Now she almost couldn't wait to be back there, surrounded by cut-price toilet paper and misshapen fruit and Autumn, Autumn, Autumn.

When her shift was over, Jules walked to the food court and ordered the five-dollar special from the sandwich place. She ripped open the package of chips as she navigated her way to the table where Dia and Alexa were waiting for her, and stopped when she reached them. "Dia," she said. "I have to tell you something."

"Juju!" Alexa crowed, waving her chubby arms and bouncing in the mall-issue high chair. "See apples."

"Yeah, you have apple, baby," Dia said, looking at Jules. "I have to tell you something, too."

Jules pulled out the chair opposite Dia and dumped her food. "Okay," she said, and she couldn't stop herself from smiling again. "What?"

Dia looked at her curiously. "Why do you look weird?" she asked. "You're all . . . smiley."

"It's nothing," Jules said, a half-truth at best. "Tell me your thing."

Dia's eyes narrowed, and then she sat back suddenly. "It's a *girl* thing!" she said. "Wait. This isn't a Delaney thing again, right?"

Jules shook her head. "No way," she said. "You know we were terrible together."

"*I* know that," Dia said. "It doesn't mean *you* still remember."

"Oh, I remember," Jules said. "But don't worry, it's not her." Under the table her knees bounced up and down. "There's this new girl at work. The grocery store," she clarified. "Her name is Autumn."

"Autumn?" Dia repeated.

"Yes. Dia—" Jules leaned her elbows on the table and put her hands over her mouth, trying to keep words in and failing.

She spread her fingers and spoke through them. "Do you believe in love at first sight?"

"No!" Dia laughed. "No. I believe in *lust* at first sight, sure. But love?"

"I know, I know, it sounds ridiculous but . . . I don't know, Dia, I don't know what else to call it. Because I think this is what it feels like." Jules tugged on her earlobe, the scarred bump where she used to have a third earring. "Love."

Dia picked up the burger on her tray and took a bite, staring at Jules as she chewed for a moment. She swallowed and then said, "Okay. Tell me about it. About her."

Jules looked down at her hands, chipped black polish and a single gold ring, warm against her dark skin. "Yesterday," she started. "One minute I'm bored out of my mind and then I go in the break room and there's the most beautiful girl I've ever seen. And I *felt* this . . . energy, or connection or . . ."

"Or what?" Dia said, a teasing lilt to her voice. "Come on. Tell me the rest."

Lex knocked her juice box over and Jules turned it right side up again, then scooted closer to the baby and lowered her voice. "Lex, your mom thinks I'm being weird. And maybe she's right, but I don't think I care. You get it, right?"

Alexa looked at her very seriously, her big brown eyes unblinking. And then she said, "Cheese, please."

Jules laughed. "I knew you'd understand."

"What does she look like?" Dia cut in. "Did she speak to you? Fill in the blanks, Jules."

"She's cute," Jules said. "Her smile is like the kind you can't ever be mad at. Her hair is all different colors. She could be in one of those old-school pinup calendars. She's like this cute, sexy, funny girl with the best smile and . . . oh." Jules twisted the ring around and around. "I think I really like her."

"And this Autumn girl, does she get to be an actual participant in this love story?" Dia raised her eyebrows. "Or are you going to have a giant crush on her and leave it at that?"

"I don't know." Jules shook her head, casting her eyes upward. "I swear—no, it's—" She stopped herself and took a breath, looking back at Dia. "When I looked at her and I felt that *thing*, it felt like it was both of us. It was, like, a real thing—I saw her, she saw me, and this *thing* happened. I know what you're thinking. It's not love. It's lust. Infatuation. But—can't it be all of that?"

Love, lust, infatuation. Autumn, bright smile, these swishy dresses beneath her Callahan's apron, flashes of leg as she walked around the store. And then the rest of her . . . well, Jules could only imagine. Would have much fun imagining in the shower later.

Dia smiled big now. "Maybe it can," she said, sounding sincere. "Autumn sounds cool, really."

"It's ridiculous," Jules said. "I'm excited to go to work tomorrow. I don't know who I am anymore."

"What are you going to do?" Dia asked, excitement in her voice now too. "Ask her out?"

Jules's hands felt suddenly clammy and she wiped them on her jeans. "I've never asked anybody out before," she realized. "Maybe I should. What do you think?"

Dia raised her eyebrows. "Why not? What's the worst that could happen?"

"She says no?" The thought of it made Jules not even want to try. God, if she said the words *Will you go out with me?* and Autumn's answer was *No*?

Heartbroken.

"So maybe she says no," Dia said. "At least you'll have asked."

"But then we'd have to work together," Jules said, "and I'd know she doesn't like me and I'll have this huge crush on her and oh my god, how embarrassing."

Dia shrugged. "If she's as cool as you say, she won't be gross about it and you'll go back to how things are at this precise moment. You know, because none of this has happened? So you don't have to freak out."

"Right." Jules sighed. "This is bad. But in a good way."

"Right," Dia repeated. "Autumn. Pretty name."

"Isn't it?" Jules said, picking up a napkin and twisting it around and around. "Autumn, Autumn. Oh, I disgust myself."

Dia laughed and Lex copied her, hers more of a high-pitched squeal. "It's okay," she said. "You're allowed to do this. I'll give you two weeks before I start giving you shit."

Jules leaned over and planted a kiss on the top of Lex's curly hair. "Oh," she said, remembering how this had started. Dia wanted to tell her something, too. "What was your thing?"

Dia pushed her fries toward Jules. "Eat first," she said. "This is big."

Jules did as Dia said, and then they left the food court, left the mall. They walked over to the nearby playground with Lex holding on to their hands, swinging up into the air between them.

At the playground Jules chased Lex around the jungle gym for a while, but before long a big kid on the slide scared Lex, and so Jules took her over to Dia in the shade. "I'm so sweaty," she said, collapsing on the grass with a groan. "It's so hot."

"Summer," Dia said, fishing a sippy cup from the back of the stroller. "Lex, c'mere. Have some water."

Jules rolled onto her stomach and propped her head up on one hand, looking at Dia. "So are you going to tell me now?"

Dia handed the cup to her daughter and watched her while she spoke. "Okay. It's about the Sun City contest."

"That?" Jules plucked blades of withered grass from the ground with her other hand. Uh-oh. Dia had this tone that usually meant she had a plan. And they hadn't talked about the contest since they were still playing. They barely talked about the band at all anymore, since Dia had ruled that it was too depressing.

Danger.

"What about it?"

Now Dia looked at her, her face set in this determined stare. "I want to enter it."

"Why?" Jules sat up, her Autumn-induced good mood rapidly shifting. "Seriously. What's the point?"

"The point is fifteen grand," Dia said. "The point is an opening slot for Glory Alabama on their tour."

Jules snorted a laugh. "Yeah, that's the dream."

"It's not a dream," Dia said. "It's for real. GA is sponsoring the contest this year, and those are the prizes. Jules, we could win all that."

"Come on." Jules tossed a handful of grass in Dia's direction and it landed all over her own legs. "Be serious. Like they're going to give fifteen *thousand* dollars to anybody."

"It's not a rumor," Dia said, taking out her phone. She messed with it for a moment, then thrust it at Jules. "See?"

Jules found herself looking at a screenshot and she had to zoom in to read it, her stomach swooping as she did so, because every word reinforced what Dia was saying.

Round One: Submit an original track.

Okay.

Round Two: You'll perform for our judging panel, one-on-one.

So maybe Dia wasn't talking shit.

Round Three: The winners will be announced at the Revelry Room on 07/27 and they'll receive $15,000 cash, the opportunity to open at one of Glory Alabama's Sunset Revue Tour dates, and more.

Whoa.

Jules shook her head and handed Dia's phone back. "So it's real," she said, dismissive, like it was no big deal, like her heart wasn't pounding. "And what, you want to enter? Okay, whatever."

Dia reached over and poked Jules's calf. "Come on."

"Come on what?"

"We should do it. Don't you think we should do it?"

Jules widened her eyes. "I think you're forgetting two years ago."

"So what about two years ago?" Dia shielded her eyes as she looked at Jules. "We went through all that and came out with nothing. What do we have to lose now? It's fifteen thousand dollars, Jules. And the chance to play with a band who came from here, who we have looked up to for *years*. Do you know what we could do with that?"

What did they have to lose? Time and energy. Each other, maybe—last time they'd lost Hanna, and Ciara, too, cut off in all the mess. And hope. Jules had learned that, to temper her hopes quickly, because life liked to squash them right when you least expected it. "News flash, Dia," Jules said, managing to not roll her eyes. "We don't have a band anymore."

Dia smiled, this sharp grin. "We have you and me."

"And Hanna?"

"What about her?"

"Well, she's the band, too," Jules said, and she meant it. They'd always made their music with Hanna; she couldn't imagine what it would feel like without her. As frozen as things were between them all, Jules remembered the good times so vividly, the way things used to be. When she was bored in class or tagging clothes or bagging groceries, thinking about those days of practicing until their throats ached and her fingers were bleeding was the only thing that got her through.

We were good, Jules remembered. *We were real. The three of us.*

"We'll find somebody else," Dia said, and she looked skyward. "Be real, Jules. You think she cares about us?"

"Who knows?" Jules said honestly. If that moment of exchanged icy eye contact at the grad party had been any indication, then the answer was no. But that had only been one moment, and she knew better than to presume to know what went on in Hanna's head. "But if—*if*—we were actually going to do this, we couldn't do it without her."

Dia hoisted a squirmy Lex into her lap, looking at Jules over Lex's head. "You know she'd eff it all up."

"Maybe not. I heard she's sober now," Jules said. Hard to believe, at first, but she'd heard it more and more. Seen Hanna at school, clear-eyed. Heard from Jesse that she no longer appeared at Saturday-night shows, or emerged from someone's messy party remains on a Sunday morning. Maybe Jules was naive, but she wanted to believe it was true. Hanna deserved better than the life she'd been giving herself. If she was sober, then Jules was happy for her.

"Yeah, I heard that too," Dia said, and her voice was hard but her eyes told a different story. "So?"

"It doesn't even matter," Jules said. "Because we're not really going to do it." Enter this contest after two years of not playing? Embarrass themselves all over again in front of the entire music crowd? In front of Glory Alabama?

But Dia looked determined still. "Okay," she said. "Here." She dug down in her pocket and emerged with a shiny coin. "Tails, we do it. Heads, we don't."

"Are you kidding me?" Jules said, and then she laughed. Of course Dia wasn't kidding; when she decided on something, she made it happen. She'd make that coin land on her side, no doubt. And Jules could say no, or she could give in to her best friend's magnetic control. "Fifteen thousand dollars? I could get a car."

"I could get a new guitar."

Jules tipped her head back and closed her eyes, the sunlight searing white and orange and gold inside her eyelids. Cracked voices. Frantically beating hearts. Nerves split open raw.

She opened her eyes. "One condition."

"What?"

"I'll do it," Jules said. "But *only* if you agree that Hanna does it with us. And only if she says yes."

"Oh, come on," Dia said, exasperated. "Talk about an *impossible* condition!"

"You don't have to convince her," Jules said. "I'll do that. I'll do the hard part. All you have to do is say yes to this."

"I . . ." Dia frowned in Jules's direction. "Do you miss her?"

Jules raised her shoulders lazily. "Well, yeah," she said. "I mean, the things she did weren't great, but we weren't perfect, either. She was our best friend." She tipped her head to the side. "Do you?"

"No," Dia said, her answer too immediate to be true. "Not really. Sometimes."

Jules seized her opening. "So let me talk to her," she said. "It's been a while. We're older now. Sometimes we're smarter. Maybe it's time to move on. Remember how much we always wanted to do Sun City? If we're going to do it, it should be with Hanna."

It took a long minute, but eventually Dia nodded. "Fine," she said, sounding only half-convinced. "But you have to handle her. And if she says no, we're still doing it."

"Only if the coin says so," Jules said. "Flip it."

It turned over twice, three times, before landing in the grass right by Lex's foot. And the force of Dia's smile could have powered the entire Golden Grove electricity grid for days.

"Tails."

Hanna

This has to be *a record,* Hanna thought. *Not even three weeks into summer break and I'm already bored out of my mind.*

She tossed a quarter in the air, again and again. The line for ice cream was long—she'd clearly gotten a craving at peak time—and even though it was cold in the café, Hanna felt the back of her shirt sticking to her skin. So far today she'd already managed to piss off her parents; they'd done nothing but shower her with questions and instructions over her morning cereal.

"Put the trash out when you're done," her mom had said. "And hang the laundry out to dry, please."

"What are you doing today?" her dad had asked. "Are you working? What time will you be home?"

"I have the morning shift." Hanna had slurped blue milk from her spoon. "And I'm taking Molly to her drama thing."

"Don't forget to pick her up," Theresa said, and Hanna raised one eyebrow.

"Why would I forget?" Hanna said. "Really?"

And then her parents had both stopped, giving her the exact same look which Hanna was pretty sure they practiced in the mirror at night. The Look meant *Don't test us*. It meant *Have you forgotten everything?* It meant *Come on, Hanna, we're only doing this for your benefit*. It was a look Hanna hated.

"Sorry," she'd said. Keep Your Mouth Shut, Hanna.

After that she'd dropped Molly off, gone to work, and spent the morning reading in the corner of the furniture store, with the creaky portable fan aimed at her face and her hopes rising every time someone passed the store.

Hanna blew her cheeks out and shuffled forward as the line moved. Truthfully, sprinkles and chocolate sauce hadn't been what she was craving at all. The longing that had risen in her in the early hours of the morning had been for the burn of whiskey, its soothing warmth, and that calm spreading through her bones. The quiet.

But whiskey was not an option, and she was out of cigarettes.

So here she was.

"Can I help you?"

Hanna looked at the girl behind the counter, ice cream scoop raised in the air like a weapon. She looked about as bored as Hanna felt, and like maybe she would use that scoop to cut someone's head off if they said the wrong thing.

"Hello," the girl said loudly, annoyed. "Can I help you?"

Hanna blinked. "Sorry," she said. *Wake up, Hanna.* "Can I have two scoops of mint chocolate chip, please?"

After she paid, Hanna wandered outside. Most of the tables were occupied with middle schoolers or parents with sticky kids, and Hanna resigned herself to sitting on the tiny patch of grass by the parking lot. She was halfway over there when a mom at the next table turned slightly from her kid and Hanna realized, suddenly, that this mom wasn't a middle-aged woman with a tired face like all the others. No, this mom was young, her curls spilling down to her shoulders and her smile shiny with lip gloss as she pulled funny faces at her kid. This mom was Dia.

Hanna stopped right where she was, and watched, because where Dia went, Jules followed. And sure enough, there she was—coming out of the café with ice cream and sodas, sitting down across from Dia, and both of them laughing. She watched Dia get up, ruffle her kid's hair, and walk off in the direction of the bathrooms. She watched as the little girl, climbing into Jules's lap now, noticed her staring and uncurled her hand to wave, beaming a big smile.

Without thinking, Hanna smiled back—it was impossible not to, with those cheeks and that happy grin—and then her mind caught up: *Oh my god,* she thought. *That's Alexa. Wait, when did she get so big?* Hanna had seen Dia with the baby around town, of course, but always from a distance and usually hidden away in the stroller, not close enough for Hanna to notice her curls exactly like Dia's and her scrunched-up nose. The last time she'd been close like this, Alexa had still been at the floppy, soft, sleep-scream-shit stage.

All of a sudden Hanna felt ancient.

When her eyes flicked to Jules, Hanna realized she wasn't the only one watching. But Jules didn't look pissed—actually, she was kind of smiling, and then she mimicked the baby's movement, lifting her hand and waving.

Hanna did that thing she'd seen in so many movies—she turned and looked behind her, to check for the person that Jules was *actually* waving at. Because there was no way she'd meant Hanna, right?

But there was no one there, and when Hanna looked back at Jules she raised her eyebrows like, *Me?*

Jules's smiled dimmed a little, but she nodded. And then she motioned Hanna over.

Mint chocolate chip dripped onto Hanna's wrist, and she lifted her arm to her mouth, licking it off. It gave her a moment to consider exactly how ridiculous an idea this was—she didn't even want to speak to Jules, she hated Jules the same way she hated Dia.

Except she loved them the same amount she hated them, and that was how she found herself walking over, gravel crunching beneath her feet, and then she was standing across from Jules. "Hi." It felt like a foreign word in her mouth, like she had to work her tongue around noises she didn't yet know how to make.

"Hey," Jules said. "I—um, do you want to sit with us? It's so busy today."

The first words Jules had spoken to her in years, and she said them almost like there was nothing bitter between them at all.

Almost.

Hanna looked in the direction Dia had disappeared in and held back the laugh she wanted to unleash. "I'd better not," was all she said.

Jules gave that smile again, cautious and amused. "How's your summer going?"

I drive my sister around, and I go to work, and I talk to myself, and I want a drink, and I would kill to talk to someone interesting, or to do something. Hanna looked past Jules. "Fine," she said. "Good. You know."

"Juju, can I have juice?" Alexa spoke in a precocious, sparkling voice and it was almost unbelievable, that this tiny human had come from Dia and could speak entire sentences now. Utterly wild.

"Sure," Jules said, and she pulled a sippy cup from the bag on the table. "Here you go."

This silence started then, stretched out and stifling and as long as the distance that had built between them. Hanna licked her rapidly melting cone for something to do, and tried not to stare too hard at Alexa. God, she was the spitting image of Dia: same curls, same medium-brown skin. But Elliot's eyes.

A cough from Jules broke the silence. "It's weird, isn't it?" She looked up at Hanna. "Lex, I mean. How big she is. Not us. I didn't mean—it's been a while, that's all. And I saw you right there and I actually wanted to—"

"Yeah," Hanna said flatly, cutting Jules off. "It has been a while." She didn't have to say what she really wanted to; Jules knew it already.

It's been a while because Dia decreed that I couldn't be around Alexa. "I have a kid now, Hanna," Dia had said, on a day when the air crackled with humidity and the windows in Hanna's bedroom were thrown open wide to the gray sky. "I'm sorry, but I don't—I can't have you around her. Not when you're drinking like this. Do you see what I'm saying? I have to make sure she's safe, Han. That's all."

Because she didn't trust me, Hanna thought. *And you picked her, Jules. Of course you did—why would you pick the drunk one over the smart one?*

That had been the real end of them. Elliot dying, Dia being pregnant, Hanna's first trip to the ER—all that had spelled doom for the band, she'd known that. But she'd thought they would still be friends, like they were before. Like they'd always be.

And then Dia had said those things. And at the beginning of junior year, Hanna stood in the back of the cafeteria watching Dia eat with Jules, so angry and so hurting at the same time, unable to make herself go over there, act like everything was normal after an entire summer of barely talking.

So they weren't together at school, and Hanna wasn't allowed to be with them and the baby outside of school, and before she knew it the silence between them was too loud to ignore.

And almost a year passed, and then Hanna went to rehab and began trying to become a person she could like. And who cared, right, about two people who didn't even know her anymore?

Me, Hanna thought. *I cared.*

"So," Jules said, and Hanna had to admire her perseverance. "What are you doing after summer? College?"

Hanna shook her head. "I have this job in Selaport. Admin. I need to earn money for now. I'm going to do the whole college application thing in a couple years, maybe. I want to major in psych and eventually become a counselor, but it takes forever, plus my grades weren't great, so I need to do some volunteer stuff or—" Hanna clamped her mouth shut. Why was she telling Jules her entire life plan? "Yeah."

"That's cool," Jules said. "Psych, huh? I can see that."

Hanna frowned. What was that supposed to mean? "Right," she said, and she could see Dia heading back over, close enough that Hanna needed to leave. She tossed the remains of her ice cream in the trash. "I have to go pick up my sister."

"Sure," Jules said. "Well, it was good to see you." It almost sounded like she was telling the truth, but what did Hanna know? Jules cleared her throat again. "Hanna, can we—"

"I really have to go," Hanna said, beginning to walk backward, and Jules nodded.

"Okay," she said. "Lex, say goodbye."

"Buh-bye!" Alexa said, and Hanna felt this pang in the pit of her stomach.

"Bye, cutie," she said, and then looked at Jules. "See you around."

That evening Hanna shut herself in her bedroom. She plugged headphones into her phone and put on some Banks and then threw herself down on her bed.

She couldn't stop thinking about Alexa. She wasn't a baby anymore, she was a full-on little kid. Dia had a, what, almost two-year-old? And Hanna didn't even know her. She could have watched her growing up; she could have been there today with Jules, on the other side of the divide.

This was the thing. She missed the music, of course she did. She missed having her hands all beat up, the performing, singing behind Dia's raspy voice.

But mostly, she missed them. Dia. Jules.

Jesus, I want a drink.

And she hated that she missed them, when they'd treated her like so much shit. Left her all alone. Or, not alone. She'd found new people to hang out with, people who didn't care how much she drank because they drank, too, and found it funny rather than alarming when she did things that ended in broken glass or scraped shins. They were fun, and not all bad like everyone else thought, and when she had to leave them behind, when she stopped drinking and couldn't be around them anymore, she'd felt bad.

No. No.

I don't need it.

I am okay.

But even though she'd liked those people, she'd never told any of them about how tired she was. How she worried about Molly being unhappy, being too old for her years because of everything Hanna had done, or what she thought about in the middle of the night when she lay staring at the ceiling. It hadn't been the same. It hadn't been *them, us.*

She felt for the fresh pack of cigarettes in her pocket, the feel of them enough to calm her for now.

"Wait until September," Hanna said, under her breath, too quiet to hear over the music in her ears. "Then you won't see them, and you'll meet new people, and things will be better."

Hanna looked out of her window, at the tree branches out of reach—green leaves already curling brown at the edges, parched by the relentless, endless sun. Being lonely was so *exhausting*. It was like being tuned into the same station, day in, day out, with no ad breaks or off switch. And listening to her same constant stream of *I'm so pathetic, I'm so lonely, why doesn't anyone like me, I should disappear, what's the point* was beyond depressing. Sickening. Hanna was sick of it all.

She sat up. *I have to do something. I will do* anything.

What?

Dia

Dia worked the afternoon shift at the bakery on Saturday, swirling strawberry frosting onto a seemingly never-ending supply of cupcakes and fixing on her Customer Smile when she had to cover the register. She much preferred being in the back, getting into the rhythm of mixing, scooping, kneading. It was meditative, almost; it gave her time to think.

As she added drops of coloring to the frosting, she thought about Hanna. Not the Hanna she'd known before, but the Hanna she didn't know now.

"What if she really has changed?" Jules had said yesterday, eating melting ice cream under the bright sun. "What if she's really sober?"

Dia wondered—how true could it really be? Hanna used to get so hammered she couldn't play properly. Every party, every show was almost guaranteed to end in disaster, Dia and Jules left to pick up the pieces.

Dia used an offset spatula to whip a pattern into the pink frosting clouds. She'd tried to slip it by Jules without her noticing, but Dia had meant it when she'd said she missed Hanna sometimes. The Hanna who was quiet, serious, and then would break out into a ridiculous impression or dirty joke when you least expected it. But Dia hadn't seen that Hanna in years, and who knew what she was like now?

She brushed blue edible glitter onto the peaks of the frosting and packed the cupcakes into boxes. It didn't matter; Hanna was going to say no. After everything? After the things Dia had said?

I'm sorry, but I don't—I can't have you around her. Not when you're drinking like this. Do you see what I'm saying? I have to make sure she's safe, Han. That's all.

It had been an easy way out, a way for Dia to distance herself from Hanna without feeling so guilty. It wasn't like she was cutting Hanna out, of course not—they could still see each other at school, and they'd hang out when Dia could get her parents to babysit, of course they would!

Pretending like she hadn't already been pushing Hanna away even before Lex was born, like she wasn't exhausted by Hanna already.

Dia put the boxes in the cold storage and stood there for a minute longer, drinking in the dry air.

Because truthfully: it was about more than the baby.

Dia had been scared.

It was New Year's Eve, not even two months after Elliot had died, when Dia had had to call the ambulance for Hanna, *praying* that her dad wouldn't be the one who arrived. They'd loaded her in so fast and sped away, sirens screaming, and by the time Dia and Jules had gotten to the hospital Hanna had had a tube down her throat and Dia was on the verge of a panic attack, thinking Hanna was about to die, too.

And then Hanna was okay, but Dia wasn't, because losing Hanna, too? It had been hard enough with Elliot, and she had liked him a lot, but Hanna was her girl, her love. So in a way it was a relief, to be able to distance herself. To know that the next time Hanna landed in the hospital, Dia wouldn't have to be the one watching her, wondering if the damage she'd done would be irreversible this time.

When her shift was over, Dia stood at her locker and texted Jules: Did you talk to her yet?

She wasn't holding out hope. Even if Hanna said yes, they'd be in trouble—the submission deadline was in four days and if they missed that, they'd miss the whole thing. They didn't have time to come up with new material, not to record and submit in four days. *Maybe* they could re-record one of their old songs—but would it be better or worse than the tracks Dia already had on her computer? And how would they even do it? As of right now, they had no drummer, no recording space; they used to record in Hanna's garage. And Hanna was going to say no, Dia reminded herself.

She leaned against her locker and opened Facebook on her phone. She'd meant what she'd said to Jules at the playground: they'd find somebody new.

Hanna could not be trusted.

So: Plan B. She went to one of the Golden Grove groups she'd made herself stop looking at, a page crowded with musicians looking for bands, making equipment trades, plugging shows. Typing fast, she wrote up a post:

Interested in Sun City? Drummer wanted immediately. No first-timers. Email diavlntn@gmail.com for details.

Dia hit Post and exhaled. When she got home, she'd go through the recordings she had on her computer—one of them *had* to be good enough to submit, to get them through the door. And then, when people emailed her about the drummer position (because they would; multiple good, ready-and-willing people would email her, right?), she could get to work on new material and a new band.

Easy.

She started to tap out another text to Jules, then paused. Jules didn't need to know about this. She could go on chasing Hanna, and Dia would deal with the reality of what was happening. It was easier that way.

So Dia slipped her phone into her back pocket, waved goodbye to Stacey out front, and headed out, her brain running with the possibilities of everything.

Elliot

Elliot watches from the edge of the yard, watches Dia dancing and playing her heart out. The party crowd is decent tonight; it's the last Monday before school starts. Everybody wants that last night, the last chance for everything they promised themselves at the beginning of summer.

When they finish playing, Dia searches him out, a light in her eyes as she stalks toward him, and the kiss she greets him with is both sweet and salty with her sweat. "Hi," she says.

"Hi," he says back, slipping a hand around her waist. Her hair is piled on top of her head and the exposed skin of her neck is mesmerizing. "I like that new song. What's it called, 'Hills'?"

"Yeah," Dia says, and she twists out of his grip, looking back. "Where did Hanna go?"

Elliot casts his gaze around. "I don't see her."

Dia tenses and Elliot bites his tongue. In four weeks he's learned that Dia does not like to be lectured, that Hanna makes this look appear on her face, that she likes people to think she's intimidating. Which she is, to Elliot at least. A girl this smart and hot and talented? There's no way he could not be intimidated.

"I can go look for her," he offers. "Hanna."

Dia shakes her head. "No, I got it."

He watches her walk away.

It's almost eleven when he sees Dia again. The party has emptied out some; there was talk of a better, bigger thing a few blocks over, but she's still here. She's sitting with her legs in the pool, staring into the water, and Elliot hands his beer to Kwame. "Hold this," he says, and he goes over.

"Hey," he says. "Did you find Hanna?"

Dia doesn't look up. "Yeah."

"Is she okay?"

"Yeah." She sighs. "Or no. Who knows?"

Elliot kicks off his sneakers, rolls his jeans up, and sits next to her, letting his feet hang in the pool. This is a fancy house; all the houses on this side of town are. His dad's realty business, the one his grandparents started after they came from Portugal, sells people these houses, the ones with the nice yards and shiny kitchens. His dad probably wants him to take over the business one day, but Elliot wants to be a writer. For now he works at the mall bookstore, which is always on the verge of closing down. "Is she wasted?"

"Of course." Dia's answer is terse. "Don't worry, though, Ciara's coming to pick us up. Take Hanna home, tuck her up in bed, and tomorrow we'll play along with whatever fairy-tale version of tonight she comes up with."

"So she drinks too much at parties," Elliot says, nudging Dia with his shoulder. "Who doesn't?"

"You don't get it," Dia says sharply. "It's not about parties. It's all the time."

Elliot frowns. "What, like—*all* the time?"

"Every night we play a show," Dia says. "And every other night too, basically. Whenever she can get her hands on it. Sometimes even when we're supposed to be practicing . . ." She shakes her head. "Sometimes you can't even tell, until she says the wrong thing. But I can't talk to her about it, because what do I know, right? Hanna says I have no idea what I'm talking about. Like I'm not the one holding her up at the end of the night."

"I'm sorry—"

"Don't apologize for her," Dia says, and she looks at him, her eyes dark pools. "It's nobody's fault but her own."

Elliot looks at his feet through the water. He's known Dia a month now, and by default Jules and Hanna, too. But Dia's known Hanna years. He thought Hanna was just one of those people, sloppy drunk. But clearly it's so much more than that.

"I didn't know," he says.

"Why would you?" Dia shakes her head again and when she looks at him this time, she smiles. "Forget it. You know what would really make me feel better?"

"What?" Elliot starts to say, but it's too late: Dia's already pushed him and he falls sideways into the pool, water rushing around him and up his nose. It's colder than you'd think and he resurfaces with a gasp. *"Dia."*

She's laughing, claps her hands. "Sorry!"

Elliot pulls himself over to her, puts his hands on either side of her legs and shakes his head, spraying her with water. "You think you're funny, huh?"

"I know it," Dia says, and she runs a hand through his curls. "Come on. Let me get you out of those wet clothes."

Elliot does not have to be asked twice.

jules

Jules leaned her upper body out of the only window in the break room, breathing in the outside air so thick it was like breathing underwater. According to Malai, there were storms rolling in all around them: "Hail and thunder and everything," she'd said, hanging out between the registers yesterday. "Saw it on the news."

"Since when do you watch the news?" Henry had scoffed, and then they'd started arguing and Jules had gone back to separating coupons.

Now, sticking her tongue out to taste the heat, Jules felt a prayer for rain forming in her. They needed it—a break from the building, crushing pressure. Relief.

Her armpits stickier than before, Jules pulled back inside and took out her phone. She tapped the back of it on her knee. She didn't even know if Hanna's number was the same.

Quit stalling, she thought. *We don't have time.*

She shouldn't have chickened out the other day and let Hanna run away. If she'd asked then, like she had planned to—well, *planned* was taking it too far. But when Jules had seen Hanna looking at them, it had seemed easy to wave her over, to start up a conversation like they spoke every single day. And she'd thought it would be easy to ask, but it almost seemed like Hanna had known what she was doing, and then she'd left, and Jules had sworn at herself.

She should have asked. If Hanna was going to say no, at least they'd have had her answer already. As it was, Jules's phone kept pinging with Dia's increasingly irritating texts, and the submission deadline was two days away, and Jules had no idea what to do except to beg Hanna to say yes.

"Easy," Jules said under her breath, and before she could put it off any longer she dialed Hanna's old number.

It actually rang—that was a start. Jules sank into the lumpy couch as she listened to the tone in her ear, going on and on. She brought her thumb to her mouth and bit her nail—maybe she wasn't going to answer. Maybe this wasn't Hanna's number anymore, and someone else was about to pick up. Maybe—

"Hello?"

Jules recognized Hanna's phone voice immediately—half polite, half *who the hell is actually calling me?* "Hi," Jules said, swallowing hard. "It's me. Jules. Hi."

Silence, except for the sound of Hanna breathing, and then, "Jules. Hi. What do you want?"

It was a question, but the way Hanna said it was flat, robotic. Like she was so exhausted and disappointed already. "How are you?"

"Please skip the small talk," Hanna said. "You're not calling me to chitchat. Are you?"

There was a sharpness to Hanna's words that left Jules irritated. Wasn't she trying to do something good for Hanna? And this was the welcome she got?

Think of the contest. You need her. "No," Jules admitted. She pulled in a breath and threw herself all the way in. "I'm calling you," she said, "because me and Dia are going to enter Sun City."

A moment of silence. "Really?" Hanna said, but her voice had lost a little of its edge. "Well . . . good for you, I guess."

"Yeah," Jules said. "You know, the prizes this year are amazing. And we always wanted to do it, so."

"Yeah, we did," Hanna said. *We,* it sounded like she was saying to Jules. *Me. What about me?*

"The thing is, you know, we're missing a drummer." Jules paused for a beat, gathered the courage to say it. "We're missing you."

Another silence from Hanna's end, long enough this time that Jules thought she'd screwed the whole thing up.

"So, what," Hanna said, and the edge was back. "You need me now? All of a sudden, I have purpose for you? Wow. Thanks!"

"Hanna—"

"No, really," Hanna said. "*Thank you.* Because the other day, when you spoke to me, I thought—huh. That was weird. Maybe she really wants to talk to me. Maybe she wants to know how I'm doing. Maybe she's heard I'm clean! Because I am, you know? I'm clean and sober now, Jules. But no. I was right. You just wanted something. I should trust my instincts more often, huh?"

Jules twisted her fingers into the hem of her apron.

Clean and sober.

Could she trust that? Could she believe Hanna when she said that?

"Hanna, it's not like that. I thought that—"

"I know I fucked us all up, but I don't think I deserve this," Hanna said, and her voice cracked. "I got clean without either of you. Because you left me. And you thought, what? You could leave me when it was hard and pick me back up when I got my shit together? I don't want to play that game."

"This is not a game, Hanna! Look—you're my condition."

A pause. "Condition?" Hanna repeated. "What?"

"I told Dia I would do it, on one condition," Jules said. "That we would ask you to do it with us. Because it was always going to be us, wasn't it? I thought—" She stopped short of saying what she really wanted to: *I miss you, Han, we both do. Come back to us.* "It wouldn't be right, me and Dia doing it on our own. So, this is me asking you: will you play with us?"

More silence. Hanna was really good at that. "It's not that easy," she said eventually, slowly. "I'm not—things are different now. We can't forget the last two years and act like everything's peachy."

"I'm not saying that." Jules pressed her hand to her forehead. "I know where we are. I know what happened. But I know I don't want to play music without you there, too."

"And Dia?" Hanna said. "What does she want? She's not the one calling me."

"No," Jules said. "But if she didn't want to do this, then she wouldn't have said yes. She'd have said no and told me to stop being annoying. Dia does what she wants, you know that."

That raised a tiny laugh from Hanna, involuntary, almost. "Right," she said. "You know, I don't need any pity favors. There are plenty of other drummers in town. You can take your pick."

"But they're not you," Jules said. It was too hard to tell whether Hanna was leaning her way, or pulling back. "Hanna, you and me and Dia, *we're* the music. There's no band without you in it, there never was. We stopped playing for a reason."

"Yeah," Hanna said. "Because Dia decided I wasn't worth her time anymore."

"That's not true," Jules said. "You know there was so much more to it than that. You know—" Jules stopped herself from saying what she really wanted to. *You know it was your drinking that broke us in the end.* She didn't *want* to blame Hanna. It was hard to stop herself, though, when Hanna was being this way. Like the Hanna Jules had known before.

Jules stared out of the window as she spoke, her last effort. "This could mean something for us," she said. "Winning. Not just the money, either—more than that." She paused, listening to a moment of Hanna's breath down the line. "Don't you want to *do* something? We were something, before. Maybe we could be that again. Hanna? What do you say?"

"I—" Hanna's sigh crackled in Jules's ear. "I don't know. I have to think."

Jules nodded to nobody but herself, a little relief slipping into her veins. "Okay," she said. That was better than an outright no; it meant Hanna was tempted, at least. Wanting. "Okay. The first round closes in two days, so—"

Hanna laughed shortly. "No pressure," she said. "All right. Two days. I'll let you know."

"Okay," Jules said again. "Bye, Hanna."

"Bye."

Hanna disappeared, replaced by silence and Jules let out a long breath as she let her head hit the couch cushions. It could have been worse. But Hanna was hard to figure out, always. She'd sounded clear, though, and Jules could imagine her, lying in her bedroom beneath the window, the way she always used to. Maybe she was telling the truth, about being sober. If she was lying, though, it wouldn't have been the first time.

Jules closed her eyes. She hoped it was true.

Hanna

Is this for real?

That was Hanna's thought as she listened to Jules's casual pleading, as she hung up, as she tossed her phone skittering across her bedroom floor. Was Jules for real, honestly asking her to come back? To play with her and Dia again, for—what?

Sure, Jules said it wasn't all about the money, but that could be her way of reeling Hanna in. Making her think it was about more than that, it was about *them*, and then when—if—whatever, at the end of it all, they could drop her as fast as they wanted to pick her back up.

For Jules to try to spin that on her, call her up out of the blue and— *she thinks she can pull me back, now she has a need for me again?* Hanna thought as she lay beneath her bedroom windows in the afternoon. She tamped down the part of her that wanted to give in to the fantasy, because none of it was actually going to become real. Her flash-forward visions of practicing, laughing together, making righteous, raucous, riotous sounds were not reality. She needed to remember that.

Do they expect me to fall at their feet and beg forgiveness? she thought. *All so they can use me to win some contest? No fucking way.*

The ember of anger burned in her all day long, while she picked Molly up, and sat through dinner with her parents, and stood under the icy cold shower before bed. She stoked the fire, justifying her rage, watching imaginary sparks fly out from old words she'd buried in her deepest heart: *I can't trust you, Hanna* and *What is happening to you?* and *Clean yourself up.*

The fire slowed a little once she was in bed, became a slow, quiet smolder that let the underlying guilt make itself known. She hated them and she blamed them, yes. But she hated herself, too. And she blamed herself. Who was the one who'd made it so they couldn't trust her? Who had pushed them so far that it was easier for them to walk away than stay and clean Hanna up again and again?

Her fault. Her mess.

Hanna lay there wide awake, Sufjan Stevens singing to her through her headphones, and trying not to think about Jules or any of the things she'd said. Around three a.m. she gave in and got up, stealing out of the house and down the street to the all-night convenience store, where she bought a pack of cigarettes, a green plastic lighter, and two candy bars from a gray-eyed boy.

She lit her first cigarette on the walk home, the click-hiss-exhale an instant sort of soothing. Hanna held her hand out and examined the way the thing looked between her fingers. She'd never been a big smoker, before. But without the drinking, she needed something else to latch onto. Her writing was the healthy version of that. The smoking, not so good. But it worked, as a way to not drink.

Four hundred and twenty-five days.

And what she wanted right now was a drink.

The sky felt close tonight, and Hanna's shirt stuck to her clammy skin. She hoped that Jules couldn't sleep either, that Dia's conscience was keeping her up.

No, she thought. *They don't care. They're right and I'm wrong, they're good and I'm the pathetic, useless failure. That's the way it is for them. Why would they ever change?*

Hanna had thought about the other day, standing there talking to Jules outside the café—she'd analyzed it and played it back and come to the conclusion that it hadn't been a ploy. There hadn't been any ulterior motive, or setup—Jules really had just wanted to say hi. It had felt almost too good to be true, if Hanna was being honest. And look. Here was the truth: Jules did want something. She always did.

Hanna got back home and walked out into the yard, where she sat in the least-rickety plastic chair. She dropped her cigarette on the ground, grinding it out with her flip-flop. Then she lit another and tipped her head back to stare into the murky sky. "You are okay," she said to the night, and she took a drag, holding the smoke in her lungs for as long as she could before letting it all rush out, leaving her dizzy. "You are not broken. You are here."

Her voice seemed tiny in the gaping dark and Hanna thought, like she always seemed to in the small, lonely moments, that the world was so vast and she so insignificant and her troubles so trivial, truly.

"Hanna?" Molly's sweet voice floated out from somewhere above, and Hanna craned her head back to find her sister hanging out of her bedroom window. "What are you doing?"

"Nothing," Hanna said. She dropped this cigarette on the ground, too, so Molly wouldn't see. "Go back to bed."

Molly disappeared back inside and Hanna dropped her head, satisfied. But barely a minute later the back door creaked open and out Molly padded in bare feet, flannel shorts hanging low on her hips. "What are you doing?"

Hanna snapped her fingers. "You are a pain in my ass, you know that?"

Molly settled into one of the other chairs, her grin lighting up the night. "I know." And then she lifted her nose in the air and sniffed noisily. "Are you smoking?"

Hanna looked in her sister's wide eyes and felt the energy she needed to lie slipping away. "Don't tell Mom," she said, flicking the lighter on and off, sparking like her nerves did at the thought of their mother. "You know how she is about it."

Molly pulled her feet up on the chair and wrapped her arms around her knees. "Can I have one?"

"No!" Hanna said. "Come on, Molls. Do you think I have a death wish?"

"That's not fair," Molly said, and the indignance in her voice made Hanna laugh. "You get to do it, so why can't I?"

"Because you're thirteen." Hanna turned the pack over and over in her hands, shaking her head. "And you're my little sister and I'm supposed to stop you from making all the mistakes I do."

"I'm going to be fourteen in three months," Molly said. "I'm going to high school. I'm not some little kid, y'know."

"Right," Hanna said. "But I'm still not going to let you smoke."

Molly made a noise. "Whatever. Why are you out here?"

Hanna shifted, wincing as her skin peeled away from the plastic. "Thinking," she said.

"About?"

"Pointless things." Hanna looked at Molly's bright-orange pedicure, and the boring state of her own feet in comparison. "You know Jules? And Dia?"

"Uh-huh." Molly jutted her chin out. "What did they do this time?"

"It's so ridiculous," Hanna said. "They want to enter the Sun City contest. And they want me to do it with them."

"Really?"

"Yeah," Hanna said. "Jules called me up today. Said all this stuff about how they miss me . . . whatever."

Molly blinked. "But they were so mean to you," she said, her younger side slipping out. "Weren't they?"

"Yeah," Hanna said. "They were."

That was the thing: Dia and Jules acted like what they had done had been necessary. Maybe a little cruel, but only in the name of kindness.

But it wasn't true. They had hurt her. Real, bone-deep, jagged hurt that never went away, no matter how much booze she drowned it in or how much she swore she was past it. How could she be? They had been her best friends. For all the shit that came with being a teenage girl, Hanna had always thought it would be bearable if she could go through it with them. Only, when it had gotten hard, they'd turned on her. And that hadn't been the promise they'd made to each other.

"So they only want you back to help them out?" Molly said.

"Yeah, I guess so." Hanna twirled the lighter between her fingers. "But I'm not doing it, so they don't get to use me."

Molly touched a hand to her hair, the blond of it darkening nearer to Hanna's natural shade. "Do you want to? If they weren't involved, would you want to do the contest?"

"No. Maybe. Who knows?" Hanna flicked the flame on, off. "I haven't touched my drums in forever. And I don't think I could do it on my own."

"Hmm." Molly tapped her feet on the chair. "Maybe—I know this is going to sound ridiculous, but listen—what if you did do it? *You* could use *them*, a little."

"What?"

"I know you miss playing music. And if you wanted to enter, you just said you couldn't do it on your own. You'd need somebody else. Why not them? You could tell them you'll do it, and they'll think they've won, but really, you're the one holding all the cards. And if you won the contest, you'd get your share of the prize money and then you could leave them."

Hanna looked at her sister with a mixture of awe and fear.

"Molly! When did you become a scheming mastermind?"

"Seventh grade," Molly said. "It was a real power struggle."

"Wow." Hanna rubbed her neck. Pretending to be okay with them, so she could get the money? That would be too far.

But Molly was right—she could just pretend. They didn't have to be friends again (like that would ever happen). They just had to be able to make music without killing each other. For the greater good. It would be a start for New Hanna, for the girl she claimed to be now. This Hanna wouldn't let herself be pushed around. This Hanna could rise above their past bullshit and do it because *she* wanted to.

At the very least, this Hanna could pretend all that was true.

Molly was looking at her expectantly. "So?"

Hanna flicked the lighter again and watched the flame burning in the darkness. "I'm tired, Molls. I'm too tired to go on being angry and alone and hating them."

She extinguished the flame and looked at her sister. "And I wasn't so good back then, either. I did awful things, too. It wasn't only their fault. But that's just how it is now."

Molly nodded, a small smile on her face. "You weren't awful," she said. "Just not the real you. It could all be different now. Isn't that what you want?"

What do *I want?* Hanna pulled at a piece of her hair, tugging hard enough that it hurt. An apology. Their *sorry*. And at the same time— their forgiveness. "I don't know what I want. I don't even know who I want to be."

Molly leaned forward, her hair swinging. "I think about what I want to be," she said. "And I can't decide. But I think when I'm older, I want to still live here."

"Yeah?" Hanna said. "Well, there are worse places to be." She looked past Molly. "I used to think I'd leave Golden after school. We talked about it, the three of us. We were gonna go to LA and live in a terrible apartment. Get terrible jobs and make music the rest of the time." She looked back at her sister, shook her head. "You shouldn't limit yourself, Molls. Think of the thing you most want to do in the entire world. If you're lucky and the world helps you out, you might actually get it."

"You could still—"

Hanna shook her head, cutting Molly off. "Not going to happen," she said, and then she stood and grabbed Molly's arm. "Come on. We should both be in bed."

"Ugh," Molly groaned, but she got up and let herself be led back into the house without resistance. Upstairs Hanna waved goodnight to Molly and slipped into her bedroom. She sank down to the floor and stretched her legs out, resting in the square of moonlight there.

Say yes, or say no.

Maybe she said yes and it went terribly, and they ended up hating each other more than they already did. *No loss,* Hanna thought. *Hate on top of hate, it is what it is.*

And if she said no—everything stayed the same. Boring, bored Hanna. No music, no nothing.

But if she said yes and it *didn't* go terribly, and they made great music and got into the contest and maybe—*don't say it too loud, don't jinx it, whisper*—won? She thought about Molly, making plans for her life. Dreaming her dreams. Hanna could still do that, if she wanted to.

She pressed her hands together. What had she told herself? *I have to do something. I will do* anything.

She got up and grabbed her phone from her bed, and she wrote the text before she could talk herself in any more circles.

Okay. I'm in.

Dia

Dia's alarm went off at seven on the days she wasn't working the early shift, and the days Lex didn't wake her. This morning it felt like she'd barely fallen asleep before it went off, her phone buzzing underneath her pillow like the most annoying gnat. "Mmph," she said into the sheets, searching with one hand. "Shut up."

She wiped her other hand across her mouth, yawning as she managed to open her eyes all the way. The light around her curtains was still muted, a fact Dia registered right as she realized that the noise coming from her phone wasn't her alarm but her ringtone.

"Shit." She fumbled her phone, yawning wide again as she glanced at Lex, still mercifully sleeping. JULES, her phone screen said, right below the time: 5:27. *Why is she calling so early?* "Hold on, hold on—" She recovered her phone and managed to answer this time. "Juliana, you'd better have a good reason for waking me up, I swear to god."

"I do," Jules said. She sounded out of breath, in movement. "I know it's early, but I'm on my way to work. And I thought you might want to know that Hanna said yes."

"Yeah, you're right, it is early," Dia said. "I was—" She stopped, rerunning what Jules had actually said. "Hold on. Go back. What?"

"Hanna's in!" The sound of a car horn came crystal clear through the phone, and Jules swore before continuing. "I got a text from her last night, this morning, whatever, and she's in."

"She said yes?" Dia sat up, a little stunned. Hanna said *yes*.

This was not how it had played out in her head.

Okay.

Forget Plan B. *(Sorry, in-box full of hopeful applicants. Your window has closed.)*

Switch to the Break in Case of Emergency plan.

"Yeah!" Jules said. "So—now what?"

Now what?

Dia was wide awake all of a sudden, her mind whirring into overdrive. Okay, okay, Hanna was in. That meant they had—she pulled her phone away from her ear to check the time, 5:31 now—forty-two hours and twenty-eight minutes until the submission window closed.

Forty-two hours and twenty-eight minutes to record themselves playing one of their old songs. They had to; they had to at least *try*. Submit their best and know that then, if they didn't get in, they'd done all they could.

(Yeah, it wasn't so much a plan as a fevered grab at the near impossible. Dia already knew that.)

Step one: Find a time to get together in the next forty-two hours and twenty-eight minutes.

Step two: Play together for the first time in two years.

Step three: Set up recording equipment.

Step four: Get a perfect-enough take.

Step five: Upload to the Sun City site.

Dia rattled through it in her head, trying to convince herself it would work. *If we focus, if we remember,* she thought, *it'll work. We'll record, and okay, the timing's not great but it's good, actually, it'll push us and—*

Better to try and fail than give up without even attempting.

(Optional Step six: Do all of the above without killing each other.)

"Hello? Dia?" Jules was saying. "Are you there?"

"I'm here," Dia said, swinging her legs out of bed now and beginning to pace in front of the window. "Okay. This is beyond ridiculous, but Jules—" Dia stopped and pushed back the curtains, allowing the rising sun to flood her room with light. "I have a plan."

Hanna

Hanna watched her parents rushing around the kitchen, the usual routine of coffee and hastily retrieved papers. She'd have to shoot now; there wasn't time to tiptoe around it.

"Hey." She leaned against the door frame, her arms folded in a careful imitation of casual. "Is it okay if I bring the drums down?"

Her parents exchanged the Look. "How come?" her dad asked.

"To play around," Hanna said. It wasn't a *lie*, really. She *was* going to be playing. She just . . . wasn't going to tell them about the rest of it right now. Because what if she and Dia and Jules found they couldn't even all be in the same room without combusting? It'd be over with before it started, and then she'd have created another reason for them to grill her for nothing. "Y'know, for fun."

"You'd have to move stuff around in the garage first," her mom said. "Clear some space."

Hanna looked between the two of them. "Is that a yes?"

Her mom got this pained look on her face, but her dad spoke first. "You'll have to clear it with the neighbors," he said. "But sure, bring 'em down."

So later, after their parents had gone to work, Hanna and Molly climbed up into the attic, taking careful steps on the beams so they didn't fall through. They brought the drums down piece by piece and put them out in the garage, and Hanna went back up for the things she hadn't mentioned to her parents, stashed in a trunk that she hadn't opened in a long time.

Inside: microphones, cables, mic stands, mixer, more cables. Almost everything they needed to record.

Because that's what Jules had said to her in a series of texts earlier this morning. That Dia had a plan—*of course she does,* Hanna had thought, *when doesn't she know exactly what she's going to make everybody do?*—and Hanna needed to dig out their equipment because they were going to record, just like they used to.

And when Jules had said that, Hanna had thought about it for a split second before texting back, *We can use my garage.* Just like they used to.

"Molly, come get this stuff!" She passed the mic stands down the ladder to Molly, and carried the rest down herself. When they had everything, she grabbed her laptop and brought it down to the garage, ready to set up.

Hanna cleared out the broken bicycle parts and other things that her dad claimed he was going to fix one day. Molly was less helping and more directing, sitting on a cardboard box outside the open garage door. "I can't believe you said yes," she said, kicking her feet in a pair of their dad's too-big work boots. "Was it what I said?"

"Little bit," Hanna said, leaning the mic stands against the wall where they blended in with a load of old shelving, where her parents definitely wouldn't notice them. "Mostly—I know I'd hate myself later for saying no. Not doing *something*."

"So, what exactly do you do when you practice?" Molly said. "How do you write songs? How do you know if it's a good song or not?"

Hanna dumped a plastic crate of photographs on top of a paint can. "Molly, could you actually help me instead of asking me pointless questions?"

Molly hopped off her box. "Will you show me how to play?" Her eyes were hidden behind pink, heart-shaped sunglasses. "Only a little."

"Sure," Hanna said. "But I need you to do me a favor."

Molly nodded. "Don't tell Mom and Dad."

Hanna stared at Molly. "How did you know I was going to say that?"

"Because you're predictable, Hanna." Molly lowered her sunglasses. "I'm kidding. What else were you going to say? I won't say anything to them."

"It's not a secret," Hanna said. "I'm going to tell them." How would the conversation go? *Hey, I'm in a band again. Yeah, I know, last time didn't go so good, what with the raging alcohol problem and losing my friends and the stomach pumping and all the rest, but this time's going to be different! How? It just is. Trust me. Oh, you don't trust me, that's the problem! Okay, well . . . trust me anyway?*

"My lips are sealed," Molly said.

"Thanks," Hanna said. "Now help me set this up."

Together they built the kit, Hanna tuning the snare and the toms, wiping layers of dust away. When they were done she ran her fingers across the crash cymbal, cool to the touch. With everything cleared away so there was enough space for them, and the drums taking pride of place, it looked like a ghost space. Ready to be haunted.

"Okay, Molls," Hanna said, and she looked at her sister. "Now all we have to do is play."

In the middle of the night Hanna stole downstairs and into the garage. She left the light off—the moon's glow came through the two small windows in the garage wall, and that was enough for her to see by. She didn't really need to see, anyway. Only enough to get over to her drums and find her seat behind them.

Hanna sat and pressed her feet into the cement garage floor. Her hands wrapped around the old sticks she'd collected from the box in her closet, soothing in their familiarity, settling the pins and needles pricking her skin.

It felt like home.

Tomorrow Jules and Dia were coming over to play and record.

Hanna smiled and shook her head at the same time. "What am I getting into?" she whispered to the snare, the hi-hat.

Was she scared? Yes. But not of Dia and Jules, not really, not much. What could they do to her now that they hadn't done already? How many other ways could they hurt her? That part was fine.

What she was more afraid of was that she wouldn't be able to do it.

What if she couldn't play anymore?

It was pointless worrying, Hanna knew. Of course she was going to be rusty—that tended to happen when you hadn't played your instrument in over a year. But that didn't mean she would have completely lost it. And she wouldn't know until she tried.

She still remembered every single song of theirs.

She still remembered the sound of Dia's voice. She heard it in her dreams, sometimes.

Hanna put one foot up on the bass pedal and applied the gentlest pressure, no noise. She turned the sticks the right way around, let them settle in her grip, extensions of her hands. And then she sat like that, still.

I am not broken.

I am okay.

Waiting.

Dia

On Wednesday morning, Dia knocked on Hanna's front door.

She would be lying if she said she was ready for this. But they had no choice. And she was trying not to think about everything that might be about to go wrong—to focus on what great thing they might be about to put into motion.

"I got this," she whispered to herself.

Of course Jules was running late. Dia could have used some best friend armor, protection for each other as they came face-to-face with the girl they were better at avoiding.

She knocked again, three quick raps this time, and then stepped back from the house as the garage door began to open.

Of course.

Dia cut across the small patch of dried-out grass and stopped on the driveway as Hanna stepped out, a hand above her eyes. "Hi," Hanna said, simply.

This was so surreal.

Dia let her gaze flit across Hanna—new nose ring, same white-blond hair—and settle on the drums behind her. "Hi," she said, an echo. "How are you?" Wow. Small talk had never been their thing, but apparently that was the best Dia could do.

"I'm good," Hanna said, folding her arms across her chest. "You know." Then one corner of her mouth quirked up, and Dia could tell exactly what she was thinking.

No, she didn't know. How could she know? It had been so long.

"Where's Jules?"

Dia shifted her amp from her left hand to her right, her guitar heavy on her back. "On her way," Dia said. "She'll be here soon."

"Good," Hanna said, and she turned her back to Dia, ducking into the garage. "We don't have much time."

Dia followed her in, and the instant hit of familiarity almost took her breath away. She tried not to let it show on her face, though. Like she tried not to let Hanna see how carefully Dia was watching her, looking for signs of . . .

What?

The old Hanna? The new one?

She wanted to believe the rumors, she really did. But she'd been through a lot of shit with—*because of*—Hanna, and it wasn't so easy. A sober Hanna was an image Dia had to work at to remember.

"Setup looks good," Dia said, to say something, and it was true.

Hanna's drums, still scratched and well loved, the mic stands placed exactly where they used to be, cables snaking over the floor. "You kept everything?"

Hanna gave her this look as she sat behind the kit. "What, like I was going to throw out hundreds of dollars of equipment?"

Dia shook her head. "Right." She slipped her guitar case off her shoulders and leaned her weight on it, Hanna watching her do it. And Dia exhaled. "Okay," she said. "I know this is weird."

"Weird?" Hanna said. "Not exactly what I'd call it."

"Strange," Dia said. *Strangers.* "Whatever. And maybe if this was another time, a different situation, we might actually do the whole thing. You know, the dredging up of everything old and saying not-nice things to each other and then promising to be different." She paused, made sure she was looking directly at Hanna when she said this next part. "But we don't have time for that. And I'm not here to go down old paths or make you do it. I'm here to play. I want to win." She lifted her chin. "How about you?"

Hanna rubbed her thumb over her bottom lip, narrowing her eyes at Dia. "I want to win," she echoed. "And I agree. I'm not here to bring up old ghosts, either."

This Hanna definitely had hints of different, that was for sure. Dia nodded. "I think we're on the same page."

Footsteps sounded outside, and then Jules was ducking under the door. "Hey," she said, out of breath, and put her equipment down with a pained look on her face. "Sorry I'm late. I forgot how much of a pain in the ass it is carrying all this stuff around."

"It's fine," Hanna said, and her voice sounded completely different now.

She was smiling. That was the difference.

"Okay," Dia said, crouching to retrieve her guitar from its slumber. "So, I have to be at day care pickup at four. It's"—she checked her phone—"nine thirty. We have six and a half hours to pull this off."

Her words were met with silence, and Dia got it. "I know," she said. "Maybe this is impossible. Maybe we are so far past dreaming it's not even funny. But we're talking about fifteen thousand dollars and an amazing show. So we can either give up now, or we can do the only thing we know how to. Play."

"We're not giving up," Jules said. "Would we be here if we weren't ready for this?"

Hanna nodded. "Improbable, maybe," she said. "Not impossible."

Dia slipped her strap over her head. "Here's what I'm thinking," she said. "We work out which of our old material we remember best and play the shit out of it until we have it as good as we can right now. Then we'll record a couple takes, not tons, because that always stresses us out and we get worse. And whatever we have at the end of this is what we submit. Even if it's truly terrible, we still do it. Then . . ." She looked from Jules to Hanna and lifted one shoulder. "What happens, happens."

"Sounds good to me," Jules said, taking out her matte-black bass and looking at it lovingly. "Hanna?"

Dia looked at her, and Hanna picked up a set of sticks and squeezed them tight enough that Dia could see her knuckles turning white. "Me, too."

Dia pulled her lucky pick from her back pocket. "All right. What's it going to be?"

They spent twenty minutes pulling up old songs from the back of their brains, listing off favorites: "Maiden Me" and "Drive By" and "Holy Water," "Honey Bee" and "Hills," "Alimony" and "Gold Ocean." Some got thrown out for being too old, too hard to remember, not the right sound. Eventually they were left with two: "Hills" and "Drive By."

"I vote for 'Hills,'" Dia said. "We wrote it near the end. It still feels like us." That, and people had really liked "Hills." Elliot had really liked it.

"I vote 'Hills,' too," Hanna said, and Dia felt a flash of surprise. Hanna, agreeing with her?

"Let's go with that, then," Jules said, and the vibration in her voice could have been nerves or excitement.

Dia couldn't tell. She couldn't tell which she was feeling more, either.

"Let's just do it," she said. "First run-through, get it out. Ready?" She looked at Jules, poised with a pick in her hand, and Hanna, with this look of concentration on her face that Dia knew so well, that she'd almost forgotten entirely.

"So ready," Jules said, and Hanna started a count, clicking her sticks together.

"—two-three-four—"

Dia

Dia scrambled to remember the exact beginning, feeling it somewhere in her brain—*there*. Her fingers slid into place and she put her mouth to the mic, drew in a breath. For not having played in so long, Hanna was steady and sure, the perfect backing for Dia to latch onto. From the moment Dia picked out those first notes, she felt it.

The glory.

Dia sang, her voice raspy and low, the right words slipping from her tongue without her having to think too hard.

> *"Ninety-eight this day*
> *Ninety-eight, what the news will say*
> *When we ran for the hills, for the hills*
> *Ran to get your girl away*
> *Got your money, made her a dress—"*

Playing was easier than talking. Talking was bitter, broken, sour, and unsure.

She watched Jules: hip out, shoulders slouched, her mouth a snarl as she backed up Dia's vocals. And she watched Hanna: eyes wild but intense, back straight, pounding out the best rhythms with her sticks, her hands. And they weren't perfect, nowhere near it, but they never had been. That was almost the entire point of the thing.

As Dia clutched her guitar (her body more used to the weight of a toddler than this, now), it felt like . . .

Awakening.

Like she'd been drifting through everything, closed eyes, tired mind, for so long, and now this explosion woke her so violently, so lovingly.

Three minutes could be both an eternity and a gasp. They careened through the middle, picked up speed as they came into the last verse—

She ain't playing you, honey
got your money, get her veil
ninety on the freeway heading straight for moonrise

—breathless, the euphoria slipping over Dia's skin like silk.

Look at us, she thought.

Listen to us.

See? They weren't complete failures. They weren't too fucked up to find this again.

They had babies and drinking problems and a whole lot of

locked-up sadness, but see how good they were? Look, listen.

Wait for it.

It was glorious, *they* were glorious; gleaming, bright shining goddesses making beautiful, messy sound and they reached the noisy end, the lucky pick almost slipping from Dia's fingers as they finished. A clashing crash of minor chords and her voice rising to a final wild yell.

Then it was over, breathlessly done, and as their noise faded, the three of them stood, watching each other. Uncertain of what had just unfolded, if it could be as simple as that, as slipping back into the skins they used to wear.

Dia's chest rose and fell rapidly, and she swallowed.

Jules broke the silence. "That was—"

She was interrupted by a small clapping and a tiny cheer from behind them.

Dia whipped around, and there, sitting on a cracked garden chair, was Hanna's little sister, Molly. "Oh my god," Molly said, and her eyes were gleaming. "That was awesome!"

"Molly!" Hanna jumped up, brandishing her sticks and crossing the few feet to her sister in a split second. "What did I say to you?"

"You didn't say I couldn't watch!" Molly protested as Hanna clamped a hand on her arm. "You said don't tell—hey!"

"Wait," Dia said. "Molly, did you really like it?"

Hanna's sister nodded. She'd looked like a little kid the last time Dia had seen her; now she looked young and hungry, one of those freshman babies ready to take the world for her own. "*So good,*" Molly said, wresting herself from Hanna's grip. "Like, I'd buy your music. If I had any money."

Dia allowed herself to smile at that. "I thought we were pretty good, too," she said, and looked from Hanna to Jules. "For a first try in forever."

"Pretty good?" Jules said, using the neck of her shirt to wipe at her cheeks. "Dia, that was fucking amazing. Didn't you feel it?"

Dia waited a moment before giving in to a real smile, a breathless laugh. "Yes! Oh, I felt it. Oh my *god*."

Hanna sat next to her sister. "I think we can actually do this," she said, and though her voice sounded nervous, her eyes looked so serious. "I think we still got it."

Molly clapped her hands together again. "So," she said. "What happens now?"

Dia looked down at her pretty guitar, the new strings she'd ordered and stayed up way too late putting on last night, the dent where she'd dropped it out of the back of Ciara's van in the parking lot of a Wendy's. So much history. And now they were making their future. "Now," Dia said, "we get to work."

Jules

They slowed down a little, went over the song in sections, picking out the errors and correcting them, tightening up the loose parts. Then they played it again and again, over and over, bursts of noise followed by short quiet, until Jules's hands were cramping and her back aching.

It felt good, though.

"That's enough," Dia said after a couple of hours. "We need to record."

Hanna pushed sweaty hair out of her eyes and got up. "Let me get it set up," she said. "We'll do one practice take, check it's working okay before we start for real."

Dia waited a beat and then nodded once. "Okay."

Jules didn't say anything, but watched their interaction with barely hidden curiosity. They were all being guarded, on their best behavior. But Hanna was pushing back a little—testing, Jules thought. It reminded Jules of the old Hanna. Except now, instead of blurting out thoughtless words, she seemed to know exactly what she was saying.

She caught Dia's eye, seeing the same wonder in her gaze. *Is she sober, for real? Maybe right now she is. But when we leave, will she stay that way? Is this all a cover? Can we trust her?*

Dia lifted her shoulders and turned away, and Jules looked back to Hanna. She was tired of not trusting her. And she wanted to believe the best. So for now, for as long as possible, she would.

Jules sank into a crouch, rubbing the backs of her tired legs. "I think we might actually—"

"Don't say it," Dia cut her off. "Not until it's done. Okay?"

Jules rolled her eyes. "Okay, superstitious. I'll shut up."

They spent a while setting up more mics, testing levels. Jules looked at the walls—no insulation—and frowned. If they had money, they could have hired a space somewhere. Other bands would be doing that. It reminded her exactly how unprepared they were. But that didn't mean they couldn't pull this off.

"It's ready," Hanna said, setting her laptop on top of a box labeled "Grandma's House" before going back to her drums. "Try once through?"

Jules stood as Dia said, "Yeah, once through."

And before Jules could even get into position, Hanna started.

It took Jules a second to catch up in her head, but as soon as her fingers found their rhythm, she was good. They were a little restrained this time, and Jules didn't know about the others, but the pressure suddenly got in her head. This was *it*. They didn't have another week, another *day*, even. If they couldn't pull together a decent recording to submit, they were going to miss their chance.

She stumbled on the chorus, earning a glare from Dia, and shook her head.

Focus.

She made it to the end without any more mistakes, and when Hanna played it back for them, checking that the levels weren't blown out and everything came through clear, it shocked Jules. "Oh, wow," she said, softly enough that the others didn't hear her over the track. "That's us."

"It's good," Dia said, nodding in Hanna's direction. "Ready for the real thing? I say we go three times, but that's it. We'll get played out after that. And we can do it and be done."

"I agree," Hanna said. "Jules? You with us?"

"I'm here," Jules said, holding three fingers up. "Three takes. I got it."

So they did it, fast and tight, and Jules managed to keep it together for all three takes, echoing Dia as she sang, her bass line playing off Hanna's drumming.

When they were done, Jules lifted her strap over her head and set her bass down, rolling her shoulders. Dia did the same, and together they moved to sit on the floor near Hanna.

Hanna grabbed her laptop and played each take back to them, the three of them listening intently. For Jules, it was like listening to forgotten girls. It was them, but in a way she hadn't heard in so long. And all she could think was: *Are we really doing this?*

Was this reality, and not some fever dream of hers?

"What do you think?" Jules asked when they got to the end. "Good enough to use?"

"I think they're decent," Dia said, always their harshest critic. "Nothing special, but good enough to give them an idea of what we're doing. Right?"

Hanna raked a hand through her hair. "The last one's the best one," she said. "We should use that one."

Jules glanced at Dia, and Dia nodded. "Can I?" Dia asked, reaching for Hanna's laptop.

Hanna dipped her chin. "Go ahead."

Jules watched as Dia pulled up the Sun City page and clicked through to the submission form. Her fingers flew as she filled in the different sections, until she stopped. "Our name," she said. "I don't think we should be Fairground this time around. I don't think that's us anymore, right?"

Hanna leaned back on her elbows. "I don't think so, either."

"So . . ." Jules looked between them. "What are we going to be?"

"Wildfire," Dia said, her mouth curving around the syllables. "I was thinking about it last night. I think it fits."

Wildfire, Jules thought. Very California, for sure. Burning, bright. Dangerous.

Was it tempting fate to name themselves after a destructive force of nature? Then again—they'd been Fairground before, and their ride hadn't been a fun one. So maybe it meant nothing, really.

"I like it," Jules said.

"Me, too," Hanna said, yet another surprise. "Do it."

Dia resumed typing, and then selected their track to add. Jules watched the upload bar speed along until their song was safely in there. And then Dia clicked Submit.

"Shit," Jules said, glancing at her phone. "With nine hours and fourteen minutes to spare."

Hanna smiled, the first time Jules had seen her do so today. "Not bad."

And Dia exhaled. "Now—"

Jules jumped in. "We wait."

jules

Jules's body pulsed with adrenaline the entire rest of the day, all night, into the next day. They had *actually* pulled it off.

Now all they had to do was hope and pray that whoever was on the receiving end of their submission heard what Jules had heard.

On the bus to work, she put her feet on the back of the empty seat in front and drummed a frenetic pattern on her knees, until the old white man across the aisle gave a very deliberate and noisy cough. *Screw you,* she said in her head. *Don't you know who you're looking at?* Then she rolled her eyes at herself.

At Callahan's, she shoved her stuff in her locker and then went out on the floor. She opened up her register and waved to Henry, changing out a display. "Hey!"

"Hey, Jules," he called back. "You ready for a rematch?"

"If you wanna lose again, sure," Jules said. Three registers down,

Autumn turned around and smiled, raising one hand. *Hi,* she mouthed, and Jules thought she might throw up.

Hey, she mouthed back.

It was painful in a sweet way, being so close to her and yet so far. Autumn, Autumn. She kept finding herself mouthing her name, tracing the letters on her palm, the inside of her forearm. It was so easy to get lost in those letters.

For three hours Jules counted coupon books and checked out the few people who came through her line, keeping an eye on Autumn's register. Her line was steady; people liked Autumn—she was new, she was sunny, she let them tell her the stories that Jules had long ago gotten sick of. And Jules got to watch, uninterrupted, getting lost in the swirl of Autumn's fingers through the air, the shake of her shoulders, the magic color of her hair.

Mrs. Doyle came shuffling up as she did every single Thursday, her cart full and colorful. "Hey there, honey."

"Hi, Mrs. D." Mrs. Doyle was Jules's favorite customer, mostly because she reminded Jules of her grandma, who'd passed away when she was eleven. The same papery, dark-brown skin, the same white hair set in an elegant twist, the same smell of talcum powder and cooking. Jules grabbed the first item and started scanning. "Ready for the birthday party this week?"

"Oh, yes," Mrs. Doyle said, in that rich, velvet voice of hers. "Elsie's going to love it. I'm making her cake today."

"Don't forget to bring me a piece," Jules said. "You promised!"

By the time she'd scanned all Mrs. Doyle's items and helped her pack them, she was five minutes late for her break. Jules closed up her register and crouched to pick up her bottle of water, and when she stood up, there was Autumn.

"Hi," Autumn said, and her cheeks were as pink as her hair. "Are you going on break?"

Jules nodded, willing her pulse to control itself. "Want to sit outside?"

They skipped the break room and walked out of the back exit, straight into the baking afternoon sun. There was a tiny, dusty parking lot, crisscrossed with tracks from the delivery truck, and Jules scuffed them away as they walked around the corner to the scrubby grass by the fire exit that no one ever used. The closest to private they would get.

Autumn sat, her legs stretched out into the grass. She had a scar on her left shin, Jules noted, and her sneakers were stained green in places. "Casualty of my little brother," she heard Autumn say, and Jules looked up to find Autumn smiling. She knew she should be embarrassed at being caught but she didn't feel that at all. She didn't care if Autumn caught her looking, trying to commit every minuscule detail of her to memory.

"How old is he?" Jules sat next to Autumn, close enough so if she shifted enough in the right direction their arms would be touching, skin on skin.

"Five," Autumn said. "He's a nightmare. But I love him."

"Big age difference," Jules said. "I have a brother, too. But he's fifteen. I love him, but he's a pain in the ass."

Autumn laughed, her mouth wide open and red inside. "Yeah. He's my half brother, but I don't call him that. He's my family, you know?"

"I get it," Jules said.

"I hate when people try to say it. My stepmom, she's my mom now. My mom died, like, ten years ago. That doesn't mean she's been replaced, but I'm allowed to love new people." Autumn shook her head as she looked at Jules. "Sorry. I probably shouldn't be saying all this. I don't know what it is about you."

"Me?" Jules shifted a millimeter closer, her breath crackling.

"Yeah, you." Autumn looked straight ahead but Jules could still see the smile on the corner of her mouth. "Whatever it is that makes me want to tell you everything."

Jules pulled in a surprised breath, summer-tinged oxygen flooding her lungs. "Oh, that," she said with a careless smile. "Sure."

"Sure," Autumn repeated. She crossed her ankles and leaned back, looking up at the cloudless sky for a moment, until she turned her gaze back to Jules.

Then they watched each other for this interminable moment; seconds, hours, days, who knew? All Jules could think was that it felt so easy, to be sitting here with this girl she barely knew and talking about real things. And the way Autumn was looking at her—the way Jules supposed she must be looking at Autumn—it was like she was lit up inside.

Maybe it *was* too much, all this, but it didn't feel that way, not to Jules.

And Autumn felt it too, hadn't she said as much?

She felt emboldened by this, by the adrenaline of playing again still short-circuiting her system. So Jules reached across and touched her fingertips to the back of Autumn's hand, and it felt like ocean water rushing over her skin. And she asked another question. "Autumn," Jules said, and she didn't think she'd ever get over that name in her mouth, "would you like to go out sometime?"

Autumn turned her hand over so Jules's fingers were turning circles in her palm. "Jules," she said, "I would like that very much."

Dia

On Sunday afternoon Dia was grabbing her stuff from the break room, ready to leave work, and at the same time checking her email on her phone for the millionth time since Wednesday.

She scanned past the sale notices, the junk, and the day care newsletter, sighing as she shoved her phone into her back pocket. Nothing.

Okay, it had only been four days. But patience was *not* her strong suit.

Stacey came through, tying her checkered scarf around her ponytail. "You're still here?"

"I'm about to leave," Dia said, pushing off the wall. "See you tomorrow."

She did leave, and walked to the stop to wait for the bus. She pulled out her phone again, habit now, and absentmindedly spun it between her fingers as she watched a guy in a Biggie T-shirt run across the street. Elliot had had that shirt, she remembered. He used to wear it all the time, even after a hole formed in the left armpit, even when Dia teased him about it.

She smiled at the stranger. Sometimes the memories hurt, but the pinprick of pain was always better than not remembering him at all, the whirlwind of everything they'd been.

(Still better: not having to lose Elliot at all. And that was why she was not with Jesse, because she could not bear that kind of pain again.)

A *ding* sounded from her phone and Dia looked down at it.

Saw one new email waiting on the screen.

Subject: Congratulations.

"Holy—" Dia jabbed her finger at the screen. "Open!"

Dear Wildfire,

Congratulations! The judges have selected you to advance to the second round of the Sun City Originals Contest. The Judges' Performance will take place on Tuesday July 10. Please look out for another email with further details shortly.

Sincerely,

The SCR Team

She read it twice, three times, before it sank in.

They'd done it.

They were *in*.

The bus was rumbling up the street toward her, but Dia got up and walked away from the stop on shaky legs, pressing her phone to her ear as she called Jules. "Answer," she said, pacing on the sidewalk, the sun hitting the back of her neck. "Come on—"

"What?" Jules answered. "Why are you calling me?"

Dia held back from yelling. "Don't be such a wench," she said. "I'm calling because I got a *fucking* email from *fucking* Sun City, okay?"

"Oh," Jules said, her voice dropping. "So? We didn't get in?"

"No." Dia's heart pounded. "We're in. We did it!"

"Wait, *what?*" Jules said, and she laughed, surprised. "Jesus, lead with that! We actually got in?"

"Yes!"

"So, what now? What next?"

"I don't know," Dia said, and she lowered her voice as people waiting at the stop turned to look at her. "July tenth. That's when the next round is. And it said we'll get another email with more details. But Jules, I mean—can you *fucking* believe it?"

"Barely," Jules said. "The tenth? Oh my god! Have you told Hanna yet?"

"No, I literally got it and called you right away," Dia said.

"Okay," Jules said. "So call her now and tell her."

Dia made a face at the sidewalk. "You call her," she said. "She doesn't seem to hate you quite as much as me."

Jules made a noise that was half disbelief, half derision. "Shut up," she said. "Don't try and pull that. You're the one acting all ice queen to her. Call her yourself. I'm not going to be your go-between."

"I am not an ice queen," Dia said, indignant. "I have been perfectly civil."

"As has Hanna," Jules said. "Now call her. Text me after. Forward me the email!"

"Fine," Dia said. "Bye."

She hung up and tapped her phone in the palm of her hand. Call Hanna. Like it was so easy. Like Hanna didn't want to scratch her eyes out.

Okay, that wasn't fair. She had let Dia in her house, and said yes to all this, and she was really doing them more of a favor than she knew. Without her, there was no way Dia would be sitting here with an email saying they were in the contest.

It still scared Dia a little, though, being around Hanna. It was a reminder of the things she'd done back then, what she'd lost, who she'd pushed away in the name of self-preservation.

But that wasn't Hanna's fault.

Dia took a deep breath and dialed Hanna, standing perfectly still this time as she listened to the ring.

"Hello?"

It took Dia a second to reconcile the soft voice in her ear with the Hanna voice she knew. "Hanna?"

"This is she."

There it was—that edge, now that she knew it was Dia on the other end. "Hi," Dia said. "It's me. Dia."

"I know," Hanna said. "What is it?"

"So—I got an email. We're into the second round of the contest."

There was a second's silence and then Hanna said, "Wait, really?" The edge dropped now. "*Seriously?*"

"Seriously," Dia said, letting herself smile a little. "We're through."

"Oh my god," Hanna said. "So—"

"July tenth," Dia said. "That's when the next round is. We'll get details later. But, yeah."

"Okay," Hanna said. "We should kick this thing into high gear, then."

Dia looked down the street, watched the trees absolutely still in the lack of breeze. "Yeah," she said. "We should. Hanna—" Dia wanted to say something, something actually meaningful, because it was going to be a long month if she couldn't bring herself to say more than platitudes.

But before she could say anything, Hanna interrupted her. "Let me make it easy for you, Dia," she said, sounding tired. "So you don't even have to ask. Ready? Yes, I really am sober. No, whatever it is you've heard I did isn't true. Yes, I'm taking this contest seriously. No, I'm not going to screw up this time. Okay? I think that covers it all."

Dia pushed a curl behind her ear, unsure where to go now.

Yes, I really am sober.

She didn't expect the rush of relief she got from hearing those words from Hanna.

"Hanna," Dia said now.

"What?"

"I wasn't going to ask," she said quietly. "I was only going to say—I mean, that's good, for you. That you're sober and everything. And I meant what I said the other day. I'm not here to drag up the past. I know you hate me, but you don't have to worry about that. All this? It's not a game to me, or whatever you might think I'm doing." She paused. "I want to make sure you know that."

Hanna's sigh crackled down the line. "I don't hate you, Dia," she said, and she'd shifted from tired to exhausted. "So don't sweat it. I'm just here for the music. Okay? Don't get all twisted up."

Dia wrapped one arm across her body, a frosting smear decorating her wrist. *I don't hate you, Dia.*

She didn't believe that at all.

Or maybe she should. After all, there was nothing for Hanna to hide behind now.

Dia nodded. "Okay," she said, trying to sound sincere. "I won't."

They were in the middle of dinner when her dad set down his fork and pointed at Dia. "Okay," he said. "What is it?"

Dia froze with her glass halfway to her mouth. "What?"

"Something's up," her dad said, narrowing his eyes at Dia. "I can tell. You're all . . . jumpy."

"Maxwell, what are you doing?" Her mom shook her head. "Can't have one peaceful meal."

But this was the thing with her dad. They were too alike; he always knew when she had something good going on, somehow could see it in her.

Dia took a sip of her water and put her glass down. "Okay," she said, and now her mom raised her eyebrows in anticipation. "So, you know the Sun City Originals contest?"

"Of course," her dad said, while her mom nodded.

"What about it?" Nina said.

Dia took a deep breath. "We kind of entered." She tried to sound casual, like it had been a whim, no big deal. "The prizes this year are big. Fifteen thousand dollars *and* the winner gets to open a show for Glory Alabama. Do you know what an amazing opportunity that is?"

Her dad snapped his fingers. "I knew it," he said. "I knew you were playing again!"

"Hold up," Nina said. "Go back. You entered a music contest? Without telling us?"

Dia picked up her fork and pushed her food around her plate. "I know," she said. "There wasn't really time. We had to get our entry together to submit really fast, and I would have told you, but—"

"We?" her mom said now. "Who's that?"

"Me and Jules," Dia said, and then quickly, "and Hanna."

Her dad nodded, his smile a thousand watts. He had always been her biggest supporter, teaching her to play, buying her books and equipment basically whenever she needed it, even when they couldn't really afford it. "It's about time," he said.

But her mom was frowning. "You have a lot on your plate already," she said. "Are you sure this is a good idea?"

"Yeah?" Dia said, trying to figure out what her mom wanted to hear. "Maybe? You know, it'll be like old times. And if—*big* if—we won, the money would be really good for us. For college, for Lex . . ."

"Like old times?" Her mom's mouth turned down, the lines there deepening. "I don't know that I like the sound of that. After everything that happened? You and your friends, Hanna—" She waved a hand toward Lex in her highchair. "This one. I don't know."

"Okay, not like old times," Dia said. "*New.* And the contest part is only for the summer. It'll be over by the time the semester starts, and I'll be totally focused on school."

"I think it sounds good," her dad said. "It's a lot of money, if you won. And besides that, it'll be good for you to be back in the scene, making music again. Guitars have to be played, not hidden away."

"I know." Dia could see her mom's brain working, coming up with more reasons that it was a bad idea, and so Dia played a dirty card. "You know, I do miss playing, Mom. It used to make me really happy. You want me to be happy, right?"

Nina gave her daughter a sharp glance. "Don't even," she said. "Dia, please do not try to manipulate me. You're better than that."

"Sorry," Dia said, not very.

"Nina," her dad said, turning to her mom. "I get what you're saying, and yes, we all know some stuff went down the last time around. But that was then, it's done now. And I get that it's another thing to take on, on top of everything else she's got, but . . ." He looked at Dia now. "I feel like you know what you're doing."

Dia let out a surprised laugh. "I do?"

"Well, you told us you would graduate, and you did. You told us you'd keep your job, and you did. You told us you'd be a good mom, and you are," Max said. "At some point, we have to think you might have learned some things."

"Um . . ." Dia knocked her hand against her leg. "Thanks."

Nina's frown eased. "Well," she said. "That may be true. I just don't want you to get overwhelmed with everything. Some things, you can't exactly drop the ball on."

Dia reached over and ran her fingers through Lex's curls as her daughter ate a handful of sweetcorn. "I know," she said. "Trust me, I know."

Her mom shook her head now. "Well, then," she said, looking from Dia to Max and back again. "I suppose it's okay."

"Really?" Dia's smile was megawatt, too. "Thank you, Mama!"

"But there are going to be rules," Nina said. "Guidelines, let's call them. One: If things start slipping around here, or at work—we'll have words. And two: Be careful. Of distractions and things and people that aren't worth your time. Because you're very special, my love. You know that, right?"

Dia looked to the ceiling. She wasn't special, no more than anybody else. Her mom only said those kind of things because she was a good mom, in the same way Dia said them to Lex. "Sure," she said.

Nina reached across the table to take Dia's hand. "And of course I know you miss playing. I was there, too. I pay attention."

"I know," Dia said, looking at her dad, too. "I love it. I love you both."

Dia

Today is a good day, Dia decided on Monday morning.

At day care Lex went in without even one single tear, a true miracle, waving as Dia blew her a kiss. The coffee place down the street had just put out lemon muffins, the glaze still warm, and Dia ate one while she waited for the bus—which came exactly on time, so that when she got to work she clocked in five minutes early. "Good morning," she singsonged to Stacey in the back, tying her scarf around her hair as she went in, and ignoring the odd look Stacey gave her.

"It's too early for that," Imelda said, pulling Dia's tasks for the morning from her board. "Be normal, moody Dia. Much better."

Dia took the order forms from Imelda's outstretched hand. "I thought perky was part of the brand," she said. "Look, I'm actually doing my job properly for once."

Imelda laughed at her. "You have a point."

Dia got to work, her good mood making her whipping a little softer, her chocolate-chip sprinkling liberal. They'd have to work out a practice schedule, start working on new material. Because they had to have new material to play for the judges, Dia didn't want them going in with anything old. It was okay to get them in, but now they needed to show who they really were, what they could do, and she knew they could do better.

She wondered, loading pans into the ovens, if Hanna had stopped writing these past two years. She always had the most heartbreaking, razor-sharp lyrics. Even at her worst, she'd produced great things for them.

Jules was right: Hanna was a part of them, for better or worse.

After her break, Dia was on counter duty, the quiet moment after the morning busyness. Usually she hated working the counter, serving customers and making small talk. She much preferred being in the back, scoring bread and loading pastries into the ovens. But today she let her good mood spill over into her *Have a great day!*, sometimes actually meaning it.

She turned the radio up a little as the bell over the door chimed, and when she looked up she gave her extra-special, real smile to one of her favorite customers. "Welcome to the Flour Shop, how can I help you?" She tipped her head to the side. "Butterscotch cookies? Or jelly doughnut today?"

"Maybe I'll get both," Jesse said. "Maybe I'll get something completely different."

"And maybe you'll get the cookies like always," Dia said. "What's up?"

Jesse ran a hand over his head. His hair had grown out as far as he ever let it, into tight spiral curls, faded up on the sides. It was a good look. Although Dia was not supposed to notice that. *Focus.*

"Nothing," he said. "What's up with you?"

"What?"

He eyed her. "You're all . . . up."

"Am I not allowed to be happy to see you?" Dia said, and then pressed her tongue against her teeth.

For god's sake, mouth. Stop saying things you're not supposed to.

Jesse leaned his elbows on the counter. "What time do you finish?" he asked. "Come by the skate park for a little bit."

"You know I can't watch you," Dia said. "It's terrifying."

"It's nothing," Jesse said, laughing. "I get hurt more at work. See?" He stepped back to lift his shirt, and on his stomach a deep purple bruise spread down from his hip to almost beneath the waist of his jeans. "That was Mickey smacking into me with a crate."

Dia rolled her eyes, even though his little trick totally worked and she could feel her pulse going up. "Oh, please," she said. "You're not going to break your neck serving pizza, though, right?"

"I'm not going to break my neck at all," Jesse said, dropping his shirt with a grin. "But it's nice to know you care."

He gave her that slow smile of his, and Dia was stuck for a moment. This was the thing: somehow it *always* tipped over from showing off, flirting innocently, to saying things they really meant and were supposed to keep to themselves.

At least Dia managed to keep it to that only. She never let herself do what she wanted to do every time he rolled up with another bruise, another break—place her careful hands on him and make sure he was okay, that he didn't hurt too much, that he wasn't about to disappear on her. She always kept her voice light when she told him how she worried, but only to hide the truth. That she was afraid of him getting hurt all the time, that the next time might be the last time, that one day he might wreck himself harder than his bike and then what would she do?

Eventually she made a face at him and said, "Yeah, I'm a sweetheart, aren't I?"

"Seriously, though," he said. "What are you doing later?"

Dia glanced out the front of the shop; it looked quiet, no one about to come in. She could tell him about the contest now, if she wanted.

But did she want to?

She knew what would happen if she said the words *We got into Sun City*. Jesse would be all psyched, and she'd let it make her feel good, and then she'd say something over the line, because she always did that when she felt good, and *then* she'd have to remember why she didn't do that.

That phone call, Dia thought. *The fresh grave. The funeral dress.*

She wouldn't say anything.

"I have to do something with my dad," she said, inventing cover for the time she'd be spending in Hanna's garage tonight while her parents were out. She opened the display case, grabbing a cookie and sliding it across the counter to him. "Here."

"Uh-huh," Jesse said, sounding like he didn't believe her, but he took the cookie and bit it in half. "So you don't have time for tacos?"

"Well . . . ," Dia said, looking at him. It was only food. They ate food all the time. She would remain in control of her mouth and her flirty, traitor brain, and they'd eat and have fun and be completely normal. "I finish in an hour."

Jesse brandished the remaining half of his cookie as he headed for the door. "See you later, Dee."

"Bye," she called, watching him leave and pinching the inside of her elbow.

Danger.

Hanna

"Don't touch that," Hanna called out, watching Ciara closely. "We have a serious you-break-it-you-bought-it policy."

Ciara pulled her hand back from the old-fashioned wardrobe. "Yeah, I don't have room for that in my house." She wandered back up to the desk that Hanna sat behind. "Don't you get bored?"

Hanna lifted her pen from the legal pad she'd been using as a sketchpad, the lines covered up with her wonky doodles. "Out of my mind," she said. "But they pay me." She glanced at her phone as it buzzed with a text, and let out a sigh.

"What?"

"Jules," Hanna said, pushing her phone away. "They're coming to my house later. To practice. I don't think I really thought this through."

No, she hadn't. She hadn't really thought past their recording attempt because, truthfully, she hadn't thought they'd ever make it in.

But somehow, thanks to some trick of the universe, they had.

And now Hanna had to, like, work with them. Practice and have them in her head and reply to their texts.

"I think you did," Ciara said, leaning her elbows on the counter. "I think you knew exactly what you were getting into. You had an opportunity and you took it. Why wouldn't you?"

Of course Ciara would think that; when Hanna had told her what she was doing, Ciara had honest to god jumped up and down with excitement.

"Why wouldn't I? Let's see—because we don't know each other anymore?" Hanna said, counting the reasons off on her fingers. "Because Dia looks at me like I stole something from her? Because being around them is kind of scary but also scary familiar?"

"Sometimes scary can be good," Ciara said, pushing up her round glasses. "You should chill. It's going to work out. You know what could happen if this all goes right?"

Hanna rolled her eyes. "And you know what might happen if it all goes wrong?" she asked. "Which do you think is more likely?"

"I was there, I remember," Ciara said. "But that doesn't mean it has to happen all over again. Two years is a long time in teenage years."

"Like you're so much older and wiser," Hanna said. "You're twenty-three."

"Exactly," Ciara said. "You're a baby to me." She paused. "You don't have to be their friend, if you really don't want to. You don't even have to like them, I guess. But you still know them. You used to be inseparable."

"I know." Hanna looked down at her nails, the black polish chipping off. *Inseparable.* Three parts of one whole. Until they weren't.

When Dia had called her to tell her they were in, it had been awkward. But civil, right? Until Dia had started talking about Hanna hating her and Hanna had found herself somehow saying that she didn't.

I don't hate you, Dia.

Was that true?

She didn't know.

It would have been easier to let Dia think she hated her. Easier, that way, to cover up her guilt and let the anger take control. But she didn't like how Dia had sounded: so superior, telling Hanna how things were when really, she had no idea. Not anymore.

When Hanna looked up, Ciara was watching her carefully. "They don't even really know you now," she said. "Not this version of you."

"I know," Hanna said. "That's the problem."

"So show them. And change their minds." Ciara stood back and shrugged. "Or don't. It's up to you. I'm just saying, *I* know this you, and this Hanna is not the kind of girl to be scared away from what she wants. Is she?"

Hanna met Ciara's gaze and held it.

Am I?

Hanna

When Hanna got home, Dia and Jules were already there, waiting for her. "Hi," she said, and curled her hands into fists, hid them behind her back. Ciara was right; she was not going to be scared off. She could do this, she could show them who she was now and let their judgmental looks roll off her. She was the new Hanna now. "Come in."

She took them through the house and into the garage, kept the door rolled down even though it was stiflingly hot. "Okay," she said as Jules and Dia got their guitars out. "So—what now?"

"Did you see the email?" Dia said. "I forwarded it to you."

Hanna nodded. In a little over three weeks they'd go and perform for the three contest judges. One original song, live and up close. And then—maybe glory. Maybe misery.

If they could get that far.

"They'll announce the winner on July twenty-seventh," Dia said.

"There's going to be a whole thing at Revelry."

"I wonder who else is doing it," Jules said, slinging her bass around her body. "Like, people we used to know. Maybe Automatic Neon?" She paused. "Maybe Ciara?"

Dia shrugged as she plugged into an amp. "Maybe."

"No," Hanna said. "She's not doing it."

They both looked at her, surprised. "How do you know that?" Jules asked.

Hanna raised her eyebrows. "She told me."

"You talk to Ciara?" Dia's voice was sharp.

"Yeah," Hanna said, adjusting her ponytail as she sat behind her drums. "When she's around, we hang out. And she's around now, so . . ."

She watched as they exchanged a look and felt a petty triumph rise. See: she wasn't the only one who'd lost something when it all went down. It had taken her time to start talking to Ciara again, but she knew that Dia and Jules hadn't spoken to her at all. Ciara said she didn't mind, things were difficult, she understood. But still—after everything Ciara had done for them? And they couldn't even be bothered to reach out, text on her birthday, keep in some kind of contact?

Ungrateful.

Jules nodded. "That's cool," she said. "I haven't seen her in so long."

Hanna picked up her sticks. "Well, she's here," she said. "No one's stopping you."

"Can we actually practice?" Dia said. "I have to pick up my kid soon."

Hanna spun her sticks. "Ready when you are." She wasn't sure if the tension in the air was good or a sign of them falling back. They were past that first shock of being together again; now was when they figured out if they could actually do this, stand each other long enough to make this work. So far it felt like one step forward, two steps back.

They played through "Hills" again a couple times, and then moved on to some of their other old material. Just trying to get a feel for it, to get back into the swing of playing consistently. It was better when they weren't talking, Hanna thought. Something about their words felt barbed. But their music felt sharpened in a good way, like a weapon, like they were protected by it.

And she felt better when she was pounding her old drums, muscles in her shoulders waking up, rhythms patterning though her hands. They still sounded so good—to Hanna's ears, at least. They still had that energy that made her want more, more, more.

After a while they stopped for a break, and Jules sat on the floor. "So we should probably get started writing new material," she said. "Right?"

"Definitely," Dia said. "We have more than three weeks; we should use them."

"I have—" Hanna stopped. "Wait one minute."

She got up and went inside the house, upstairs to her room. She opened the bottom drawer of her nightstand and let out a long, slow breath as she placed her hands on top of her notebooks.

They weren't just writings; they were her lifeline, in a way. Her way of taking control, turning her inward hate into something good, writing her way from confusion to some kind of clarity.

There was a lot in here. Dark things, secret things, wild things. Words she hadn't planned on showing people.

Except, when it came down to it, this was not *people*. This was Dia and Jules.

And as confused as Hanna was about where exactly she stood with them, what she really felt, she knew that they would understand all of it. Her words, her lyrics. This was how they got each other, wasn't it?

Show them, Ciara had said.

She was in these notebooks, the old her and the new. Maybe this was the perfect way for them to see how much she had truly changed.

So she lifted out a small stack and held them close to her chest as she ran back downstairs, back into the garage. "Here," she said, holding them out in Dia's direction. "These will help."

It took Dia a second, but then she took the pile from Hanna and when she looked up, it was with genuine surprise. "Oh," she said. "You still write?"

Hanna folded her arms and nodded. "A little." Every single day.

Now Dia's mouth curved into the smallest smile. "Thanks," she said. "Jules—we can start from here."

Jules nodded and looked at Hanna. "You always were our poet."

Hanna smiled back, instinctual. "Yeah," she said. "I always was."

Elliot

It's kind of hypnotic, watching the skaters go back and forth on their boards, from up on the hill. Like the tide rolling in and out, Elliot thinks.

"Have you seen Graceland play before?" Jules asks him.

"No. I don't really go to a lot of shows," he confesses. "It's not really my scene."

"She kind of does that, doesn't she?" Jules stretches her legs out on the grass. "Makes you do things you didn't think you would."

True.

They're sitting on the hill above the skate park, waiting for Dia to get off work so they can go see Ciara's band play. It's kind of fun, being with the band. Like a new world. Dia knows all these people, and Elliot follows behind her everywhere they go and pretends like he knows what he's doing there. He hit the jackpot, he thinks—this guitar-playing, song-writing, determined force of nature, actually with *him*. Not that they have touched the words *girlfriend* or *boyfriend*. Dia doesn't seem to care, and Elliot just wants to keep what they have for as long as he can. "Do you have plans?" he asks Jules now. "For the band? After school or whatever?"

"*Dia* has plans," Jules says, and then smiles. "I'm kidding. We talk about it. Going to LA after graduation. But then maybe we could stay here and become the best here, instead of being nobodies in that city. People might pay more attention then."

"Do you want to do that?"

"Yeah. You know, I want to prove everyone wrong. Black girls playing alt music?" She pauses. "People still think it's weird, and it'll be ten times as hard for us as some straight-white-boy band with a fraction of our talent. I want to show them they're wrong. We have as much right to be there as anyone else." She looks at Elliot and shakes her head. "But who knows? It's all, like, a thousand years away."

"Right," Elliot says, although he's a junior and they're sophomores. So for him, graduation is only several hundred years away.

"And who knows what might happen before then?" Jules is looking down the hill as she says this, and Elliot looks, too. Hanna's down at the bottom, talking to a girl on a bike. Jules is frowning, and Hanna's flipping her hair, and Elliot isn't sure what to say. He's both part of this and not, and whenever Dia brings Hanna's drinking problem up now, Elliot stays quiet. She never really wants him to say anything, anyway; she just wants to say things out loud, things she won't say to Hanna.

Then the girl on the bike rides away, and Elliot notices Jules's gaze following her. He smiles and nudges her with his elbow. "You like her?"

"No," Jules says, but she begins playing with her hair. "Shut up."

"Who is she?" Elliot nudges her again. "Come on . . ."

Jules shakes her head and looks up at the sky. "Delaney Myers," she says. "But she doesn't even know I exist."

"So make her know," Elliot says.

Jules laughs and looks at him. "Oh, easy as that?"

He thinks back to meeting Dia at that party, the way he'd almost missed his chance, how he wouldn't be sitting here with Jules if she hadn't appeared out of the night and he hadn't asked her name. "I mean, think about it," he says now. "You can sit and keep pining over her, or you can try." He looks to where the girl—Delaney—is now. "She's cute. Why don't you just ask her out?"

"I don't even know if she likes girls," Jules says, and she makes a face.

Elliot grins. "You'll never know if you don't ask."

"But what if she shoots me down?"

"So? She's just one person," Elliot says. "You get over her and find someone new."

"But . . ." Jules's eyebrows pull together. "She's Delaney. She's perfect. I want *her*."

Elliot laughs at her stricken expression. "It's not that deep, Jules. I swear. Just ask her!"

"Hey!"

Elliot turns and Dia's walking toward them, wearing those

skintight jeans again, and now he no longer has to wonder about taking them off.

They've had sex a handful of times now, in off-limits rooms at parties, once in her bedroom while her parents were at work. The first, third, sixth time for both of them, better every time. And now, when Elliot sees Dia, all he can think about is how she's the only girl he's seen naked and it is everything he dreamed and more. About the stretch marks all across her hips and thighs that shimmer like lightning in a summer storm sky.

"Hey," Jules says, standing up and dusting the grass off her legs. "Ready?"

Dia nods. "Where's Hanna?"

"Down there." Elliot points, and when a shadow flashes across Dia's face, he takes her hand and pulls her close and pinches the inside of her elbow, softly. "It's fine."

"Yeah, yeah," she says, but then she kisses him. "Let's go."

The four of them meet Nolan on the way, take the bus across town, and get their hands stamped at the club where Ciara's band is playing. Hanna really isn't too bad; Elliot keeps a cautious eye on her all night, still. At one point they end up getting drinks at the same time—Cokes—and Elliot's talking to her about baseball—she's an Angels fan—when she suddenly shakes her head. "You don't really like me, do you?"

"What?" Elliot says, taken aback. Where is this coming from? "No. I mean—yes?"

"It's okay," Hanna says, resting her elbows on the sticky tabletop, a dreamy look in her eyes. "I'm messed up. You can think that."

"I don't—"

Then she reaches into her shirt and pulls a tiny flask from her bra, and bares her teeth at him. "Tell her if you want. I don't care."

She walks away, this blond ghost, and Elliot clenches his fist. *Tell her if you want.*

He finds Dia and the words are on the tip of his tongue, but the music's loud and she kisses them away.

jules

Jules had never been on a real date before. She had never stood on the front steps of another girl's house, dressed in nice clothes, wearing makeup, and knocked on the door. She had never had the door open to reveal someone's mother standing there. So when that happened and this imposing woman looked at her, inquisitive, Jules had to wipe her suddenly sweaty hands on her pants.

"Hi," she managed to force out. "Is, um, is Autumn home?"

"You must be Jules," Autumn's mom said, and the icy facade disappeared as she broke into a smile about as bright as her blond hair. "Come in, come in!"

Jules tried to keep calm as she stepped inside. She could already tell it was too hot for the jeans she'd put on, and she'd gotten her period about fifteen minutes before leaving the house, and the bus had been late, and and and . . .

But the hall of Autumn's house was enough to distract her, because it was filled with . . . *everything*. Kitschy velvet portraits lined the floral-papered walls, and the shoe rack by the door bore a dozen pairs of sparkling stilettos. An orange table held a variety of china figurines, and each stair had its own vase of fake flowers. Jules took it all in, scanning and then finding Autumn's mom staring at her expectantly. "You have a lovely home," Jules said, her inflection almost making it a question—*Is that what you want to hear?*—and Autumn's mom beamed.

"Oh, thank you, sweetheart!" She spoke with this southern curve to her voice, Texas or Mississippi or somewhere else Jules had never been. "I know it's a little much, but I love a house full of pretty things. Makes it so much easier to get up in the mornings, doesn't it?"

"Mom, please stop talking." Autumn descended the flower-packed stairs, the skirt of her sky-blue dress swirling. "Jules does not need a lesson on Dollywood chic."

Jules tried not to look too taken aback by Autumn and her radiance, but in that dress, with her mermaid hair all swept up and the flash of thigh and her mouth so shiny red—god, she was beautiful.

"I don't know what you're talking about," Autumn's mom said. "Everybody needs that lesson. But fine, I won't keep you." She lowered her voice a touch. "Back by eleven, okay? And keep your phone on."

Autumn rolled her eyes but smiled, passing her mom to stand by Jules, and even that close was almost too much; what was Jules going to do when they had to sit by each other? "Yes, okay."

"All right!" Autumn's mom clapped her hands together. "Have a good night."

Jules remembered her manners at the last second. "It was nice to meet you, Mrs. Holloway."

"Oh, you too, honey. You two have fun," Autumn's mom said, and waved them out of the door. "Bye!"

The door shut firmly, leaving the two of them standing on the porch. There was a beat of silence before Autumn began laughing. "I'm sorry," she said. "I know, she's kind of a lot."

"Your mom?" Jules said. "I like her. Does she know this is a date?"

Autumn tipped her head to the side. "Yes."

"Okay," Jules said. "I didn't want to say anything wrong, or . . . you know."

"Not everybody from the south is like *that*," Autumn said. "And besides, I tell her everything." Then she gave Jules this long, up-and-down look. "But now we're done with her, can I tell you how good you look?"

Jules dipped her head, her face on fire. "Not as good as you," she said, looking back at Autumn. "Although, I feel bad. I should be taking you somewhere fancy in that dress."

"Don't be silly." Autumn shook her head. "It doesn't matter where we go. I just want to go somewhere with you."

A roller-coaster swoop in the bottom of her stomach. "Okay," Jules smiled. "You like Giorgio's, right?"

Jules wondered if the other people on the bus could tell they were on a date, or if what she felt crackling in the air was for her and Autumn only.

They got off and walked the few blocks to the pizza place, where they got a table out in the courtyard surrounded by families and other kids their age throwing balled-up napkins at each other. Jules asked the girl who brought their drinks if Jesse was working. "Not tonight," she said. "Can I get your order?"

They ordered the veggie deluxe, because Autumn didn't eat meat, and fried mac and cheese because—*fried mac and cheese*. When their food came their server gave them garlic fries, too, and when Jules said they didn't order fries, the girl gave her a sly grin. "On the house," she said. "Enjoy."

She walked away and it took Jules a second to figure it out, right as Autumn said, "Why did she do that?"

"Because we're on a date," Jules said. "And I think she's probably one of us. Me. I mean, she's queer."

Autumn turned to look after the girl and then looked back at Jules, a delighted expression on her face. "Huh," she said. "That's so nice!"

"Isn't it?" Jules said. Golden Grove was a pretty decent place to be, as a baby gay. Their school had a decent QSA, and coming up through the music scene there had been enough older girls for Jules to see and know that she, too, could come out and live a relatively okay life in town. She'd never had this, though—an actual date with another girl. This was another level.

Autumn did this thing of drawing the cheese out with her teeth and snapping it with her finger that was equal parts funny and mesmerizing. Jules wiped her fingers on her napkin as she chewed a bite of pizza. "So your mom—stepmom—where's she from?"

"A tiny town in Georgia," Autumn said. "She always says she had to get out because it wasn't big enough to hold her. Like, did you see the shoes?"

"Oh, I saw them," Jules said. "Impressive."

"I know." Autumn smiled. "She's so . . . she does exactly what she wants, you know? She wears ridiculously high heels and fake lashes, and her outfits have a ton of cleavage always, and she dances in the kitchen every single day. I want to be exactly like her when I grow up." She tipped her head to the side and studied Jules. "What do you want to be when you grow up?"

Jules lifted a corner of her mouth. "Financially stable."

"Ha! The dream," Autumn said. "Okay. Really, though."

"Really?" Jules blew out her cheeks and looked to the sky, streaked with deepening blues. "I have no idea. I don't even know what I'm interested in anymore. Like, my favorite class at school was math, but that's about all I've got."

"When I was a kid, I wanted to be a prima ballerina," Autumn said. "That was before I realized there are a very limited amount of fat girl ballerinas in the world, and that you have to actually be good at dancing."

Jules laughed. "What now, then? Besides your mom, of course."

"I want to be a nurse," Autumn said. She touched a hand to a pink curl. "When my mom—not Sasha, my first mom—was dying we practically lived at the hospital, and the nurses are the ones who keep you going. They would bring me books and let me sit in their station, take me down to the cafeteria in the middle of the night. They do all these things you don't even realize, and they help you get better, too. Well. When they can."

Jules looked at Autumn, marveling. How good was this girl? Smart and sweet and a heart of actual gold.

And honest. Autumn was spilling her soul, and Jules was lying.

Autumn gave her a funny look. "What?" she asked. "Do I have food in my teeth?"

Jules took a breath. "I used to want to be famous," she said in a rush, the truth now. "Maybe famous isn't it—known. I used to want to be able to stand on a stage somewhere and play music and have all these people sing the words back to me."

Autumn's eyes lit up with curiosity. "Music?"

"Yeah," Jules said, her palms sweating.

"Used to," Autumn said. "You don't want it anymore?"

Jules looked away. "It's a dream, isn't it? A little kid thing. Like you wanting to be a ballerina," she said. "People don't really get to have those dreams come true. It's a story they tell you so you'll believe in magic a little longer."

Autumn shrugged and leaned her elbows on the table. "Maybe, maybe not. Ballerinas are real, right? You can go and see them dancing. All those people on TV, on the radio, in magazines . . . they're real people. Once upon a time it was a dream for them, too. Somebody has to make it—it could be you. Then maybe . . . I would get to be the girl with the rock star." Her cheeks glowed pink.

"Maybe," Jules said, her face warm, too. *God, I wish.* But then she pressed her hands together. "I used to be in a band, actually."

"No way," Autumn said. "Tell me about it."

So Jules did tell her the story, the most bare-bones version she could manage without skipping over any of the important details. She tried not to get distracted by Autumn's face, either, intently watching her, and when Jules was done talking Autumn shook her head. "Wow," she said. "That's so cool. And also kind of shitty. But still cool. Don't you want to play anymore, then? Make another band or something?"

Jules drummed her fingers on the shiny silver surface of the table, watching her distorted reflection in it. "Actually, we just started playing together again," she said. "The three of us. Hanna's sober now and we're trying to make it work. It's going okay so far. We—" Should she mention the contest? No, not yet. In fact, maybe she wouldn't tell Autumn until the whole thing was over. *Yes,* she thought, warming to the idea. *What if we win and then I tell her? And she'll be so surprised because she'll have no idea, and imagine her face!* Autumn would be delighted, and Jules would get to feel like a true rock star goddess. Yes, this was a plan. "Yeah, it's going well."

"That's awesome," Autumn said. "Seriously."

Jules played with her straw. "It feels good," she said. "Playing again."

"So how do I hear you?" Autumn raised her eyebrows. "You have a Soundcloud? YouTube?"

"You wish," Jules said. "We shut it all down before. And Dia has all our original recordings, and good luck trying to get them out of her."

"Fine," Autumn said with a laugh. "I'll just have to come to one of your practices."

"Maybe," Jules said, nervous even at the thought of playing before this girl. "One day."

Autumn smiled, white teeth behind her red lips. "Okay."

Jules shook her head. "I've officially talked about myself enough. Okay. Moving on."

"Let's get dessert," Autumn said. "And I'll bore you to death talking about me. Deal?"

Jules laughed. "Okay. Deal."

They took the bus home, sat across the aisle from each other, and Jules asked delicate questions about Autumn's mom, her first mom. And Autumn answered equally delicately.

How did she die?

Pneumonia.

What was her favorite music?

Jazz. Dizzy Gillespie.

How much did Autumn miss her?

So much. Like you wouldn't believe.

Eventually they were back right where they'd started, outside Autumn's front door, and Jules was supposed to say goodbye but she didn't really know how to. "Full disclosure," she said, looking Autumn right in the eye. "I've never been on an actual date before. I'm not really sure how I'm supposed to do all this."

"Full disclosure?" Autumn smiled. "Me neither."

Their laughter died out quickly, giving way to fast breaths and Jules's heart pounding so hard she was sure the entire world could hear it. She lifted her hand to brush a strand of blue hair from Autumn's forehead. "Full disclosure," she said. "I would really like to kiss you right now."

"Full disclosure," Autumn said, her voice a little shaky. "I've never kissed anybody." She took a step closer and her voice evened out. "But I would really like to kiss you, too."

The moment before it actually happened was the longest time in Jules's entire life, this space of *Should I be doing this?* and *Yes, of course* and *What if I ruin it all?* and *Autumn, Autumn, Autumn.*

And then they were kissing. Her mouth on Autumn's. Her hand under Autumn's chin, and Autumn's hands on her waist and it was quick, sweet, and Jules was going to leave it there, not turn Autumn's first kiss into something too much, but Autumn had other ideas. Because it was Autumn pulling Jules closer, Autumn opening her mouth, Autumn sighing in this way that made Jules slide her hand to the back of Autumn's neck and slip her tongue across her lower lip. Jules felt like she was underwater. All she could see and feel and think was this girl and maybe she wasn't really in love yet, but oh, maybe she was.

Hanna

"Jules, could you please concentrate?" Dia snapped her fingers in front of her friend's face. "This is serious."

"I'm *listening!*" Jules rolled her eyes. "Jesus, Dia. A girl could change her mind, you know. I could be sleeping right now, but here I am. For you, out of the goodness of my heart."

Hanna listened to their bickering and pulled at the neck of her shirt. They were out in Dia's yard so, Dia said, Alexa could run around outside.

Hanna had nodded at that, acted casual, but most of her was panicking because she had to be on her best behavior, didn't she? Dia hadn't said they could have their writing session at her house without knowing what that entailed, had she?

So this was Hanna's test: prove she could be good and sensible and *not dangerous* around Alexa. Which, really, wasn't hard, because the only time Hanna had really been dangerous, out of control, was when she was drinking and now she had four hundred and thirty-four days without that and all she had to do was be normal.

("Normal.")

"It's two in the afternoon," Dia pointed out. "And don't act like you're so selfless. I know you want that prize money."

"Who doesn't?" Hanna lay out on the blanket Dia had put down. "Fifteen thousand dollars. It's a lot."

"What do you think it's like to be rich?" Jules stretched her feet out near Hanna's face, and Hanna shifted away. "Sorry. Can you imagine? For some people fifteen grand is nothing. A night at a club buying bottles. A ten-minute shopping trip. A tenth of a car." Jules laughed. "I could buy *ten* cars."

Jules was right, Hanna thought. Fifteen grand could buy ten rusted-but-still-pretty used cars, perfect for cruising from Golden Grove all the way to wherever Hanna wanted.

Dia clapped her hands together. "How about we stop talking about money we don't have and try to do some actual work?"

"You are so boring sometimes," Jules said, and Dia smacked her. "It's true!"

Hanna made herself sit up and grabbed one of her notebooks. "Where do you want to start?"

Dia pulled her acoustic guitar into her lap and put her sunglasses on top of her head. "I was thinking we'd all pick out some of your lyrics that we like and see what fits with some of the ideas I have. And then we can . . ."

Hanna let Dia talk and nodded every so often, to show she was listening, but really she found her attention going to Alexa.

She was at the bottom of the yard, involved in some kind of game that Hanna couldn't quite work out: first she picked up a bear, and then she filled a bucket with a handful of dirt, and the bear went to the robot with a teacup on its head, and repeat. But Hanna found herself mesmerized, almost, watching this tiny human that came from Dia carrying out this operation so seriously, pausing every so often to call out, "Mama, watch!" She definitely saw Elliot there—in her smile, the shape of her eyes, and it was like remembering he was gone all over again. Almost three years, now.

Look at her, Hanna thought. *She walks and she talks and she's an actual person. And I missed it all.* She had missed all the times Dia must have been so excited—and all the times she struggled, too, and things got hard. Jules had been the one there for her.

"Hanna?" Dia's fingers waved in front of her face. "Are you paying any attention?"

Hanna started. "Sorry," she said, and looked at Alexa as she spoke. "I was thinking about Elliot," she said without thinking, only hearing herself a second after the words were out.

Fuck.

See, she was getting better at the whole watching-her-mouth thing, but sometimes she *couldn't* contain it.

She turned back to look at Dia, her eyes wide. "She reminds me of him."

Jules shot Hanna this warning look, like *What the hell are you doing?*

But the corners of Dia's mouth lifted ever so slightly. "I know," she said, wistful. "There's something about her, right? Like the way he was."

"Does she know about him?" Hanna said, filter fully disengaged.

Dia nodded. "As much as she can understand. I show her pictures and stuff," she said, turning to watch her daughter. "We talk about him."

"I can't believe she's going to be two," Jules said, and she called Alexa's name. "C'mere!"

Alexa scrunched her face into a frown. "I'm busy!" she called out, and Jules burst out laughing.

"Oh, yeah," she said, looking at Dia. "She's your kid, all right."

Dia rolled her eyes but smiled. "Let's work," she said.

This time Hanna paid attention, picking through her notebooks and unearthing words that she barely remembered writing. She might have said she hadn't if the proof wasn't right there in front of her, in that scratchy black pen with the looping letters.

Dia picked out melodies on her guitar and echoed them with her voice, shaping sounds into Hanna's words. Jules noted down every little change, the lift in the second verse, where Hanna said she wanted to add a fill, added words when Hanna's weren't quite perfect.

Hush, pretty baby
Haven't you heard?
About the fight last night
The mess your mama don't like
I'll show you where to go
To find your diamonds and gold—"pearls?"
And honey, we'll sleep till it's hunting time

Dia tightened her D string and played a line, switched to chords, and sang along. "'Hush, pretty baby / Haven't you heard'—like that?" she said. "Kind of a gothic, heavy feel?"

"I like that," Hanna said, and she sat up. "With really intense drums, like . . ." She demonstrated, hitting her hands on her knees. "Jules, what do you think?"

"Yeah, I'd make the bass kind of intense, too," Jules said, nodding, and they went back and forth with all these different ideas—"Maybe in the bridge have it all disappear, real quiet, and then back to loud?" and "Play that again, but an octave up," and "Wait, I'll come in there."

It was getting easier, being around Dia and Jules. It was like they were actually—well, not friends, but not enemies. Not actively hating each other.

She didn't have to second-guess everything they did, waiting for the punchline, the hidden camera or whatever.

She was supposed to be there for the music, but sometimes Hanna found herself thinking about more than that—about being friends again. Was that something she wanted, though? Was that ball even in her court?

Maybe.

After a few hours Hanna and Jules left and set off walking home. Hanna pushed her hair behind her ear and tried to ignore how badly she needed to cut the dead ends off, searching for suitable small talk to fill the silence between her and Jules. "That was good, right?"

"Yeah," Jules said. "You two didn't bite each other's head off, and we actually got some writing done. I give us a B-minus." And then, with barely a pause: "I want to ask you something. But you don't have to answer if you don't want to."

Hanna looked at their feet, walking out of sync, and shook her head. She knew exactly what Jules wanted to ask. "We can go there, if you really want," she said. "You want to know why I stopped drinking, right?"

Jules paused as a bus roared past, and when it was gone she said, "Actually, I want to know why you started."

Hanna took a breath. She had talked so much, at rehab, and that had been good, but it wasn't like this. It wasn't telling one of the girls who used to know her better than she knew herself.

She stopped walking and perched on a low wall outside a pretty house. "I felt all this pressure," she said, shielding her eyes as she looked up at Jules. "To be this person I wasn't. My mom was always getting at me about my grades or my hair or something. And I started to feel . . .

sad all the time. But I didn't feel sad when I was drinking, and I could forget the pressure, and I could be this version of myself who didn't care about anything. And we were always at parties or shows, it was easy access, and it was this thing I could hold on to—when I felt bad, when I was hating myself, I could figure out that it was only five more hours until I could get a drink, and then I could get through those hours."

Jules nodded slowly. "Okay," she said. "So why *did* you stop?"

"I wanted to be better," she said. "That was it, really. I wanted to be proud of myself. But I had nothing to be proud of. I lost my best friends, I lost my music, I made my sister scared of me. I lied *all* the time. I kept trying to quit and falling back into it. I didn't like myself when I was drinking, but I didn't like myself when I wasn't, either, and at least when I was drunk it was easier to forget. But there's this thing sometimes, where you think you've hit bottom and then you fall a couple hundred feet below that and you're, like, is this it? Is this me?"

Lying in another hospital bed. Looking out and locking eyes with Molly, her scared face. The scratch in her throat as she'd tried to say, *I'm sorry, Molls, I'm so sorry.*

Is this me?

She chest hurt at the thought of talking about the Molly of it all, and so she skimmed past it. Not a lie, more an . . . omission of the truth. She'd tell the whole story one day.

Instead she said, "I really thought about it, if this was going to be me for the rest of my life. How much I didn't want that. And my parents, they wanted me to go to rehab, and I thought—what's one more failed attempt? But that time I didn't fail. So—recovery. Sobriety." She held her hands out. "Here I am."

"Here you are," Jules said.

"I counted it out," Hanna said, and the memory of that first week of rehab flashed so close to the surface. "One hour without a drink. Then an afternoon. A whole day. Seven days. And it hurt, in ways I didn't know it would. Physically, in my head . . . it's like this other version of yourself is in there with you, pushing and pushing and pushing you to give in. And when the anxiety hits, the depression, what do you do? The thing you used to make yourself feel better is gone now. You can't have it." She exhaled slowly. "But now it's been four hundred and thirty-four days. And sometimes I think, it would be nice to have a beer, a little something, just to take the edge off. When my mom starts picking at me, when I fail a test, when I hear a song that reminds me of us back then. When I feel like shit and the effort of trying to stay clean feels like a waste of energy because I'm never going to be anything but a fuck-up—my head says, *Would it be so bad? Wouldn't it make you feel better?* But it's never *just* one drink, not for me. That would be it, and I'd be right back exactly where I *don't* want to be. So. I keep counting."

Jules looked at her for a moment without saying anything, and Hanna almost began to regret saying any of it. But then Jules shook her head. "Hanna," she said, "I'm really happy it's working out for you."

Hanna shrugged. "I got myself in, I get myself out. Besides, I still have plenty more changing to do."

"Well, we all do," Jules said. "But, fine, if you won't be proud of yourself, am I allowed to do it for you?"

"I am proud of myself," Hanna said. "Sometimes."

I am okay.

I am not broken.

I am here.

Sometimes.

jules

Jules was in a good mood.

Writing with Hanna and Dia yesterday had been so good, working old parts of her brain that were suddenly wide awake and itching to create. And hanging with Hanna like they were kind-of-friends again—that was cool. On top of that, she was still electric all over from her date with Autumn. From the kissing of Autumn, the holding hands with Autumn, the kissing Autumn again.

She was maybe in too deep.

But that didn't stop her from texting Autumn at the end of her shift at the mall: lunch?

Autumn's reply flew back: where?

Jules tapped her phone against her lips. The Gardens, she wrote back. I'll bring sandwiches, you bring a smile.

Autumn: ☺

The bus ride over gave her plenty of time to overthink things. Like—she hadn't actually seen Autumn since their date the other night. And she didn't know what she was supposed to do now—a kiss hello would be way too much, right?

But would Autumn expect Jules to kiss her again?

Was she supposed to ask Autumn out again, for a second date, officially?

Would Autumn ask her?

Would *Autumn* kiss *her*?

Stop. Over. Thinking.

She got off the bus and went into the park, found an empty bench next to a cluster of palm trees. She sat and quashed the impulse to rub her sweaty palms up and down the sides of her thighs. Why was she so nervous now?

Should I hug her?

This was all new to Jules. She had nothing to compare it to, no expectations of her own to temper. It was times like these she wished she could pick up her phone and text Ciara, ask for her older-wiser-queer-girl wisdom. But that wasn't possible. Add that to the list of things she regretted, mistakes she'd made and wished she could undo.

Chill, she told herself as she waited. When she saw Autumn approaching, she waved and was rewarded with Autumn's smile.

"Hi." Autumn smiled, and Jules's nerves stilled.

"Hey," she said, holding a hand above her eyes to shield from the sun. "I got you extra peppers."

"My favorite," Autumn said, and she sat on the bench by Jules's side. "I'm starving."

They ate their sandwiches and talked about nothing in particular—made fun of their manager, Greg, talked a bit about the band. Jules almost told Autumn about the contest, let it slip, but she caught herself and remembered her plan. Tell her when it was over, when (if) (no, *when*) they had won. She felt giddy at the mere idea of it.

"So it's good," she found herself saying. "Practice and everything. It's fun."

"I have a question," Autumn said. "How come you picked Dia? Over Hanna?"

Jules put a hand over her heart like *ouch*. But it was a fair question. "I knew Dia first," she said. "She's like my sister. I loved Hanna, but—Dia was having the baby. Hanna was . . . I was tired of her." That was the honest truth, even if it wasn't *nice*. "It was easier without her. It was easier to be with Dia. It's shitty, because I never wanted to give up on Hanna, but—how long do you wait? I don't know." She rubbed her neck, guilt seeping in. Autumn would think she was terrible now. "I tried, before everything. I did."

"I get it," Autumn said, and then she screwed her face up. "Or I guess I don't, exactly. But I understand what you're saying."

"You'll like Dia," Jules said. "When you meet her."

"Good," Autumn said, her smile back.

Okay, Jules thought. *This is good.* They were talking and Jules had yet to say or do too much, and Autumn was laughing, and this was all excellent. "The other night," she said, balling her trash up. "I had a really nice time."

"Me too," Autumn said, but her smile dimmed a little. "Can we talk?"

"Uh . . ." It slipped out before Jules could stop herself, and her knees started bouncing again. In what world did *can we talk* ever lead to anything good? "Aren't we talking now?"

"I mean, like, talk about us," Autumn said, and she dipped her chin. "Or, me."

"Okay," Jules said. "What about us? And you? Did I do something wrong? Do you not want to go out again? That's fine, okay, whatever you want." Lie—it was most definitely not fine with Jules. This was supposed to be their beautiful beginning, not a messy crash and burn already. So what had Jules done to screw it up?

"Breathe," Autumn said with a smile. "You didn't do anything. I mean, except take me on the best first date I could have asked for. I'm—" She paused. "It was my first date."

"Mine, too," Jules said.

"Yeah, but, I'm not the first person you've dated. Right?" Autumn said. "I didn't . . . I don't know what this means. Like, I think I've had crushes on other girls before, but I never thought about it too much. But then there's you, and it feels like so much more. So maybe I'm gay? Or maybe I'm bi. Or maybe I'm something else entirely. Or maybe I don't even know yet. Am I supposed to know yet?"

Jules lifted one shoulder. "I don't know. That's all yours. No one else has to know or not know what or who you are."

"But it matters, right?" Autumn said, and her cheeks were flushed pink. "Does it matter to you? I don't even know if I'm supposed to talk about this with you, like—is this so neurotic to you? You must think I'm ridiculous."

"As if," Jules said with a laugh. She plucked at the fraying threads in the ripped knees of her jeans, her heart slowing as she realized that this wasn't Autumn ending things. She just wanted to *talk*. "I think you're amazing."

"Stop."

"Stop what?" Jules said. "Being honest?"

"You know what I mean," Autumn said. "I'm asking you a question."

"Does it matter to me?" Jules said. "I don't think so. Maybe you're gay. Maybe you're bi. Maybe you're something else entirely. But you're still you, right?"

Autumn pulled at a purple curl and smiled. "I guess."

"Okay." Jules smiled back at her.

"I think I'm a little nervous," Autumn said quietly. "That's all. Your first kiss is supposed to be fun, right, not send you spiraling into slight existential crisis. Not that it wasn't fun," she added quickly. "Because it was. *So* much fun."

Jules smiled slyly. "I try."

"Shut up." Autumn moved her hand to Jules's knee, playing with those fraying threads, and the palm of her hand brushed the bare patch of skin and Jules's entire body felt warm. "Would it be okay if we—went slow?"

"What kind of slow?" Jules said carefully. The last thing she wanted was to go backward, for this to turn into what she'd had with Delaney—all hidden and cold and more fighting than fun—but she also didn't want to give up on this the way she had with that. She put her hand on top of Autumn's and raised her eyebrows again. "Like, would it be okay if I . . . asked you for an official second date?"

"Hmm, let me think. . . ." Autumn's eyes sparkled. "Yes."

"And if I wanted to kiss you on that date?"

"That would be a definite yes."

Jules grinned. "And if I wanted to come see you on your break tomorrow with the best brownie you'll ever eat in your life?"

"Like I'm going to say no," Autumn said, and she turned her hand over underneath Jules's, threaded their fingers together. "You're good at this."

"What?"

"Talking." Autumn scrunched her nose up as a bee buzzed past. "I like that."

"You can talk to me about anything you want," Jules said. "I mean it."

"Wanna walk?" Autumn said, turning to admire the flowers. "I never come here. It's really pretty."

Jules reached over and pushed Autumn's hair behind her ear. "What if I wanted to kiss you now?"

Autumn smiled, half visible to Jules. "We can do that, too."

"C'mere." She and Autumn had just had a serious talk about serious things and it hadn't involved any sniping or snapping or deliberately poking sensitive topics. It had been honest and real and—this was what it was supposed to be like, wasn't it? *This* might be a healthy, respectful, real relationship.

She kissed Autumn on the cheek first, where her skin smelled like lemon. Maybe it was magic or maybe it was luck. Either way, she was not giving up.

Dia

They fell into a pattern: practice in Hanna's garage, go to work, practice again, live their lives for an hour or two here and there. Dia found herself exhausted from staying up late, playing in the living room while Lex slept, then getting up early to get to the bakery. Sometimes her dad passed by her, going out or coming in from his shift, and he'd stop and listen as Dia played him something, nodding or giving a suggestion. "That's good," he'd say. "What about the chorus?"

But for Dia, the exhaustion was worth it every time they played, every time she opened her mouth to let their words slip out, when they ended practice aching and sweating. And she looked forward to practice now—for the music, and for the fact that it no longer felt like a battle between her and Hanna. She wasn't sure, but she thought they were kind of . . . becoming friends? Ish? In these time-pushed circumstances, it was hard for her to hold on to the grudge, to remind herself again and again why she'd cut Hanna out.

Because, more than anything else, this Hanna seemed entirely different to Dia now. Different from both the person she'd been when she was drinking, and even the person she'd been before that. This Hanna was someone who Dia found smart and a little tough and, truthfully, intimidating.

They were at the Golden Music Supply Store, a little over a week out from round two now, walking the aisles. Dia had Lex in the stroller, occupied with her phone, and Jules and Hanna followed behind her, talking over each other.

"I'm saying, we sound better when we slow the end down," Hanna said. "Otherwise it all gets rushed and all the detail gets lost."

"We just don't have it yet," Jules said.

The store was this kitschy palace of everything and anything you could ever want for your alternative musical needs. Dia ran her fingers over the top of a display case, peering at the mandolins inside. A poster of Glory Alabama hung above the case, their faces decorated with the swirls of their signatures. "Well, we'll clean it up," she said, staring up at the four women's faces. She'd always been amazed that they'd come from the same place as her: sat in the same classrooms, hung out at the same skate park, bought their strings from this very store. "Messy is not acceptable."

Hanna made a face that Dia ignored, and Jules said, "I still like 'Pretty Baby' best."

Their writing sessions had been good; so far they'd come up with a handful of skeletons of new songs, and now they were trying to pick which two to focus on. They kept going around in circles, though, bickering over the smallest aspects of each one.

Dia kind of liked it. This was what they used to do, dissect their music into tiny pieces and then put those pieces back together again, a broken puzzle. It was fun.

"I'm starving," Dia said, turning in the direction of the guitars. "Can we get food when we're done?"

She headed down the narrow aisle, the others following. "I have a question," Jules said from behind. "And don't laugh at me."

"Shoot," Dia said.

"What are we going to wear?"

Dia stopped in front of a corkboard layered with flyers and old posters. "We'll wear whatever we normally wear," Dia said. "Be us. Y'know?" And then she turned back to look at the two of them, both in ratty cutoffs and sneakers and hair pulled back. She looked down at herself: same cutoffs, flip-flops, a tank that had once upon a time been white. "Okay," she said. "So, maybe not *exactly* what we always wear."

"Wait," Hanna said, looking offended. "What's wrong with my clothes?"

"You have a stain on your shirt, for one," Jules said, and Hanna looked down, screwing her face up.

"It's bleach," she said. "Fine, maybe we *do* need to think about this."

Dia clapped her hands together loud enough that the other people in the store looked over at them. "I'll add it to the list," she said, ignoring the groans from both Hanna and Jules at the mention of it. They did the exact same thing every time Dia got out her notebook to write something else down or check something off that list.

"You two are working my last nerve today," she said, but only half meant it. "Come on. I need strings and picks and then food."

"All right, I'm going." Hanna's white ponytail almost hit Dia in the eye as she stomped ahead. "Hurry up, Jules."

Jules looked after Hanna, then at Dia. "She has a real attitude these days," Jules said. "I like it."

Dia shoved her toward the accessories. "Go!"

After tacos, Jules left for work, and Dia and Hanna were heading home. "Are you getting the seven?"

"Yeah," Hanna said.

"Me, too."

They walked to the bus stop in silence. When they got there Hanna scanned the times and Dia perched on the bench, checking that Lex was still sleeping. Out like a light.

She looked up at Hanna, whose nose ring flashed in the sun. "I've been meaning to ask," Dia said. "When did you get that pierced?"

"What?" Hanna said, and then she touched a hand to her nose. "Oh, that. I think it was six months ago or so . . . January?" She sat down next to Dia and stretched out her legs. "I felt like doing something fun."

"Did it hurt?"

Hanna nodded emphatically. "Like a bitch," she said, and then she laughed. "But you've given birth, so . . ."

Dia smiled, scraping her shoe on the asphalt. "Yeah, that hurt. I'd rather get a needle shoved through my face than do that again."

Hanna turned a fraction. "Hey. I, um—I meant to say sorry. For bringing Elliot up last week. I don't know what I was thinking."

Dia felt that reflexive rush of slight nausea she got whenever Elliot's name came up. Yeah, it had kind of taken her by surprise when Hanna mentioned him, but it shouldn't have. Dia had always thought Hanna's tendency to say whatever came into her brain was a side effect, but clearly it was all Hanna.

And it wasn't like Hanna hadn't been there, too—hung out with Elliot at parties, laughed at his awful jokes. She'd sat with Dia in the hospital waiting room. Helped pick out her dress for the funeral. She'd known him; she was allowed to talk about him. "You don't have to apologize," she said. "He's not a banned topic. It's okay." She focused on a scar on her knee, tripping her fingers along it, and then looked back at Hanna. "It's weird. Because we weren't actually *together* together. It wasn't like we'd been dating for two years and he was my first love and everybody knew it. I wonder if that's what we would have become. Or maybe we would have carried on for a couple more months and then ended. I didn't know him, really *know* him. Not beyond that infatuation stage."

"Right," Hanna said. "I get it."

"It's like . . . me and Jesse, we're not together," Dia said. "But I know him so much better than I ever knew Elliot. And I have this everlasting link to this boy who's gone now and sometimes I don't know what I'm supposed to do with that."

Hanna nodded. "She's cute, though," she said with a smile, holding a hand up to shield her eyes. "Your link. Smart, too."

Dia exhaled. "Yeah, she is."

"So . . . ," Hanna said, and Dia knew exactly what was coming next. "What *is* the deal with you and Jesse?"

Dia rubbed her thumb on that scar. "When we met I said we could only be friends. Because Lex was so little and getting through school was the most important thing, and it felt weird to start going out with somebody when I was still the Girl Who Had the Baby by the Dead Boy. Sensible, right?" She paused. "But now Lex is almost two and I'm doing okay with her. I graduated. I have an okay job. Every reason I gave him is kind of . . . not a reason anymore."

Hanna raised her eyebrows. "So . . ."

Dia closed her eyes. "I have this fear," she said, and it was the first time she'd ever said it aloud. "That something terrible's going to happen to Jesse. And I don't think I could deal if it happened all over again. The funeral, the way everyone looks at me, the complete empty space where he's supposed to be in the world. I wasn't even in love with Elliot and it was awful. I can't imagine how it would be with Jesse."

"Because . . . you're in love with him?" Hanna said. "I thought he was just, like, the hot guy you keep around to flirt with."

"He's that, too," Dia said. "It's easier that way."

"It doesn't sound easier."

Dia opened her eyes to look at Hanna. "No," she said. "It doesn't, does it?"

"I know it was bad," Hanna said, "when Elliot died. But it was an accident. What are the odds of Jesse dying, too? Really."

"I don't know," Dia said, and she didn't know why she was telling any of this to *Hanna* of all people, either. Maybe because Hanna knew, too, what it was like to feel out of control. To feel like there was something bigger than you that you wanted to run from but could not escape.

Or maybe because Hanna was the one who'd borne the brunt of Dia's fear, taken the worst of it without ever knowing. And, Dia was seeing now, that hadn't been fair to her. As much as she'd been trying to protect herself, she'd been hurting Hanna, too, and she'd still done it. Hanna—now, and as the girl she'd been—deserved more than that.

Dia breathed out, focused on their conversation. "I know it seems ridiculous. But there's nothing in the world that can tell me one hundred percent that he'll be fine."

Hanna shrugged. "Everybody dies sometime. You and me, we'll be gone one day. It is what it is."

"Reassuring," Dia said, her palms itchy. Hanna was talking about the gray of life that Dia didn't ever think of. To her, it was all or nothing: you survived or you didn't. You were here or you weren't. It could hurt you, or you could cut yourself off before it even tried.

But deep down she knew Hanna's version was closer to reality. You hurt and you healed and you felt joy and sorrow in the same breath. That was what Alexa taught her every day.

But it was still hard.

Hanna smiled now. "All I'm saying is—for all the time we get on this planet, you might as well try being happy for as much of it as you can."

"I *am* happy."

"You know what I mean."

Dia pulled on her curls.

Yeah, she knew.

Dia let a silence develop for a minute, easing the stroller back and forth with her foot, the space between her and Hanna comfortable. Who would have thought, only three weeks ago, that this scene would ever unfold?

"It's going good, don't you think?" Dia picked at her scraped-off nail polish, a casualty of her guitar. "The music and everything."

"Yeah," Hanna said. "Better than I ever thought. You don't think so?"

"No, I do," Dia said. "Sometimes I think we might actually do it. Win. Get the money and the prize and be back to where we were. But better," she added, seeing Hanna's eyebrows raise. "Different."

"A lot is different," Hanna said.

"Right." Dia stared ahead, at the asphalt wavering in the heat. *Say it out loud, Dia. She deserves to hear it.* "It's really good, Hanna. That you're sober." She looked at Hanna now. "I mean it."

Hanna's smile was slight. "Four hundred and forty-four days."

"You count every day?"

"It works for me," Hanna said. "I picked it up in rehab."

Rehab?

Dia tried not to let the shock show on her face, pretty sure she was failing. "You went to rehab?" she said. "I didn't know."

"Why would you?" Hanna said, and shrugged. "Last year. Spring break."

Dia's mind began to run, trying to understand what more could have possibly happened to push Hanna into rehab. If everything she'd known Hanna to do hadn't been enough, if choking on a tube down her throat hadn't been enough? Maybe she'd done something truly terrifying. Maybe her parents forced her to go.

And then she thought: did it really even matter why? Four hundred and forty-four days was a long time. Hanna was sober, and that was not easy. She deserved less of Dia's skepticism and a lot more respect.

"Well, I'm glad," she said. "That it helped. And that you went." She swallowed hard, and said it before she could change her mind. "I'm sorry, you know. For how it all went down back then. It was messed up, the way I . . . cut you off."

Hanna looked surprised, like she'd never imagined hearing Dia say those words. "Thank you," Hanna said, and her smile was slight. "But I messed up, too."

"We all did," Dia said. "We were young and stupid." The next part came out without Dia overthinking it, the most real thing she'd said to Hanna in years. "And I was really scared, Hanna. That you were going to end up doing something to yourself that you couldn't undo."

Hanna nodded slowly, her eyebrows pulling together as she looked at Dia. "I know," she said softly. "Me, too."

Dia felt the air go out of her and all she could say was, "Okay." And Hanna seemed to understand, nodding again.

And then they sat in silence, waiting for things Dia couldn't even name.

jules

On Monday they were back in Hanna's garage, running through one of the loose ideas that they'd turned into a third real song. Jules could feel her fingers starting to harden, old calluses coming back to life, and she loved it. She loved the way it felt to play and shout and sing and dance, to feel like there was more to her life than work and school. She stepped onto a plastic crate, pretending it was a riser and she was playing to a crowd of thousands at, like, Coachella or some equally huge festival that Jules would always *say* was so cliché but would really kill to be at, and howled the last line, closing her eyes. The reverb faded and Jules opened her eyes to the disappointing view of the garage door. She jumped down and wiped the sweat from her forehead. "I like this one," she said. "Makes me feel like . . . I need to go to a strip club and then maybe kill a guy."

"FYI," Dia said, "if you kill somebody please don't tell me about it.

That way I won't have to lie on the stand."

Hanna grabbed her crash cymbal to stop it. "Jules, if you kill someone, I *will* go on every single murder show and talk about how I knew you when you were a good girl." She held her hands to her heart. "Honestly, she was the sweetest thing. Troubled, though. I'm not surprised she killed him."

"Make sure they use good pictures of me," Jules said. "You know you pretty white girls always get your, like, sorority pictures everywhere, not your mugshots. That's what I want."

"We'll make sure to remember that," Dia said, lifting her guitar over her head. "But can we get back to work now?" She got out the notebook Jules had begun to hate and sat cross-legged on the cement floor. "We have just over a week. We should decide what we're going to play."

"I think we should do 'Bones,'" Hanna said, playing with the end of her braid as she sat on an amp. "I think it shows our growth."

"But 'Pretty Baby' is really good, too," Dia said. "Intense, and it has some good technical parts in there."

"What about the one we just did?" Jules asked. "That's really good."

"But it's not ready," Hanna said.

Dia shook her head. "And it's not right for this."

Jules looked between the two of them and exhaled. Well, mark this day. Hanna and Dia, agreeing.

This was like a miracle.

Without Jules really noticing, things had changed. At the very least, Dia and Hanna weren't fighting, only bickering, picking at each other with sharp barbs.

Jules had seen worse from them, much worse.

And now things seemed to be going okay. Better than okay. Good.

She drummed on her knees. "Fine," Jules said. "'Pretty Baby' is technically good and I love it, but 'Bones' shows us off more. And the lyrics are on another level."

Dia nodded once. "Okay, then. 'Bones.'"

The door that led into Hanna's house opened then, and Molly poked her head out of it. "Hanna!" she said, sounding breathless. "Mom's going to be home in twenty minutes."

"Shit." Hanna stood, suddenly jittery, shoving her sticks in her back pocket. "Okay, we have to go. Or, you have to go, I mean."

Dia crossed her arms and stared at Hanna. "Hold on," she said. "What?"

"My parents don't exactly know about any of this," Hanna said. "So—"

"So what?" Jules said. "We used to practice here all the time."

Hanna screwed up her face. "Yeah, and that was before I went to rehab, and now the rules are different. I can't do *whatever* I want anymore, so—"

"So you're lying to your parents?" Dia said.

Hanna took a too-long pause. "It's not a lie," she said eventually. "They just don't know. Yet."

"Hanna! Are you kidding me?" Dia shook her head even as she got up. "Of course not. I should have known. Look, I don't want to tell you how to live your life—"

"Okay," Hanna said sharply. "So don't."

Jules unplugged the cables and lifted her bass over her head. "It's fine," she said loudly, to fill the sudden silence between them all. Had she jinxed it by thinking about them getting along? "She knows what she's doing. Right, Han?"

Hanna pursed her lips. "Right."

"And Dia is not trying to be overbearing, only watching out for you," Jules said. *"Right?"*

"Sure," Dia said, more as a sigh than anything else.

"Excellent," Jules said. She flipped the catches on her case closed and gave them both a sharp look. "So, we'll pick this up tomorrow. Yes?"

Dia did this exaggerated head roll but when she looked at Jules again the annoyance was gone. "Yeah," she said. "Okay."

"All right," Jules said. "Get your stuff and let's go."

Hanna grabbed one of the amps and moved it to the back corner, pulling a blue sheet over it. "Tomorrow," she said, "twelve?"

"Yeah," Jules said, waiting as Dia got all her stuff. "We'll be here."

Dia looked over at Hanna. "So you know," Dia said, "this is a bad idea. You should really—"

Jules took Dia by the elbow and yanked the door open, waving back at Hanna as she steered Dia outside. "Okay, we're done. Bye, Hanna!"

Dia pulled herself out of Jules's grip as the door crashed shut behind them. "Ow! You are, like, annoyingly strong."

"It's carting all those frozen peas," Jules said, flexing. "Truth."

Dia looked back at the house. "I don't like this," she said.

"What?" Jules said. "You think we're gonna get her in trouble?"

"I think she's going to get herself in trouble," Dia said. "Like always."

"She's not such a pushover now, is she? She does what she wants." Jules looked at Dia. "Reminds me of someone."

"Shut up," Dia said, but without any meaning. "I don't lie to people."

"Oh, really? I don't think you want to hear what I have to say about your boy Jesse." Jules swung her case over her shoulder. "Let's give her a break. Maybe she really does know what she's doing." Jules wanted to believe that, but the doubt in her voice was clear.

Still, she turned away from the house and began walking to the bus stop. "We're not in charge of her," she called back to Dia. "It's her life."

Jules went home, up to her room, where she propped her guitar against the wall and stood in front of her closet, shaking off the feeling of practice and Hanna's panic.

So Hanna's parents didn't know. Hanna obviously had a plan and knew what she was doing.

Or, that was what Jules was choosing to believe.

Instead of that, she tried to focus on what she was going to wear for the movies with Autumn. She stood in front of her small closet for ten minutes, black on black on black looking back out at her. Not like Autumn, with her rainbow of dresses and lip gloss in a thousand shades of Kiss Me. Jules tugged at the hem of a worn-out jersey and wrinkled her nose. But you know what? Autumn saw her all the time at work and if she liked Jules in her Callahan's apron, she should like her in anything, even band practice clothes.

So instead of changing, Jules pulled her braids up into a high pony, put on more deodorant, and switched her flip-flops for high-tops.

Down in the kitchen she saw the remains of her dad's best pasta, roses in a tall vase, and two notes on the refrigerator. From Danny: *Out w/people, back by 10.* And from her parents: *Gone for dessert, don't wait up!*

Jules smiled and plucked one of the flowers out of the vase to smell. Sometimes they were so cute it hurt.

She wrote her own note and slipped it under a strawberry magnet: *Movies, see you in the morning!*

She left and hopped on the bus again, and it didn't take long to get there, but when Jules walked up to the theater somehow Autumn had beaten her there. "Hey!"

Autumn looked up from her phone and her face broke into this beaming, beautiful smile. "Hi." Today her dress was orange and off her shoulders, revealing the faintest swimsuit tan line, and her lips were the same purple as her hair.

Jules closed the distance between them. "Hey," she echoed. "How was your day?"

"Same old," Autumn said, catching a strand of her hair before it got stuck in her gloss. "Yours? Did you have a good band practice?"

"Yeah, it was good," Jules said. She kept her face neutral so as not to give away her secret.

The more they practiced, the better she felt about their chances of winning, and that meant she was getting closer and closer to her fantasy of telling Autumn all about it.

Autumn smiled with shiny white teeth. "Could be worse," she said. "Ready?"

"Ready," Jules said, and without thinking about it too much, she reached for Autumn's hand, her own warm fingers wrapping around Autumn's cool ones.

But only for the briefest of seconds, before Autumn snatched her hand away, leaving Jules holding nothing but air.

Jules looked at her and Autumn was already shaking her head, her mouth this small smile. "Sorry," she said. "I didn't mean to do that. Here, let's go."

Autumn held out her hand, but Jules didn't take it this time. "You didn't mean to do what?" Jules said, and her voice came out louder than she intended, and her face was hot. "What? You don't want to hold my hand?"

"No," Autumn said, looking confused. "I mean, yes. I mean— Jules. I think it was just a reflex."

A *reflex?* "Really?" Jules said. "What, so your instinct is to not want to touch me?"

"I didn't say that." Now Autumn's eyebrows drew together and she looked up at Jules like she wasn't sure what was happening. "I'm not used to it, is all."

Jules shook her head. "You know, if you don't want to do this, you don't have to. I'm not interested in making you be with me if you don't care."

"Jules!" Autumn's mouth dropped open. "When did I say I didn't care? All that happened was that I took my hand away, and I didn't even do that on *purpose*, okay? I want to be with you and I want to hold your hand, so will you let me now or do you want to stand here and fight all night?"

A girl passing them by gave Jules an odd look, and Jules folded her arms across her chest, looking at her feet. "Stand here and fight," she said to the sidewalk. That's what she and Delaney would have done.

But Autumn was not Delaney.

"Oh, stop," Autumn said. "I'm not fighting with you, silly girl. Okay?"

Jules fought a smile and looked up at Autumn. "Okay."

"You are trouble," Autumn said. "Let's go in."

Neither of them attempted anything this time—they just went into the theater and bought their tickets and food, and then found their seats.

Halfway through the movie, Autumn placed her hand, palm up, on the armrest between them. And Jules took the invitation, laced her fingers through Autumn's. Her heart moved out of her throat and settled in its rightful place.

But this small voice in the back of her head whispered to her. *This is all you're good for. In the dark. Who's going to claim you out there, in the real world?*

Autumn shifted, leaned her head on Jules's shoulder, the strawberry of her shampoo so sweet.

This girl, Jules thought, defiant, shutting that voice up. *She will.*

Dia

The sun beat down on Dia's shoulders as she sat outside, watching Lex kicking a ball around the yard. She rolled her wrists, hearing the clicking of ligaments, and blew out a sigh between chapped lips. It was a day off from the Flour Shop, but she'd run errands all around town while Lex was at day care, and then gone to Hanna's for practice. At least her parents were both at work now—it meant that there'd been no one to judge Dia for feeding Lex a Happy Meal for lunch and then planting her in front of cartoons while Dia lay on the couch, staring at the ceiling, asleep with her eyes open. Sometimes the only thing to do was put aside all her worrying about being a Good Mom and settle for being Okay-Ish and Trying Really Hard at It.

Now she watched Lex playing, and when her phone started buzzing on the step beside her, Dia didn't even raise her head to check the caller, just put it to her ear and answered. "Hello?"

"Dia Valentine," Jesse's voice said. "Where the hell are you?"

Dia slipped a hand to the back of her neck and smiled at the concrete. "Home," she said. "And hi."

"I didn't mean now," Jesse said. "It was more of a figurative *where are you*, y'know? Because you've been completely MIA the last couple weeks, Dee. What's up with that?"

"I got stuff going on. You know me," Dia said, watching a lone white cloud scudding across the otherwise unblemished sky.

"Well, forget that and come hang out with me," he said. "I haven't seen you in forever, and I'm bored."

"You only think of me when you're bored?" Dia said. "Real nice."

"Not true. I think about you all the time," Jesse said, and Dia heard it in his voice, how halfway through he realized what he was saying and slowed like he was trying to pull the words back into his mouth. But by then it was too late; they were already out, and they had already wound their way into Dia, catching her breath and her words in her throat.

"We'll go to the Gardens," he said now. "You and Alexa and me. What do you think?"

What did she think? Dia pressed one hand to her chest, gazing in Lex's direction. She thought that he was so good to her, and she missed the way he looked at her, and what better way to spend her afternoon than with this boy and this little girl?

"I think that sounds perfect."

Dia saw Jesse from the bus, sitting on the wall by the south entrance. They got off and she took her time walking over, because he hadn't noticed them yet, and when he didn't know she was looking was when she could really look. He'd cut his hair short again, and his left elbow had a bandage wrapped around it, the white stark against his deep brown skin. For a moment Dia imagined what would happen next if she were his girlfriend: she would walk over and touch his arm, kiss him hello, and he'd smile at her.

What would it be like to kiss Jesse Mackenzie?

That, she'd imagined many, many times before: staring out of the window in school, mindlessly piping cookies at work, with her hand between her legs at night.

"Mama, go," Lex's impatient voice said, and Dia shook herself out of it.

"Okay, baby," she said. "Whatever you say."

Jesse had seen them now, and he hopped down from the wall, wincing a little as he put pressure on his left arm. He bent down to greet Lex first. "Hey, kiddo," he said. "Dope hat."

"Hi," Lex said. "We going to see the bugs."

"Well, duh," Jesse said. "They're the best thing here."

He stood and smiled at Dia, heartbreaking as always, those almost-black eyes, his full mouth. "Hi."

"Hi." Dia tipped her head to the side. "Let's walk."

They followed the long path into the wildflowers; Dia let Lex out of the stroller and she went ahead of them, flitting from flower to flower like a little honeybee. "What happened to your elbow?"

"That? It's fine," Jesse said. "A sprain."

Dia looked sideways at him. A sprain. Like it was nothing at all. "What did you do?"

"It's nothing, for real," Jesse said. He put his arm straight up in the air, waving it around. "See? I messed up a landing, got a little bruised. These are the perks of riding."

Dia sighed. "Sure."

"It's one of those things," he said. "You start riding, you're going to fall down. It's worth it, a couple breaks and batterings every once in a while. You still get back on the bike at the end of it all."

"Hmm." Dia reached out but stopped short of her fingers grazing his arm. "You scare me, sometimes." *All the time, every second of every day* was what she didn't say.

"It'll heal," Jesse said. "You don't need to worry."

"I can't help it," Dia said, and she looked away, at Lex wandering close. "Not when it comes to you."

Jesse didn't say anything, and now Dia was the one wanting to pull the words back out of the air and swallow them down.

Then Jesse said, "When's Alexa's birthday?"

"The twenty-second," she said. They kept walking, Dia making sure Lex was always in their sight. "I wonder about who she's going to be," Dia said. "You know? What she's going to like, what she's going to want to be."

"Whatever it is, she'll be the best," Jesse said. "With you being her mom? For sure."

They walked beneath a sickly-sweet arch of flowers. "What did you want to be?" Dia asked. "When you were a kid."

Jesse blew his cheeks out and began ticking them off on his hands. "First off was astronaut," he said. "Classic. Then it was soccer player, chef, and I *think* doctor. Then I landed my first three-sixty whip and I decided I wanted to be a pro rider." He dropped his hands. "*Then* I realized I was nowhere near good enough, and so I moved on to architect."

Dia flexed her fingers on the stroller's handlebar. "Lex, don't grab," she called out. "Gentle, remember?" Lex bounced her head, nodding, and Dia kept an eye on her as she meandered closer.

"Look at her," Jesse said. "She used to be a tiny thing and now she walks and talks and understands what you say to her. Dee—you're, like, imparting knowledge to her."

"With great power," Dia said, and she almost felt like she could cry. "She's so amazing."

"You made her," Jesse said, and he nudged her shoulder with his. "That's pretty amazing, too. And one day you'll have that house with the big yard and all that. Everything you want."

Dia glanced sideways at him, the most she could bear to look at him right now. "Yeah. We'll see." She spotted Lex crouched in the flower beds. "Lala, come this way."

Jesse cleared his throat. "You know, I didn't know if you'd answer when I called," he said. "Kinda feel like you've been avoiding me lately."

"Avoiding you?" Dia repeated, surprised, and then she thought about it for a second. With practice and work and writing, she had been extra busy. And then there was the fact that Jesse didn't know about any of it.

"Yeah," he said, turning so he was walking backward and looking at her. "I go into the Flour Shop, you're not there. I ask if you wanna hang, you say you're busy. You know."

Dia smiled.

Maybe she should tell him now.

Everything was going so well, and the day was nice, and maybe she didn't *need* to be so afraid. Maybe she could tell him, and he'd be happy for her, and she'd—

What? Say something she shouldn't?

Would that be so wrong? What had Hanna said? *For all the time we get on this planet, you might as well try being happy for as much of it as you can.*

She felt the sun on her shoulders, the music in her head. She felt good, today.

"Okay," she said. "You want to know the truth?"

Jesse looked at her, uncertainty in his eyes. "Do I?"

She laughed now. "It's good," she said. "Me and Jules and Hanna— we entered the Sun City contest. And we got through the first round, so—"

"Wait, wait, wait." Jesse stopped. "You entered Sun City? You and Jules and *Hanna*?"

"Yeah."

"Hanna Adler? Hanna who you don't talk to?"

"Yes!" Dia said. "Except, I do, now. Talk to her."

"Okay," Jesse said. "And that's where you've been, being in a band and entering contests and not telling me about any of it?"

"I guess...."

Jesse took a step back and threw his hands up. "Why didn't you tell me about any of this? *Dee*. What, you just give me cookies to shut me up and send me on my merry way without thinking this might be of interest to me? I can't believe you!"

He sounded so serious and Dia would have fallen for it without the cookie talk and the way he started to laugh at the end. "Shut up," she said, his laugh infectious. "See, maybe *this* is why I didn't tell you, because you always make a big deal of everything."

"For real, though," Jesse said. "Why didn't you say anything?"

"Superstition," Dia said. It wasn't a complete lie, not really. "You know."

Jesse shook his head. "You never cease to amaze me."

Dia's pulse skipped and bounced, staccato sharp, and she turned her attention to Lex to get away from his gaze. "Stop."

He cleared his throat. "So, Hanna," he said. "What's that like?"

They looped all the way around the gardens as she told him all about Hanna, the difference between the girl Dia had known before and the girl she knew now. About practicing, and how she'd missed it all.

They walked back by the rose garden and Dia watched Lex carefully as Jesse talked to her and her mind wandered again, to what it would be like to kiss him.

Stop wondering, a whisper in the back of her mind said. *Do something about it.*

"Dee." Jesse's voice interrupted her thoughts. "Are you listening to me?"

Dia stopped walking, stepped away from the stroller. "Jesse."

"What?"

She looked at him for a long moment, and he stared back at her, those eyes that seemed to read everything. Fathoms deep and holding things he'd told only her, quiet truths Dia had entrusted to him. God, he was pretty, but god, he was everything else, too.

"Dia," he said now. "What is it?"

She took another step closer to him and before she could talk herself out of it, touched her hand to his chest. "Hi," she said.

For a moment she thought she was making a huge mistake, him staring down at her and not moving at all, but then he started to smile. And electricity crackled across her skin as he put a hand on her waist. "Hi," he said back.

She was afraid to breathe in that second, afraid that any move she made would shatter this moment they were in. Because she was being reckless, she knew, dangerous.

The sun surrounded Jesse in a halo, set him alight, and Dia rose up on her toes, lifted her chin, felt the ghost of Jesse's breath across her lips. *I am going to kiss Jesse Mackenzie,* she thought.

And then: "Mama!"

"Fuck," Dia breathed, and at the same second Jesse's hands stilled on her body. He dipped his head, resting on her shoulder, and Dia felt him shaking before she heard his laugh. Without meaning to she wound her arms around him, her hands on the back of his warm neck, pulled him closer. "Oh, this is funny?"

He lifted his head and widened his eyes at her. "Come on," he said.

"It's pretty funny. It's perfect."

Dia saw them standing there with their arms around each other, her chest against his, entangled and unaware and unashamed, and then Lex called again. "Look! Ladybug!"

"Listen," she said, keeping her voice low, just for him. "This is not over."

"No?"

Dia stroked her fingers across the nape of his neck and he smiled. "No," she said. "I promise."

She pulled away from him and headed to her daughter. "Where is it?" she said. "Show me."

While Lex found the creature again, Dia looked over her shoulder and Jesse was standing there, watching them, shaking his head like he couldn't believe her. Dia knew what he was feeling; she couldn't believe herself, either.

It was already a memory to her, running her fingers across the back of Jesse's neck, his hand on her waist. *Did I really do that?* she thought wonderingly. It was an impulsive decision, so unlike her.

But all summer long she'd been doing things she normally wouldn't, letting herself risk things. And this—it felt good, real. And this relief at touching him at last, the way he laughed into her skin.

She looked back at her daughter, reached into the flowers with her, and smiled.

It felt inevitable.

Hanna

"You think you're ready for high school, Molls?" Hanna picked up her sweating milkshake. "You can ask me anything. It's really not so bad." She ignored the look Ciara gave her. What? If Hanna took out the drinking and the friends falling apart and the loneliness, then— actually no, it was that bad. But she wasn't going to scare Molly with her horror stories.

Molly shook her head. "I'm not that nervous," she said. "I'm kind of excited."

"For high school?" Ciara made a face. "You're braver than me, kid."

They were sitting on the hill overlooking the skate park, watching the people down there and recovering from a morning at the mall picking between a hundred identical pairs of jeans for Molly. It felt weird for Hanna to be imagining Molly going back to school and not thinking about it herself. Real life, she guessed.

"I think I want to try out for cheerleading," Molly said, tossing her hair back in the most perfect way and looking at Hanna. "What do you think?"

Hanna tipped her head to the side. "You don't need my permission," she said. "Do what you want. I think you'll be a badass cheerleader, though."

"They'd be ridiculous not to pick you," Ciara said through a mouthful of fries.

Molly smiled and sounded relieved when she said, "Okay. I'm going to do it."

"I can't believe you're going to be a freshman," Hanna said.

"Me either," Ciara said, crossing her long legs. "This time last year you were all braces and pigtails. Now you're a cheerleader in cooler jeans than me."

"Shut *up*," Molly said, so thirteen. "God, you two are embarrassing."

Hanna slung her arm around her sister's neck and tugged on her ponytail. "It's my right."

"Whatever." Molly wriggled out of her grip, but she was grinning when she stood up. "I'm going to talk to Portia, she's down there."

"All right," Hanna said. "Don't go anywhere else."

"I won't."

She watched Molly head down the hill and then said to Ciara, "I forget that's she not a little kid. Sometimes she acts like she is, and she's just my little sister, and then sometimes she comes out with this wise-woman talk and I'm like—Molly, is that you?"

Ciara laughed. "This is what happened to me with *you*," she said. "When we met you were, like, fourteen! Now you're as legal as me. With a real grown-up job and everything."

"I know," Hanna said, groaning at the thought of her office employment, creeping ever closer. "But it'll only be for a couple years, until I have some money to pay for college and get my shit together."

Ciara nudged Hanna with her shoulder. "I think your shit's pretty together now," she said. "You're sober, you graduated, and you're still alive."

Hanna raised her eyebrows at that. "Real high bar."

"I used to worry that I'd come home from touring and you would be dead," Ciara said bluntly. "So whatever you might think about yourself, I'm pretty fucking glad that you're still here."

Hanna put a hand to her chest and pressed against the sudden sharp tension there. Sometimes she forgot—all the ways she'd hurt the people around her, all the ways she'd let everybody, let herself, down. But Ciara was right: she was still here. And maybe she did have her shit together. She was making music again, even; two months ago she wouldn't even have *dreamed* that could happen.

Things could change; people could change. *I have changed,* Hanna thought.

I am here.

I am okay.

She linked her arm through Ciara's and shifted closer. "Thanks."

"No sweat," Ciara said breezily. "Now, I need music updates. Since you won't let me hear anything or insert myself all the way into this venture for some reason."

Hanna shook her head. "You know I want to," she said. "But it feels like it has to be the three of us doing this, on our own. As much as I would love your genius input, obviously."

"Your ego stroking is duly noted," Ciara said. "I can't believe that, one, you're talking again, and two, that my protégées are moving on without me!"

Hanna pulled away from Ciara, twisting to face her. "I know," she said. "It took me a while to believe it would work but—" She paused and swallowed. "I really missed them. I hated some of the things they did to me, but I missed them, too. Even though part of me wanted to hold that grudge until the end of time."

"Scorpio," Ciara cut in. "Typical."

Hanna smiled. "Right. But we make good music together. We're magic at that. And it's good to be back with them and not hating them all the time. So . . . I don't know, maybe I'm naive, but I don't think so. Right?" She shook her head. "I had to let them back in, knowing that it might all blow up in my face, but it didn't. That's more brave than stupid, right?"

Ciara looked at her, levity replaced with intensity. "They're being good to you, yeah? And you to them?"

"Yeah," Hanna said. She thought of the apology that had slipped from Dia's lips, taken her so much by surprise that she hadn't even known how to process it, was still processing it. "We're good."

"Then yeah," Ciara said. "More brave than stupid."

Hanna poked Ciara's knee. "I know it's weird," she said. "They kinda cut you off, too."

Ciara shook her head, the ring through her lip flashing. "There was a lot happening," she said. "They needed space, just like you did. They know where I am, when they're ready. I'm waiting."

"Right," Hanna said, and she put her head on Ciara's shoulder, watching tiny Molly down below under the sun. "Waiting."

jules

"Have a good day," Jules said, her cheeks aching. "Thanks for shopping at Callahan's."

She watched the customer wheel their cart away to the outside world and sighed as the front doors swished open. Escape: so near, so far. Her fingers plucked bass lines in the air, her new nervous twitch. She'd rather be practicing than working, but—

"Hey!"

Jules jumped. "Henry! Stop doing that."

"What?" Henry said, shrugging his shoulders. "Just trying to get your attention."

"You don't need to scream in my ear to get it," Jules said. Two registers down she saw Autumn turn around and laugh. "What do you want?"

"I heard you're doing the Sun City contest," he said. "That's cool, I didn't know you guys were even playing again."

"Oh," Jules said. *Shut up, Henry.* "Um . . ." She glanced over at Autumn again, whose face bore confusion now. Oh, no no no. He was ruining her surprise! "Keep your voice down," she said. "Who'd you hear that from?"

Henry shrugged. "I dunno, around," he said. "You think you'll win? I heard the prize is fifteen grand." He slapped his hands together. "That's a lot of money."

"Yeah, it is," Jules said, and now Autumn was leaning out of her lane. No, no—if she heard him and asked, then he'd tell her and it would completely screw up Jules's plan—she'd never get her rock-star goddess moment when she told Autumn they'd won, and—

"Henry," Autumn called over. "What's the contest?"

Okay, it was over.

Henry turned. "They have it every year," he said. "The radio station runs it. You know, you enter a song and the winner gets played on the radio and stuff. But this year it's like a way bigger deal, because Glory Alabama—you know them, right?—they're sponsoring it this year." He turned back to Jules. "So, you think you'll win?"

"What's the prize?" Autumn called again, and this time she was looking at Jules.

She swallowed. In the grocery store, wearing her polyester apron, was not how she'd envisioned this moment going. "The winner gets to play a support slot for Glory Alabama when their next tour comes through," she said. "And . . . fifteen thousand dollars."

"Whoa," Autumn said, and Jules couldn't tell whether her surprise was at the money or that she was just finding out about the whole thing right now or some combination of the two. "That's amazing."

Jules bit her lip. So this wasn't how she'd wanted to tell Autumn, and probably she'd have some explaining to do later. But it was all out there now. "Isn't it?" she said, but then there was a customer heading her way, and when she looked back over, Autumn was busy, too.

Jules exhaled as she began scanning items. Okay. Autumn didn't seem annoyed. Confused, maybe, but once Jules explained, she'd get it. "That'll be thirty-seven eighteen," she said. "Cash or credit?"

The afternoon passed fast, busier than usual, and when Jules got a breather again she looked to Autumn's register. But it was already closed up, no sign of Autumn. She looked down the aisles closest to her and then called out to Malai down by the paper towels. "Hey, where did Autumn go?"

"I think she's finished," Malai called back to her. "She just went out the back."

She'd left without saying anything?

Jules paused for a second before closing her register, too, and heading out past Malai. "If Greg comes out, tell him I'm on my break," she said.

"Sure," Malai said. "No problem."

Jules walked as fast as her tired feet could carry her, and when she got to the break room she was relieved to see Autumn at her locker. "Hey," she said, slightly out of breath. "Are you leaving?"

"Yeah," Autumn said, pulling a pink backpack from her locker.

"That's what I usually do when my shift's over."

She hadn't looked at Jules. So maybe she *was* pissed. "About the contest—"

"What about it?" Autumn stuffed her apron in her backpack. "It sounds amazing, really. I hope you win."

"I hope so too," Jules said, and she couldn't help her smile. "Okay, I know it's stupid, but that's why I didn't tell you. I wanted to wait until after, so that if—no, *when*—we won, I could tell you that. But Henry kind of ruined it."

"Don't blame him," Autumn said.

Jules bit her lip. "Are you mad?" Jules regretted the words as soon as they left her mouth.

"Am I *mad*?" Now Autumn looked at her. "I don't get you, that's all. It seems like you say one thing and then do another, and I don't like it. I mean, you said I can talk to you about anything, so that's what I've been doing, even when it's not easy for me to do it. But then it's like, you get to keep secrets from me? And I'm not supposed to be annoyed by that either? I thought we were all about being honest with each other."

"We are," Jules said, taken aback.

"You get to be mad at me over whatever, like that stupid thing at the movies, so why can't I be pissed about this?"

"I was going to tell you," Jules said, stepping closer. "When we won."

"And what if you didn't win?" Autumn asked, her voice sharp. "Where you still going to tell me? Or were you just going to let it slide?"

"I . . ." Jules hadn't really thought it through that far. She'd gotten hung up on the part of her fantasy where Autumn started kissing her. "I don't know. I thought it would be fun to, like, surprise you with the news. I wanted it to be exciting. Maybe that was a bad idea. . . ." It certainly seemed that way now, her reasoning sounding flimsy even to her own ears. She twisted her fingers together. "It made sense at the time, but now . . . I guess I was wrong. I'm sorry."

"Fine. It's fine," Autumn said, and she slammed her locker shut, pushed past Jules. "I have to go."

"Autumn, wait—"

But Autumn walked out, the door swinging closed behind her. Jules looked up at the water-stained ceiling and groaned. Again and again, her ridiculous, overblown, romantic fantasies came crashing down around her. Why hadn't she just told her about the contest in the beginning? *Why?* Now Autumn was upset, and even though Jules had been trying to do something right, she'd screwed that up again, too.

She headed back out to the floor.

Dia

Dia had gone to bed on Tuesday happy. She'd fallen into a deep sleep and dreamed of being back in the Gardens with Jesse, standing in that exact same spot, except that this time she was actually kissing him.

Her mouth on his. His arms wrapped around her, her hands on his chest.

Her hands skimming skin and—

Bone. Bones under her fingers, and blood, and Dream Dia had looked around and they weren't in the Gardens anymore, they were in the middle of a road and there was a car flipped on its side and underneath that car was the body of the boy she'd just been kissing. And Dream Dia had tried to run, but her feet were suck to the sidewalk, stuck *in* it, and she could only watch as Jesse's crushed body was pulled from beneath the wreckage, zipped into a body bag, taken away.

She'd woken up with her heart racing, panicked breaths rasping from her, and it had taken her a minute to work out why she was in the middle of an anxiety attack, what in her mind had thrown her into the deep end and left her to wake up struggling against the water.

"Elliot," she'd said aloud, throwing the covers off. *"Jesse."*

She'd rolled over and looked for Lex in her crib, calmed herself breathing in time with her baby. *It's a bad dream,* she thought. *It doesn't mean anything.*

Lex's chest rose, fell, and Dia twisted her fingers into the sheets.

It did mean something, though. It was everything she'd feared, the entire reason she'd been keeping Jesse at a distance for years now, the reason she'd cut Hanna off. Her brain had conjured her this perfect reminder, a heart-splintering shock to say, *You know this is a bad idea. Do you want him to die, too?*

The dream—nightmare—played on her mind all week. On Friday morning they had an early practice at Hanna's, and Dia was all sorts of out of it, messing up the lyrics not twice but *three* times, and completely blanking on the end of "Pretty Baby." She wiped her hands on her thighs and shook her head, tried to rattle the music back into place that way.

"What is up with you?" Jules asked as they were packing up.

"Nothing," Dia said. "I'm fine, I just . . . messed up a couple times." *I just can't stop thinking about the next funeral I might have to go to.*

Jules clipped her case shut. "All right," she said, but she was looking at her phone instead of at Dia.

"Is it Autumn?" Hanna asked, teasing.

Jules stiffened. "No," she snapped, shoving her phone away. "It's nobody."

"Jesus," Hanna said. "What is wrong with you two today?"

"What's with all the questions?" Jules said. "God."

Dia held in a sigh. This was just frayed nerves, old ways rubbing up against new girls. Nothing to worry about. "All right, I gotta go."

"See you later," Hanna said, twirling a stick between two fingers.

Dia left and caught the bus over to work, stashing her guitar and amp in the back room before settling into her schedule for the day: three rainbow birthday cakes, six dozen frosted sugar cookies, and many, many chocolate fudge cupcakes.

While mixing ingredients, Dia felt her nerves calming a little. Sugar and butter. Eggs cracked. Flour sifted. She separated the batter into bowls and added coloring, drop by single drop. Too much and the intensity would be over the top, cartoonish instead of whimsical.

When she took her break, she checked her phone and looked at the last text she'd gotten from Jesse: Come by the skate park tomorrow, if you can. We'll hang.

She hadn't replied yet.

She hadn't even seen him, not since Tuesday. Now that he knew about the band, it was easy for her to hide behind it, tell him she was so busy and so sorry and maybe tomorrow, always tomorrow. But she'd been texting him enough that he didn't think anything was wrong, she was pretty sure. He didn't know that she was freaking out.

That all she could think when she saw his name on the screen was that she had made a terrible mistake.

She had already lost one person. And she hadn't even *loved* Elliot. It sounded awful, but it was true—she had liked him a lot, and she could have loved him, too, but she'd never even gotten the chance. And it had taken her months to put all of that feeling together, to recognize that she wasn't a horrible person for thinking that, and that it didn't make her missing him any more or any less, that she was allowed to be sad.

So what would she do if it was Jesse? A boy that she *did* love, that she had been in love with for so long now. People liked to talk about loving and losing—but Dia would rather not have him be hers and still have him be whole than be with him. Jesse was already getting hurt all the time; what more would it take for the worst to happen to him? What if being with her was the thing that *made* it happen?

She leaned against her locker, and all her breath left her as she realized the truth.

It's me.

I'm toxic.

Dia destroyed good things. Elliot. The band. Hanna, too, in a way. People got close to her and became broken. So it was up to her, wasn't it, to make sure she didn't inflict all the damage she was apparently capable of. To take herself out of the picture and leave people alone, let them go on to goodness without her dragging them down.

A quiet part of her said: *No, this isn't real, this is not rational thought.*

But the bigger, more afraid part of her overruled that logic, made her think about what more might happen if it *was* real and she tried to ignore it.

Dia slid down the metal, her hands on her knees. Think of all the pain she could have saved if she'd realized the truth of herself sooner.

But she knew it now. And she could still spare Jesse.

Back in the kitchen, she pulled her cakes out of the oven perfectly risen and started decorating her cookies—the initials *ANW* iced in pale pink on each one—and Dia's hands were steady enough now to get it perfect.

When the cookies were done she finished off her rainbow cakes. Pipe a single stripe of red at the bottom, and orange above it, yellow, sky blue, grass green, lavender, deepest plum. Spin the cake and smooth the frosting out, blurring the edges between one color and the next. Fill the top with sugar-heart decorations and box it up ready for it to go to a loving, hungry home.

She barely noticed the afternoon passing as she worked, and when she was finished she stood away from her bench, watching the glitter on her hands shift in the bakery lights. "What's up?" Stacey said, passing on her way to the ovens. "You need something?"

"No," Dia said, shaking her head. Sometimes the hardest choices made for the easiest decisions.

What she'd done with Jesse had been wrong. She'd put her hand on his chest and her mouth almost on his and set into motion something that she couldn't contain.

But she'd fix it. She'd leave him alone, even though it was the last thing she wanted to do.

She looked at Stacey and smiled. "I'm all good."

Even though she was breaking her own heart.

* * *

After work Dia headed over to the skate park.

She walked, feeling the heat of the sun on the back of her neck but also smelling the trees and the flowers and that summer-asphalt scent. She climbed the hill that hid the skate park in its dip and looked out at the sun beginning to set, the kids below rolling back and forth on rattling boards and bikes. Two girls practiced tricks on dirt mounds, following each other at shocking speed, whipping perfect circles in the air. Dia watched with her heart in her mouth as they left the earth again and again, a flood of relief each time they landed and continued on, no damage, no pause.

Dia hitched up her shorts before she sat on the grass, scanning until she picked out Jesse on his bike, flying over a bench with the wind molding his shirt to his body. She knew she had to actually go to him, tell him that she'd lied, that what she'd started in the Gardens was, in fact, over. But she wanted to wait a little longer in the world where that was still a possibility, where he still thought things were changing.

He really was good, she realized as she watched him. More than that—he looked alive out there. He said he wasn't good enough to go pro, and Dia had no way of judging, really, but he was beautiful in the air.

A group of girls with their boards under their arms crested the hill, their noise breaking Dia's reverie, and planted themselves on the grass. A couple of them looked at Dia, nodding in recognition, and she gave a cautious smile back before standing.

She made her way down to the asphalt and hovered on the edge of everything, waiting for Jesse to notice her. It took a minute, but then he saw her; Dia saw him seeing her, the way he smiled and changed his direction. *No,* she thought. *Don't give me that smile. Save it.* For a cowardly second she wanted to leave, put as much distance between her and this place, her and him, as possible.

And then Jesse skidded to a stop only inches away from her. "Hey," Jesse said, and there was that smile. "There you are."

Her stomach twisted almost violently, the longing that she usually kept so far down thudding into her chest. "Hi," she said, and she couldn't help smiling back at him. But then she remembered why she was there, and shook the smile away. "I need to talk to you."

"Okay," Jesse said, sounding unconcerned. He even rolled his bike closer and did that looking-up-from-beneath-long-lashes thing that usually made Dia literally weak in the knees. "What's up?"

It was easier with the park and all its people, the noise, behind them. She made herself look him in the eye as she told both the biggest lie and realest truth. "I made a mistake. The other day. With you." She forced herself to keep looking at him, even as this confusion came over his face. "I shouldn't have tried to kiss you. I—we should stay the way we are. Friends. It's not a good time. I have a kid and a job, and now the band to think about, and college . . . I think it would be better if we . . ." She tried to find the right word and finally settled on "Didn't."

Jesse was silent for a minute, a painfully long minute. "If we didn't," Jesse said slowly, looking up at her. "But the other day, you—"

"I know," Dia said.

"And now—"

"It was a mistake," Dia said again, folding her arms across her stomach, protective. "And I'm really sorry. But it's for the best."

"Okay," he said again, flat now. "If that's what you really want, Dee."

"It is." *And it's not.*

He nodded, and the riders whipped past in the background, and Dia felt sick. Eventually Jesse spoke again. "Can I at least get the real reason?" he said, his eyes so serious. "Or do you want me to pretend I believe what you said was it?"

Dia swallowed. "That is it," she said. "That's the reason."

Jesse shook his head. "I know you, Dee," he said. "You don't do anything you haven't already decided you're going to do. And Alexa didn't appear between then and now. None of what you said is new. It's the whole reason we're not *already* together, right now."

Dia blinked. "I don't know what you want me to say." No, she knew; she just couldn't say it. How could she say *I'm afraid that if I kiss you, you'll die? If you touch me, you'll be broken?*

"The truth," Jesse said. "Or should I tell you what I think it really is?"

Dia shifted. "What?"

He stood now, leaned over his handlebars. "I think you're scared," he said. "And you don't ever want anyone to know that. I get it. I don't know what you're scared of. You think we won't work out? Or maybe it has nothing to do with me really. Maybe it's about Alexa. Maybe it's Elliot." He said the name carefully. "You tell me, Dee. I just know that sometimes I see this look on your face and then you cover it up so fast, and—you have this thing about you, where you know exactly what you're doing and why, and sometimes I think I'm the one thing you can't put in its place. The way you feel about me is the one thing you can't put away somewhere."

"You're right," Dia said, and Jesse started to look hopeful just as she said, "You don't know. You *don't* get it. I have to think about the future. I have a kid—"

"I know," Jesse said, "and you're a fucking *awesome* mom. And she's the coolest kid I ever met. But is this what you're going to do forever? Use her as your excuse?"

"She is not my excuse," Dia snapped, and she felt her throat constricting. "She is my *reason*. I am her mother, the one parent she still has in the world, and I have to be *everything* for her."

"I know," Jesse said. "But what about the contest? What if you win? Are you going to give up on the band because of her? Give up on that again, too?"

"Don't *even*," Dia said. "You don't know what it was like. You don't know shit." She heard her voice, and god, she hadn't meant for it to be like this. But maybe this was what it would take to make him understand that he was better off without her. "You think you know me, but you don't. You never will," she said, digging her nails into her palms. "So think what you want about me, come up with whatever reason is enough for you, if you can't accept that *I don't want to be with you*." She threw her hands up. "I'm not listening to this anymore."

"Fine. Do what you want, Dee," Jesse said, and he sounded so done with her. "Like you always do."

She shook her head at him and swallowed the beginnings of the crying her body wanted to do. "Whatever, Jesse."

She turned on her heel and stomped back up the hill.

The truth, he'd said. Like she could give him that—like he wouldn't hear what she had to say and not think she was out of her mind. Even she wondered if she was crazy, but what was crazy, really? It was a word people used, Dia thought, to make others seem unimportant, not worthy of listening to. And maybe this fear of hers wasn't "normal," but that didn't make it any less real.

It wouldn't be real enough to Jesse, though. Not enough to make him stay away, the way she needed him to.

And it was done now, wasn't it?

Wasn't that what she'd wanted?

Dia got to the top of the hill and allowed herself to stop for a moment, long enough to breathe in dusk air and exhale sorrow. In her chest, her heart beat on, battered and bruised but still steady.

I did the right thing, she told herself. *He'll get over it. He'll get over* me.

Dia wiped her hands over her eyes and dragged a hand through her hair. She had to go home, take care of her kid, get ready for their final practice on Monday. Because if there was one thing Jesse was really wrong about, it was that she was going to give up on the band again. She had not come this far to let it go. Not this time.

Hanna

Monday was their last practice. They played "Bones" over and over, at Dia's command: "Again, I messed up the second verse." "Again. Hanna, that ending was sloppy." "Again! Jules, you come in with vocals on the second chorus, can you please try to remember that?"

Hanna pounded her drums and ignored the burning in her shoulders. Dia was on fire today, pushing them so much. But that was what they needed: to play hard, loud, sweat it out and let everything out before tomorrow. Tomorrow, when three people who didn't know about them were going to judge them, literally, and ask them questions, and maybe find them wanting.

But if they did, it wouldn't be for lack of trying. It wouldn't be because they hadn't put their all into trying to make this happen. Hanna was sure of that, if nothing else.

She kicked a little more energy where it was needed and pulled way back when it wasn't, listening to Dia's voice crack over Jules's bass line. Sometimes Hanna had to focus in order to not hear the words, because they became a distraction. Lyrics she'd written in the dark quiet of her bedroom, not expecting to hear them set to any music but her own, if she'd even gotten around to it the way she'd always told herself she would. And now in Dia's voice, over music the three of them had written together, the inner workings of Hanna's mind laid bare—it was shocking, to her own ears. But she loved it, too. To finally have it out there and her words not festering any longer, it was good. Sometimes, when she let herself, she even felt proud.

They hit the end and came to a stop, shuddering cymbals and fading reverb. Hanna swiped strands of hair out of her face, hot with her sweat and exertion, and waited for Dia's verdict. Dia turned around, glowing and breathing heavy. "All right," she said. "That was better. Let's take a break, and—"

The inner door flew open, taking them all by surprise, and Hanna whipped around. "Molly! What are you doing?"

Her sister held out her phone. "Mom's coming home early!" she said. "I only just saw her text, but it was twenty minutes ago, so—"

"Shit." Hanna sprung to her feet. "*Shit*. You need to leave."

Jules widened her eyes. "Hanna. You still haven't told them?"

"Now is *not* the time, Jules." Hanna dragged a hand through her hair, spinning around. "Did you not hear me? We gotta *go*."

"What's the big deal?" Dia said, doing the opposite of leaving. "What do they think you've been doing, anyway? You have an entire drum kit set up in your garage."

"They think I got it out for fun," Hanna said, and the longer her friends looked at her, the higher she felt her pulse climbing. "They're not here when we practice. It's *fine*."

"It's clearly not fine," Jules said, but at least she was lifting her bass over her head. "Why don't you tell them? Is it us?" She pointed at Dia. "Are we the problem?"

Hanna glanced at Molly and then at them, wringing her hands together. "No," she said. "I wanted to do this first and see if anything would happen before I made them all—"

She stopped, then, because her mom was pulling into the driveway, and even from where she was standing, Hanna could see the confused look on her face. She exhaled slowly, loudly. "Well, fuck."

Hanna

"Hanna?" Her mom was standing in the open garage door now, this iciness to her words that froze Hanna. "What's going on?"

For a minute Hanna thought about lying, but what was the point? It was pretty obvious what was going on. And it was fast becoming pretty obvious to her that her plan had been a bad idea. But she could still explain, tell her mom exactly what and why and hope for some reprieve.

Her mom was looking at her expectantly, one penciled-in eyebrow raised, and Hanna took a deep breath. "Hi," she said. "You remember Jules and Dia. Obviously."

Her mom gave her friends half a glance before closing in on Hanna again. "Of course," she said. "Hello, girls."

Jules kind of coughed, looking down at her feet, and Dia said, "Hi, Mrs. Adler."

"Hanna," her mom said, ignoring Dia. "What is this?"

"We're . . ." Hanna made herself stand up straight, look her mom right in the eye. "We're practicing. Music. You know."

"Right," her mom said, and the facade cracked. "Inside, now. You too, Molly."

Hanna shot a glance at Dia and Jules and lifted her shoulder apologetically as her mom swept through the garage and into the house. *Sorry,* she mouthed, and Jules looked confused while Dia looked tired, and then Hanna followed her mom into the house.

"Close the door," Theresa said when she and Hanna and Molly were in the kitchen. She dropped her bag heavily on the floor and turned around, fists on her hips. "And start explaining, Hanna."

"It's not what you think," she started. "It's only—you know the Sun City contest? It's a really big deal this year. So . . . we've kind of . . . entered it."

"I don't understand," her mom said slowly, in a way that meant she understood perfectly but did *not* like what she was hearing. "You and those two are friends again, then? After all the trouble you caused?"

Hanna caught that *you.* "That was a long time ago," she said. "And I was going to tell you, but I didn't want to make you . . . worry for nothing." Yeah; that was a good angle. "I knew you would think about what happened before and all that, and I didn't want to bring it up to you if there wasn't going to be anything for you to worry about."

"So instead you lied?" Theresa leaned against the counter, her eyes sharp on Hanna. "How long has this been going on?"

"Not that long," Hanna said, shifting her weight as she scaled the timeline of her deceit down. "Only, like, a few weeks."

"A few *weeks*? Hanna." Her mom shook her head. "I don't understand you. I don't understand what you think you're doing. Every time you lie to me and your dad, you set us all back. Because now I wonder—what else have you been lying about? Can you see that, Hanna? I don't want to have to think like that, but when you violate the trust that we have only just built back up, I have to."

"I'm not lying about anything else," Hanna said. "And I wasn't even lying about this, more . . . not telling the whole truth. Because I knew you would think it was a bad idea anyway."

"Of course I think it's a bad idea!" Theresa said. "I know you love to play music, Hanna, but am I the only one who remembers what happened to you when you were involved in all that? You are doing so, so much better now, and the last thing I want is for you to slide back into that place you were in before. But this seems like a good way for that to happen, doesn't it?"

Hanna folded her arms. "I'm not drinking," she said bluntly. "I'm not going to drink. I just want to make music. I want to be *happy*."

"And maybe I could believe that if you hadn't gone behind our backs to do all this," her mom said, waving in the direction of the garage. "Having them over here only when we're not around, bringing your sister into this—"

"She didn't make me do anything," Molly interrupted. "And Mom, you should hear them, they're so good!"

"That is *not* the point," Theresa said. "Molly, go upstairs."

"But—"

"Upstairs!"

She waited until Molly was gone before turning back to Hanna. "I'm sorry, but I don't think this is a good idea. I think it needs to be done, now."

The way her mom said *I'm sorry* made it clear she was anything but. "Done?"

"Finished," her mom said, slicing her hands through the air. "No more."

"No!" Hanna clasped her hands together, pleading. "Mom, we get to play to the judges tomorrow, and then that's it. We might actually win. And it's so different now, I'm so different now, you know that."

But her mom shook her head. "I *don't* know, Hanna," she said. "When you lie to me, you make me think that you're not so different."

It landed like a barb in Hanna's heart, but she tried again. "I should have told you, I'm sorry, I—I didn't want you to think all of this stuff, but please, Mom, it's not what you think and it's—"

Her mom held her hand up, stopping Hanna. "This is what I mean," she said. "*Trust.* Maybe if you'd come to me first, we could have discussed this and worked something out. But you lied, and *now* you want me to believe that it's not a big deal. That's not the way it works, Hanna. And I'm saying *no.* I don't want you doing this."

Hanna shook her head, desperate. "You can't stop me," she said. "I'm eighteen."

Her mom raised her eyebrows and let out a bitter laugh. "Oh, is that where you want to go with this? Okay, then. Yes, Hanna, you are eighteen. An adult. But you live in my house, so you play by *my* rules. If you want to do your own thing, then you need to do it outside my house. That's the way it is."

Hanna's mouth dropped open. "You're kicking me out?"

"No," Theresa said. "I am telling you the rules. In *my* house, you will not lie to us, and you will do as I say, and I say you can't do this."

"That's ridiculous," Hanna said, clenching her fists tight and giving in to sudden anger. "You can't do that."

"I can and I will." Her mom crossed the kitchen and put a hand on Hanna's cheek, and Hanna could see deep into her eyes then. Anger and fear, both in there. This rush of guilt washed over Hanna.

She should have told the truth from the beginning. It wasn't even that big a deal. And now it was *this*, it had become this, because her mom *couldn't* let her have this *one thing*. "I will not lose you again, Hanna. I saw you disappear right in front of my eyes, and I had to watch them stick a tube down your throat to get you back from the poison you put in yourself, *twice*, and I had to put my seventeen-year-old daughter in rehab. I'm sorry if you think I'm overreacting, but you are my *daughter* and I will do whatever I have to to keep you with me."

"Mom," Hanna said, and unexpected tears spilled over, the weight of them slipping down her cheeks. "I just got this back. Dia and Jules, they're not—I was so lonely and now I'm not," she said, her voice cracking. "It's only tomorrow and then we'll be done, no more practices, I promise." A rash promise to make, but right now she wanted to get her mom to stop and consider. Hanna did not want to leave, she didn't want this to be the thing that pulled them apart, but god, she was so *exhausted*.

But her mom shook her head again. "I'm sorry, Hanna," she said. "This is the way it's going to be. This is for your safety."

Hanna stepped back, out of her mom's grasp, and the last thread of self-preservation snapped. "I don't get you," she said. "What else do you want me to do? I got sober and I let you search my room whenever you wanted and I earned your trust back, but because of this one little thing, it's all gone? That's *bullshit*."

"Excuse me?" Theresa said. "You better watch yourself, Hanna."

"Why bother? You watch me *all the time*," Hanna said. "I'm sick of it. When are you going to let me live my life again? Am I supposed to stay here and do whatever you say whenever you say it so that one day you'll think I'm good again?" She pulled in a ragged breath. "I will never be good again, will I? I'm the bad daughter, the one who drank and drained you and hurt your precious baby, the one *good* child you have. You want me to go? Maybe I should. Go and leave you all here so you can live a nice tidy little life without my mess to ruin it for you. And you can tell all your friends that you tried your hardest but I was just too out of control. That would be nice, right?"

"You think I *want* you to leave?"

"I don't know, Mom," Hanna said. "You don't really seem to want me here."

"When your father comes home—"

"He'll say exactly what you say," Hanna said. "That's how it works."

"I have had enough of your attitude right now."

Hanna whipped around, heading back outside. "Or maybe you've had enough of me."

"Where are you going?" her mom snapped to her back. "Hanna, get back here. Hanna!"

Hanna

Breathe.

Breathe.

Hanna went back into the garage to find Dia and Jules all packed up, and Jules looked at her. "What did she say? Are you okay?"

"Oh, it's fine," Hanna said, clenching her fists. "You know, she thinks I'm a liar and a drunk, but what else is new?" Her nails dug into the palms of her hands and she shook her head, trying to shake out the whisper of *whiskeywhiskeywhiskey*. "You should really go."

"Yeah, we're going," Dia said. "Wait—she said that to you?"

"It's literally nothing new," Hanna said. "It is what it is, okay? Can you—" She stopped and tried to slow her breathing. "I need you to go, *now*."

"We're *going*," Dia said again. "All right?"

Jules and Dia exchanged a look that Hanna was pretty sure she wasn't meant to see. "So, tomorrow—"

"I don't know why she's so pissed," Hanna said, whirling her hands through the air. "I was going to tell her. I was just *waiting*."

"Right," Dia said. "But—"

Hanna rounded on her. "But what? But I didn't? But I'm a liar anyway, so who would even believe what I did or didn't plan to do?"

"Did I say that?" Dia picked up her guitar case. "There's history, that's all."

"Oh, of course you would take her side," Hanna said. She looked up at the ceiling and let out half a breath of unamused laughter. "You think you're so much better than me, don't you? You think you're so clever with your little comments and rolling your eyes when you think I can't see, like, *Hanna, you messed it up again!* I get it, Dia, okay? I'm a fuck-up and I always will be to you, but god, you are not perfect either."

Dia stepped back. "Again, did I say that? No." She shook her head. "We're leaving now. You can call me later, when you've calmed down."

"I'm calm," Hanna said, her teeth gritted. "Don't I look calm to you?"

"You look like you need space," Jules said. "Or maybe you should give your mom the space."

"It doesn't matter what I do or where I go," Hanna said, pacing now. "There's always something with her. I'm always screwing up in a thousand different ways. And then she tries to tell me she's only *worried*, she's *concerned*, always has to bring it back to the fucking drinking. That has nothing to do with this!"

Dia looked at her. "You're right," she said. "Maybe that has nothing to do with this. Because you're sober right now, and yet here you are, screaming at us and talking about your mom when you know what, yeah, she probably is worried about you and you're lucky, you know? Not everybody has a mom like that."

"She should take a tip from you," Hanna said, and she let out a bitter laugh, looking at her hands. "Give up on me. Cut her losses. Worked out okay for you, didn't it?"

"Give up on you?" Dia said, her eyes flashing. "Wow, Hanna. So why the fuck am I here? Did I imagine all this, the last month?" She looked at Jules again and back at Hanna, her eyebrows pulling together. "You think that I *wanted* to cut myself off from you? No. But there's only so long you can let yourself be hurt by someone who doesn't want your help, and you didn't want it, not at all. So what were we supposed to do? Stand by and watch you kill yourself?"

"You didn't have to abandon me!"

"Well, I'm sorry it felt like that, but I did what I thought I had to do," Dia said. "And I don't want to do it again, I don't want to give up on you and on this, and live and die in this town. I want more than that, and so do you, and you've been telling me all this time how different you are now, so *prove it to me.*"

"I can't! You won't ever believe me," Hanna said. "You and your fu—"

"Hey!" Jules said. "*Stop.* Both of you, stop! We didn't spend the last month busting our asses so you can force us into imploding now."

"It's always my fault, isn't it?" Hanna snapped, and Jules glared at her.

"I didn't say it was anyone's fault," she said. "I just want this to *stop* before it goes too far and we can't come back from it."

The air shimmered with the heat of her outburst and Hanna felt the shake in her hands.

But she already wanted to peel the words back from the ether and swallow them whole. Choke on them.

Dia exhaled loudly. "Tomorrow is important. We have worked too hard to mess it up. So we're leaving, and you do whatever you need to do to remember why we're doing this, and then you call me later. Okay?"

Hanna looked past her. She knew Dia was right. Why couldn't she *shut up*? Always running her fucking mouth, ruining all the work she'd done to make people believe she'd changed, to make *herself* believe she was different now.

Well done, Hanna: you're truly living down to everybody's low expectations.

Congratulations.

"Come on," Dia said to Jules, and Hanna wanted to say something, but all the fight had vanished and she only wanted to give herself to the floor beneath her.

Jules looked back at her before they disappeared. "Think about tomorrow," she said. "That's what we wanted before. We might get it now. Think about that, okay?"

When Hanna gave one sharp nod, she tasted the salt of her tears. *Fuck.*

"Okay," Jules said. "Call me if you want."

Hanna watched them leave and sank to a crouch, pressing her hands to her eyes as she rocked on her heels. The taste of her words was metallic, and she wasn't sure if she was going to throw up or not.

"Get inside." Her mom's voice was like nothing she'd ever heard before, and now Hanna was pretty sure she was going to be sick. "Now, Hanna."

She stood slowly and waited there, surveying the mess of their practice, the mess she usually tidied and hid so nobody would be able to tell. There it was, a month's worth of back and forth and testing new boundaries and releasing so much history into the stale garage air.

Was it all over, now?

"Hanna."

She turned and looked her mom dead in the eye. "You don't have to yell," she said, knowing she was only making things worse. But she kind of liked it. "I'm right here."

Hanna skipped dinner. She sat at the top of the stairs instead and listened to her parents arguing about her.

She's lying to us again, her mom kept saying. *How do we know she's not lying about other things too?*

"You could ask," Hanna said under her breath. Unlikely.

Let's not get ahead of ourselves, her dad said. *She's come a long way.*

That was nice, her dad sticking up for her.

And it only takes one slip to bring her crashing down, her mom said. *I'm not taking any chances.*

Hanna got up and retreated to her room. Now she was calmer, she could understand what her mom had been saying—the trust thing. She had lied. She had broken their trust. But if she'd asked, told her parents that she wanted to play in a band again, she knew what they would have said. She knew what her mom would have done.

She lay on the floor beneath the window, evening light playing over her body.

But making music again felt like surfacing after a thousand hours underwater. They didn't get it and they didn't ever let her explain it.

Her phone buzzed for maybe the fifth time in twenty minutes. Hanna looked at it, then put it facedown on the floor. Dia and Jules were freaking out, she was sure.

She was freaking out, underneath it all. Because tomorrow was important. If she didn't go, then she'd be letting the others down, and tanking their shot at fifteen grand and the Glory Alabama show.

If she went, and her mom found out—and she'd find out; wasn't today evidence enough for that?—then she'd lose her family. Even more than she already had.

Her phone buzzed again: voice mail, from Dia. She listened to it: "Hey, it's me. I'm—sorry for being shitty earlier. I just want to make sure you're okay. Call me or text me or something."

Hanna tossed her phone aside. What was her punishment going to be? No car privileges. Curfew. Walk a straight line, touch your nose, blow into this. Maybe.

Her palms itched. In the trunk of her dad's car was a bottle of Jameson that she knew he thought she didn't know about. She could go out there and take it, drink the whole thing and forget about all this until some point further in the future, leave it for Future Hanna to deal with.

More of her than she liked said, *Yes, do it.* The idea of oblivion was so enticing.

Four hundred and—what was it?

She stayed in her room, weighing the idea and mindlessly watching makeup tutorials and chain-smoking out of the window until the rest of the house was asleep and quiet. Then she made her decision.

Nothing was going to change unless she made it. And she'd been doing everything her parents' way for so long now, but it didn't make a difference.

Time to try something new.

She looked around her bedroom, surveying all her stuff in the moonlight. Clothes on the floor and books stacked against the wall and her small desk with her laptop on it. The lamp on her nightstand, pictures of her and Molly at various ages tacked up on her closet doors.

She took a deep breath and then started with the pictures. Took them down one by one and laid them on her bed. Then she started on the insides of her closet, throwing all her shorts and underwear and shirts on top of the pictures. The couple crumpled dresses on the bottom, shiny, tight things from her darkest days, she left.

Hanna was half under her bed when she heard the creak of her bedroom door, and then Molly's voice. "She didn't mean it," her sister whispered, and Hanna could hear the nerves in her voice. "You don't have to do this."

Hanna came out with the biggest duffel she owned and dust on her hands, looking over at Molly in the darkened doorway. "Were you listening earlier?"

"Behind the kitchen door."

Of course; she'd learned that habit from Hanna. "She meant it, Molls." Hanna forced a smile. "Don't worry about it, though. I'll be fine."

"Where are you going to go?" Molly asked, playing with the drawstring on her pajama shorts. "Don't do this."

Hanna ignored her question and started shoving her clothes into the bag. "I'll be fine," she said again. "Trust me."

"I do," Molly said quietly. "Hanna. I do trust you, you know?"

Hanna paused her packing and turned around. She was never sure with Molly, when she said things like this: did she mean it, or did she just want to make her big sister happy? After what Hanna had put her through?

Hanna liked to believe it was a little of both, mostly.

So she said, "I know, Molls." She crossed the room and pulled her sister in close, planted a kiss on the top of her head. "I know."

Elliot

OCTOBER

Elliot shifts into third and tries to ignore the rattling sound coming from somewhere in the car. It's not his, it belongs to his cousin Ana, and it's kind of crappy, but he wanted to take Dia out without taking the bus. So now he owes Ana thirty bucks of gas money and an unspecified favor, but it's worth it. It was even worth Dia's dad grilling him at their front door: "You drive safe? No texting, right?" he'd said. "You don't drink and drive, drive while you're high?"

"No, sir," Elliot had said. "Wouldn't even think about it."

Now Dia rolls down the window and sticks her hand out. "Sorry about my dad," she says. "He does that to everyone I get in a car with. He's an EMT, so, you know, he sees it all the time."

"I get it," Elliot says, taking a right. "I passed, though, right?"

"You wouldn't be driving me if you didn't," Dia says, and she reaches across, rubs her thumb at the corner of his mouth. These little things she does, possessive things—Elliot loves them.

They pull in to this burger place; it looks like the diviest thing ever, but Dia's eyes light up. "Let's get one of everything," she says. "It's all so good."

They get their food to go and drive to a spot high up on the edge of town and sit on the hood of Elliot's cousin's car while they eat. The sky darkens and the town lights up beneath them. So it's not the classiest date ever, Elliot knows that, but it doesn't really matter. That's not what he and Dia are about. This is good.

She's in the middle of a story about Ciara and a broken-down van when her phone rings. Elliot watches her take it out, frown, and silence it. "What was I saying?" she says. "Oh, so yeah, we're driving and all of a sudden we can't see anything, there's smoke *everywhere*—"

Her phone rings again. "You can answer," Elliot says.

"It's just Jules," Dia says, and cuts it off again.

Then it rings, again, immediately.

"Maybe you should answer," Elliot says, and this time Dia looks at him and puts her phone to her ear.

"What?" she says, impatient. "Juliana, I'm busy."

Then her face falls. Elliot wipes his hands on his jeans as Dia begins chewing her bottom lip. "What? Where are you? I don't know where that is. Whose house? Slow down."

After a minute more of conversation, she hangs up and fixes Elliot with a moody stare. "Hanna?" he says.

"She caused a scene, Jules said." Dia tugs a hand through the ends of her curls. "Smashed a window, and the girl whose house it is, is freaking out, and Hanna's pretty much blacked out and Jules can't get her to leave. So . . ."

Elliot rattles the car keys. It's either leave Hanna to self-destruct or try to help. "Let's go get them."

jules

It was ten on Tuesday morning. Hot, but not as hot as it was going to be, Jules knew.

And she was standing outside Revelry, clutching her bass, staring up at the marquee.

They'd had their name up there before, as Fairground. The first time it had ever happened they'd taken about a thousand pictures, posed beneath it. Today it was empty except for the words LIVE MUSIC.

Jules scuffed her feet on the sidewalk and took out her phone for the thousandth time since leaving Hanna's yesterday. Still no response.

No texts, no missed calls. Nothing to answer the question Jules had asked around six in the morning, when she was too wired to sleep: *You are coming, right, Hanna? You are going to be there?*

Nothing from Autumn, either. No *good luck* or *You'll kill it!* No anything.

(Did she deserve good luck from Autumn?)

"Hey."

Jules looked up and Dia was right there. "Hey," she said. "Have you—"

"No, I haven't heard from her," Dia said.

Jules resisted the urge to toss her phone across the street and instead folded her arms over her chest. "She'll be here. I know she will." She was trying to convince herself as much as Dia, because she knew nothing. She hadn't heard from Hanna all morning, all last night. And the Hanna she'd seen yesterday had been a stranger. No, not a stranger. Someone she knew far too well and had hoped to never meet again.

Jules looked at Dia, and she was staring up at the marquee the same way Jules had been. "It's been so long," she said without looking at Jules.

"I know." Jules looked down at the sidewalk, gray and dirty and already beginning to shimmer in the heat. "She has to be here. Right? Otherwise—what's the point of any of this?" If Hanna didn't show, and they didn't play, and they didn't win, then what was the entire point of everything they'd been doing?

Maybe there wasn't one; maybe it was too naively hopeful, way too made-for-TV-movie for Jules to think that there was some grand meaning to this whole thing. Maybe it was just that they'd tried to do something and failed and that was it.

"Then there's no point," Dia said. "We fail. That's it."

But Jules refused to accept it. Dia was wrong, she had to be wrong, because Hanna *was* different now. Sober and changed, and she wanted this exactly as badly as they did. Didn't she? "She'll be here."

"Keep telling yourself that," Dia said, and she didn't sound angry, only tired. "We should go check in."

Jules looked at her and their eyes met, and Jules felt about as exhausted as Dia sounded. *Come on, Hanna.*

She nodded. "Okay."

Inside they signed in and were led into the warren of back corridors and left to sit on folding chairs at the end of a line of people. Guitars littered the hall, scattered between flannel-clad musicians who seemed to collectively turn and look at them. Scanned them and assessed their competition, it felt like to Jules. She fixed her face in a blank, I-don't-care expression and stretched her legs out, looking at her beat-up boots. "We have time," she said under her breath, so the person on her left didn't hear. "She has time."

"Thirty minutes," Dia said. "You think she's actually coming? Or you think she's going to screw us over?"

"She's not screwing us over."

"What if she is?" Dia said. "What if this was her plan all along? Tell us she wants to play, get us this far, and then make us lose. Payback. For what we did to her."

Jules screwed up her face. "What would be the point?" she asked. "Seriously. What does she get from that?"

"She gets to hurt us the way we hurt her."

"No." Jules shook her head. "She wants this as much as we do. You can see it, when she's playing. When we're writing together. Don't you feel it?"

"Yeah," Dia said, more a sigh than a word.

Jules turned toward Dia, the two of them shielding each other from the jagged whispers and sideways glances. "You don't think she might—" She felt cruel even saying it, doubting Hanna this much. "Relapse?"

Dia's eyes widened. "God. No. No? I hope not."

Jules leaned forward and looked down the corridor, resisted the urge to get out her phone and call Hanna for the millionth time. So if she wouldn't miss this, and she wasn't downing vodka somewhere, then—where the hell was she?

"This is exactly what I expected, in the beginning," Dia said, her voice low. "From Hanna. This is exactly the kind of shit I thought she'd pull. And before, this would have made me feel good, you know? Knowing that I was right about her all along. But now I feel like . . ."

Jules looked at her. "Like what?"

"Like . . . *really*? She spent all that time telling me how different she is. I *believed* that she's different. And yet, here we are." Dia pulled at her curls.

"She *has* changed," Jules said, and she wasn't sure if she was trying to convince Dia or herself. "She has."

Dia was silent for a moment, and then she nodded. "I know."

They waited while names were called, while groups filed in quiet and came out swaggering. They moved down the line, closer and closer to the backstage door. Jules looked down this hall, at the old posters and album artwork and flyers papering the length of it. They'd walked this hall so many times. They'd been on that stage and in the crowd and up on the balcony.

Why didn't any of that make her feel less sick?

The door opened and the girl with the clipboard came out. "We're running a little behind," she announced, pulling a pen from behind her ear. "Don't worry, we'll get to everybody. Washington Forth, you're up."

They waited.

Jules bounced her feet on the sticky floor, her knees jittery, her hands plucking at her clothes and her hair as the time ticked up to eleven. When she looked at Dia her head was tipped back against the wall, her lips moving silently. Jules could make out what she was saying; *comeoncomeoncomeon*. Same thought running on loop in Jules's head.

Jules leaned to speak in Dia's ear. "We still have time," she said. "She can still be here."

Dia pulled away. "She didn't *know* we'd have time," Dia said flatly. "She should be here by now. She's not coming."

And Jules couldn't fight that fact anymore. Dia was right; Hanna didn't know about any reprieve. Eleven, that's when they were supposed to have been up, and Hanna should have been there. "Shit," she said, gripping her knees. "*Fuck*. What are we going to do?"

"Wildfire? You're up."

The girl with the clipboard said their name like a question, her voice going up at the end, her eyebrows rising to match. Jules supposed she was right; what kind of name was Wildfire, anyway?

What kind of broken band were they, anyway?

She locked eyes with Dia and they took the same deep breath, steeled themselves with the same strength. "We got this," Dia said, quiet, to Jules. "Let's go in there and lay it all out, the two of us. That's all we can do."

Jules picked up her bass. "Let's go."

They walked, instruments in hand, up to the clipboard girl. "All right," she said, snapping strawberry gum, the smell of it enough to turn Jules's stomach. "You have—"

"Wait!"

A clattering commotion, someone yelling, "Watch it!" and someone else saying, "Ow! My *foot*!" and Jules wasn't sure whether to be relieved or mightily pissed off as she turned to watch Hanna, here, *finally*, sprinting down the hall.

"I'm here!" she said, out of breath, heading to them with what seemed like half her drum set in her arms. "Wait, I'm here."

She came skidding to a stop and bent over, her head almost between her knees. "Jesus Christ, Hanna," Dia hissed. "It's about time."

Jules pulled Hanna to standing. "Get it together," she whispered. "We need you."

She looked back at clipboard girl, her mouth curled into a sneer. "Ooo-kay," the girl said, dragging the sound out. "So, anyway . . . you have fifteen minutes to set up, and then the judges will come in. Good luck." She sounded so utterly bored, and Jules hated her for a second.

But there was no time for that, and no time to talk to Hanna, either, because they were through the door now, and in the wings, and in the dark Jules could only see the gleam of Dia's eyes and the white of Hanna's hair, and then the brightest lights bathed them as Dia led them out onto the stage.

Elliot

OCTOBER

Elliot crawls along the street. "Which number did she say it was?"

"She didn't," Dia says. "She said—"

She cuts off, and Elliot sees why, sees Jules standing on the sidewalk in front of a landscaped front yard. "I'm gonna go a little farther," Elliot says, because the street is crammed with cars parked up and down, and if he parks too close and someone hits this car, he's going to pay.

"Okay," Dia says, and then in the same breath, "I can't leave her alone for one night. Jules is supposed to be taking care of her, you know? This is fucking ridiculous, I cannot—" She cuts herself off. "Whatever. Let's go get her."

Elliot parks and they walk back down to the right house, and Jules is still outside waiting for them. "I know, I know," she says as they get near. "I was supposed to keep an eye on her, I know."

"It's not your fault," Dia says. "She always does this."

"What happened?" Elliot says. "She smashed a window?"

Jules shakes her head. "A mirror," she says. "In the bathroom."

"Did she get hurt?" Elliot says, imagining the force it takes to crack the glass. "Did she, like, *smash* smash it?"

"She threw a bottle at it," Jules says, and she looks at the ground. "The whole thing shattered."

"Why the fuck would she do that?" Dia says, but Elliot knows enough now to know that it's not a real question. "Where is she now?"

"She wouldn't let me take her home," Jules says. "The girl who lives here is *pissed*."

Dia rolls her eyes and Elliot looks between the two of them. "Let's just go get her out as fast as possible," he says. "Minimal collateral damage. I mean, minus the mirror. And the bottle. And herself."

They split up—Jules takes the kitchen and the backyard, Dia and Elliot take the living room and the upstairs, because, as Dia says, "Hanna has never met an off-limits sign she didn't completely ignore."

She's not anywhere they look. Upstairs, downstairs, outside, upstairs again. Jules is with them now, checking under the bed of the master bedroom. "Where the hell is she?" she says, and Elliot can hear the panic in her voice. "I left her dancing in the kitchen."

"You can't take your eye off her," Dia says. "You know that."

Elliot opens the closet, a last resort, and of course, there she is. Slumped against the wall with a pile of knocked-down clothes blanketing her. He looks over his shoulder. "I got her."

Dia comes over, stands by him, and Hanna looks so peaceful that Elliot is almost afraid for her, for what she's facing when she wakes up in about 0.2 seconds.

"Hanna," Dia hisses, crouching. "Get up."

Hanna's lips move, but no sound comes out and her eyes stay shut.

"Hanna, I swear to *god*." Dia jabs Elliot's ankle. "Help me."

Together they pull Hanna up to standing, and Elliot puts her arm around his neck as she starts mumbling. "Leave me alone," she slurs— or, he thinks that's what she's saying. "Tired."

"Yeah, well, I'm tired too," Dia snaps, taking the other half of Hanna's weight. "Jules, get the door."

They maneuver her out of the bedroom, down the stairs, through the hall. Jules has Hanna's bag, something that Elliot thinks might have been Hanna's shirt earlier tonight because now Hanna has on a men's button-down and the thing Jules is holding is stained red. "I think she's bleeding," Elliot says.

"Hey!"

Jules looks back at them, her eyes wide. "That's the girl," she says. "We should be gone, like, now."

"Get back here!" A white girl with long, blond hair and angry eyes jumps in their path. "She owes me, that crazy bitch! She *trashed* my house. I want my money."

"We're really sorry," Jules says, and she grabs the front door. "We're going, we won't come back, we're really sorry—"

"I *want* my *money*."

"It's only a mirror," Elliot says, and he notices the curious circle forming around them. They should really get out, before this turns into something.

"It was an *antique*."

"Well, you should've taken it down before you threw a party," Dia says, out of breath, and the girl's eyes go wide, and Jules puts herself between them.

"Go!" she says, and Elliot does what she says, dragging Hanna out of the house and through the neat yard—more collateral damage— while the girl keeps yelling at them but does not follow.

"Way to defuse the situation," Elliot says.

Dia glares at him. "Help me get her to the car."

It takes forever to get her up the street to the parked car, but eventually they get there and Elliot bears Hanna's weight while he fishes the keys from his pocket. "Lay her down," he says, and Jules is on the other side, coaxing Hanna toward her. Eventually she's stretched out across the back seat, and now Elliot says again, "I think she's bleeding." He starts to check her over but Jules shakes her head.

"She's fine," she says. "She spilled wine on her shirt."

Dia almost chokes. "Where the fuck did she get wine?"

"Where the fuck does she get everything?" Jules shoots back.

It's dark and Elliot's adrenaline is running high. He looks back toward the house, checking that no one is coming after them. "Antique," he says. "How much, do you think?"

"Did you see that house?" Dia says. "We don't have the money, trust me."

"We better pray she doesn't find out who we are," Jules says, and she rubs her face. "Can we take her home? I'm tired."

Dia gets in the back, lifting Hanna's head and laying it on her lap. "You get shotgun," she says, and then she looks at Elliot for the first time in what feels like hours. "Thank you."

He shrugs. "No big deal," he says, like he carries half-comatose girls out of parties every weekend.

Elliot drives them back to their side of town, five miles under the speed limit, Dia's dad's words echoing in his head. The radio is on low and Jules flicks from station to station. In between snatches of sound Elliot hears Dia talking quietly, and at first he thinks she's telling Hanna off. But when he listens, he hears it, this sweet, low whisper:

"It's okay, Han, you're okay. Why do you do this to yourself? It's not good, it's not good. You scare me when you're like this. I know, shh, it's okay. We're taking you home. You'll be okay."

He turns the radio up and keeps driving.

Hanna

They flew into fast motion, plugging in amps, testing mics, setting up the cymbals and snare and kick pedal around the house drums. Hanna would have preferred her own kit, but she had no way to bring it all, and usually she could get by with the basics and her own essentials. She steadied her hands, shivering with the adrenaline surging through her, and sat. In front of her Jules looked over to Dia, stage left. "Give me an A?"

Hanna settled her sticks in her hands, gave the snare an experimental hit. Her heart was battering her ribcage still, her lungs burning from having to run all the way from the bus stop to here with her equipment weighing her down and her head playing *latelatelate* on a loop.

"Hanna." Dia looked over her shoulder. "All good?"

Hanna thought of the bag she'd packed last night, now stashed at her job.

She'd gotten two, maybe three hours sleep once she'd finished packing. Wide awake at five a.m., she'd wondered if she was making a huge mistake. On the bus, making her way here, she'd still been unsure. *I can go back,* she'd thought. *Mom will never know.*

But right now, on this stage with these girls, she knew.

This was right.

"All good," Hanna said.

This disembodied voice interrupted. "Hello," it called out. "All set up? It sounds good from here."

Hanna held a hand up and squinted against the lights. Where was that voice coming from?

"Yes," Dia said into the center mic. "We're ready."

"Thank you," a different voice said. "So—Wildfire, is it? Before we get started, one question from me: give me some of your influences."

Hanna caught Jules's glance back at her; she looked as off-kilter as Hanna felt. But Dia stepped closer to her mic and cleared her throat. "Hi. Um, influences—Sleater-Kinney, Melissa Auf der Maur, Sade, Kacey Musgraves, Christina Aguilera—"

"Interesting," the second voice said.

"Okay," the third voice said. "What are you playing for us?"

"This song is called 'Bones.'"

Dia turned to her, and Hanna looked to Jules. They looked perfect: focused, cool, their all-black outfits, their shiny guitars. Hanna locked eyes with Jules and saw everything she needed right there.

She rolled her shoulders, steeled herself, lifted her sticks.

Four sharp clicks and Hanna dropped, feet first, into the noise.

Their hours of practice had made them sharp, clean, in sync with each other. And Hanna let herself be suspended in the music, her aching muscles light now, but her breath coming in gasps between fills. She sank into Dia's voice, her own lyrics.

"In the forest,"

Dia sang,

"Bones break like branches
Weighed down with words
And under the night is awake
Waiting to break."

Jules brandished her bass and pressed her mouth to the mic, and Hanna felt their ghosts watching, the past ephemeral versions of her playing right in this same spot.

"I call the witches and
They say they won't know me
Not without blue blood and moonlight
Moons under the skin of my loves."

Dia vibrated at the front of the stage. Hanna could see the energy coming off her and fed from it. Jules's jersey twisted around her waist as she bounced one foot off the floor, wrenched her guitar away from and then back against her body, and Hanna thrashed against the drums, releasing every ounce of her pent-up explosive anger on it.

> *"All the honesty*
> *In the woods and the world*
> *Isn't going to save me*
> *She can ride that horse until she dies*
> *She can follow that river*
> *Into deep darkness."*

Hanna pounded the drums, cracked skins, weathered cymbals, and felt the air stop around them. Suspended in this place, this sound, for a fleeting moment. This really was it. Not the end.
Everything.

> *"In the forest*
> *In the dungeon*
> *Wherever wildflowers grow*
> *That's not where I'll be*
> *When you're not watching*
> *The witches take me*
> *To the forest of ever after."*

Dia's voice ended it, the only sound above the fade of their music, and Hanna dropped her head forward, her chest heaving, her hands shaking.

This is everything.

"Thank you," one disembodied voice said, and Hanna almost hated whichever one it was for the interruption of this moment. "We'll be in touch."

Dia

They broke everything down as fast as they could, in uncertain quiet. By the time they were done the judges had disappeared, and they left the stage, wound their way back through the club, and finally spilled out into the sunlight.

Dia took only a second before she began tearing into Hanna. "Are you fucking kidding me?" she yelled, and Hanna didn't even look afraid, but the guy crossing the street away from them did. "Are you *fucking kidding* me, Hanna? You really had to pull a stunt like this on a day like today? What were you doing? What were you *thinking*?"

And Hanna spoke over her, trying to answer her: "I know, I'm sorry—"

"You're *sorry*? Yeah, you'd better be! You almost cost us—"

"I know, I really didn't mean to—"

"So what *did* you mean to do? You don't text, you don't call—"

"That wasn't my fault, the traffic—"

"What were we supposed think? You didn't even—"

"And I had to—"

"Why didn't you call me? Call Jules? We—"

"But I got here, didn't I? We did it, isn't that what you—"

"What I wanted was—"

"*God, stop!*" Jules pushed herself between them, held her hands out while she whipped her head, looking from Dia to Hanna and back to Dia again. "Breathe. Please."

Dia did as Jules said, pulling in sticky summer air and breathing out the taste of exhaust. Hanna was watching her carefully, face flushed red.

Dia looked away. Her clothes were sticking to her. Her stomach felt empty.

But they'd done it. That was real.

"Okay," Jules said now, stepping back. "Better?"

And now that Jules was out of her way, Dia set her stuff down, reached out and grabbed Hanna, pulled her into a viselike hug. "I didn't think you were coming," she said into Hanna's hair. "I thought I was right about you all along." She closed her eyes. "Thank god you made me wrong."

Hanna's laugh was pure surprise. "Okay," she said. "I'm sorry."

"I'm sorry, too," Dia said, meaning it, so sincere, and she hugged Hanna tighter. "But don't do that ever again."

Dia pulled back, pulled a caught curl from her lips and looked at Jules, the surprise emblazoned across her face, too. "I'm hungry," she said now, feeling a little delirious. "Are you hungry?"

"Starving," Jules said.

Hanna pulled cash from her pocket. "I'll buy," she said. "And then I'll explain."

Dia picked up her guitar and her amp, and tilted her face up to the sun. Nothing was ever easy with them. But easy wasn't always good.

"Let's go."

Hanna

In the gas station across the street from the bar they got dollar hot dogs and chips, Skittles, and a bunch of candy bars and sodas. "And a pack of Marlboro Lights," Hanna said as they piled their stuff on the counter.

The guy behind it didn't ask for ID before getting the cigarettes and sliding them across to Hanna. "Eighteen seventy-nine."

Hanna started to pay, then swore. "Can I get a lighter, too?"

They paid and left and then, without even talking about it, they crossed back over to Revelry, lugging all their equipment behind them. This time they walked down the sidewalk to the tattoo shop and slipped through the alley that led to the parking lots behind the buildings. It was what they used to do all the time, when they couldn't get in or had opened for Graceland. They'd go out to the parking lot of whatever venue they were at and sit on the curb with their legs stretched out onto the asphalt as they waited for Ciara to take them home, giddy and happy.

So that was what they did now, the three of them in the corner of this empty lot, surrounded by guitars and drum paraphernalia.

Hanna peeled the cellophane off her cigarettes but didn't open the pack. "I think it went okay," she said, turning the pack over in her hands and looking straight ahead. "We kept it together. We played as good as we ever have. We have a chance, I think."

She turned her head, Dia and Jules both looking at her. "I'm sorry," she said, meaning it. "You want to know what happened?"

Dia dipped her chin, and Jules almost smiled. "Shoot."

Hanna took out a cigarette, tapped it against her palm, and started from the beginning. "My mom said I couldn't do the contest. She doesn't trust me, and I get it, I do. But I'm also tired. I don't know what else to do to make them trust me. She said as long as I lived in her house, it was her rules, and she said no. No band, no music." She lit the cigarette. "'If you want to do your own thing, then you need to do it outside my house.' That's what she said. So, fine. I packed my stuff and I'm out."

Her words were met with the rushing of traffic out on the road and the faintest noise from the club.

Then Dia shook her head, her face confused. "Wait, what?" she said. "You left home? Like, gone?"

"Where are you going? What are you going to do?" Jules grabbed Hanna's knee. "Oh my god, Hanna, are you for real?"

"Because of *this*?" Dia said. "Hanna."

She shook her head, a lazy curl of smoke twisting from her lips. "Because of everything," she said. "I've been good, you know? Since rehab, I've tried *so hard* to be the best version of me. I got my grades up. I got my license. I've never missed work, not once. I stopped going out anywhere, really, so my parents would know I wasn't doing something stupid somewhere. I hang out with Molly, I try to keep my self-destructive ways to the absolute minimum, and yet—none of it is enough to make them stop looking at me the way they do."

"What way?" Jules asked.

"Like I'm the biggest disappointment of their lives." She flicked ash to the ground and scratched at the back of her knee. "They're not wrong. I've done a lot of bad things. But I never could get it right with my mom, even before the drinking. And playing music with both of you again, it's like—the best thing that's happened to me in forever. And I'm supposed to give that up?"

Hanna put her cigarette out. Then she told them everything: that she'd gotten up this morning and acted completely normal at breakfast, had apologized for her words yesterday.

Her mom had taken Hanna's hand. *You understand,* she'd said. *You understand why I want this for you?*

"Yes," Hanna had said. "I get it."

And her mom had said, "Your part in the band is over. We're agreed?"

"Yes," Hanna had lied. "It's done."

"We'll discuss this more tonight," Theresa had said, and then left for work.

Molly had eaten cereal as she'd watched Hanna packing up the parts of her drums that she could take. "You're really doing this?" she'd asked, plucking at her bottom lip.

"Yes," Hanna had said, coming back into the house. She'd checked her reflection in the hall mirror, checked she looked ready for their performance. Then she'd looked at her sister and tried her best to smile. "I'm not going far, Molls. And I'll call you tonight."

"What about Mom and Dad?"

The note Hanna had left on the table wasn't exactly subtle.

I'm sorry. I have to do this. I can't stay here when you won't let me breathe. And I don't want to lie to you anymore, but I don't know how not to. I wish I could say this to your faces but I don't think I could. So instead, let me call this the last time I'll lie to you and break your trust. I have to do this. I love you.

Hanna

"Don't worry about them," she'd said. "They know this has nothing to do with you."

And then she'd hugged Molly goodbye, kissed the top of her head, and hauled her ass to the bus stop.

"I went by work first," she said, wrapping up. "It was the only place I could think to go. I had to get away. Then Ciara picked me up to bring me here, and we hit traffic. There was an accident on Piper and everything was backed up, and then I didn't even have any service to text or call."

Dia shifted. "What about last night?" she said. "You never texted me back then. You had service then."

"I know," Hanna said, scuffing her feet on the asphalt. "I didn't know what I was going to do. So . . . I didn't know what to say."

"I really thought you weren't coming," Dia said, leaning back. "So, you're actually moving out? Where are you going?"

"Ciara's. At least, for now. It's not that big a deal, really," Hanna said, and part of her believed those words. "Plenty of people are out on their own at eighteen. In a few weeks I'll be working full time. I can rent a room somewhere and . . . I'll eat ramen and cereal for every meal. It's a rite of passage, no?"

Dia and Jules exchanged a look, and Hanna turned her lighter over in her hands. "What?"

"Nothing," Jules said, but Dia exhaled loudly.

"We were worried," she said. "That you might have—slipped."

"Slipped?"

"Had a drink." Dia squeezed her elbows to her ears. "But I'm glad you didn't."

Hanna thought of that bottle of Jameson, the one she'd managed to keep just out of her reach. "I don't do that anymore," Hanna said. Well: she didn't know the future, what might happen, but for as long as she could, she would keep herself away from that bad habit. She didn't want there to be a *next time* for any of the things she used to do. She didn't want there to be another time for somebody to find her.

She pulled her feet in so she was cross-legged and looked at the pack of smokes. "There's something I haven't told you," she said. "I know you'll think I'm terrible."

"I'll reserve judgment until I hear what it is," Jules said. "And so will Dia, won't she?"

Dia held her hands up. "Swear."

Hanna took a deep breath. "I didn't just decide to quit drinking," she said. "Molly found me in my room one night. I had been drinking, obviously, and I passed out, and when she saw me I wasn't breathing. She called 911. So I got to do the whole ambulance-ER-stomach-pumping thing for the second time. Except this time it was so much worse, and I didn't even think that was possible but it was, because this time my sister had to see me doing it. She had to make the call." The guilt sat in her stomach, jagged. "But that's what made me want to finally stop. I couldn't believe that I'd let Molly do that, be the one to find me, like—what if it had been worse?" She looked at Dia and Jules. "I didn't believe in wake-up calls before, but that was totally mine."

Jules's eyes looked full of sorrow. "Why wouldn't you tell us that?"

"Because I hate it," Hanna said vehemently. "I'm so ashamed of it. And I wanted you to think that I turned myself around and got better all by myself. But really, it was only because of this terrible thing I did."

"You didn't have to. Quit," Dia said, breaking her silence. "How many times did you try before? But this time you *did* stop. You decided to do that. I don't think that's anything to be ashamed of."

It was as if the pressure, the guilt wound tight within her, suddenly snapped, and Hanna found herself wiping away leaking tears. She had nothing to be ashamed of.

I am okay.

"You don't know how much I needed to hear that," she breathed. "God."

They sat in silence a while, the rushing cars, snatches of music from the club and the road.

Dia looked up at the sky. "Look what we did," she said. "At the beginning of summer, could you even imagine this? Look what we put in motion."

"*Let's enter Sun City*," Jules said, in a perfect imitation of Dia. "*What's the worst that can happen? Oh, yeah, Hanna gets kicked out of her house, no big.*"

"I never said that," Dia objected. "I said, what do we have to lose?"

"Same difference."

Hanna drummed on her knees. "It'll make a good story," she said. "When we're famous."

"A great story," Dia said. "Teenage mother, out and proud lesbian, reformed bad girl. We'll be on every blog worldwide."

"We should celebrate," Jules said. "We actually *did* this. Let's do something good."

Dia rolled her eyes. "Like what?"

Jules began reeling off ideas, Dia shooting every one down until Jules accused her of being a downer. They worked their way through their candy stash, melting chocolate under the hot sun, and Hanna laughed along with them, hard enough to make her stomach ache. And she felt both so overwhelmed with everything and so overcome with gratitude for these girls that she didn't know what to do.

So she ate her candy, and sat with them, and it was good.

Dia

Dia had to leave for work after a while; when Dia asked, Hanna insisted she was okay, and Jules rolled her eyes when Dia hesitated. "Go already," she said, flicking her hand in Dia's direction. "We don't need you getting fired, we have enough drama already."

"All right, I'm out," Dia said, stealing a Reese's cup for the bus ride. "Both of you text me later, okay? Okay, bye!" She turned, and then whipped back, unable to keep the shit-eating grin off her face. "Can you believe we pulled this off?"

Hanna raked her hands through her hair, shaking her head. "I can't," she said, her smile as wide as Dia's. "It's too much."

Dia really left then, had to rush for the bus with her guitar smacking against her back and her stupid heavy amp bashing her legs.

It only took ten minutes in the bakery to make the morning feel like it was years ago, moons away. Imelda had her running around on a rush order, and she spilled an entire vial of food coloring over her hands, her skin tinged blue no matter how hard she scrubbed. When she was working the counter, she looked up and saw Jesse walk past with two guys whose names Dia could never remember. He didn't stop, and he didn't look in, and it took Dia a split second of hurt to remember what she'd said to him.

Of course he didn't stop. It wasn't like he was going to come in to flirt over cookies like normal, was it?

She pressed her knuckles into the hard plastic of the register and swallowed hard. Sacrifice, that was what this was. She couldn't have everything she wanted, nobody could. And she wasn't the only one losing things; Hanna was losing her home, wasn't she? So she should suck it up and forget about him. Remember the feeling of singing her soul out this morning, feeling so really and truly awake for the first time in years.

At least he was safe from her.

Dia let out a slow breath.

After her shift, she headed to day care. When Lex came running out, Dia picked her up and swung her through the air, making the silly growling sounds that made Lex laugh so much. "Ready to go home, Lala?" she said, and smoothed her hand across Lex's curls. Maybe she didn't completely understand why Hanna's mom had given that ultimatum, but she partly did. She knew what it was like to want only the very best of the world for your kid. To want to cling to them, curl them tight against you and keep the entire world out, if that was what it took for them to stay safe.

She kissed a graze on Alexa's knee, and thought about it as they walked home. See, you couldn't keep them safe, not completely. The world always got its way somehow, in painful bruises or boyfriends dropping dead, girls who wouldn't love you back, or obsession, even addiction.

Dia called out when they entered their house. "Mom? We're home."

No answer, and Dia moved toward the stairs, almost bumping into her dad as he came down them, mid-yawn. "Hey," she said. "Where's Mom?"

"Taking a bath," Max said, scrubbing a hand over his face. His knot of locs had fallen to one side and he had pillow creases in his cheek, but then his eyes lit up like Christmas morning. "Wait—how did it go?"

"It was . . . good," she said. Trimming the truth a little, for the sake of brevity. "We did what we wanted to. It's up to the judges now. If they liked us or not. But even if they don't, we showed them exactly who we are." Dia cut herself off, wary of saying too much, jinxing it. "I'll tell you at dinner. What are we having?"

"Tacos," her dad said, yawning again. "I'm going to get started now."

She took Lex out in the yard while her dad made dinner, chased her back and forth. Her dad called them in after a little while, and Dia strapped Lex into her high chair as her mom came in wearing sweatpants and an army T-shirt, a silk scarf wrapped around her hair. She pulled plates from the cabinet and Dia filled glasses with iced tea and the four of them sat down to eat.

Dia filled her parents in on as many details of the day as she thought necessary, leaving out Hanna's superlate arrival but leaving in her issues with her mom. Nina's forehead wrinkled as Dia talked and then she shook her head. "That girl," she said, and Dia thought she was about to go off about how bad she was, all the things she'd heard a thousand times before from a thousand different people, but then Nina said, "She doesn't have the best luck, does she? You tell her if she needs anything, we're here. Okay?"

Dia raised her eyebrows. "Seriously?"

"Yes, seriously," her mom said. "What?"

"Nothing," Dia said. "But . . . it's Hanna. Usually you tell me how I should be careful with her and all that. Now it's different."

Her mom lifted one shoulder. "You know, you've been spending a lot of time with her, and you don't do that with people you don't trust," she said. "So if you trust her, I suppose I can, too. And if she's going through a hard time, we can be good people and try to help her out. Besides, she's just a kid. And now she's a kid out on her own. If it was you, I'd want someone to help you, too."

Dia smiled. "You're good people, Mama." Then she looked at her dad. "I'm glad you let me stay," Dia said. "I know it wasn't what you wanted for me, having a kid, and everything with Elliot made it all worse and . . . I don't know. I don't know what I would do without you."

"Are you for real?" Max said. "In this family, we stick together. That's the way it is. Maybe we tell you things you don't like sometimes, maybe you do things we don't like sometimes, but that's life. We're all we have, right here."

Dia looked at Lex. *We're all we have, right here.* And how lucky they were to have it all.

Hanna

Hanna stood on the sidewalk outside Ciara's place, the same small, one-story house she'd rented ever since Hanna had known her. Ciara had been nineteen then—see? Only a year older than Hanna was now. This could be her life. Why not?

This whole thing felt both incredibly final, a Big Deal, and also the most overdramatic thing she'd ever done.

Everything and nothing all at once.

She felt seven years old, stuffing a backpack full of Pokémon cards and Oreos, seven pairs of socks and one shoe, and "running away" to the house of the woman who used to watch Hanna after school. Like back then, some small, childish part of her believed that she'd only last until dark before her mom turned up to collect her, arms outstretched as Hanna cried, shocked by herself. The rest of her, though, knew that she had crossed a line that maybe couldn't be uncrossed.

Hanna was at the top of the steps when the door opened and Ciara stepped out onto the porch. "There you are!" she said. "Didn't you get my text?"

"Hi," Hanna said, letting Ciara kiss her cheek. "Um, no. I turned my phone off."

"Like, *off* off?" Ciara shuddered and took one of Hanna's bags. "I would die."

"Yeah, well, I'm avoiding the fallout." She could only imagine the scene that would happen when her parents got home and discovered her gone, the note. She didn't want to hear any of it.

Hanna followed Ciara inside and when the door closed behind her, she felt this jolt, all her adrenaline halting in her veins and pooling in the bottom of her stomach.

I am here.

I am okay.

"Lucky for you," Ciara said, "I am currently between roommates. So instead of staying on the couch, you can have an actual bed."

Hanna swallowed past the knot in her throat. "Thanks," she said. "For the bed, and letting me stay, and . . ." She blew her cheeks out. "It's been a day."

Ciara stood in between the middle of the living room and put her hands on her waist. "What do you want to do?" she asked. "You want to talk about it? Want to talk about playing? Want to talk about nothing at all?"

"Honestly?" Hanna said. "I want to eat. I'm starving."

"Let's order in," Ciara said. "Chinese?"

"Perfect."

"You can go put your stuff in the other room," Ciara said, crossing into the little kitchen. "I'll order."

Hanna nodded and hauled her stuff down the hall, past Ciara's bedroom and into the small room at the end. It was empty except for the bed, a nightstand, and an unplugged lamp.

She set her bags down, put her equipment in the corner, and closed the door. Then she plugged the lamp in and flicked it on, the warm bulb emitting a surprising amount of light. It wasn't dark yet, but getting there; the sky outside the window was more navy than light, orange-tinted clouds dropped here and there. She'd stood in the window at work and watched the world go by all afternoon, telling herself over and over that she could do this.

Hanna sat on the edge of the bed and exhaled into the emptiness. *What have I done?*

When she turned her phone on it took a minute for the messages to come through: three texts from Dia, one from Jules, one from Molly, two from Ciara. Four missed calls from her dad, seven from her mom. Two voice mails.

She took a second before listening, running her hands over the sheets. Fresh, she could tell, they had that laundry smell. Ciara was so good to her.

Hanna texted Molly back first, short and sweet: Hey Molls, I'm at Ciara's. I hope you're not getting the fallout, if you are, I'm sorry. Call you later, I'll tell you all about playing today, it went good :) love you xoxo

Then: voice mails.

The first was long, and Hanna held her phone away from her ear so she could only half hear what her mom's angry voice was saying: *This is beyond a joke, Hanna* and *Do you think this is funny?* And *This is exactly what I'm talking about, you have to take some responsibility for your actions, you think they don't affect anyone but you?* and *How am I supposed to trust you when you do this?*

Yeah, that was basically everything Hanna had expected.

The second voice mail was shorter. Her mom, again. But different this time. This time she sounded like she'd been crying, and Hanna's heart ached but did not break as she listened to Theresa say, *Please call me. We can talk about this. I love you, Hanna.*

Hanna tossed her phone onto the bed. She loved her mom. Under it all, she did love her. But god, she hated her, too.

She changed into pajama shorts and a T-shirt, and joined Ciara back out in the living room. "Okay, sunshine?" Ciara said from her place on the couch. "You look awful."

"Thanks, and screw you," Hanna said, and Ciara laughed.

"Sorry," she said. "Food will be twenty minutes."

"I turned my phone on," Hanna said. "My mom is an excellent emotional manipulator even through voice mail."

Ciara made a face, one hand playing in her hair. "Mothers," she said. "Complicated animals."

"So very true." Hanna sat down next to Ciara and put her feet in Ciara's lap. "Thank you," she said, closing her eyes as she leaned back. "I know I'm a pain in your ass."

"No pain," Ciara said. "Well, sometimes a little. But you know me, Han, I'm a glutton for emotional distress. Can't give up on the people I love. That means you."

Hanna opened her eyes and looked at Ciara. "I know," she said. "You're the only one who hasn't."

"I don't know about that," Ciara said. "You spent all day with a couple of girls who could have iced you all the way out. You have Molly on your side, always. We're here, aren't we?"

Hanna nodded, and a surge of shocked sadness caught her. She had to look to the ceiling so the sudden tears threatening wouldn't spill over. "Right," she said, pressing her nails hard into her palms. "You're right."

"I always am," Ciara said. "You want a glass of water?"

She nodded. Ciara *was* right; Hanna was not alone. This wasn't like before, and she wasn't the same girl as before.

No; that wasn't right. Because she was the same. She was still Hanna with the drinking problem, Hanna who hated herself a lot of days, Hanna who would love nothing more than to give in to her addiction sometimes. What was different was how she dealt with all that now. She had changed, and she had stayed the same, and maybe Ciara or Jules or Dia didn't get that. But Hanna knew herself now, for better or for worse.

Mostly better.

Elliot

NOVEMBER

"I think I want strawberry," Dia says, putting her hand on Elliot's shoulder. "Or cookie dough. Or both."

"Both," Elliot says.

"Good plan."

She steps up to the counter and orders for both of them, caramel swirl with hot fudge sauce for Elliot, and then they take their ice cream outside. She climbs on top of one of the picnic benches, sits on the tabletop. "Are you coming tomorrow?"

Elliot sits on the bench between her legs, looking up at her. "Yeah," he says. Is that even a question by now? Every weekend Dia goes somewhere, to play a show, to watch some other band, and almost every weekend Elliot follows her there. "Ciara's band is really good."

"Ciara's band is excellent," Dia corrects. "God."

Elliot laughs. "Sorry."

"You know, she took a chance on me," Dia says, digging her spoon into her ice cream. "She gave us our first show. Without her we'd still be playing in Hanna's garage."

"Your hero," Elliot says, deciding to sidestep Hanna for today. That night at that party is still making him uncomfortable. He had to lie to his cousin about the stain on the back seat and beg her not to say anything to his parents.

(Dia keeps saying Hanna is fine, that she has it under control, that he doesn't need to worry about it.)

(Elliot's pretty sure she does not have it under control, but then again, what does he know? He's known Hanna for four months; she's known Hanna for years and years. Who knows better, really?)

"I really think out of everybody here, maybe Ciara could be the one to actually make something out of music," Dia says, waving her spoon in the air. "Besides us, obviously."

"Obviously." Elliot takes a bite of his sundae. "What's the plan, then?"

Dia's eyes flash and she puts her shoulders back and Elliot hides his smile by pressing his face into her knee. God, she's so hot and determined and he's pretty sure he's going to be left behind in her dust, but at least one day he can say he knew her. "Okay," she says, "so this year, we keep playing around town and playing with Graceland. That way people get to see us. Then next year we level up, you know? Start getting our own shows outside town—"

Elliot nods and asks questions in the right places and listens to Dia's entire plan for Fairground's world domination. She thinks about the future; so does he, a lot, and Elliot likes that they have this in common.

"What about you?" Dia asks. "What's your plan?"

"I don't know," Elliot says. "I think I want to write a book one day."

That takes Dia by surprise. "Really?" She reaches out and runs a hand through his hair. "You write?"

"I try," he says. The most he's gotten so far is half-finished short stories, but it's a start.

"So what, you gonna go to a fancy writer school?" Dia teases. "Learn all about those boring books everyone pretends are genius?"

"I'll probably stay close for school," he says. "If I get the scholarships I need. That's the only reason I'm still playing baseball."

"Wait," Dia says, eyes wide. "I didn't know you were, like, scholarship-money good. I'm really dating a jock, aren't I?"

"Admit it, you like the way I play," Elliot says, abandoning his ice cream to slide his hands up her thighs. "Home run after home run."

Dia bursts out laughing. "That is the cheesiest shit I ever heard," she says, and Elliot can't help but laugh too.

"See?" he says. "I got it all. I'm an athlete, I'm a writer, I'm a comedian."

"Yeah, yeah." Dia leans down and puts her hands on either side of his face. "You're a prize."

jules

Now that it was over, their big moment, the throwing themselves in front of three strangers and screaming *choose us*, Jules felt . . . restless. Like, she had all this extra energy coursing through her and nowhere for it to go. Their practices had come to an abrupt stop with the loss of their usual rehearsal space. "We'll find somewhere," Hanna kept saying. "We'll pool our money and hire some place."

"Sorry, what money?" Dia had said. "My kid is about to be two. I have to buy textbooks. My funds are *extremely* limited."

"We'll work it out," Jules had said.

But so far they hadn't. Instead they'd been wasting time around town: hanging around the music store, rifling through clothes they couldn't afford at the mall, watching Lex run around the playground. Jules had been working, and pretending things were okay with Autumn, and that her omission of truth wasn't still hanging between their every interaction.

It wasn't working.

A week later the three of them were at the movies, mostly for the AC, but they left halfway through. "Why do they always have to kill the black girl?" Jules said as they crossed the lobby. "And why can't the women ever talk about anything other than some guy?"

"And why can't the girl ever be the badass hero?" Hanna said. "How come she has to spend half the movie training some guy to be as good as her and the other half either falling in love with him or being killed?"

"Hollywood," Dia said. "They don't get it."

They went over to the nearby McDonald's instead and sat outside eating fries and drinking milkshakes, Hanna smoking. Jules squinted against the setting sun and looked at Hanna, about to ask the same question she'd already asked a dozen times over the past two weeks. "Did you talk to your mom yet?"

"No." Hanna dipped a fry into Dia's chocolate shake. "She's left me, like, a hundred voice mails. I know I should call her back. But I'm waiting."

Dia's brows sloped together. "For what?"

"Until I know what I want to say," Hanna said, and then she looked into the distance. "It's harder than you'd think. To not say what you really want to, even when you *know* what you want to say is the worst thing. Even when it's going to cause trouble. You have to hold it in. I'm not very good at doing that."

Jules and Dia exchanged a look. "You're better at it now than you ever were before," Jules said. "Trust me on that."

"Sometimes it's okay to say the thing that causes trouble," Dia said. "Sometimes the trouble needs to happen."

Hanna looked at Dia. "You really think that?"

Jules raised her eyebrows, curious to hear Dia's answer, too. That was so not a Dia thing to say. Then again, this whole summer was not what any of them had planned. Things were different now, in so many ways.

"Yeah," Dia said. "Sometimes I do."

Hanna ate another fry. "I think I'll keep waiting."

"Waiting, waiting," Dia said. "Is this all we do now?"

"A week and a half," Jules said.

Next Friday was the show at Revelry, where they'd announce the winner of the contest, and Jules almost had to throw up every time she thought about it. "I know we keep saying it doesn't matter," Jules said, and she twisted her fingers into the ends of her braids, the way she always did when she was nervous. "I know we keep saying we'll still play and it's not the end of us as a band and everything."

Dia looked at her. "But?"

Jules pulled her hands from her hair. But she *really* wanted to win. Who wouldn't? She wanted to walk around with the invisible approval on her, to play a show with her idols. Okay, and also—she wanted to drive around in the car she would buy with her share of the money blaring Formation with the windows down and waving her middle finger in everybody's faces. "You know," she said eventually. "I *want* it."

"What would you do?" Dia asked. "With the money."

"I want a car," Jules said. "I'd take us everywhere."

"When we win you will," Dia said. "We'll get matching rides. Red. Yeah?"

"Can we talk about something else?" Hanna asked. "This is giving me hives."

"What's left?" Jules said. "You don't want to talk about the contest, or your living situation. Dia doesn't want to talk about *anything.*" She rolled her eyes when Dia kicked her. "Oh, please. You've barely said a word all day." *And I have nothing good to say about me and Autumn,* she thought.

She needed more food to keep from thinking about it all. "I'm going to get an apple pie. Anyone want anything?"

"More fries," Dia said.

"Coke," Hanna said. "Large."

"Coming right up."

Jules went inside and got in line behind two younger girls whispering in each other's ears. When she got to the counter she ordered and then turned, leaning her elbows on the counter and looking at her friends outside the window.

Listen to that—*her friends.*

Hanna and Dia, sitting by themselves, laughing at something. Two months ago this would have been impossible to imagine, because of what had happened two years ago.

But two years was a long time. Long enough for things to change again and again, a thousand times over. For Jules to realize that fighting was not her fantasy. For Dia to raise a precocious, perfect kid. For

Hanna to get sober and get smart and become this new-but-the-same girl.

Long enough for all of them to realize that there was nothing they could do to each other now, ever, to fully break them.

And win or lose, they still had their music. Nothing and no one could stop them. Jules knew that now.

jules

Jules was at the grocery store early on Thursday morning, yawning as she listened to Henry and Malai bickering across their registers. "Can you shut up?" she called after a while. "You two are so annoying."

"Says you," Henry fired back. "You wanna go? Freezer race, you and me, winner takes all."

Jules raised her eyebrows. "Takes all what?"

"Uh . . ." Henry tapped his chin. "All . . . the vending machine food you can get for ten bucks."

"I'd rather have the ten bucks," Jules said. "Pass."

She started tidying the pamphlets on the end of her register, lining them up by height, until she sensed a customer waiting. "Sorry," she said as she turned. "I—Autumn."

Autumn leaned on the plastic barrier shielding the screen between them. "Hi," she said, her voice a little unsure.

"Hey," Jules said, surprised. "What are you doing here? You're not working today."

"What do you think?" Autumn said. "I came to see you."

Jules's heart tripped over itself. "Oh." Oh?

Her nerves jangled. Things were not so great with them, not since Autumn had found out about the contest and Jules's secret keeping. They were still talking, texting, but—she could feel it all between their words, Autumn's uncertainty and her own anxiety squeezing in the air around them. Jules had apologized, and Autumn had said that it was fine, she was fine, but Jules couldn't quite believe it. Surely Autumn was still mad, really, and just telling Jules everything was okay; surely this was all a sign that they weren't working out, not Meant To Be; surely Autumn was going to end things with her any day, any minute now.

(Jules knew those thoughts were ridiculous, but in some moments she'd find herself thinking that what was *really* ridiculous was thinking Autumn would ever want to be with her in the first place.)

But that was how it had worked before, wasn't it? With her and Delaney. Every conversation they'd had could be twisted and turned into a fight, and Jules had become an expert at it. But Autumn was *not* Delaney. Right?

"Are you seeing the others today?" Autumn tucked a strand of hair behind her ear. Her hair was loose, the colors faded to soft pastels from their former bright rainbow.

Jules nodded. "At eight."

"Before that?"

Jules looked around, but it was quiet and no one was paying them any attention. "I'm not doing anything."

That earned a smile from Autumn, a fraction of her megawatt version. "Okay," she said. "Will you come over? When you're done here?"

"Come over?"

"I think we should—talk," Autumn said. "When do you finish?"

Jules looked at her watch. Grocery store time did not work like regular time; more like time in the fairy stories Jules had read when she was younger, slipping back and forth and stretching out so long. "Four hours," she said. "Four more hours?"

Autumn winced in sympathy. "Will you come?"

"Sure," Jules said, but all she could think was, *It's too late. I broke things before we could even get started.*

What happened to the girl who'd asked Autumn out with so much confidence? What happened to the magic?

Jules glanced around again—no sign of customers, and the others were paying them zero attention. No one to witness her crashing and burning in such quiet, careful style. "I'll be there."

"All right," Autumn said, already beginning to walk away. "See you later."

The bus let her off half a block from Autumn's house. At the door she hesitated before ringing the bell, and then bounced on the balls of her feet in the time it took for Autumn to come to the door. When she opened it, she was smiling, and Jules smiled back, a reflex.

"Hi," she said. "Sorry I'm late."

"It's cool," Autumn said, and led Jules inside. "Do you want something to drink?"

"Sure." Jules took a second to adjust to the brightness of the hall, all the knickknacks and everything, and followed Autumn to the kitchen. "Is your mom here?"

"No, my parents are at work, and my brother's at day care," Autumn said, leaning into the refrigerator. "They won't be home for hours."

Jules shrugged her backpack off. "What do your parents do, anyway?"

"My dad's a construction manager. My mom works in some snobby law office, and she does hair and nails on the side. I know," she said. "Of course, right? She wants to open her own place one day. She'll be able to service all your acrylic and peroxide needs."

Jules pointed at Autumn's hair. "Does she do that for you?"

"Yeah." Autumn handed her a Diet Coke. "Couldn't stop her if I tried." She laughed softly. "Um, I have to switch the laundry real fast. You want to go up to my room? It's the second door on the left."

Jules followed the directions, up the decorated stairs and onto the landing, the walls of which were painted as bright as the ones downstairs.

Autumn's door had an *A* painted in blue. Jules opened it, and if the rest of the house was a neon Palm Springs pool party, this was the morning-after meditation. Jules exhaled as she stepped inside—*This is Autumn's bedroom. I am in Autumn's bedroom*—and gazed around. The walls were a soft, pale gray and the only clutter was a pair of shoes by Autumn's closet. Otherwise, everything was neatly in its place: the perfume bottles placed at measured intervals along the windowsill gleamed; the pictures above her bed were framed. And the books in the tall case were arranged by color. By *color.*

Jules went to them and ran her finger lightly across the shelf of spines that shifted from blue to green. "It's impossible to find anything," Autumn's voice came from behind. "But it looks so pretty."

Jules turned. "You're a neat freak, aren't you?"

"Little bit. My mom has the rest of the house to fill with all her stuff. But this is mine." Autumn sat on the edge of her bed and looked up at Jules. "So."

"So . . ." Jules glanced out the window. From Autumn's room you could see houses, trees with their leaves curling brown in the heat, some kids playing in the street. She looked back at Autumn. "Are we over?"

Autumn startled. "What?"

"It's okay," Jules said, and she meant it. It was only her own fault, pushing Autumn too much, lying to her. If Autumn wanted out, Jules understood. "I know I screwed up. I'm sorry. But it's okay."

Autumn's eyes widened. "Slow down," she said, her voice high. "Why would we be over? Do *you* want us to be over? Did I do something wrong?" Then she held her hands up. "Actually, no. I don't think I *did* do anything wrong. I think I got upset about the contest thing, and then you got weird, and started avoiding me, and now here we are. Am I right?"

Laid out like that, it sounded bad. "No. Maybe." Jules paused. "Okay, yes."

"Do you even know why I was upset?" Autumn asked. "I'll tell you. You didn't tell me this big thing and it made me feel like I wasn't important to you. Like maybe I was thinking that we meant more than we really do. That's why."

"Are you kidding me?" Jules said, her surprise real. "Autumn. You couldn't possibly think we meant more than *I* think we do. Oh my god, the first day I saw you I thought—" She stopped herself. But then Autumn's words in the break room came back to her: *I thought we were all about being honest with each other.* "I thought you were amazing. I felt like I fell in love with you the second I saw you, and I'm telling you that even though it's ridiculous and embarrassing because it's the truth."

Autumn's cheeks were bright pink. "Jules—"

"You want me to be honest, right?" Jules said. "Okay." She took a deep breath. "Let me tell you about my ex."

When Autumn's eyebrows rose Jules held her hands up. "Wait. See, I went out with this girl for, like, six months last year. I'd had a crush on her for literally years. I really liked her and she really liked me. But we were *so wrong* for each other." She shook her head and smiled tiredly. "It was obvious after a couple weeks. We should have broken up right then. But I liked her, and she was the first person I'd dated, so I wanted it to work. And I always wanted her attention, I wanted her to be . . . sweet to me. Because I—" Jules ignored the heat in her cheeks. "I like the romance—flowers and hand holding and everything. But she wasn't like that, it just wasn't her. And when she tried, I'd pick apart how wrong whatever she'd done was."

Autumn brought a hand to her hair, nervous. "Okay," she said.

Jules looked out the window again. "I do this thing," she said. "I think everything should be perfect and magical and then when it's not, I decide it's not worth my time. But really, I don't think what I'm waiting for is a fairy tale. I think it's just someone who wants to try as hard as I do. You're just you and I'm just me, and if it works or not is up to us, not some magic. I'm sorry I didn't get that before. I really am sorry."

The space between them felt so full, and Autumn stared Jules down, and the scrape of branches against the window was the only sound beyond the blood rushing in Jules's ears.

"Okay," she said eventually. "I accept your apology."

Jules felt a snap in her chest, palpable relief. She did? "You do?"

"I really like you, Jules," Autumn said, her eyes bright. "But god, you like to make things complicated."

Jules laughed. "I know."

"You're lucky I'm the kind of person who doesn't give up on things when they're not perfect and magical." Autumn said. "If that was me, I wouldn't be here. My life has not been perfect and magical. But it's still good."

"Yeah," Jules said. "I get it."

"But from now on," Autumn said, "talk to me. Don't pick a fight. I don't like fighting."

"Okay," Jules said, nodding quickly. "I can do that."

Autumn leaned back on her elbows and Jules tried not to let her eyes linger where Autumn's skirt rode up. "Oh, Jules," she said, and the smile she gave now was her full dazzling brightness. "What am I going to do with you?"

She stood and took three steps across the floor, planting herself in front of Jules. "You make me nervous," she said. "Not because I don't want this, but because I want it so much. And it's all new to me. I've never kissed anyone but you, and I've never kissed anyone with people watching me, and I've never held anyone's hand and been like, *This is my person.* But I want to do all those things with you."

Jules tipped her head to the side. "It's okay," she said. "I get it. It's new to me, too. Being public. Letting people see. And I get how it feels scary sometimes. I don't want to make you do anything you don't want to, that you're not ready for."

"I know you don't," Autumn said, and she put both her hands on Jules's waist. "But I do want to do them. If I screw up—it's not because of you. Okay?"

"Okay."

"And if I screw up, will you let me know?"

"Yes," Jules said, and she felt confident now, all the uncertainty gone and this magnetism in its place, heat from Autumn's hands on her. "And you'll do the same for me, right?"

"Yes."

Jules smiled, relief that they were finally, definitely on the same page flooding her. She put her hands on either side of Autumn's face and kissed her once, quick and sweet. "I feel so lucky," she whispered in the space between their mouths.

Autumn's fingers tickled at Jules's waist in a way that made her squirm. "Please stop talking and kiss me properly," Autumn said.

Jules felt both like she would come alight and come undone at Autumn's touch. She felt suddenly nervous again—like she didn't know where to put her hands or what to do with her body, even as her body seemed to decide for itself, pressing closer to Autumn, even as she kissed Autumn again, her tongue tracing Autumn's lower lip.

Her heart was racing. *Stop thinking.*

Stop thinking stop thinking.

Why am I so nervous?

Is she nervous?

Her skin is so warm.

I think I love her.

They broke apart. "Jules," Autumn said, her cheeks pink, her voice hoarse.

"What?" Jules said, her voice a whisper in response. "What's wrong?"

"Nothing." The back of Autumn's hand brushed right where Jules's cutoff's ended and her whole body bloomed warm. "Nothing at all," Autumn said, and swallowed hard. "I, um . . ."

"Is it the kissing?" Jules asked. "We can stop."

"No, no," Autumn said. "That is the opposite of what I want."

Jules wondered if she was hearing the meaning in Autumn's words right. "So . . ."

"Full disclosure," Autumn said. "I really want to do more than kiss you."

"Like—" Jules couldn't help her laugh. "That's a nice way to put it."

"Shut up," Autumn said, and this time she pinched Jules's thigh, the gentlest pain. "I'm saying I *want* to. If you want to. You know, take our clothes off and . . . other things."

Now Jules's heart rate kicked up a thousand percent. She touched her thumb to Autumn's chin. "You know we don't have to do anything."

"You're not listening," Autumn said, and she stepped back. Her hands went to her shirt and she tugged it free from the waist of her skirt, lifting it to flash the smallest amount of peachy skin. "I *want* to. Get it?"

Jules wet her lips. She'd done under-the-clothes fooling around with Delaney, in the back of her car at night only, hands cramped behind zippers and underwear. And she was pretty expert at getting herself off, but that was a different matter entirely. But Autumn looking at her like that, taking off their clothes in Autumn's room in afternoon sun, seeing each other and doing things to each other?

That was another level.

This was intimacy. Sleeping together.

Sex.

And god, she wanted to.

"Do you? Want to?" Autumn held her hand out to Jules. "Have sex with me?" An invitation. And a nervous look that fluttered over her face, like maybe she was doing the wrong thing, which was so not true that Jules almost wanted to laugh.

But instead she took Autumn's hand and pulled her close again, their bodies pressed together, and she pressed her hand flat against the bare skin under Autumn's shirt. "Yeah, I do," she said. "Are you sure?"

"Yes." Autumn said, and then her usual sweet smile turned wicked. "Yes!"

Jules cut her laugh off by kissing her, and her fingers fumbled for the hem of her own shirt. She found it and broke away from Autumn to pull it over her head and toss it aside, and Autumn did the same, revealing an emerald-green bra with all sorts of lace and ribbon that left Jules feeling too plain in her black sports bra. But the way Autumn took her in made her feel more than enough.

It was only a trip and fall to Autumn's bed, and once they were on her rose-colored sheets everything seemed to slow and speed up at once. Fast: Autumn tracing circles around Jules's belly button, Jules sliding her tongue at the back of Autumn's knee, the time it took to unbutton her shorts. Slow: Autumn shimmying out of her skirt, the kiss Jules gave Autumn as the sunlight hit her eyes, the touch of Autumn's hands on her breasts. The sound Autumn made when Jules touched her for the first time, surprised and breathless and quiet. And the satisfaction Jules felt, pride as she made this girl she was half or wholly in love with squirm and moan at her touch.

It was the best kind of careful and careless at the same time, accidental elbows and knees and giggles as they shifted around. A hurried apology at a sharp intake of breath and then *No, no, good* in response. Skin on skin and mouths on skin and hands on everything everywhere.

Jules had never done this, had kind of believed she'd have to wait years and years to find something like this. Someone who would let her see them so bare, who she would show herself to in spite of nerves, uncertainty. She tickled the bottoms of Autumn's feet and got a laugh in response, and then she slid her hands up Autumn's legs, dropped her head to blow on Autumn's soft inner thigh. Autumn tensed, Jules felt it, and she raised her head. "Okay?"

"Yes."

"Do you want me to—"

Autumn's eyes closed, a somehow pretty sheen of sweat on her cheeks and a breathless voice when she said, "Keep going. Do *not* stop."

Jules slipped her hands around Autumn's beautifully round hips and kissed her thigh, her slick skin. And for her first time giving oral, she thought she did pretty good. Or from Autumn's gasping reactions, it seemed that way. It was not like she imagined, like things she'd read online had told her it would be: it was *better*. And when Autumn reached down, her fingers grasping for Jules, and when Jules reached up and twined her fingers through Autumn's, it hit her.

This was it. Real romance. Not just the sex, but the laughing at each other, spilling their fears, talking about laundry and color-organized books. It wasn't magic; not everything was glittery and gold all the time. And declarations in the pouring rain and flowers on her doorstep—the idea of them paled in comparison to the reality of this, Jules realized. This everything, and this right now—Autumn's fingers threaded through hers, this most intimate stolen moment that was theirs and no one else's—what more had Jules been aching for?

And she had it now, and maybe it wouldn't be a forever thing, the end of all her longing. Jules had no idea. But this, right now, was enough.

Jules was enough.

Dia

The morning of Lex's birthday broke bright and clear. When Dia's alarm went off, Lex was already wide awake, bouncing around in her crib with bedhead curls sticking in every direction. "Mama!" she squeaked. "Hi."

"I'm up!" Dia rolled out of bed and padded over to the crib. "Hey, do you know what day it is today? It's your birthday! How old are you?"

Lex scrunched her face up before answering, "Two!"

"That's right, my baby genius, you're two today." Dia lifted her out and smushed their faces together. "Let's go get some birthday breakfast."

Her dad was already at work in the kitchen, but he abandoned the stove to come over and plant a kiss on Lex's head. "Happy birthday to my favorite grandbaby!"

"I'm two," Lex said, proudly holding up her hand and actually showing three fingers. Dia folded one down and smiled.

"That's right," Max said, rescuing pancakes from the stovetop. "Are you hungry?"

"For chocolate-chip pancakes?" Dia said, pretending to gnaw on Lex's hand. "Always, right, Lala?"

They ate breakfast outside, all four of them. Her mom put sliced bananas on Lex's plate, and Dia added a giant swirl of whipped cream. Birthday rules.

After breakfast Jules arrived with Autumn in tow, and they spent an hour setting up in the yard—streamers strung from the fence, balloons tied to the lawn chairs, and their table draped in paper tablecloth and so much glitter. It wasn't a real huge party, more of a come-to-the-house-there'll-be-food-and-music thing. Lex was only two, Dia figured; there wasn't much point in going over the top. But it was one of the rare times where Dia could make magic. For Lex, she'd make magic whenever she could.

Dia was setting out the food when the doorbell rang and Hanna came in, Molly following. "Where's the cake?" Hanna said. "I'm here for the cake."

"You have to wait," Dia said. "Molly, help yourself to drinks, they're outside."

"Cool," Molly said, strutting off in that self-conscious, attention-seeking way that was so thirteen-year-old.

Dia turned to Hanna. "Does your mom know she's here with you?"

"Yes," Hanna said, rolling her eyes. "Molly told her. She said Mom went all quiet first, and then super enthusiastic, and the only thing she said to Molly was to be home by dinner." They both watched Molly in the yard. "She gets so much more freedom than me. But she deserves it."

"You deserve it, too," Dia said.

Hanna nodded but said nothing, and Dia grabbed her arm, pulling her outside. "Come on. This is supposed to be fun!"

By two their little yard was as full as it ever was—mostly with her mom's friends, her dad's EMT crew and their older kids, neighbors (including Waffles the dog playing gently with an overexcited Lex), and a couple of moms from day care watching their kids running through bubbles.

After Dia spilled soda on her shirt she went to change, tossing the dirty clothes in her overflowing hamper. Before she went back out, she went in the bottom drawer inside her closet and took out the baby book that she'd never quite finished. But still, she allowed herself the luxury of five minutes sitting there, paging through the pictures with her messy writing underneath: *Forty weeks pregnant* and Dia holding her belly for the camera. *Alexa's first day home*, a tiny ball of a baby in a too-big onesie and mittens. After a while it became just pictures, hastily pasted in: Lex standing with Dia's hands hovering, ready to catch her, and sitting in a kiddie pool in the backyard, and with cake smeared all over her face from a year ago.

Her baby was two and she'd so far managed to keep her alive, relatively unharmed, and seemingly happy. Dia didn't really believe in a god or heaven or anything, but she closed her eyes anyway and thought words that she couldn't say out loud to anybody: *She's amazing, Elliot. You'd think so if you knew her. Or maybe she wouldn't even be here if you were still here. I don't really know what might have happened if you hadn't gone and died on me. But it doesn't matter. You changed my entire world and I'll never get to tell you what that means to me. I have this piece of you, though. She's here, and I'm here, and you're not, but we're okay. We'll be okay.*

She opened her eyes and laughed at herself. "Get it together, Valentine," she said, running a careful finger under each eye so as not to smudge her mascara. "Jesus."

Dia left the book on her bed and went out again. When she got to the back door, she called to Jules, "Come help me with the—" She stopped. "Oh."

Jesse was out in the yard, and from where Dia stood it looked like he was rescuing a balloon that'd gotten free and tangled in the tree that trespassed over from the neighbor's yard. She watched as he reached for it, stretching high, his shirt riding up showing yet another bruise, on his back this time. He got it and handed it to one of the older kids, and Dia leaned against the door frame. "When did he get here?"

"I don't know." Jules was at Dia's elbow now, and she followed her gaze. "Like, ten minutes ago?"

"Oh," Dia said again. "Okay."

"What?" Jules looked at her. "Is he not supposed to be here? Is something going on with you two?"

"Nothing's going on."

"Your face says you're lying," Jules said. "Did he do something?"

"He didn't do anything," Dia said, and that was the truth, at least. "Forget it. Come light the candles with me."

Everyone crowded around as Dia sat with Lex on her lap and helped tear open some of her presents, and then pretended she wasn't getting emotional while everybody sang "Happy Birthday." She pressed her face close to her daughter's so they could blow out the candles together, and whispered in her ear. "Happy birthday, Lex. You're my best present every year."

They passed around cake, vanilla with strawberry buttercream, and someone—Hanna, Dia suspected—turned the music up, A Tribe Called Quest soundtracking the afternoon turning to evening. People began to drift home, full up and happy. Dia snapped picture after picture on her phone: of her dad holding on to one of Lex's shoes while she ran circles around him; her mom swinging Lex high in the air; Jules smushing a kiss on Lex's cheek while she giggled.

She wrapped up pieces of cake and gave them to people on their way out, thanking them for coming. She watched Molly and Autumn showing Lex how to thread daisies into a chain. She watched Jesse petting the dog and talking to Candy with the leash in her hand. She didn't mean to avoid him, and she didn't want to push things. He had come to her house, though. He was on her territory.

Why is he here? Dia thought. *He's supposed to be done with me. What is it going to take?*

Dia took a piece of cake and held it carefully on her way over to Jesse. "Hi," Dia said. "Sorry to interrupt."

"It's cool," Candy said, clipping the leash onto the dog's collar. "I have to go pick up Christopher from work now, anyway. Thanks for having us, Dia. I think Alexa's having a great birthday."

"I think she cares more about the fact she got to see Waffles than any of her presents," Dia said with a laugh. "See you later."

Candy waved as she led the dog away, and Dia looked at Jesse. "Lex loves that dog," she said. "You know how she is."

"It's a pretty cute dog," he said. "I can see why she's so into it."

Dia smiled and then looked at her feet. "What are you doing here?"

"Well, I don't like to miss free cake," Jesse said, and he wasn't exactly smiling, this guarded expression on his face. "Aren't we supposed to be going back to the way things were?"

"I . . ." Dia wasn't sure what to say to that.

Jesse nodded toward Alexa. "And you don't turn two years old every day, right?"

"Right," Dia said. *Of course he came,* she thought. *Of course.* Because he was a good person and Dia had told him to come, months ago, and so even though things were weird, he was still here. Because he didn't want to miss her kid's birthday.

"I had a gift already," he said. "I wanted to make sure Alexa got it."

"Oh. Thank you," Dia said, and then, "Here." She presented the cake to him. "I know it's not butterscotch cookies, but we were all out."

Jesse waited a long beat before taking it from her. "Thanks," he said, and then he looked at her properly for the first time all day. "How did it go? Round two?"

Dia pulled in a slow breath. "Okay," she said. "Good. I think."

"Good," he repeated, nodding. "All right. I gotta go. I'm supposed to be at work in fifteen minutes. I . . ." He ran a hand over his head. "Sorry if I made it weird coming here."

"It's okay," Dia said again, and she silenced the part of her that wanted to ask him to stay, to talk about things, because she didn't have the words and she knew, really, that she should let him go.

So instead she nodded and said, "Thanks for coming," before walking away, back to Lex.

When everyone but her friends had gone and the yard looked like a whirlwind of glitter and ice cream had hit it, Dia changed the music to Carly Rae Jepsen and started cleaning up. Her mom and dad had taken Lex on a walk around the block, to try to calm her down from everything, and it was nice to breathe for a minute.

"What do you want to do with the leftovers?" Hanna said. "In the fridge?"

"Yeah," Dia said, grabbing a trash bag. "Tupperware is under the sink."

She started gathering up all the torn wrapping paper and paper plates while Molly helped Hanna box up the food and Jules . . . well, Jules didn't seem to be doing anything but sitting and watching the others work. "Juliana," Dia said, "can you get off your ass and help?"

"I am helping," Jules said, kicking her legs out and folding her hands behind her head. "I'm observing. Making sure you get everything."

"You're being obnoxious," Autumn said, hands full of streamers. "I don't make out with obnoxious people."

"Go *get* me a soda," Dia said. "That's helpful."

Jules groaned. "Fine," she said, standing.

Dia cleared the table of debris while Jules did as she said, and when she came back with the soda they both sat in their plastic chairs. Dia put her feet in Jules's lap as she read the happy birthday texts from cousins she hadn't seen in years and her aunt who'd recently learned how to use emojis. "People love birthdays," she said to Jules, flicking from her texts to her email. "It's like—holy shit."

"Your aunt Jeanie said holy shit?" Jules said. "Wow."

"No," Dia said, and she opened the email that was from Sun City Radio, her fingers slipping on the screen. "Hanna! Come here, *now*!"

Jules sat up. "What is it?" she asked. "Is it the contest?"

Hanna came over, and Molly and Autumn stopped cleaning up to look over. "What?"

Dia cleared her throat and began to read: "'Dear Wildfire: We are so stoked to let you know that you have made it into our top three!'"

"We're in the top three?" Hanna asked, her eyes wide. "Wait. Read that again. We're in the top fucking three?"

Dia started laughing and couldn't stop, and then to her surprise Molly took the phone from her hand and took over.

"Listen," she said. "Okay . . .

"Dear Wildfire:

"We are so stoked to let you know that you have made it into our top three! And here's our surprise: round three includes YOU becoming part of the lineup at next week's show at the Revelry Room! You'll perform for an audience of real live music fans and Glory Alabama themselves! The judges will take this performance along with everything else into consideration before choosing the winner. We'll be in touch with more details very shortly. Congratulations!"

When Molly stopped reading there was silence, until Hanna said, "Wait, what? Perform?"

"That's what it says," Molly said, looking around at them. "What?"

Dia took her phone back and ran over the words again and, sure enough, right there it said it: *round three includes YOU becoming part of the lineup—*

Part of the lineup?

"Oh my god," she said, her heart pounding. "A *surprise*? What do they think this is, a reality show or something? We have to perform next week? Like, in front of people? In front of Glory Alabama?"

"No," Jules said, shaking her head. "No way. They would have told us that already. Wouldn't they?"

Hanna tugged at her hair. "Oh my god," she said. "We haven't performed for real people in *years*."

"Fuck," Dia said, starting to panic a little, and she looked up at the others. "What are we going to do?"

Autumn lifted her hands filled with paper the same colors as her hair. "Isn't this good news?" she says. "Isn't this what you wanted all along?"

Jules cracked her knuckles. "Not exactly."

"What are we going to do?" Dia repeated.

"You're going to play," Molly said confidently. "You're going to show them what I saw for an entire month. What's the big deal?"

They were silent for a minute, and Dia could almost feel them all spinning through what this really meant.

Jules blew out her cheeks. "Well, Molly's right," she said eventually. "We're going to play, aren't we? What other choice do we have? We've done it a hundred times before. And we did it last week."

"In front of *three* people," Hanna said.

"Three, three hundred, what's the difference?" Jules's grin was shaky, and Autumn put a hand on her shoulder. "Come *on*. Okay, we weren't expecting this, but! We can do it. What, are we going to pull out now because we're scared?"

"I'm not scared," Dia said immediately. Okay, so that wasn't completely true, but it felt like Jules was issuing a challenge, and Dia was not one to back down from a challenge.

Not anymore.

"I am!" Hanna said, raking a hand through her platinum hair. "We haven't played a *real* show in years. And GA are going to be there, watching us? We can't."

Dia took a deep breath and surveyed the wreckage of the yard, her friends standing there, Autumn and Molly waiting expectantly.

"Yeah, we can," she said, and the initial rush of panic was replaced with adrenaline now. They were going to play a show in front of an actual audience—wasn't this everything they'd really wanted?

Dia looked at Jules, at Hanna, and gritted her teeth. "We better get back to practicing."

Hanna

Hanna rushed home to Ciara's house and used the spare key to let herself in. Ciara was sitting on the couch with her laptop, coffee in one hand, and looked up when Hanna came clattering in. "What?"

"Can I borrow your van tomorrow?" Hanna asked, her words tripping over each other. "It's an emergency."

Ciara's eyebrows shot up. "Emergency?"

After Hanna explained everything, Ciara nodded and got up. "Okay," she said. "We can do this. One minute." She disappeared into her bedroom and Hanna sank to the couch. In less than a week she was going to be on a stage, in front of hundreds of people, playing while Dia sang her words. Playing to people who either wouldn't know who she was or would remember her, Hanna the drunk. No big deal, not at all.

She scratched her nails on the arm of the couch and took a deep breath, held it for three, let it out.

I am okay.

Look at it this way: the people who didn't know her couldn't think anything about her, not anything that mattered. And anyone who did remember her, who might look at her and get that light in their eyes as they recalled her alcohol-fueled screw-ups—what did they matter, either? They didn't know her. No one really knew her, not anymore. Only Dia and Jules, Molly and Ciara. Only the people who actually mattered to her. Those were the opinions she cared about, and everybody else? Fuck 'em.

Ciara came back then and Hanna jumped to her feet. "I switched my shift," Ciara said, slipping her phone into her back pocket. "We'll take care of it, first thing tomorrow."

"You don't need to come—"

"Will you shut up and let me be a part of this?" Ciara said. "Shit, Han, I have restrained myself from pushing into your whole reunion operation this long. I am only so strong!" She grabbed Hanna by the shoulders. "And you know you can practice here, right?"

Hanna tried to frown, but it gave way to a smile. "You're sure?" she said, relief flooding her before being swallowed up by all the adrenaline currently flooding her system. "Thanks, C."

"No sweat," Ciara said. "This is what we do. Right?"

Hanna met Ciara's gaze and nodded. This is what they did, favors pulled and good faith given because they all wanted the same thing at the end of everything: a chance to try. "Right."

* * *

On Monday morning Hanna opened the door to her house while Ciara sat in her idling van at the curb. "Molls?"

Molly appeared in the kitchen doorway. "I can't believe you're doing this," she said, her face fixed in worry. "Mom's going to lose it when she sees."

"Tell her to come talk to me," Hanna said, heading out to the garage. "Besides, they're mine. I paid for them. I'm taking them."

She opened the garage door from the inside, rolling it up and letting the sun in, and then Ciara got out of her van. The three of them carried out the remains of her drum set and loaded them into the back, and when they were done the garage looked strangely empty. "All right, Molls," Hanna said, and she grabbed her sister in a vise-grip hug that Molly had no chance of wriggling out of. "I have to go, but I'll text you later?"

Molly frowned once Hanna let her go. "What should I say?"

Hanna knew right away that Molly meant *What should I say when Mom asks me what the hell happened?* She looked up to the sky for a second while she thought, and then back at her sister. "Tell her I said I had something important to give you," Hanna said. "And you didn't know I was here for the drums, and you had nothing to do with it. Okay?"

Molly nodded reluctantly. "Okay," she said. "Bye, Han. Love you."

"I love you too, Molls," Hanna said, starting toward Ciara in the van. "Talk later."

jules

It had taken some convincing on Hanna's part, getting them to agree to come to Ciara's place. But Hanna had said Ciara wasn't mad, and even though it didn't stop Jules feeling bad—after everything Ciara had done for them, they'd still faded from her life like it was nothing, Jules's second-biggest regret—she believed it. Hanna had stayed close to Ciara. And if she said that Ciara wasn't mad, then maybe it was true.

So on Monday afternoon, they took the steps up and knocked on Ciara's door. It opened as soon as Jules's knuckles left the wood, Hanna standing there looking wired. "Come in," she said, impatience in her voice. "Set up, I want to get going."

Jules exchanged a look with Dia, a *who is this girl again?* look of awe. "Okay," Jules said as they entered Ciara's house, began unpacking their guitars. "Whatever you say, captain."

Ciara's house looked the same, Jules thought, but as she looked around she began to notice the changes. Gray walls instead of green, the posters replaced with framed art prints. The rug on the living room floor was white and fluffy instead of multicolored knit. Jules lifted the corner of it, though, and underneath was the chunk of wood missing from that same floorboard. She smiled: Dia had dropped a plate there, shards scattering over the floor, and only after they'd cleaned up had they noticed the board.

She put the rug back and plugged in. Dia was ready; Hanna was sitting behind her drums in the corner, and she lifted her sticks, eyes gleaming.

Two songs—that was what the follow-up email had said. Each of the final three acts had to perform two original songs, and then the judges would decide who was going to win.

So they ran through "Bones" and "Pretty Baby," their obvious second choice, over and over, knowing them almost too well. It was the intense focus of knowing they had only five days now, the anxious energy from before having dissipated; or, it was finally falling into the band they were, who they were now.

Jules didn't know which for sure, but she did know that they didn't make any mistakes. Didn't slip up or forget anything, didn't get into any bickering arguments or snap at each other the way they usually did. They kept going until Dia made them stop, wary of getting played out.

"I think we're ready?" Dia said, sounding unsure but looking determined. "Yeah."

"Ready?" Jules said, pulling her braids into a twist. "We can't be ready. We still have five days."

"You know what I mean," Dia said. "We were already ready. This is just extra. I don't want us to freak ourselves out by practicing too much."

Hanna held her sticks up. "You're right," she said. "Let's take a break, at least."

They sat on the couch, pushed back to make space, and drank sodas from Ciara's fridge. "This is weird," Jules said, breaking the silence. "It feels like no time has passed."

"You can tell it has," Dia said. "Look at Hanna's roots."

"Hey!" Hanna said, then tugged at her hair and sighed. "It's true. I really need to fix this situation."

Jules looked at her. "Let's do it now," she said, the idea catching her. It was the kind of thing they used to do all the time: hair dye over kitchen sinks, makeup sessions in Dia's bedroom, late night secrets in between. "We'll help."

"Really?" Hanna sat up. "You want to?"

"Why not? We're done here," Jules said, glancing at Dia to check. "We'll kill each other if we keep going. Let's do this instead, and we'll practice again tomorrow to be sure."

"Yeah," Dia said. "Sure."

Jules got up right as the front door opened, and there was Ciara silhouetted in the doorway.

She let out a little shriek upon entry and raised her aviators. "For the love of all that is holy," Ciara said. "Would you look at you three together!"

"Ciara!" The name burst free of Jules's mouth without her even meaning to say it, and she threw herself into Ciara's outstretched arms with such force that Ciara stumbled. "Hi!"

"Hi, pudding." Ciara returned Jules's bear hug with equal enthusiasm. "Oh, god, you're taller. When did you get taller?"

"I missed you," Jules found herself saying. "I'm sorry." Was that all? Was that everything she had?

But Ciara touched her cheek. "It's okay," she said. "I know."

It was Dia's turn to be enveloped in Ciara's arms next—arms even more covered in tattoos than they had been before, Jules noticed—and then they stood there, all looking at each other and laughing. "Congratulations, mama," Ciara said to Dia. "I heard you got yourself a beautiful little one."

"She is beautiful," Dia said. "She just turned two, can you believe it?"

Ciara shook her head. "I really almost can't," she said. "You'll have to tell me all about her." She narrowed her eyes. "But what are you doing sitting around? Aren't you supposed to be practicing? I want to hear you!"

"We're taking a strategic break," Hanna said. "We're going to fix my hair."

"Oh, really? Hmm." Ciara shimmied her shoulders, bare in a skull-emblazoned halter top. "Now that I can help with. But! Only on the condition that you play for me later," she said. "And catch me up on everything I've missed. And I mean *everything*. Deal?"

"Deal," Jules said, in unison with Hanna and Dia.

"All right then." She whipped around and headed back out the door. "Come, my loves! To the beauty supply."

Jules looked at the others, the biggest smile on her face. "I forgot how much I fucking love that girl."

They piled into Ciara's van—like old times—and headed downtown. Inside the beauty-supply store they wandered the aisles looking for bleach powder, developer, rubber gloves. "You know, you could try a little color," Ciara said to Hanna. "Blue tips?"

Hanna shook her hair out. "Maybe," she said. "Jules, what do you think?"

"Why not?" Jules said. "If you want."

"We'll go look," Dia said, grabbing Jules by the hand and dragging her into the next aisle. Heads bent low by the boxes of Hot Red and Purple Orchid, Dia whispered to her. "She's not mad, is she?"

"Ciara?" Jules said. "No. She's not."

"Okay," Dia said. "I needed you to say it."

Jules reached out and flicked Dia's elbow. "Don't push it," she said. "Right now we have a really good thing going. Don't jinx us."

"I would never," Dia said, rubbing at her elbow. "And ow!"

Jules started down the aisle, toward the pinks and blues. "Oh, you princess."

She scanned the array of colors, mentally pairing each with

Hanna's face and either casting aside or plucking a box out. When she couldn't decide between Coral, Capri, or Lagoon Blue, she went to find Hanna and Ciara. But as she passed the makeup aisle, a too-familiar voice caught her and Jules had to look.

Down there by herself was Delaney Myers. Standing the way she always did: back arched, one hip jutting out, her head tipped ever so slightly to the side, in case anybody was looking. Which Jules was, she supposed, but not *looking*. Because this was the first time she'd seen Delaney since graduation and it felt strange. Like, as if there used to be a piece of invisible string between them, pulling taut and falling slack but always connecting them, that now had been sliced in two. Jules felt no pull, not in that bittersweet way she always used to.

Delaney hadn't seen her. Jules watched her for a moment, bending down to pick something off the bottom shelf. Before this summer Jules might have found some reason to walk down there, shut off her brain for a minute, and give in to loneliness. But now Jules had that thing she'd always been needling Delaney for, and she regretted the time they'd spent pissing each other off and pretending it was what they wanted. Delaney deserved better, too.

"Hey," Jules called out before she really thought about it.

Delaney heard and turned and smiled like there was nothing out of the ordinary about this. "Hey," she called back. "What are you doing here?"

"Hair dye," Jules said, and pointed at her braids. "Not for me."

Delaney nodded slightly. "Right. For your girlfriend?" she said, and then grinned at the face Jules knew she must be making. "I heard you were seeing some pretty girl with amazing hair. Am I wrong?"

Jules looked up to the pockmarked store ceiling, trying not to laugh. "No, you're right."

"That's good," Delaney said. "I hope she's good to you."

"She is," Jules said, and watched Delaney carefully. "Are you? Good?"

Delaney nodded. "Yeah. I am."

Jules smiled, and she hadn't realized how good it would be to ask that question and get that answer. To even talk to Delaney like they were only some version of friends. "All right." She lifted her hand to wave goodbye. "See you around."

"Yeah," Delaney said, waving too. "Have a good summer."

And then Jules kept on walking, pulling her phone out when it buzzed in her back pocket.

Autumn had perfect timing. Hey, her text read, hope it's going well! Malai lost big this morning so next taco trip is on me. It was accompanied with a selfie, Autumn peeking over a twenty-dollar bill.

Jules shook her head. I was just talking about you, she wrote back. You're so cute it should be illegal.

I know, Autumn's response came. But you love it.

Jules glanced over her shoulder, back in Delaney's direction. What they'd had and what she had with Autumn—they were an entire world apart. She and Autumn weren't perfect, not close. They made mistakes, and made up, and they were both figuring it all out. And it was better than Jules could have ever imagined.

Jules snapped a picture, a silly face, and sent it to Autumn. Then she headed up to the counter, where the others were already congregating. "Hey," she said. "Did you choose a color?"

Hanna nodded, glancing at Jules as Dia and Ciara stacked boxes on the counter. "You okay?"

Jules let out a slow breath, imagined herself tangling her fingers in the sweet pink and ocean blue of Autumn's hair. "Yeah," she said. "Perfect."

Hanna

Hanna stood in the bathroom that night, turning this way and that, watching the way the light changed on her new Special Effects Nuclear Red hair.

"Are you sure?" Dia had asked, a brush loaded with red dye in her hand. "Once we start, there's no going back."

Hanna had taken a deep breath and nodded. "Do it."

It was almost a shocking difference. Hanna was so used to the bright white—it had been her calling card since she'd first locked herself in the bathroom with the bleach at thirteen. But shock was what she needed. Because the girl with the platinum hair was not really her anymore. She didn't know if she was this girl, either, but she could try it out for a while. Experiment with who, exactly, Hanna Adler was right now.

She pulled her hair into a ponytail, admiring the jewel-bright shimmer as she did so. Then she took her phone out of her pocket and checked the list of missed calls: all from her mom, none since last week. Only a handful of texts, sent at times of the morning Hanna thought of as night. Just checking in, they said, or some variation of.

Hope your day went well.

The weather's nice today.

Nothing from today, no sign that her parents had noticed her heist—or that they had decided to do anything about it, at least.

Hanna bent over the sink. It had been two weeks now. For the sake of harmony: time to yield.

She watched her new self in the mirror as she dialed. It only rang for a second before her mom answered, this cautious voice. "Hanna?"

"Hey, Mom."

"Hi. Did you get my messages? I left a lot," Theresa said, and then, "You came home today. What were you doing?"

There it was. Hanna knew her mom couldn't keep away from that.

(Hadn't she known, really, as she'd been dismantling her drums that it would lead to this? Wasn't that a little bit why she'd done it?)

(Maybe.)

"I'm sorry," Hanna said, flexing her free hand. "I should have called you back sooner. I was . . . I've been trying to get my head straight."

"Hanna—"

"I want to talk," Hanna said, watching her mouth move in the mirror. "Not on the phone. At home, with you and Dad. Would that be okay?"

There was a long silence, and then her mom said, "Of course it would. Come by tomorrow. For dinner?"

"Sure," Hanna said, and it felt strange to be doing this, arranging dinner dates at her own dining-room table. "See you then."

She hung up and checked her reflection again. The red, she loved, but she wanted more. More different.

She opened the door. "Ciara! I need your help."

The first thing Molly said when she opened the front door was, "Your hair!"

Hanna touched a hand to her head, a little self-consciously, grateful for the distraction from the unsettled feeling she'd gotten from knocking on her own front door. "Oh, yeah."

"It's so short! And red!" Molly said. "You didn't tell me you were doing it."

Hanna let the ends run over her fingertips. Last night she'd made Ciara cut off five inches. The ends now hovered above her shoulders, falling in her natural waves. "It was a spur-of-the-moment thing," Hanna said. "I didn't plan it. I would've told you if I had. Stop hassling me."

Molly gave a defiant toss of her head. "Fine," she said.

"Hanna?" her dad's voice rang out. "Is that you?"

She steeled herself, fixed a smile on her face, and followed Molly inside, into the kitchen. "Hi, Dad." She was not a hugger at the best of times, and she leaned against the door frame, waved at her dad sitting at the table. "Hi, Mom."

Theresa came away from the sink, a pitcher of water in her hands.

"Hanna," she said, and there was the tiniest hint of warmth there, and then her eyes widened. "Your hair!"

"Looks good," her dad cut in, nodding approvingly. "Different."

"Yes," her mom said, her smile wavering. "That's what I was going to say. Sit!"

"Sure," Hanna said, pushing down her laugh. How easily everyone was shaken by a box of red dye and pair of scissors.

But aside from that, things were not as terrible as she'd expected.

They playacted regular through dinner: passing food, Molly making faces across the table, her parents making intermittent conversation. Hanna ate and wondered if this sense of surreality was evident only to her, or if they all appreciated the play they were putting on.

Once they were finished, Hanna got up to clear the plates. "Molly, help me out," she said, but her dad cleared his throat.

"Actually, Molly, will you give us a minute?" he said. "Take your laundry upstairs."

Molly rolled her eyes. "Fine." But as she stood up, she shot Hanna a worried look. Hanna nodded at her and mouthed, *It's okay.* Because it was true. Hanna had been at this table with her parents wearing those Very Serious faces many times before: after the ER that first time, and when Elliot had died, and after the ER that second time, and when they'd told her she was going to rehab. She'd lived through those talks and she'd live through this one, too.

Four hundred and sixty-eight days, she thought.

I am here.

I am not broken.

I am okay.

Once Molly was gone, up the stairs, her parents turned all their attention on her. "Hanna," her dad said, and he looked so, so tired. "We need to talk about what's going on."

"Where are you staying?" her mom asked. "Not with Dia? Jules? I called their mothers."

"You called their *moms*?" Hanna said, and she wasn't sure why she was surprised. "I'm staying with Ciara."

"With Ciara?" Her mom pressed her lips into a thin line, and Hanna could imagine the conversation in her head: *At least she has a safe place to stay. But Ciara's a part of the whole music thing. She's older, though, and maybe she'll teach Hanna something about responsibility. Or maybe she'll be a bad influence.* "Okay," was all her mom said eventually. And then she sat up straight, eyes bright. "What are you *thinking*?"

Hanna swallowed her nerves and looked her mom right in the eyes. "I am thinking," she said, "that you gave me an ultimatum and I made my choice. That's what you're supposed to do, isn't it? When someone says do this or that. You pick one. I picked the one you didn't want. That's it."

"Come on, Hanna," her dad said, raking a hand through his graying hair. "Take this seriously."

Hanna looked at her hands for a minute, spread flat on the warm wood of the table. Then she looked up and blinked slowly. "Take this seriously?" she said. "Trust me, I am. I'm trying to make up for *years* of not being serious." Her mom started to say something, but Hanna shook her head. "Can I talk for a second, please?"

Her mom's eyebrows rose, but she nodded anyway. "Sure," she said, acerbic. "Talk."

Hanna leaned her elbows on the table and spoke with her hands, too. "I know," she started, her voice as clear as she could make it. "I know I've done things in the past that made it hard for you to trust me. I've done things that have made it hard for me to trust myself, but I'm trying really hard to do the right thing. I know you don't like the idea of me playing music again, and I'm sorry that I lied to you about it. I think I knew you wouldn't want me to do it, and I didn't want to give you the chance to tell me that.

"And Mom, I know you were only trying to do what you thought was best for me. But what you think is best for me and what I think are so different. But you gave me the option to stay here and go back to the way things were before, or leave and do what *I* want to do. So I left, because I *can't*, and I don't want to, go back to the way I was. I don't mean the way I was when I was drinking, I mean the way I was, like, *two months* ago. When I was lonely *all* the time, and constantly trying to do things to make you happy, and not making myself happy at all." Hanna looked around the kitchen, the walls familiar sunshine yellow, the cabinets worn with years of their touch. "I haven't been happy in so long. Making music again—I remembered what it's like to have something I actually care about. And I knew you wouldn't understand." She shook her head, looked back at her parents, watching her warily.

"Me and Dia and Jules, yeah, we've had our problems. The problems that I had, that I have, are not because of them. They're not because of the music. My problems are because of *me*, and who I am, and how I chose to act. I'm not choosing that way anymore. That's the real thing. I could be anywhere doing anything and still be falling apart if I didn't choose every day to be sober and to be different than the girl I was." She took a deep breath and met her parents' gazes for the first time since she'd started speaking. "I know I can't make you trust me, or trust that I'm doing the best thing for me, but I'm asking you to. I'm asking you to at least try."

Her dad watched her as she stopped talking, this look in his eyes like he was really processing what Hanna had said. But her mom looked upset. "I don't know, Hanna," she said. "I think you're right—we don't agree on what's best for you. But I think that we can *talk* about it all and come to some kind of agreement about the music and what you're going to do. Yes, Benjamin?" But then she carried on without giving Hanna's dad a chance to answer. "But in the meantime, I think you should come *home*."

Hanna supposed she should have been relieved to hear that, but she wasn't.

She liked being out of the house, being responsible for herself with no one to approve or disapprove of her actions. Being on an equal level with Ciara instead of constantly watched over by her parents. The idea of coming back filled her with a sense of overwhelming claustrophobia. "Thank you," she said. "Really, I mean it. But . . . I don't think I should come home."

"What?" her mom said, lips disappearing into a thin line again. "Hanna."

"You said it, that day," Hanna said. "I'm eighteen, I'm an adult. Old enough to learn what it is to take care of myself. I don't think it's good for me to be here anymore. Not that I don't love you and miss you," she said quickly. "Because I do, of course. It's only been two weeks but I do miss you. But also—it's only been two weeks, and I feel so much *better*. I think that being here with you watching me all the time makes me do things I shouldn't. Does that make sense?" She leaned her chin on her hands. "The truth is, I like it with Ciara. I like cooking for myself and coming home when I want and saying and doing things without wondering how you're going to react first."

"You might like it now, but it's a novelty," her dad said. "You won't like it so much when most of your paycheck's going to rent and you have to deal with mold and no one's there to do your laundry for you."

"Yeah, but who likes that stuff?" Hanna said. "You just do it, right? Because you don't have another choice."

"You have another choice," her mom said, and she sounded a little shocked. "Hanna, sweetie, do you really feel like we're always watching you?"

"You are," Hanna said. "But I don't blame you. This is what I'm saying. I did things to make you have to do that. But now it feels like we're stuck in the routine of you not trusting me and me desperately wanting to *make* you trust me, and I really want to stop."

Her dad cleared his throat. "Living by yourself," he said. "That's a big jump. Responsibility."

"I know," Hanna said. "Once I start my job, I'm going to have some money. Ciara's looking for a roommate, and she says I can live there officially if I can work it out. And I have to do it sometime—leave here. Now I feel like coming home would be a step backward. I want to keep going forward." She shifted, her new shorter hair creating this breeze around her neck. "I want to know who I am on my own."

They talked a while longer, and eventually her parents were . . . not on her side, but accepting. Accepting that she wasn't coming home and that she wasn't giving up music and that, maybe, she was not exactly who they thought she was.

But Hanna was more than ready to start becoming who *she* really wanted to be. It was only the beginning of a much longer conversation, Hanna knew, but at least it was a start.

"This Friday," her mom said, when Hanna was getting ready to leave. "You can come for dinner again, if you'd like. Maybe we can talk some more."

Hanna gave a small smile. "Okay," she said. "But this week, I can't. Next week, though."

"What are you doing this week?" her dad asked, as they walked out to the hall.

Hanna cleared her throat. "It's, uh . . . the contest. This thing at Revelry, where they're going to announce the winner."

Theresa gave this soft smile. "Sounds fun," she said, and those two words alone were enough to let Hanna know she was trying. Would this last, her trying?

Hanna knew better than to hope, and yet, she still did.

"Maybe you can come by on Saturday instead," her mom said. "It's okay if you don't. Door's open."

"I will," Hanna said. "I have to get the rest of my stuff, too."

"Don't worry about that," her dad said. "We're not kicking you out. You can leave things here until you have space for them."

Hanna nodded. "Thanks," she said. They were at the door now, and this time she did hug them both, hard and fast, and felt tightness in her chest. Inside this house it was all she could do sometimes to breathe. Outside, the air came so much easier.

"I'm going to say bye to Molly," she said, and she ran upstairs. Molly's room was empty, and so Hanna turned and pushed open her own bedroom door. "Molls?"

Her sister sat on the bed, cross-legged with her back against the wall. "You're not coming home," she said, flat, accusatory. She looked over at Hanna. "That sucks."

"I know," Hanna said. "You get why I'm doing it, though, right? It'll be better this way."

"No, it won't," Molly said. "You're supposed to be *here*. What about when I start school? Who's going to help me? What if I need you?"

Hanna went to her, sat down on the bed. "I'm right here, Molls. You need me, anytime, anyplace, you know I'll be there. And I'm only a bus ride away. You can come hang with me and Ciara whenever you want."

Molly's lip shook. "Promise?"

"I swear." Hanna shifted; she already felt a little out of place in this room. "It's weird, Molls. I feel like a grown-up and a little kid all at the same time. Like, I don't know what the fuck I'm really doing, but I know I have to do it."

Molly turned to her. "Can I come on Friday?" she asked. "I really want to see you all play."

"I'll see what I can do," Hanna said.

She scanned her room, the memory of so many years and so many versions of herself lingering in here. The Hanna who read horror stories under the covers by flashlight; the Hanna who hid bottles under her bed and kept the curtains closed against the light; the Hanna who listened to melancholy voices singing in the quiet dark hours of the night, and scribbled her own words to get them out of her head.

She got up and crouched in front of her nightstand, opening the bottom drawer. The last of her notebooks were still in there, and she lifted them all out. "You want some advice, Molls?"

"From you?" Molly said, and pretended to cower when Hanna whipped around to glare at her. "Kidding. What?"

Hanna looked at her not-so-little sister, delicate and not, strong and not. "Life is too many strange and beautiful things to use it being unkind to yourself." She paused. "People will try to make you into somebody you're not. Even the people who are supposed to love you for who you are. Sometimes it feels like it would be easier to become that person. But that won't make you happy. And if you can, being happy is the most important thing. So do what you have to so that the world does not get you. Do you hear me?"

Molly looked like she wasn't quite sure what to make of Hanna's words, but then she nodded once. "I hear you."

Dia

The moon was bright in glimpses between clouds, hanging low over Dia in the backyard. It was Thursday night—or Friday morning, now—and she'd spent hours lying in a puddle of her own sweat before accepting that she wasn't going to sleep. So she'd grabbed the baby monitor and her acoustic, crept downstairs to sit out on the back steps.

She'd thought she'd get some relief, but the air was thick like a storm was about to roll in—that's what they'd been saying on the news all week. But they said that all the time, talked up these big thunderstorms, told everybody to be ready for the rain, and then they never came. *No storms,* Dia thought. *They only wish for it.*

When the back door creaked open, Dia jumped, putting a hand to her chest as she twisted around. "You scared me," she said.

"I could say the same," her dad said. "What are you doing out here?"

"Can't sleep," Dia said.

"Nervous?" Her dad sat down beside her, the reflective stripes on his EMT uniform shining.

Dia ran her thumb across the strings of her guitar. "A little," she said, honestly. "Mostly not. I just want to do it, you know?"

"I know," her dad said. "I'm sorry I can't be there." Neither of her parents could; they'd both been excited when Dia had told them about Friday, and then her dad had realized he was scheduled to work and her mom would have to watch Lex so Dia could go.

Never mind, Dia had said. *It makes me nervous when you watch, anyway.*

"It's all right," Dia said now, reassuring again. "You got all those people who need their lives saved. I guess it's an okay excuse."

Max smiled, and he looked exactly like Lex when he did that: same crinkled corners of their eyes, same apple cheeks. "I'm real proud of you," he said. "You know that, right? No matter what happens tomorrow, you did this."

"I know," Dia said, quietly, into the night. "Hey, you want to hear what we're playing?"

Max held his hands open. "Hit me."

So Dia played a concert for her audience of one, under the clouds, and the moon winked in and out of sight, and she felt the anchor of the earth release her the slightest amount.

Elliot

NOVEMBER

"We're Graceland!" Ciara says from the stage. "Thanks for listening!"

Elliot sticks his fingers in his mouth and whistles; next to him Jules has Dia on her back, and they're both cheering.

They've come out of town tonight, to Longport, where almost all the houses are the fancy kind. This one has a huge pool with a slide, a trampoline, a giant oak with a tire swing hanging from a thick branch. The yard is full of people, and Elliot recognizes fewer than usual.

Hanna throws an arm around Elliot's neck. "Elliot!" she yells directly in his ear. "How much you wanna bet I can do a backflip on that thing?"

She's pointing at the giant trampoline, and Elliot frowns.

"Don't worry," Hanna says. "All that's in my cup is soda, I swear. Here! Try it."

She thrusts her red cup at him and Elliot looks at Dia, who hops down off Jules's back. "I'm good," he says, but Dia takes the drink. She swallows and her eyebrows rise.

"See?" Hanna says with a gleaming smile. "No lie."

"Okay," Elliot says. "Ten bucks."

Hanna leads the way and climbs up on the trampoline, tugging her jeans up. "Watch this," she says, and Elliot does watch as she executes not one but two perfect backward somersaults.

"She did a lot of gymnastics when we were kids," Jules says, and Elliot shakes his head as Hanna climbs back down.

"Unfair advantage," he says, but he hands over the ten bucks.

"I never said anything about being fair," Hanna says as she tucks the money inside her shirt. "Thanks!"

Now Dia's the one with her arm around his neck. "See?" she says to him as the others begin bickering about something. "She's not always so bad."

Like he's the one saying she is. But Elliot decides not to say that. Hanna is in a good way tonight and Dia's laughed more than he's ever seen her before and things are really good. Instead he says, "I'm going to get a drink," and kisses Dia's cheek. "You want one?"

"Beer," she says, and then frowns, and Elliot sees her eyes go to Hanna. "And a water."

"Coming right up."

When he gets back outside, Dia and Jules have joined Hanna back up on the trampoline. He can see them, rising and falling out of the deep blue sky, hair flying everywhere, laughter pealing over the music.

He makes his way through the yard, and when he's almost to them someone comes running past him—Ciara. She hauls herself up on the trampoline, too, and the four of them soar through the air.

"Having fun?" he calls up to them.

"Take a picture!" Dia calls back.

He does as she says, capturing them in blurry speed on his phone, and when he looks at the picture he can almost see the magic they possess, right there on the screen. For all the heartache and mess and drama—shit, he gets it.

These girls are something special.

Dia collapses, breathless, and tumbles to the ground. "C'mere."

It's almost midnight and Elliot already knows he has no chance of getting home before curfew, but fuck it. She's lying in the grass now and Elliot lies next to her, smiles as she hooks her leg around his. There's probably an empty bedroom they could make good use of—

"I know exactly what you're thinking," Dia says. "Dirty."

"I know what *you're* thinking," Elliot says.

"What?"

"Something about the band," he says. "You always are." He touches a finger to her temple. "If I opened this up, it'd all come spilling out." He lifts himself over Dia and stares down into her unblinking eyes. "You're really beautiful," he says, and maybe he's kind of drunk but it's true. "Really really."

Dia laughs, and the sound vibrates through his hand. "Thank you."

"I think you're made of magic," he says. Okay, he's definitely drunk, but it's still true. "You and Jules and Hanna. When I see you with them, doing this thing you love, you're so *alive* and it's like I'm seeing the truest you and"—he should probably not say this but it's true—"I think I could be in love with a person like that."

"Elliot," Dia says, her smile so wide, and then she kisses him until they're both breathless, and when he speaks again he puts his lips to her throat.

"Made of magic," he says, the words pressed into her skin. "All of you."

Hanna

They stood together, the three of them, across from Revelry with the traffic rushing between. The marquee was all lit up tonight, in bright white: SUN CITY AND GLORY ALABAMA PRESENT THE ORIGINALS CONTEST.

"So it's not *our* name," Hanna said. "But one day it will be."

They waited for a break in the traffic and then ran across the road, headed into the club. First they had to sign in, and Hanna tried to see the other names on the list, but the girl with the clipboard—a different girl this time—was too fast, whisking them through to backstage before Hanna could look. "Did you see?" she asked the others as they made their way through the maze of hallways. "Who else is on the list?"

"No," Dia said. "But it went up on the website last night."

"Who is it?" Jules said. "Do we know them?"

"I don't know them," Dia said. "Knoxville Slums is one. And then Ursula Arrival. I don't know if that's a group or a person."

Hanna lifted one shoulder. "Never heard of them," she said.

A guy with the sharpest eyeliner Hanna had ever seen met them backstage, checked them off his list, and pointed them in the direction of the dressing rooms. "You're in room three," he said. "Sound check in five minutes."

They dropped their stuff in the dressing room, the flaking white walls and barely illuminated mirror unchanged since their last time here. Sound check blurred by, but afterward they waited in the wings to watch whichever act was checking next. They shouldn't have, Hanna realized, as soon as this group of punk people came out and launched into noise. "Oh," Jules whispered. "They're good."

"They're *really* good," Hanna said.

"Forget them." Dia turned on her heel and started back to the dressing room. "We're the shit, remember?"

Hanna tried, but she was too nervous.

It was better once they were back in the dressing room, door closed to the world. Jules played music out of her phone, a drop in the ocean of sound pushing up against the door, but enough for them. They spilled makeup across the dressing table and painted each other's faces: gold cheeks and red lips, radiant highlights and clear, sticky gloss. They changed into shorts, boots, and high-tops, black shirts: one Nets jersey, one scooped black tank, one cropped, bone-illustrated top.

In front of the mirror they stood together, and as Hanna smoothed her hands across the flash of soft stomach visible between her shorts and her shirt, she took them in. "We almost look like an actual band," she said to their mirror selves, her shoulder knocking against Jules's arm. "We almost look like we know what we're doing."

Dia teased her fingers through the ends of her hair, big and loose for tonight. "Illusion," she said. "The art of fooling everybody, including ourselves." And then she turned to Hanna, half a smile on her face. "C'mere, you have lipstick right *here*."

Jules bounced on the balls of her feet. "I want to go see," she said. "Only for a minute."

So they went out, crept around the side of the stage and inched back the curtain, stood and looked out on the swelling audience. Hanna's palms started to sweat as she took it all in: the lights, the throbbing noise. People crowding right up to the stage, and filling up the balconies, and still more coming in. She needed a nicotine hit. "There's a lot of people here."

"Glory Alabama are watching somewhere," Dia said.

"Where?" Jules asked. "Oh, I think I might throw up."

Hanna wiped her hands on her thighs. The last time she'd played in front of an audience this big, she'd been halfway to blackout and barely able to get through the song.

Not this time.

She scanned the crowd for Ciara's tattoos, Molly's blond halo, but couldn't find them. They were here, though; she could feel it.

And then the lights went down and the cheers lifted.

"All right, people! Are you ready for a show?"

They paced, prowled backstage while bigger local band Wednesday Street took to the stage and warmed everybody up with electronica-infused grunge.

They stood in the wings as the MC introduced the contest acts, gave the whole spiel: *Money! Fame and glory! Everything you could ever want!*

Knoxville Slums went out first. Rattling punk sounds, screamed vocals—this was the band they'd seen earlier. Hanna cracked her knuckles over and over, listening to Dia talk loudly, right in their ears. "It's a Flogging Molly–meets–Rancid thing," she was saying. "Basic. And *so* old."

"We're better!" Hanna said over the noise, to her hands. "Right?"

"Right!"

Ursula Arrival were cleaner, to Hanna's ears, but had way less stage presence. One of their singers froze every time she opened her mouth, her entire body still as she sang, but their guitarist could shred, Hanna had to give them that. "We're better," she said again, a mantra, rolling her sticks between her palms.

Jules knocked her hip. "Say it again."

"*We* are *better* than *them*," Hanna said, turning away from the stage. "Got it?"

Dia ran her hands along the neck of her guitar. "This will sound wrong," she said. "But—I almost don't care if we win or not. I *care*, I *want* to, but—"

"It's more than that," Hanna cut in. "Right?"

"So much more!" Jules said, and they were all a breath away from yelling to be heard.

Hanna pushed her hair back. "I'm really glad you made me do this," she said. "I'm really glad I wasn't too afraid to try! And that you see me now. I see you now." Dia and Jules were looking at her, full attention, and Hanna's heart was humming. "We made mistakes and we did terrible things but that's not all that we are. That's not who we are. Fuck. Am I even making any sense?"

Jules laughed, hard, and Dia smiled as she nodded. "Total sense!" she said, throwing an arm around Hanna's neck.

Ursula Arrival screeched to a stop, and the crowd's cheers were noticeably less than they had been for Knoxville Slums.

"We are going to rip the sky open," Hanna said, and Dia leaned in. "What?"

The MC walked out, mic to her mouth. "Okay! Now we have our last Sun City hopefuls. They've been around the block and they're back again—make noise—"

Hanna put her mouth to Dia's ear. "We're going to rip open the sky!"

"—for Wildfire!"

Dia

Dia pulled away from Hanna, electricity coursing through every inch of her. "Whatever you say!" she yelled back, and then she looked at Jules. "Ready?"

"We got this," Jules said.

Dia tugged her shorts up, shook her hair around her face. The MC was leaving the stage now, people were clapping and yelling and it was for them, this time, no one else.

She steeled herself, pulled her spine up tall, and took a step.

When she walked out, it was with the confidence of a girl who'd done this a hundred times before. Tonight the lights were bright enough to dazzle, throwing shadows into the corners of her vision, but it didn't faze her.

Dia stepped up to her mic, center stage. "Hi," she said, to

instantaneous cheers. Gratifying. "We're Wildfire." She laughed, raspy. "Maybe some of you here used to know us, before. But you don't know us now. You'll find out."

Without waiting for another response from the crowd, without having to check that Hanna and Jules were ready because she already knew they were, she ripped into the beginning of "Bones."

Two songs could be both an eternity and a gasp. Long enough to lay your heart bare, but so fast that if you blinked, you might miss it.

Dia pulled words out of the back of her throat. She danced, on the spot, her legs shaking, and over to Jules, to Hanna, as far as her cables would allow. They ran into each other and landed back down, and the heat of her body set Dia alight.

She played for the girls they used to be and the ones they were now, and all their fallen-apart pieces that had gotten lost or ruined or discarded along the way.

She played for her baby at home, sleeping, dreaming dreams that Dia couldn't even know yet.

Her arms ached and her hips shook and every muscle in her felt awake.

"Bones" became "Pretty Baby" before she knew it, and the lights shifted through the spectrum and she was performing now, not just playing: she was taking her hands off her guitar and lifting the hair off the back of her neck, closing her eyes and tipping her head to the ceiling, snaking her body to the thrum of Jules's bass line.

This is it.

This is what it feels like.

To be alive.

Dia opened her eyes and looked out on the crowd, as far as the lights let her see. Opened her mouth wide enough to swallow the sun and sang.

"'Hush, little honey, I know you heard about the fight last night / the mess your mama don't like—'"

She turned up to the balconies, slapped her hands on the strings, a burst of perfect sound. "'Wait till I get home, I'll show you where to go—'"

Dia felt alone and surrounded all at once in that moment, as she sweated through her shirt and smeared the makeup she'd so carefully painted on earlier.

And though the crowd was giving her their everything, so much energy, Dia barely needed it. All she needed, she had, up onstage with her.

"'Everything I ever wanted,'" Dia sang, the truest words. "'You don't own what I give, when it breaks you, give it all to me, baby pretty baby—'"

And then it was over. The lights, the purple and red and white strobing lights, flashed before cutting out, plunging the whole place into blackness.

And cheers, stomping feet, roaring applause.

Dia bent double, breathless, spent, and then Jules was grabbing her hand, dragging her offstage, and the thought, again: *This is it.*

This is what it feels like.

* * *

They crashed into each other offstage, sticky hugs, breathless laughs. "Holy shit," Hanna kept saying, over and over with her hands spinning through the air.

"Holy oh my god," Dia said. "Was that really us?"

"It was the most us possible," Jules said, lifting her hair off the back of her neck and fanning her face, laughing. "I want to do it again."

"I want to do that every night," Dia said, throwing her arms to the ceiling and rising up on her toes. Her skin felt raw, too tight for her body, every movement testing her limits, every rub of her clothes burning. And this whole place felt too small to contain her, pushing back against her, and how dare it, how dare it try to put a limit on what she was feeling right now. "I need water. You coming?"

But then the guy with the amazing eyeliner was there, directing them away from the stage and talking a mile a minute into his headset. "No, they can't come in without their passes. I don't care who they say they are, we have security for a reason. If they're Glory Alabama people—wait, how many lights are out? Call Karla down, she'll take care of it—"

Dia slipped away before they got to the dressing room. "I'll be back," she called in Jules's direction, and then she was half running away. "I'm coming back!"

She headed through the familiar maze of darkened back hallways and out into the empty lobby, pushed through the doors to the main room, the other side of the stage where people now were yelling and clapping for Violet Ocean as they came onstage to close out the night.

The crowd was looser right at the back, where Dia was, and it wasn't so hard for her to work her way over to the bar that ran along one side of the room. "Hey!" she yelled when she got there, leaning her elbows in something sticky as she signaled the bartender. "Water?"

"Dia!"

She turned at the sound of her name. Wasn't expecting to see Jesse standing down the bar from her, saying her name again, but there he was.

"What are you doing?" he said, raising his voice over the band and closing the three feet between them. "Shouldn't you be—"

Dia cut him off, yelling at him. "You came!"

"What?"

She couldn't tell if it was the high from that performance, or being tired of the pretending, or pure adrenaline that made her do it. Made her grab his arm and pull him toward the door so fast that he spilled his drink, through the lobby and into a corridor lined with posters. "You came," she repeated, the door swinging shut, leaving them in this private space. Muted noise from the stage, dimmed red lights over the doors. "That's what I said."

Jesse was wiping his spilled drink from his black shirt, but he looked up at Dia when she said that and kind of shook his head, and when he spoke he sounded so frustrated. "Like I wouldn't, Dee."

She allowed herself a long look at him, all of him, his broad shoulders and warm brown skin and his pretty eyes all confused.

"Dia," Jesse said. "Can we—"

"You want the truth?" she said suddenly, her voice raw. "Okay. It's not about Lex or the band or college or whatever of the thousand excuses I've given you. It's the way you look at me, Jesse, and no one else ever looks at me like that, and what if I lose that? What if I lose you?" She shook her head. "And I don't mean what if we don't work out, or we get together and then hate each other in six months, or anything like that. I mean what if I lose *you*." She held her hands out, palms turned up like some kind of prayer. "The last boy I was with died, Jesse. He *died*, and I never got to know what we might have become, and more than that, who *he* might have become. I am so scared that if you and me happen, something terrible will happen to you and then you'll never get to become the person you're supposed to be. And I'll be left here wondering what's so wrong with me that every boy I touch dies."

Jesse looked at her. "That's what you think? Dia. Nothing's going to happen to me."

"You don't know that," she said. "You cannot *know* that. And I *can* know that this fear is not reality but it is so real to me." She closed her eyes and tipped her face to the ceiling. "I had this dream, this nightmare, that you died, and it brought back so much of what happened to Elliot and—it didn't matter that it wasn't real. Because it was real in the moment I woke up, the moment that I *knew* that you were both dead. And then I remembered that you're not, that *you* are still here, and in that second I thought I would do anything to keep you here. So, if that meant us not being together—I had to do that."

"Why are you only telling me this *now*?" Jesse said, his confusion evident in his voice and his posture and everything about him. "Why didn't you say any of this before?"

"Because I was scared," she said, her blood rushing. "But I'm tired of being scared, and I'm tired of not telling you the truth, and I love you, Jesse, *I love you*."

She let the words hang there between them, heavy enough to almost be tangible, and Jesse looked stunned. "What?"

"I love you." Dia took a breath, took in the quiet all around them, opened her eyes and look at Jesse again. "Some days I see you and I feel like—oh my god, I love this boy, and I just want him to be okay, and what if these bad things come true and I never told you the truth and I never said sorry and I never said that I love you so much it doesn't feel real, sometimes. What would I do then?"

Jesse pulled in a ragged breath, took a step back from her. "You'd do fine," he said. "Exactly like you are now. Without Elliot."

"Elliot is not you," Dia said. "And I wasn't fine for a long time. I'm clearly not fine now, unless my brain is trying to tell me something else with this death dream." She touched her hands to her face, ignoring the sticky sweat under her arms. "But tonight I feel like I can do anything. So I'm telling you, before I get scared again and let you go."

He looked at her and she couldn't tell whether he was believing her or not, the way his mouth was set in such a straight line. "Dee."

"Jesse."

"You love me," he said. Statement, no question.

Dia answered him anyway. "Yes."

"Dee," he said.

"You came to my kid's birthday," she said, lowering her voice. "You came here. You are too good, Jesse Mackenzie."

"Dia, stop," he said, and her heart skipped a beat and her brain said, *This is it.*

This is where we end.

And if it was: at least she had been unafraid.

But then he closed the space between them again, the electric air keeping them apart, and she felt his touch on the back of her hand. He shook his head, looking down at her. "Dia Valentine, you are a pain in my ass."

And then his hands were holding her face and his mouth was on hers and it was the thousand times they'd never kissed in one moment. It was the hours spent watching him ride and the late-night texts and the things she'd told only him.

It was her hands on his hips and his tongue in her mouth and her heart at a thousand beats per minute. The dim recognition of her back hitting the wall, his body pressing her into it, and a noise of disappointment when he stopped kissing her, a noise that became a grateful sigh as his lips touched her throat.

And it was a thousand hours in three minutes of the most delicious kissing Dia had ever experienced. She wanted to keep doing it, all night. But she had other things to do, other people to be with. So even though it physically pained her, she pushed him away. "I'm calling a time-out," she said, breathless. "I have to go back, I have to find Hanna and Jules and—I don't even know. And so this is time-out."

Jesse slid one hand from her waist to the small of her back and used the other to catch her chin. "I didn't get to say," he said. "You were fucking amazing up there."

Dia resisted the urge to kiss him again and instead ducked out of his embrace, laughing as she twisted away and began walking down the hall. "I know," she said. "We were *fucking* amazing."

jules

Jules watched Dia run back into the dressing room and grab Hanna's hand. "Let's go dance," Dia said. "It's Violet Ocean. Remember when we used to come see them here?"

"Can't forget," Jules said. "Let's go."

They left their instruments and wound their way out of backstage and into the crowded main room. They fought their way through until they found Ciara and Molly, and screamed and shook and made themselves a place in the heart of the crowd. Dia's lipstick was smeared and her eyes wild, and she spilled a plastic cup of water over Jules as she pulled Dia in to jump with her, but Jules didn't care, only laughed and danced harder.

And then Jules found Autumn, in one of her pastel dresses with her rainbow hair, and kissed her like she'd never meant anything so much in her life. She brought her into their circle and they danced as the Violet Ocean bassist climbed up on a riser, caught up in the heat of everything, wrapped up in momentum and movement and sheer exhilaration. And it wasn't the moment she'd ached for; it was a thousand different, infinitely better and sweeter moments, every single second of it.

So they danced more, sang along with the crowd, became messes of sweat and pounding feet and raw throats.

And then the band finished their encore, left the stage to be replaced by the MC, and holy shit there was Astrid Parker, the lead singer of Glory Alabama, standing and breathing and *existing* in the same room as Jules. The crowd died down a little, and Jules felt a squeeze of her hand, looked to see Hanna standing next to her and staring at the stage. "All right, you've been patient," the MC was saying, a teasing lilt to her voice. "Very patient! But now, finally, it's time to announce the winner of this year's Sun City Radio Originals contest. The winner of *fifteen thousand dollars*!"

Cheers, a wave of applause as the MC handed over the mic to the other woman. "Hi!" she said, moving to center stage and laughing as the crowd erupted again. Jules let out a yell, too; she couldn't stop herself.

When the noise died down a little she spoke again. "I'm Astrid Parker"—more yells—"and on behalf of all of Glory Alabama, I want to say how impressed we are with the talent we've seen and how glad we are that we decided to do this. You have blown us away and we're so stoked to know that Golden Grove is still producing amazing musicians. So—"

"Get to the point," Dia's whisper came, and Jules shook her head. She was both nervous and not, because if they lost, nothing would change, except everything that they had changed for themselves already.

But if they won—

"I can't take it," Jules said, and her shoulders bumped up against Dia on one side, Hanna on the other. "This is too much."

She rose up on her toes, and the crowd was getting loud again, impatient, hungry. "Okay, okay," Astrid said, laughing, and the rest of Glory Alabama joined her onstage, waving at the audience. "We'll put you out of your misery."

Dia reached for her hand, and Jules reached for Hanna, and the three of them took the same breath.

And Jules looked at her friends, new from old, and the girl she had fallen in love with, and the world around them that she had longed so hard to know again, and she exhaled.

Epilogue

It's sunny when Dia gets out of class.

She slips her biology textbook into her bag and makes her way across the courtyard, over to the parking lot. There's a party she's invited to tonight, but Dia has gone to exactly two parties in the entire first year of college, and both of them were a bust. Besides, she has other places to be, better things to do.

Jules is already there, leaning against the driver side of the dark-red Jetta that she calls her baby. "What took you so long?" she says, holding her hands out. "We're on a tight schedule."

"It was my last final," Dia says. "What was I supposed to do, get up and leave?"

Jules opens the car. "Get in," she says. "Come on!"

They drive across town, Jhené Aiko playing out of the slightly crackly car speakers. Dia rolls the window down and lets her hand float in the wind as they pass through the Nice Side of Town. She checks her phone: eta? also do you want the red cups or blue? the first message says, and the second: also the doctor took my cast off finally so want to come watch me ride tomorrow?

"Jesus Christ," Dia says under her breath. He's trying to irritate her on purpose, she knows, but he's so very good at it.

It's okay. She's spent almost a year with him. He gets hurt, he gets better. She helps him change bandages or clean cuts, sees the way his body heals. And she doesn't get those bad dreams anymore.

"Jesse?" Jules swings a left.

"He wants to know, do we want red cups or blue?"

"Red," Jules says. "Definitely."

Dia replies to him and then puts her phone away, propping her feet up on the dash. "So Ciara's in charge of food, and Jesse's getting the other stuff, and Hanna's setting up at their place already. What else?"

"Once we get the cake, we're set," Jules says.

"Aren't you forgetting something?"

"What?"

"My child?"

"Oh, shit." Jules makes it through a yellow light and glances at Dia. "Okay, I did not *forget*, it momentarily slipped my mind."

Dia laughs. "Relax," she says. "Let's go get her."

At day care Lex comes running out, her hair bouncing off her shoulders. "Hi, Mommy!"

"Hi, Lala!" Dia holds her hand out for her daughter to take. "Ready for the party?"

"Is there gonna be pizza?"

"Oh, yeah," Dia says as the cross the parking lot. "So much pizza. More pizza than you can imagine."

"Nuh-uh," Lex says, her eyes wide. "Really?"

"Really really." Dia clips her into the car seat and then gets in the front. "All done."

They go to the Flour Shop to pick up Autumn's birthday cake, and then they drive over to Hanna and Ciara's new place—or, not so new; Dia keeps calling it that, even though they moved in eight months ago. Hanna's out in the yard, setting out blankets and chairs and at the end, a makeshift stage formed from cheap pallets. "Me and Molly worked all day on that," she says, proud, as Lex jumps on top of it. "Tell me how good I am."

"Very good," Jules says. "Okay, so, I'm going to get Autumn and we'll, like, waste some time while people get here and then I'll text you when we're coming back."

"Waste some time?" Dia says, raising her eyebrows. "Jules, you know you can say the actual words, right? We don't need euphemisms."

Jules sticks her middle finger up. "I'm going now."

Dia helps Hanna with the rest of the setting up, and when Ciara comes back they help her unload the car. Dia gives Lex a giant lollipop to occupy her for a little while.

Jesse turns up with the cups and everything else that was on the list Jules gave him. "Hi," Dia says. "Can you do me a favor?"

"Another one?" Jesse says. "What?"

She touches her lips. "Kiss me right here."

"Oh, that I can do," he says, and he does, and Dia thinks she'll never get tired of him.

When it gets a little later and everything's ready, people start arriving. Not tons of people—Autumn's friends from school, a couple of Ciara's new bandmates, a select number that Jesse rolls around at the skate park with. It was supposed to be a surprise party, except for when Autumn's mom told Jules that Autumn *hates* surprise parties, and so now it's just Autumn's birthday.

When Autumn walks in they all yell, "Happy birthday!" and she blushes.

"Thanks," she says. "This is too much!"

Ciara's hooked up speakers to pipe music into the yard, and Dia sits on the grass with Lex. Summer break's about to start and she's going to be busy busy busy, still working at the bakery, and with the band, and the internship she got at a tiny local indie label, thanks to Astrid Parker.

After they'd won, and then later on, after they'd played the most amazing show of their lives opening up for Glory Alabama, Astrid had given Dia her email. "Frontwoman to frontwoman," she'd said to a dazed Dia. "If I can help you with anything, let me know. You remind me of me."

All year long they've been emailing, Astrid answering all of Dia's questions about the business, production, marketing, what it really takes to succeed. She even helped Dia get the internship—because as much as Dia still loves playing, now she's thinking about what kind of career she might be able to make out of all of it, too.

Once Lex has eaten her body weight in pizza and cake and starts falling asleep, Dia calls her parents.

They meet her out front and her dad takes Lex, puts her in the back of the car. "I won't be super late," Dia says to her mom.

"It's fine," Nina says. "You officially finished freshman year today, it's Autumn's birthday, you have fun! We'll take care of the baby."

"She's not a baby," Max says, and he kisses Dia on the top of her head. "Listen to your mama. Have fun."

She blows a kiss as they drive away, and walks back into the yard.

The music gets turned down, and the three of them get up on the makeshift stage, and Dia arranges her dress so she's not flashing everybody while she plays. "Hi," Jules says. "So, Autumn wanted us to play for her birthday, and I do what she tells me to, so here we are." That makes people laugh, and Dia shakes her head, the curls she's pulled around her face fluttering in the breeze. "We're going to do some songs you'll hear on our new EP, if you feel like getting it."

"Come see us next week, too!" Dia says, fishing a pick from her pocket. "You won't regret it."

Hanna cracks her fingers, sitting behind the keyboard they got a few months ago and have been experimenting with ever since. "Ready?"

Jules turns so she can see both of them and nods. "Ready."

Dia looks at their friends, their family, the hungry hearts waiting for them to begin. Her lips are dry and her fingers ache already, in the best way. She closes her eyes for only a second, watches the lights behind her eyelids strobe, and she can almost smell the sticky heat, the sweat of being onstage.

She opens her eyes. Jesse gives her that smile, the one she thinks will never stop breaking her heart, and Ciara holds up her phone, ready to record them. The lights strung up across the fence, around the two spindly trees Hanna so proudly looks after, light up everything in beauty, and Dia fixes her fingers on the fretboard of her new acoustic, a richer sound than she's been used to. It's worth getting used to.

She smiles. "Ready."

Acknowledgments

Everyone says the second book is the hardest, but for me it's also the most proud I've ever been of anything. I loved writing this book, and I hope it finds a way into people's hearts.

Thank you to my editor extraordinaire, Elizabeth Lynch. You let me write my messy girls and make them a thousand times better.

Thank you to Suzie Townsend for taking me on and supporting TIWIFL so much.

Thank you to Jennifer Johnson-Blalock for everything.

Thank you to everyone at HarperTeen who made this a real book: Renée Cafiero, Claire Caterer, Bess Braswell, Audrey Diestelkamp, Gina Rizzo, Vanessa Nuttry, and especially Michelle Taormina for such a glorious cover.

Thank you to my all my friends: To my UK babes for all the whatsapp procrastination and deep dives on Kristina's balcony. Thanks especially to Ali Standish and Carlie Sorosiak. To everyone in AMM for several thousand hours of slack chats and making me laugh a ridiculous amount. To all my friends in the 17s, especially Laurie Devore and Kiersi Burkhart. To Rachel Lynn Solomon—thank you for letting me cry in your direction so much. Thank you to Courtney Summers for all your support. And to everyone I couldn't possibly name who has shared their excitement for this book somewhere—it honestly keeps me going.

Thank you to my sensitivity readers, including Elizabeth Roderick, for giving your time and expertise to help me make this book the best it could be. Any errors in authenticity are mine and mine alone.

Thank you to Pretty Little Liars for keeping me halfway sane during the winter of 2016 while I wrote and rewrote this book. Mona forever.

Thank you to Christina Aguilera, Sufjan Stevens, Kacey Musgraves, Beyoncé, JoJo, and many, many more for keeping me company for so many years.

Thank you to my family for supporting me always.

Thank you to all the women who've picked up a guitar and a mic.